ASH AND BONES

A CITY OF SACRIFICE NOVEL

by Michael R. Fletcher

For the Extraordinary Fellows of Arcane Sorcery.

This is a work of fiction. Names, characters, business, events, and incidents are the products of the author's imagination. Any resemblance to actual persons, living or dead, Dyrk Ashton or otherwise, or actual events is mostly coincidental. Has the author done a butt-ton of drugs? Well, his lawyer says he prolly shouldn't answer that. The real question though: Is this the place for such rambling?

Editor: Sarah Chorn
Cover Art and Typography: Felix Ortiz

Books by Michael R. Fletcher
Ghosts of Tomorrow
Beyond Redemption
The Mirror's Truth
Swarm and Steel
A Collection of Obsessions
Smoke and Stone – City of Sacrifice #1
Ash and Bone – City of Sacrifice #2
Black Stone Heart – The Obsidian Path #1
She Dreams in Blood – The Obsidian Path #2
The Millennial Manifesto
Norylska Groans (Co-written with Clayton W. Snyder)

TABLE OF CONTENTS

WHAT HAS GONE BEFORE

Some folks requested I include a recap of *Smoke and Stone*. You don't have to read it if you don't want/need to. I have attempted to include enough refreshers throughout the book that you should be able to dive in without reading this. That said, if you want a quick refresher, here it is!

A Quick Refresher on Bastion:

Surrounded by endless desert, sands stained red by the blood of billions, Bastion is the last city of man. Created by the gods, the city consists of concentric rings, each populated by a highly stratified caste. The closer one lives to the Gods at the centre, the more important one's existence, the better one's life.

The Loa, priests of the banished Mother Death, fight to free Bastion from the stone grip of the nahual. Unlike the nahualli, whose sorcery relies on narcotics, the Loa channel their blasphemous powers through stones and crystals, the very bones of the earth.

Crude and uneducated, the Growers of the outermost ring work the fields and farms that feed all the city. Bound by the laws laid out in the *Book of Bastion*, they live hard lives with few luxuries. Considered too stupid to raise their own children, Grower babies are taken to crèches to be raised by the nahual of Her Skirt is Stars, the god of childbirth.

In the next ring inward, the Crafters take the raw materials supplied by the Growers and fashion them into the clothes, tools, and meals that keep Bastion functioning. Compared to the Growers, the Crafters live relatively easy lives. They learn trades, earn money, and are allowed to raise their own children.

The Senators' Ring is home to Bastion's lawmakers.

The Bankers' Ring is responsible for the city's economy.

The nahual of the Priests' Ring are responsible for enforcing the holy scriptures of the *Book of Bastion* and shepherding all the city's souls.

The Gods' Ring at Bastion's heart is home to the gods. They rarely venture forth. Only the Heart's Mirror—the Voice of the Gods, and High Priest of whichever god currently rules the pantheon—is permitted entrance.

The Story So Far...

Born to the wealth and comfort of the Priests' Ring, Akachi was sent to Bastion's outermost ring to train as a nahualli, a sorcerous priest. After five years in the Northern Cathedral, studying as an acolyte, he is now a nahual of Cloud Serpent, the Lord of the Hunt. Yet he still lives in the shadow of his disappointed father, Cloud Serpent's High Priest.

For reasons unknown to Akachi, Bishop Zalika chooses him to reopen a long-abandoned church in the Wheat District, one of the most dangerous neighbourhoods in the Growers' Ring. In recent months she's sent half a dozen priests to the church. All have been assassinated by Loa heretics.

Assigned a squad of Hummingbird Guard led by the indomitable Captain Yejide, Akachi is attacked en route by a mob of filthy Growers, or 'Dirts,' as Yejide calls them. Barely escaping with his life, Akachi arrives at the Cloud Serpent church to find it in a horrible state of disrepair.

Nuru, born to the poverty and despair of the Growers' Ring, is a street-sorcerer in the Wheat District. She lives with the boys she grew up with in the crèche. Chisulo, with his need to always do the right thing, is the gang's leader. Bomani loves a drunken brawl more than anything. Omari, the gang's Finger, is a talented thief. The massively muscled Happy wants nothing more than to sit on his stolen box and drink whatever concoctions Nuru has brewed. Scarred Efra, a diminutive woman with a quick temper and penchant for violence, exists on the periphery of the gang. Not quite one of them, she disappears for days on end, often returning looking like she lost a fight with a rabid cat. Together, they hold three streets of turf, dealing forbidden narcotics grown in plots hidden in the fields beyond the district's tenements. Haunted by dreams of a colossal spider with the body of a beautiful woman, Nuru plans to carve the thing from her nightmares. She hopes to use her power as a nagual—a shape-shifting sorcerer—to *become* the creature. Unfortunately, as a Grower, Nuru has no access to the tools and paints required to complete such a difficult carving. She becomes increasingly sure Efra will play a part in acquiring what she needs.

When Bomani is murdered by Fadil, the leader of a competing gang, and Efra is taken hostage, Nuru sees her hopes of completing the carving in danger. She and her boys rush to save Efra. They find her beaten and bloodied, but hardly broken. After, Nuru doses Efra with a blend of narcotics so she may walk in her dreams, learn more of this dangerous woman. She discovers that Smoking Mirror, Bastions god of discord, has taken an interest in Efra. Trapping Nuru in the dream-world, the god shows her glimpses of a possible future. The Loa heretics are inciting the Growers to rebellion. Soon, the Turquoise Serpents—Southern Hummingbird's elite warrior priests—will come to the outer ring to crush the Dirts. She sees a city blanketed in ash, the fields burning. The slaughter will be terrible.

Protect Efra, Smoking Mirror commands Nuru, *or Bastion will fall.*

During Akachi's first night in Cloud Serpent's church, he dreams of a scarred girl. She will bring death and ruin to beautiful Bastion. It is, he realizes, a vision sent by his god. As a priest of the Lord of the Hunt, he must track this woman, stop her before she destroys the city. While searching the district for the scarred girl, one of Akachi's Hummingbird Guards is attacked and wounded by a drunken Grower. The *Book of Bastion* states that any attack against a nahual is punishable by death on the altar. After sacrificing the man, a horrendous and scarring event, Akachi learns the true cost of his responsibility. Feeling stained, somehow lessened by what should have been a holy experience, Akachi turns to his narcotics to escape. He walks the dreams of the local Growers, hoping to find the scarred girl.

Saddened by Bomani's death and knowing it was her fault, Nuru brings the gang together in a spiritual ritual of healing. For the first time including Efra, she hopes to bind the woman to her purpose. During the ritual Nuru shows her friends the carving she cannot complete. She explains her need for proper tools, all of which are forbidden to Growers. The gang discover themselves confronted by a temple-trained Cloud Serpent nahualli. The sorcerous priest wrestles control of the dream-world from Nuru. Omari is gravely wounded during the fight. Bearing the mark of Smoking Mirror, a rectangle of solid black tattooed on the inside of one wrist, Efra banishes the nahualli from the dream-world.

Knowing they are hunted by a priest of Cloud Serpent, Efra forms a desperate plan. She and Nuru will journey to the Crafters' Ring—which is strictly forbidden by the *Book of Bastion*—to steal the tools Nuru needs. Omari remains unconscious, beyond the reach of Nuru's sorcery.

Garrotting a couple of Crafters for their clothes, the two women enter the Crafters' Ring and steal the tools and paints. They leave behind a trail of corpses as Efra is unwilling to chance being caught. Where Efra is untouched by the deaths, each is a wound in Nuru's soul. Though she tells herself she *needs* these tools to save her friends, the cost is too high.

Finding the ignorant Dirts in the dream-world, Akachi is stunned when the scarred woman defeats him. Knowing his prey is close, he commands his squad of Hummingbird Guard to do a door-to-door search. Ignoring Captain Yejide's warning that the district is too dangerous, he splits the squad up to cover more ground.

Loa assassins ambush Akachi and Yejide with their blasphemous sorcery. Several squad members are slain. Though he survives the attack, Akachi does not escape unscathed. Touched by amethyst, the stone of self-destruction, he plummets into depression. Fleeing his responsibilities and the awful cost of his choices, Akachi turns to narcotics, walking the edge of brain-burn. Hallucinating uncontrollably, he visits the under-world. He witnesses the assassination of the leader of the pantheon, Father Death, at the hands of the Loa. A new godling is born, Face Painted with Bells, and she holds the realm of the dead, awaiting the return of Mother Death.

When a Hummingbird Guard reports that a Grower named the Artist is responsible for most of the forbidden tattooing in the Wheat District, Akachi remembers the rectangle inked into the scarred woman's wrist. In the desperate hope the Artist might know Akachi's prey, the young nahualli decides to pay the man a visit.

After Nuru and Efra return to the Growers Ring with their stolen tools and paints, the gang huddles in a tenement basement. Under the influence of a massive dose of narcotics, Nuru works to complete the carving. After days of constant effort, she finishes only to discover the woman half of the spider looks terrifyingly like her. Realizing Omari is dying, the gang decides to visit the Artist, a mysteriously educated Grower. Ascending to the street, they find ash falling from a smoke-throttled sky. The fields are burning, and the Loa have risen in open rebellion.

Meeting at the Artist's tenement, Nuru's gang does battle with Akachi and his squad of Hummingbird Guard. Under the influence of a suicidally dangerous blend of narcotics, Akachi calls his allies through the veil separating realities. He becomes a monstrous creature with the speed of a puma, the strength of a bear, and the armour of a pangolin. Equally dosed, Nuru uses her carving as a focus. She is horrified to discover she has carved Mother Death, the banished Queen of Bastion.

Powerful as Akachi is, the young nahualli is no match for a god, even one as starved and weak as Mother Death. Akachi is defeated and left for dead. Captain Yejide, whom he believes he has fallen in love with, and her squad are dead. Yejide's soul is now trapped inside Akachi's obsidian dagger. After a procession of Growers carries him back to his church, Akachi is visited by his god as he lays dying on the altar. He learns that the gods play a game of manipulation, warring through their worshippers rather than coming into direct conflict. Each of the gods has chosen a Heart, someone to represent them in the coming war. The last Heart alive will ascend to become the new Heart's Mirror, the previous one having been murdered by the Loa.

Cloud Serpent has chosen Akachi to be his Heart. Cleansed of his doubts, Akachi's faith is born anew in the heat of divine light. He learns that Efra is the Heart of Smoking Mirror and that Nuru is Mother Death's Heart. For Akachi to ascend and become the new Heart's Mirror, he must stalk and kill the women.

Gutted by the loss of her friends, Nuru flees with Efra. Though ignorant of the roles they will play in the coming war, the two women swear to bring down the nahual, to free the Growers from oppression.

The gods are once again at war.

AKACHI - VENOMOUS PURPOSE

Obedience lies at the heart of faith.

—The Book of Bastion

Lying on the sacrificial altar, Akachi's mangled left hand caught his attention. Appalled at the loss, unable to accept it as real, he wriggled the stumps of his fingers. They itched, the ghosts of ants on flesh.

His sacrificial dagger lay upon his chest. He lifted it with his undamaged hand. No longer could he feel its deep evil. The souls of Yejide, the woman he loved, and Nafari, his only friend, were trapped inside.

Levering himself to a sitting position, Akachi groaned in pain.

Mother Death.

Nuru, the filthy street-sorcerer who was the god's Heart.

Violent little Efra, the Heart of Smoking Mirror, the Obsidian Lord.

They will pay.

They would all pay. As Cloud Serpent demanded.

The gods saved us. We owe them everything.

Jumoke, the acolyte Bishop Zalika assigned to Akachi when she sent him out to the Wheat District, entered the hall. Approaching the altar, he bowed low. "Are you hungry, Pastor?" he asked as if nothing had happened.

He wasn't.

"Fetch me clean robes," said Akachi. "I hunt a god."

Swinging his legs off the altar, he sagged. Jumoke caught him, kept him upright. Cloud Serpent had closed Akachi's wounds, but he was still weak from blood loss.

Betrayed by the weakness of flesh.

"You must rest, Pastor," said the acolyte.

Nodding, Akachi allowed himself to be led to his chambers.

Jumoke helped him to bed, bowed again, and left.

Akachi slept.

Waking to discover a platter of bread and fruit, he ate and again slept.

Akachi woke to empty silence.

No distant chatter of Hummingbird Guard as they cared for their weapons and armour.

Dead. All dead.

Failure, and second chances.

He earned the first, and didn't deserve the second. But the gods worked in mysterious ways, or so said the *Book of Bastion*. Perhaps this was all according to some divine plan beyond his understanding.

The desire to hunt, the itching hunger at the base of his skull, cut through Akachi's thoughts. He needed to prowl the streets of the Growers' Ring, stalk through the sad, empty dreams of the Dirts until he found the two women who killed him. He would open them wide, expose their sinner hearts to the light of the gods. For the Heart of Smoking Mirror, the scarred Dirt who murdered Captain Yejide, Akachi's love, sacrifice upon the altar would suffice. For the achingly beautiful Heart of Mother Death, something altogether more terrible was required.

Much as that relentless hunger consumed Akachi, he remained weak.

The stumps of the fingers of his left hand tingled and itched, a reminder of his failure to banish Mother Death. Two pale scars in the dark oak flesh of his chest were all that remained of the grievous wounds the god inflicted when she impaled him on barbed spiders' legs. He remembered hanging there, a helpless bug, writhing in agony. She broke him, tore everything he was. Two matching scars adorned his back, where he couldn't see them.

Rising gingerly from bed, Akachi flipped the long knot of tangled braids over his shoulder. The bones of rats and snakes, tied into his hair, clacked and rattled. Many were broken, pale fragments trapped in the chaos. Long past time to replace them, he couldn't remember when he'd last undone the braids, had his hair brushed out and cleaned.

Still wearing the robes he died in, Akachi stank.

Everything stank.

Blood and smoke and death.

Hands on the walls for support, Akachi staggered to the church's kitchen. The stone, still cold from the night's chill, felt rough and raw, far from the perfection the *Book of Bastion* proclaimed it to be.

Hearing Akachi's entrance, Jumoke turned from the meal he was preparing and studied the nahual with a critical eye.

Reaching forward, the acolyte poked a finger through the tattered, blood-stained hole where Mother Death impaled Akachi. "I don't think these are worth mending."

After torturing the Artist, warring in the street with the Dirt gang, being maimed and killed by Mother Death, and finally visited by a manifestation of Cloud Serpent, little remained of Akachi's banded red, white, and black robes.

Collapsing into a chair, Akachi sat in silence as Jumoke set a plate of sunken fruit and stale hardbread before him. The food held no appeal. Then again, the acolyte could have laid out the finest feast, and Akachi still wouldn't have been interested.

He remembered the dry weight of scales, the viper rearing back, foot-long fangs dropping into place. The stabbing agony as Cloud Serpent sank those fangs into Akachi's torn flesh, pumped venomous purpose into his blood.

What was sustenance in the face of obedience and service?

Nothing. A distraction.

"I need to go," said Akachi, rising from the table. He leaned against it, eyes closed, waiting for the dizziness to pass.

"You need to sleep," said Jumoke, "to heal. In the morning, if you can stand without wobbling, maybe then you can leave."

Too tired to argue, Akachi said, "Wake me when the sun rises."

"Of course, Pastor."

"You're not going to wake me, are you."

"Of course not, Pastor."

"You're a terrible acolyte."

"That," said the boy, "is why the Bishop sent me with you."

Akachi heard the grin in the lad's voice.

Jumoke helped him back to his chambers and into a change of clothes. Tutting and muttering like Akachi's grandmother, he made sure the blanket was tucked in just right before puttering about tidying.

Akachi fell asleep before the boy left the room.

He dreamed. The ruffle of wind through his feathers. The stench of smoke and ash. Following the curve of the Grey Wall separating the Growers from the Crafters, he flew to the Northern Cathedral. Grower districts passed by beneath, all the same yet all different.

Within the cathedral he found the halls, long and empty, haunted by the ghosts of fallen nahual. Stairs disappeared into the deepest bowels of the earth.

Akachi hesitated at the top of the steps.

I remember these.

They led to the underworld.

It felt different this time, thinner and less real. There was a truth here, but not the truth of his previous journey.

Can there be more than one truth?

That seemed wrong. Truth was an absolute. It was stone, like Bastion. Truth was the word of the gods, not subject to the whims and foibles of mortals.

Truth and untruth.

Right and wrong.

Good and evil.

The Book left no room for doubt.

Last time, confronted with these stairs, he'd immediately headed down. This time, a lurking fear, like murky water of an unknown depth, filled him. No dead and forgotten gods would bear mute witness to his travels. But to ignore such a vision would be foolish.

Akachi's missing fingers itched. He scratched at the stumps.

Even in my dreams.

Decision made, he descended the winding stair.

Dream, or vision? Pactonal manipulation, or sending of the gods?

The thought haunted him. How could he know which this was?

When he passed by the ancient library, the first of the cathedral's basements, he recognized where he was.

Reaching the second basement, the dispensary where the narcotics for the cathedral's nahualli were prepared and stored, Akachi paused. The thought of all those sorcerous tools quickened his heart. Foku. Ameslari. Jainkoei to open his soul to the will of his god. His ruined hand shook.

He wanted all of it.

Cloud Serpent healed me of weakness, cleansed me of such base needs.

Breathing deep, Akachi slowed his heart.

He had devoured the last of his jainkoei as he lay dying on the altar.

I'll need more.

That was common sense. As a nahualli, a sorcerous priest, narcotics were the path to power, the tools with which he thinned the veil between realities.

I have prey to hunt.

Desiring the narcotics needed to complete his task wasn't weakness. It was logic. It was sense.

Leaving the stairs, Akachi headed toward the dispensary.

Bishop Zalika stood waiting.

She held a staff in her right hand. Large as she was, it stood a full head taller. The top, a carved eagle's talon, clutched a misshapen red stone. The rock pulsated like a beating heart.

"Long ago," said Zalika, "when the world was young and alive, The Lord, Father Death, had a brother." Her words were the dry rumble of desert thunder.

This is no pactonal sending.

This wasn't the Bishop. Something spoke through his memory of the woman.

"The brother was The Fifth Sun," Zalika recited. She stared at nothing, made no sign she knew Akachi was there. "The Movement. Naui Olin. He Who Goes Forth Shining. Father of the Day. Lord of Eagles. Flint Tongue."

How many times had Akachi wondered at the lack of a sun god?

This is Cloud Serpent! He speaks to me once again!

To be so blessed tore Akachi's heart with joy.

"The Fifth Sun was loved and worshipped by all," intoned Zalika.

"I've read the Book many times," said Akachi. "I've seen no mention of this god."

"The Lord, god of rot and ruin, dwelling forever in the dark of the underworld, grew jealous of his brother," continued Zalika, as if she hadn't heard him speak. "The two argued and fought. Father Death murdered his brother, cut his heart out."

"Was this removed from the Book?" Akachi asked. Some of the older copies had material no longer included. "Or do you quote Loa blasphemy?"

Still not making eye contact, she hefted the staff with its pulsating stone. "Father Death mounted the bloodstone heart in the claws of an eagle as mockery and created the Staff of the Fifth Sun. The staff was bequeathed to his highest nahual, a soulless katle, as a gift. She used it to control the weather. Though she brought countless seasons of bounty, she also turned the staff against any who challenged her." The Bishop droned on, lacking the usual loathing she bore for Akachi. "Every use further angered the sun. Godless, abandoned, the sun raged, striving to burn this world free of life. Day by day, year by year, the world died. The katle was murdered, assassinated, and the staff disappeared from the memory of man. It was hidden away, far out where nothing mattered, where no one would look for it."

She's speaking for me, not to me.

He was here, in the cathedral basement, and yet he wasn't. A dream that was both less and more.

"It's in the Northern Cathedral," said Akachi, understanding.

"Bring the staff to the place of eternal night," she said, staring vacantly at nothing.

A riddle? The place of eternal night?

It was so unlike Zalika, who spoke in blunt barbs of dislike.

In the Temple of Revelations, Sin Eater's greatest church in the Priests' Ring, nahual were forbidden false light of any kind. The temple, a reverse pyramid sunk into Bastion's floor, had twelve basements. The dark of the lowest level was said to reveal the sins of even the most holy man. Only Sin Eater's High Priest could enter, as such soul-deep revelations would break a less devout mortal.

Was that what she meant? He'd never heard of it being referred to as 'The place of eternal night.'

"Is that from the *Book of the Invisibles*?" Akachi asked.

"The Queen's Heart must die."

Mother Death, the Queen of Bastion. Nuru, the street-sorcerer, was her Heart.

"The Destroyer seeks the end of all," said Zalika. "The final blasphemy, the murder of an entire pantheon."

Akachi reeled. Cloud Serpent had told him that Efra, Smoking Mirror's Heart, would bring about the fall of Bastion, that humanity would die because of her. The Lord of the Hunt wanted Mother Death's Heart thrown from the wall and the Queen banished, but Akachi had thought that Efra and Smoking Mirror were the real threat.

"Has something changed?" asked Akachi. "I don't understand. I thought—"

Zalika lifted the staff and brought the heel down hard. It rang like stone on stone.

Akachi woke to the stench of ash and burnt meat. Rising, he went to the church's entrance. While hardly invigorated, he no longer staggered with exhaustion. Everything ached, a dull heat throbbed through his limbs like the threat of infection.

Bastion burned.

A pall of smoke bruised the sky. It looked solid, a reverse landscape of blue-stained grey. Hills and mountains stabbed down toward the earth. It felt like he might reach up and touch them. Fat flakes of ash fell, blanketing the world in heavy silence.

It's a god, hanging over the city, devouring all sound.

Was there a god of smoke? Searching his memory, he found nothing. Many carried smoke-related references—Smoking Mirror, and the like—but no god claimed smoke itself.

'The Heart's Mirror is dead,' Cloud Serpent had said as Akachi bled out on the altar. 'Assassinated. Father Death has fallen. The pantheon has no leader.'

Akachi witnessed The Lord's demise at the hands of the upstart godling, Face Painted with Bells, during his hallucinatory journey into Father Death's domain.

Was that yesterday? Two days ago? Three?

Time was mud.

Standing sheltered in the doorway, gazing into the filthy streets of the Wheat District, the church behind Akachi felt like a waiting grave.

The Hummingbird Guard Bishop Zalika sent to protect him were dead. Even Captain Yejide, who he thought he may have loved.

Did she love me?

No way to know.

Nothing but doubt. Not of his feelings, but of hers. She never expressed anything beyond a desire to protect him. That was her job, her god-given task. Sometimes, however, he'd swear she looked at him like he was more than an assignment.

Or was that pity?

He'd been spiralling toward brain-burn, heavily dosed on narcotics for days on end. That week was a blur of hallucinations and failure.

Maybe she thought him a fool.

Maybe I was.

Akachi stared into the ash.

Maybe I am.

But he still loved her, still carried her soul in the sacrificial dagger.

Maybe it doesn't matter what she felt. Maybe it only matters what I feel.

They were all dead. Was it his fault? Could he have done things differently?

As Akachi lay on the sacrificial altar, feeding the gods, Cloud Serpent had come to him, a beautiful viper. The gods hadn't seemed displeased.

What were a few lives to the Lord of the Hunt?

The god hollowed Akachi like a master craftsman carving a flute. He recalled feeling gutted of fear and doubt, every last emotion torn from him as Cloud Serpent filled him with divine purpose. The purpose remained. He knew what he had to do. While he still felt hollowed, it was a different kind of empty. A lonely empty.

The presence of Cloud Serpent was infinitely more addictive than any narcotic.

How many nahualli brain-burned on jainkoei, desperate to feel even a hint of their god's attention?

Knowing exactly what your god required of you was one thing—a gift he never thought to achieve—but being the centre of divine attention was unlike anything Akachi ever felt. He would do anything to have that again.

The feeling was difficult to describe, impossible to define.

Aspects of it mirrored some of what Akachi felt for Yejide.

Was it a kind of love?

Or perhaps need?

Did it matter? Was there a difference?

He didn't know, couldn't tell.

I love Yejide and I need her.

Could you have one without the other?

She didn't need me.

No. She did not. Captain Yejide didn't need anyone. She was strong.

ASH AND BONES

So strong.

Did that mean she didn't love him?

"You're stalling," Akachi whispered.

Cloud Serpent had come to Akachi, manifested here in this church. And then there was the dream last night. The two felt completely different. Why hadn't the god told him everything when he was here?

Had Akachi misunderstood? Was that not a message from the Lord of the Hunt?

No pactonal, no matter how skilled, could have fooled him so completely. It was a proper vision, a divine sending. It had to be.

The subtle change in message, however, haunted him. Who was the real threat, Nuru, or Efra? The answer seemed obvious. Nuru was a street-sorcerer, and Heart of Mother Death. Surely that banished god's return, and the resulting rise of the Loa, was more dangerous than some scarred Dirt with no sorcery. As Smoking Mirror's Heart, Efra had to die. In the end, only one Heart could remain and ascend to become Heart's Mirror. But at least the Obsidian Lord was a part of Bastion's pantheon.

Smoking Mirror's choice baffled Akachi. It made no sense. The girl was nothing!

Reaching his ruined hand beyond the shelter of his church, Akachi watched flakes of ash gather in his palm. The air stank, clawed the back of his throat leaving it raw. He felt like he'd caught one of those colds that occasionally swept through the cramped acolyte dormitories of the Northern Cathedral. In the distance, a muted scream of agony, cut short, killed the beautiful silence. Great billowing clouds of smoke rolled down streets and alleys, cutting visibility to a score of strides. Shapes moved closer, staggering or sprinting. Fighting.

Voices raised in anger, incomprehensible bellowing, followed by more screams.

Jumoke approached to stand behind Akachi. "Pastor, you should return inside," he said. "The Growers are rioting. If they see you..."

Wiping his ash-stained hand on his robes, Akachi re-entered the church. A smear of grey cut through the red, white, and black bands of his vestments. A flash of dull anger, quick to fade.

The Heart of Cloud Serpent should be immune to filth.

He wasn't.

Soon, he'd venture out into the smoke and soot.

"Perhaps," said Jumoke, as if reading his thoughts, "you should wait for things to settle down."

What should he tell the young acolyte?

"I must report to the Northern Cathedral," said Akachi. "Bastion is in danger. Mother Death has gained a foothold in the city. Her Heart is here. The Loa will rally behind the street-sorcerer. The Hummingbird Guard will not be enough to hold the ring." He recalled his dream of Southern Hummingbird's elite troops. "We need the Turquoise Serpents. All of them. The Dirts must be pacified."

Jumoke glanced past him, frowning in distaste at the world beyond. "It's too dangerous. Once the smoke clears the Growers will return to their tenements. Invisibility emboldens the criminals among them."

"Fetch my narcotics," Akachi commanded. "Whatever is left."

He prayed there'd be enough to allow him to thin the veil and reach his spirit animals. Flying to the Northern Cathedral would be faster and safer than walking.

Dipping a quick bow, Jumoke bustled off to the chambers at the rear of the church. Though only a year or two younger than Akachi, he seemed like a child. There was a wide-eyed innocence to the boy that miraculously survived the events of the last week.

He didn't see what I saw.

The acolyte hadn't witnessed the horrors, the violence and murder. He hadn't seen Mother Death standing in Bastion's holy streets. Akachi had left with Captain Yejide and the surviving Hummingbirds to question the Dirt known as the Artist. He returned alone, splashed in blood and on the brink of death.

It seemed so unreal.

The burning itch returned in his fingers and he scratched at it without thought, startled to again discover them missing. Cloud Serpent healed the killing wounds in Akachi's chest and left him with this reminder. Why, Akachi wasn't sure. He had no doubt the god could have made him whole, could have healed the lost fingers.

He left me crippled because I failed him.

Akachi should have defeated the street-sorcerer, once again banishing Mother Death to the bloody Desert. He should have cut Efra's heart from her chest, sacrificed her on the altar.

He wanted to protest. It wasn't fair! He'd been unaware he faced the Hearts of both Smoking Mirror and Mother Death! He hadn't understood. No one warned him!

It didn't matter.

His first real test as a man and as a nahual, and he failed both his god and his father. This second chance was more than he deserved. His lost fingers were a small price to pay.

The sounds of violence escalated. Peering through the smoke and raining ash he saw figures struggling. A squad of Hummingbird Guard, discernible only by their flawless efficiency, battled a mob of Growers. The nahual were deadly, bludgeoning Dirts, shattering skulls with ebony cudgels, smashing bones and joints. Growers littered the ground, clutching wounds, or lying motionless. And still they came, a wave of stinking humanity, clawing and punching, screaming with insensate rage.

Helpless, Akachi watched as the occluded shapes dragged down one of the Guard and smashed their head in with a fist-sized stone. He wanted to charge into the chaos, shred the veil between realities, unleash the blood-hunger of Gau Ehiza, his puma animal spirit. He couldn't. No narcotics swam his veins. He was a nahualli, untrained in physical combat.

Akachi ground his teeth. One by one, the Guard fell.

Coward, he berated himself.

No. To charge out there and die in the street would be purest folly. He alone knew the truth. Cloud Serpent gave him a task, commanded him to hunt the Hearts of Mother Death and Smoking Mirror.

Two stupid Dirt girls.

Except they weren't. Even ignoring the fact Nuru was a street-sorcerer, the women were backed by gods. They fought the same war he did, for the same prize. The last Heart alive would go to the Gods' Ring and ascend to be Heart's Mirror. They'd be granted immortality and become the Voice of the Gods. Their own god would rise to rule the pantheon, replacing the fallen Father Death.

They play the same game.

Game. War.

Was there a difference?

As long as mortals did the fighting and the gods remained aloof, Bastion would survive. Another war among the gods would surely destroy the city, end humanity.

This was how it had to be, humans acting as extensions to the will of the gods.

Blood in the streets, running deep in gutters lining every alley and building. Never a precious drop wasted.

The last of the Hummingbirds went down under the weight of Grower numbers. The Dirts hefted limp corpses, paraded them like trophies. In moments, the street was again empty, the victorious chanting fading to nothing.

Do they even know why they fight?

The fools smashed churches, goaded on by Loa manipulators, ignorant of the consequences.

They fight a war that could end all Bastion, snuff the last spark of humanity forever.

"Pastor?" called Jumoke from the church's main hall.

Akachi returned inside.

"I found a small amount of aldatu, and jainkoei," the acolyte informed him.

Hunger stabbed through Akachi, and he struggled to crushed it. He hadn't thought there was any jainkoei left.

Weaving through the assorted detritus, Jumoke deposited the narcotics atop the blood-stained sacrificial altar. Some of those stains were Akachi's.

Is it sacrilege to use an altar as a simple table?

About to scold the boy, Akachi saw the badly blended pile. The cured mushrooms had been hastily ground together with the jainkoei. Pale flecks jutted from the mess. He must have prepared this days ago, back when he rode the ragged edge of brain-burn. He had no recollection of making the blend, nor what he intended it for.

The aldatu, a powerful hallucinogen that thinned the veil between worlds, he'd need to become the blood-tailed hawk. The jainkoei, he did not.

The hunger returned, creeping like a beaten dog. Desire. Longing. A need to open his soul to the will of his god. Anything to once again be the centre of Cloud Serpent's attention, if only for a heartbeat.

Akachi despaired he'd ever feel that again. He *craved* it. This tiny amount of jainkoei would give him the smallest taste of what he desired.

"I can fish out the jainkoei," offered Jumoke.

Akachi swallowed. It was the right thing to do. Save it for later. Never ingest narcotics beyond what you require for the sorcery. Over and over the teachers beat that into the acolytes.

"No," said Akachi, swallowing his doubts. "Leave it. I…" The dream. Zalika. The staff. The Northern Cathedral. "I may need Cloud Serpent to guide me." He darted a glance at the acolyte. "The Loa incite the Growers. The ring is dangerous."

Jumoke nodded agreement, face expressionless. "Of course."

How could Akachi explain? He'd battled Mother Death, the most ancient god, and been slain. The Lord of the Hunt intervened, manifested right here in this very church, and brought him back. He was Cloud Serpent's Heart, tasked to hunt and kill the enemies of Bastion.

He alone among all the nahual understood how serious this Grower uprising was.

No one else knows Mother Death has returned!

And yet, he had no idea what to do. Yes, he must hunt the two Dirt women, but which was the priority? What if they split up? Cloud

Serpent's command amounted to a rather vague *get it done*. Even the dream hadn't told him what to do with the staff.

Vision, he corrected. *Not a dream.*

He wanted to search through the *Book of Bastion*, hunting for references to the Fifth Sun.

He felt utterly lost.

Being Cloud Serpent's Heart made him neither wise nor knowledgeable. He was the same untested priest who left the Northern Cathedral barely a week ago. His experiences changed him, but gave no answers.

Should I pass along what I know?

Who should he report to?

The Hearts of the other gods were out there, somewhere in Bastion. Though the sects of nahual worked together to shepherd the souls of the city, they each served their own god. It was an uneasy alliance at the best of times, politicking and manipulation smouldering in the background. Now, with The Lord dead, those embers would spark to life. That smouldering strife would escalate to a true inferno. Alliances would form and be broken. Assassinations and backstabbing would become commonplace.

Trust was a luxury only enjoyed during times of peace.

Each sect will hunt and kill the Hearts of the opposing gods.

Akachi was now a target, someone worth killing.

Bishop Zalika's god was dead. Much as she hated him, she might be one of the few nahual who had no cause to wish him harm.

The dream. She wouldn't willingly give him the staff. He knew that to be true.

Is she still a Bishop?

If not, who ruled the Northern Cathedral?

Too many questions and no answers.

He needed to go to the Cathedral as much to learn the state of the ring as to warn whoever was now in charge.

What happens if your god dies?

He shuddered at the thought. To be cast away like that. One

moment she was the highest ranked nahual in the northern quarter. Now, was she even a priest?

It doesn't matter. Zalika doesn't matter. Only Bastion matters.

The gods played their game through their mortal representatives, but if the city fell, everyone lost. Nothing would survive.

Reporting what had happened to a ranked nahual, Akachi realized, would be a mistake. It would draw attention he could ill-afford.

He'd find the Staff of the Fifth Sun and resume his hunt for Nuru and Efra.

The more he thought about it, the more confusing everything became.

How can the Hearts of two competing gods travel together?

Did the women not know? They were ignorant Dirts, after all. Maybe they didn't understand what was at stake, didn't realize that, in the end, only one of them could survive to be Heart's Mirror. Perhaps they used each other, plotting betrayal when the other was no longer of use. The small scarred one, Efra, seemed capable of such behaviour.

Nuru, the beautiful one, clung to some desperate code of conduct. Closing his eyes, he saw her. She was stunning, the kind of impossible beauty that hurt. Then, when the god came, she was terrible. Jagged legs, barbed with obsidian. Spider's body, bulbous and glistening. And yet still Nuru, the same long hair the colour of rich loam. Flawless skin, the limitless black Akachi imagined only blind people saw.

She'll learn or she'll die.

Seeing the irony, Akachi quirked a sad smile.

The two women couldn't be more different. Efra, Smoking Mirror's Heart, would never let a thing like friendship stand in the way of what she wanted.

Scooping up the narcotics, he shoved them into his mouth and chewed.

Seeing Akachi looking for something to drink, Jumoke said, "The church well is full of ash." He winced a shrug. "Sorry."

Akachi waved it away and choked down the blend. "Stay here until I return."

"I shall protect the church with my life," swore the acolyte.

"No. If the Growers come, I want you to flee."

Jumoke flashed a quick grin. "Yeah, I'm going to loot the church and run away." The boy studied Akachi, mouth set at an odd angle, like he was trying to decide whether to speak further. "Try not to get killed. Again."

Akachi grunted a laugh. "How did I end up with you as an acolyte?"

"Probably crapped in the Bishop's breakfast."

With a nod, Akachi exited the church.

Even through an impenetrable haze of smoke and ash, the sun's heat crushed him. Falling ash collected on his head and shoulders, dusting his hair grey, staining his vestments. Guessing the time was impossible. One patch of sky, a smear of blood, seemed slightly brighter than the rest.

Akachi coughed, spitting.

Ash-choked wells.

Burning fields.

Is it already too late?

Was Bastion doomed?

The gods would never allow that.

And yet Cloud Serpent said that both Efra and Nuru had the potential to destroy Bastion.

The narcotic mix coiled in his blood like an angry snake, twisting reality, thinning the veil between worlds. There, through the smoke and ash, he saw his spirit animals prowl, awaiting his call.

Fetching the carving of the blood-tailed hawk from its place in his belt, Akachi focussed on it, let it become his world.

The screams and sounds of violence faded.

The smell of burning fields was replaced by another, deeper odour.

Death. Sun-rotted meat. Ash-thickened blood.

Colours dimmed as his peripheral vision shrank to a narrow predator's focus.

With a scream, Akachi took to the air.

NURU - MIRRORED BLACK

Just as Father Death rules the underworld, each god possesses its own reality. Once populated by trillions, the gods stripped them clean of life in their eternal hunger. Now, only those hoarded souls, harvested from Bastion, remain.

Farmed.

Rationed.

The hunger of the gods is never sated.

Only Mother Death, the last of the Rada L'Wha, the one god truly of this *reality, has the wisdom to save humanity.*

—The Loa Book of the Invisibles

Nuru lay on the floor in the dim basement of an abandoned Grower tenement. The grit of filth and ancient stone stabbed through her thread-bare thobe.

How long had she lain here, afraid to close her eyes, yet praying for sleep?

Exhaustion left everything dreamlike, unreal. Giving up, she pushed herself into a sitting position. Though the last of the night's chill pimpled her flesh, the day's heat trickled down the shallow steps. Throat dry, she coughed.

"You're awake." A shape moved in the dark. Efra.

"Yeah." She felt parched, cracked like sun-baked mud. "Can't sleep. Every time—" Her chest tightened.

Every time she closed her eyes, she saw them.

Bomani, murdered by Fadil's gang, his blood staining the street.

Omari, gaunt and sunken, dead in a basement, broken by that Cloud Serpent nahualli.

Happy, a sacrificial dagger shoved into his heart.

Chisulo, shattered, his chest caved-in fighting a nagual monster.

Over and over she watched him step between Efra and the Cloud Serpent sorcerer. 'Get behind me,' he said. No hesitation. He could do no less, make no other choice. He would protect his friends no matter what it cost. And she saw herself kneeling in the street, the carving of Mother Death before her, as her friends died.

"We have to move," whispered Efra, as if she feared the Birds might hear.

And go where?

Nothing mattered. Why continue? Everyone was dead.

Everyone, except scarred and murderous little Efra. In a single week she spilled more blood than Bomani managed in years of gang-related violence and drunken street brawls.

Not just blood. Deaths, too.

Quick as Bomani was to violence, he had no taste for murder.

Efra killed without hesitation.

Your own hands are hardly clean.

Using her nagual power to become a deadly viper, Nuru had killed Sefu to rescue Efra.

And you helped her kill. You held down helpless Crafters while she choked the life from them or smashed their skulls.

Efra stood motionless, an outline, waiting. She bore Smoking Mirror's mark, a black rectangle tattooed into her wrist, and yet she hinted at a willingness to betray the god.

He's a fool if he thinks he owns her.

Of course, if he offered Efra something she truly desired—security, safety, control, or power—then perhaps Nuru was the fool for thinking she might still turn on him.

"You ready?" asked Efra.

"What's the rush?"

"We are hunted."

"The priest who hunted us is dead. Everyone is dead."

Mother Death ran him through twice, vicious barbed legs tearing great holes in his chest. Nuru remembered the glory of the moment, feeding off the nahualli's blood, the contempt with which she cast aside the ruined remains of him. They left the priest bleeding out in the street. No way he survived such wounds.

Efra grunted dismissal. "He was just a priest."

Nuru blinked at the shape of her. The sun must be rising. She could now make out hints of detail. Efra stood with her arms crossed protectively over her chest, impatience writ in the set of her hips.

"*Just* a priest? He was a temple-trained nahualli of Cloud Serpent, Lord of the Hunt."

"Just a priest," repeated Efra. "Just a man." She snorted. "A *boy*. It's the god we should fear. He will send more priests."

As always, Efra was right. That young priest—she didn't know his name—was nothing. Another corpse. They were hunted by an entire priesthood. They were hunted by a god.

There were nahual more terrifying than the priests of Cloud Serpent. The nahualli of Father Death tore souls from people, tortured their victims for an eternity in The Lord's underworld. She once heard that a Sheep District rose up in rebellion and a nahualli of Sin Eater brought plagues upon them. A dozen streets of bloated corpses and not a single death beyond. The nahualli of every god, even one as seemingly benign as Precious Feather, were capable of terrible sorcery.

Do all the gods hunt us? Have we united them in purpose?

"Do you think word has spread?" Nuru asked. "Will all the nahual be looking for us?"

Efra tilted her head in thought. With a finger, she traced the scar from one temple, through her lips, to the opposite side of her chin. "No," she said. "If the gods aren't already at war, they will be soon."

"They will wage war on Mother Death."

Efra glanced up the steps to where the tenement above grew

brighter with the rising sun. "You're wrong. It isn't us against them."

"No?"

"It's everyone against everyone."

Nuru squinted at Efra, trying to read some hint of expression. "How do you know?"

"Smoking Mirror spoke to me. Stone and smoke and sand." She shuddered. "I dreamt mirrored black, slicked in blood. A war of dead, and a burning night sky."

The Obsidian Lord speaks to her.

From anyone else it would have been a lie, or insanity. With Efra, Nuru had no choice but to believe her. She'd walked the woman's dreams, witnessed Smoking Mirror show Efra flashes of possible futures. The god had confronted Nuru there, held her trapped in Efra's dream-world. *She is my Heart*, he said. *Protect her or Bastion falls.*

That had been before Nuru finished the carving of Mother Death.

Had Smoking Mirror not known what Nuru worked at?

What if I was wrong? What if Mother Death wasn't part of Father Discord's plan at all?

Nuru had assumed the god knew everything, was somehow behind Mother Death's return to Bastion, but Smoking Mirror made no mention of the banished god.

What if he hadn't known? Could Mother Death be manipulating Smoking Mirror?

That felt wrong. The nahual often spoke of the Obsidian Lord as an ancient trickster and master manipulator whereas Mother Death was only ever spoken of in tones of horror and fear. She wasn't subtle. She brought death and destruction.

Back before she began carving the god, Nuru had known, deep in her bones, that Efra was important. She remembered feeling that Bastion would somehow provide an answer and Efra would play a part.

And Efra had. She got them into the Crafters' Ring. She got Nuru the tools and paints to complete the carving.

Was that Mother Death influencing my decisions?

She recalled the rush of fear when she learned Fadil's gang took Efra, the panic that her one chance at completing her carving might be taken away. She pushed Chisulo to charge off and rescue the girl even though Efra was barely part of the gang.

After, Efra somehow became a central figure, even taking command and giving orders.

We went to see the Artist because of Efra.

That had been her decision.

Nuru's friends died because of Efra.

No!

Nuru crushed the spiralling anxiety. That wasn't all Efra's fault. She was being unfair, blaming the girl for things no one could have foreseen.

She is my Heart, Father Discord said of Efra.

Am I with Efra because this is where Mother Death wants me, or because this is where Smoking Mirror wants Efra?

Nuru's mind reeled, flitting from possibility to ever more outrageous possibility. And yet, no matter how insane it all felt, at least two gods had entwined themselves in her life.

What *wasn't* possible?

Mother Death, the banished Queen of Bastion, was deranged from countless millennium spent scrounging an existence beyond Bastion's Sand Wall. She survived by devouring lesser gods and the souls of those cast from the city. But she was ancient. Ancient beyond even the other gods if the Loa were to be believed. Nothing survived that long without some deep cleverness.

She is my Heart. What did that mean? It sounded like the Obsidian Lord chose Efra for something. *Protect her or Bastion falls.* Was that still true? Had it ever been true, or had the god lied?

Whatever Father Discord was up to, he wasn't finished. A shiver of terror ran through Nuru. Every Grower knew better than to draw the attention of the nahual. How much worse was it to be the focus of a god?

Efra stood waiting. Her words sank in.

"Everyone against everyone?" Nuru asked.

"The gods are at war, but they can't fight each other for fear of destroying the city." Efra turned to face Nuru, eyes like shards of shattered glass in the dark. "We are their weapons. They fight through us."

"To what end?"

Efra hesitated. "Father Death is dead."

The Lord dead? Impossible!

"How do you know that?"

Efra waved away the question. "The gods war to see who will replace him. The winner will be the new head of the pantheon. Either everything changes, or we'll see another ten thousand years of the same."

"Smoking Mirror told you this?"

"Maybe."

Maybe?

"Did he mention a god's Heart?" Nuru asked.

"A what?" asked Efra, looking bewildered. "Heart? I don't think they're flesh and blood like us."

"Something I heard once from a nahual," lied Nuru.

"Either way," continued Efra, giving Nuru a confused look, "it means the gods are not a united front. They have bigger problems than two Dirt girls."

Nuru was less sure.

Efra saw her doubt. "The fields are burning. The Growers riot in the streets. If the nahual don't regain control, the whole city will burn or starve, or both." As if eager to be moving, she looked over her shoulder, up the worn steps. "If they regain control, nothing changes. Growers work the fields. Bastion continues stagnating."

If we win everyone starves and dies?

"How do you know that?" Nuru repeated.

"Smoking Mirror showed me," she said, voice devoid of emotion. "Sin Eater wants to crush the Growers and Crafters, bleed them of temptation. Enforced purity, flawless adherence to the Book. Lashes for unclean hands and stained thobes. Daily confessions. Whippings for impure thoughts. Hobbling. Breaking bones. Driving tiny spears of wood through the corner of the eye to lance sin at the source. There are plants that will lock you inside yourself, make you empty and obedient, the perfect Dirt. Sin Eater is obsessed with purity. His nahual will devour our flaws, free us from the freedom to make mistakes."

Father Discord said all this?

A scream echoed down the steps.

"Maybe we should stay here," said Nuru.

Her world was dead, gone from her. Or maybe she was gone from it. She couldn't tell. Somehow, when she and Efra passed through the Grey Wall into the Crafters' Ring, they broke something ancient and precious. When they re-entered the Growers' Ring, it wasn't the world they knew. It was smaller, greyer.

We left one reality and returned to another.

Everything that happened after—the deaths of her friends, the fighting and rioting in the streets, the fields burning, Mother Death—it was all Nuru's fault.

They broke the laws of nature, the rules of the world. They did the forbidden and Bastion paid a terrible price.

We never should have left.

Offering Nuru a hand, Efra pulled her to her feet. "Let's go. It's getting louder up there."

She was right.

"Isabis," said Nuru, tuning to squint into the dark corners of the room, searching for her snake.

"You have to leave her."

Nuru swallowed rising fear. "No."

"If the Birds see you with a viper around your neck, they'll kill us and her. If you love the snake, you have to leave her."

Nuru darted an angry glare at the scarred girl. *What the fuck do you know about love?*

Efra was more like the snake. Though, come to think of it, sometimes Nuru felt like Isabis was aware of her beyond being a source of warmth on a cold night. Not that Isabis loved or cared for her, but at least the snake seemed to acknowledge that they existed together, depended on each other somewhat.

Not Efra.

Efra could walk out of here and never look back. A week from now she probably wouldn't remember Nuru's name.

You're being unfair. She saved your life.

And she cried after Chisulo's death. That meant something, right?

Efra tugged Nuru toward the stairs. "Come on."

She was, Nuru hated to admit, right. She was always fucking right. Isabis would draw attention. Even if the Birds weren't specifically looking for them, wandering around with a viper curled around your neck was too much.

Grinding her teeth, eyes stinging, Nuru allowed herself to be pulled up the steps.

"I'll find you," she called into the dark. "I'll come back."

She swallowed her grief. Isabis was more than a snake. She was the last connection to Nuru's old life. "Stay safe," she whispered.

"No one is going to wander into a dark basement and mess with a deadly snake," said Efra. "We on the other hand are going to get our skulls smashed in by Birds. She's safer without us."

She probably meant it to be comforting.

Already Nuru missed Isabis, the cold emotionless solidity of the reptile mind. So like Efra. Kill for a purpose. Kill because you're annoyed. Both were capable of doing either.

The air grew thick as they reached the ground floor, smoke clawing at their throats, the heavy stench of scorched stone. Heat sucked the moisture from Nuru's flesh, the air from her lungs. The sky, a bloody wound of cancerous smoke stained red by the occluded sun, clawed at her senses. The world felt wrong. Crushingly wrong.

All my fault.

Growers were forbidden from leaving the ring. It was in the Book. Why did she ever think things could improve?

Nothing ever *gets better. Not until you're dead*, was the Grower joke that wasn't a joke. A cowardly mocking of the nahual claim that if they led good lives, if they were meek and obedient, they'd be reborn closer to the gods. Flakes of ash danced in the air, swaying like drunken Dirts, piled in ankle-deep drifts in the streets. Footprints cut weaving paths. After a life-time of bare feet on gritty stone, each step felt strangely soft.

Nuru stared at a long mound of ash, mind working at the mystery of what caused it. She realized it was a corpse, still and buried.

A woman, bloodstained thobe torn and filthy, sprinted past. Three men, gaunt and stripped near naked, chased after her, hooting. They reached for her with wrinkled hands, fingers like leather. Hungry eyes, feral. They knew what they wanted.

Nuru made to step out, to stop them, to slow them so the woman might escape.

Efra dragged her back into the shadow of the entrance, clamping a hard hand over her mouth. "Don't," she breathed into Nuru's ear. "I'll have to kill them."

She will. She'll kill them all.

Nuru knew a moment's hesitation. Fight free. Catch the men's atten-tion. Let Efra do what Efra did. Make fucking sure they died. But then she remembered the bodies Efra left in the Crafter's Ring. Choked cold, still as stone. Eyes wide. Blood and bone and brains.

The hesitation cost her the chance, and the men were gone, hooted cries fading away.

"They're going to—"

"Better her than us," snapped Efra. "Later, when your blood is thick with whatever it is you need to shred the veil, we can crush them. Now, we have to run."

Gripping Nuru's hand tight, Efra pulled her into the street, away from where the men went. Something long and sinuous twisted through the smoke far above. Like an unseen snake parting tall grass, its passing roiled the clouds. As long as ten men lying head to toe and as wide as three, smaller shapes flitted and darted about it. They reminded Nuru of those tiny birds that always harassed hawks.

Impossible, she thought.

With no narcotics in her blood, the veil remained an impenetrable wall. She couldn't see it, much less thin or reach through it. Was there another sorcerer nearby? She couldn't imagine what the thing could have been. Not even the largest constrictors were that big. Was it Loa, nahualli, or something else, something from *outside*?

Through Nuru, Mother Death gained entrance to the Last City. What if other spirits, demons and dead gods, also found some way in?

This is the end.

She remembered thinking that.

The city will fall, everyone will die.

It was all her fault.

Growers ran past, darting terrified glances over their shoulders, eyes wide with terror. Not chasing, but fleeing. More came. Scores. Crammed shoulder to shoulder, they filled the street. A young man stumbled and fell, clawing at those nearest. He went down, disappeared from sight. Without breaking pace, the crowd surged over him.

The Hummingbird Guard followed, tight formations of red leather armour, ebony shields, and blood-spattered cudgels. They smashed bones and joints, caved skulls, and left death in their wake. Where the Growers screamed in rage and fear and fought like cornered animals, the Birds worked in grim silence. Nahual of Father War, The Left Hand, they were priests of Bastion's God of Terror.

A nightmare of violence in crimson armour, blackened by blood-thickened ash, the Birds did their god proud. The wet *slap* of wood on flesh, a litany of prayer. The splintering *crack* of bone, a benediction. The screams of the broken, a song of worship offered in exaltation.

Without warning, Efra dragged Nuru into the street, bulling her way into the mob.

Nuru's world became the thunder of raw sucking breath, the stench of panic and sweat. Shoulders jostled her, an elbow catching her on the cheekbone. When she staggered, dazed, Efra kept her up, kept her moving. Sodden pulp squishing between her bare toes, sharp stabbing pain in the arch of her foot. Glancing down she caught a glimpse of ruined skull, bent at an odd angle, eyes gaping lifeless wide, as she stepped on the face.

Choking ash and smoke. Too hot to breathe, nostrils clogged shut. Sparks fell from a flaming sky, burnt holes in thobes, left scorched wounds in flesh. A savage crush of gaunt bodies. Each struggling inhalation hurt. It felt like her lungs were filled with silt.

The gods burn the world.

Sin Eater would purify the wayward Growers with fire, cleanse them of their Dirt lives.

Helpless and lost, Nuru allowed Efra to drag her through the crowd. The scarred woman screamed insults and threats at those around them or at Nuru. Sometimes Efra shoved people aside, drove viscous little punches under ribs, jabbed fingers in eyes, or did whatever she deemed necessary to keep moving forward.

Efra kicked a man in the back of the knee. When his leg buckled, she put a hand on his shoulder and used him to propel herself past.

A flash of black caught Nuru's eye, the rectangle tattooed on the inside of Efra's right wrist.

Smoking Mirror's mark.

Father Discord. God of Strife. The Enemy of Both Sides. She was perfect for him, an unstoppable force of chaos.

And you carry Mother Death in your heart.

The Mother of the Universe. The Destroyer. How could a god be the embodiment of two such opposing concepts? And if Efra was perfect for Smoking Mirror, what did that say of Nuru? Had the Mother chosen wrong? Could gods make mistakes?

Or did she know something Nuru did not?

Nuru stumbled as Efra yanked her around a corner and into a less crowded street. Her shoulder ached like the joint had been pulled half out.

"Run, you fucking bitch," screamed Efra, "or I'll fucking leave you!"

They ran.

They sprinted past streets filled with warring men and women. Growers dragged down Birds with their bare hands, beat them to death with crude clubs. The Guard fought with inhuman precision, killing efficiently, but grossly outnumbered. Piles of refuse burned, further fouling the already wretched air. People lay sprawled in ash, Bird and Dirt alike. Some were still. Others moaned or crawled, sobbing for help.

"Mom!" cried a young Bird, face a bloody mess, one eye a gaping wound, both legs bent awkwardly beneath him. "Mommy!"

A Grower came out of the smoke and crushed his head with a rock.

In the distance, the Grey Wall towered over squat tenements. Though they took whatever streets seemed least dangerous, Efra kept turning them in that direction. If breaking the holy scripture of the Book the first time caused all this, what would happen when they once again passed through into the Crafters' Ring?

Stumbling with exhaustion, they slowed. On this street, Growers huddled in their homes. There was no open fighting.

Efra pulled Nuru to the next corner and stopped. Peering around it, she swore.

"Birds at the gate," she grunted between breaths. "Fuck."

Nuru fell against the wall, let it take her weight. Numb from horror, she said, "Are we on the same side?"

"Of what?" Efra asked, distracted.

"This war."

Pulling back from the corner, Efra studied her.

Is she deciding, or deciding whether to lie?

"I see you thinking about that," said Nuru.

A hint of a smile teased Efra's lips, gone before fully formed. "I thought we were. But the fact you're asking makes me wonder."

Better than an outright lie, but less than helpful.

Eyes narrowing, Efra asked, "Why wouldn't we be?"

Nuru grabbed Efra's arm, pulled up the sleeve, exposing her tattooed wrist. "Smoking Mirror." Releasing the arm, she touched her own chest.

"Mother Death."

"So?" Efra's brow crinkled in confusion. "We make our own choices. If Smoking Mirror thinks I belong to him, he's a fool. Does Mother Death own you?"

"No."

"Exactly. It just means one of us might have to betray a god." Efra winked. "Maybe both of us." She bit her lip, teeth worrying at the ridge of scar. "The gods made this city to save humanity, but they also built these ringed walls. They trapped the Growers in this life. You think they have our interests at heart? Me either. So fuck them."

For an instant Nuru imagined a world without gods. If humanity were free to decide its own path, what would it choose?

It was a fool's dream. It would never work. Bastion would fall without the gods. Even if it didn't, humanity would still be trapped in here, surrounded by endless desert and the souls of all the world's dead.

She's right. We have choices.

But what choices would Efra make? She was self-centred and dangerous, willing and able to do anything if she thought it would improve her situation.

Can I trust her?

Did it matter?

"What do we do?" Nuru asked. "We lost. Everyone is dead. It's just us. We're helpless."

"Lost? Helpless?" Efra barked a harsh laugh. "Maybe we didn't win, but we didn't lose."

Nuru wasn't so sure. "You said there were Birds at the gate. We're stuck here. We'll never get out of the ring."

"We'll find another gate."

"They'll all be guarded," argued Nuru.

Hissing through her teeth in frustration, Efra looked up and down the street. "We have to find a Loa church. They've been preaching the return of Mother Death for a thousand generations. Well, she's back, and we have her. They'll feed us. They'll get us out of the ring."

A lone Bird, bleeding from a score of wounds, staggered from an alley. A half dozen Growers followed in pursuit. They caught the woman, pulled her down. Nuru watched as they bent the woman's limbs until the joints popped, a sick parody of what the Birds did to punish violent Growers.

"We'll die out here," she said. "We should wait. We should hide until this passes."

"This won't pass," said Efra. "Not for a long time. Not until a great many Growers are dead. Not until we've been crushed back to meek servility. It that what you want?"

Meek servility. That didn't sound like Efra. She must have heard it somewhere. Maybe from a nahual.

Recalling the Crafter women with their children, Nuru whispered, "No."

"We tear this down. All of it. The nahual think this is their war. Mother Death thinks it's hers. It isn't, it's *ours.*"

"How are we going to find a Loa church?" Nuru asked.

Once again grabbing her hand, Efra flashed a quick grin. "Easy. We'll ask."

AKACHI - A WORLD OF ENEMIES

It is easy to underestimate tecolotl and their pathetic dependence on stones. However, much as many nahualli learn several arts, there is nothing stopping a tecolotl from learning true sorcery. This combination of pure art and foul blasphemy births nightmarish results.

In the third millennium, during the Senatorial Wars, nahualli Raziya, a Loa infiltrator and skilled tecuhtli, intercepted a wagon of sacrificial daggers bound for the Priests' Ring. Combining the art of the tecuhtli with her tecolotl talents, she used kyanite to force the souls stored in the daggers into the corpses of those she'd sacrificed. Having created an army of undead, she then used hyraceum to bend the trapped souls to her will.

Though Raziya began with only a handful of corpses, each person slain rose to join her army. Within a week, one third of the Senator's Ring was under her control and populated almost entirely by corpses. Were it not for the intervention of the Turquoise Serpents, the ring would have fallen to the Loa.

—The Book of Bastion

A blood-tailed hawk, Akachi spiralled into the air, powerful wings pulling him higher. Distant fields still burned, adding to the pall drowning the city. If there were nahual out there fighting the flames, they were losing.

Predatory eyes caught every movement beneath him, the crashing war of small men. The hawk didn't care, but the man at the heart of the bird studied the weft and wane of battle. The Hummingbirds fought with consummate skill, worked in tight formations, but the sheer mass of

Grower flesh took its toll. Again and again he witnessed squads falling back, pressed into dead ended alleys, cornered and butchered.

They're losing.

The Growers fought without finesse, but from this vantage he realized they fought with surprising intelligence. Their movements were too planned for such a chaotic struggle.

They aren't that smart. They aren't that organized.

Akachi glanced toward the Grey Wall, hoping for some sign that the Turquoise Serpents, Southern Hummingbird's elite, had arrived. The smoke was too thick.

Dim shapes, drained of colour, surged about like terrified field mice. Dirts swarmed a church of Precious Feather. Beautiful women, dressed in revealing robes cut to best accentuate their varied shapes and features, fled the temple only to be trapped in the courtyard. One of the women stepped forward, blue-black hair like that of a puma spilling about her shoulders. Jainkoei and aldatu in his blood, Akachi saw the veil around her twist like gossamer threads of silk. She twined reality about her fingers, weaving the very fabric of the world. With a gesture, she scattered two carved wooden figurines in the ash before her. Uncertain, timid as their nature demanded, the Growers slowed. The Precious Feather nahualli opened the veil with a practised twitch of slim fingers and called through her allies. The carved totems became real. A leopard, mighty muscles rolling, prowled ready. Long arms strong enough to tear a grown man apart, a massive gorilla beat its chest and roared in challenge.

Peyollotl, Akachi mused. And a skilled one, if she could control two totems at the same time.

As he flew past, several jaguars and a monstrous lumbering crocodile charged from the smoke to attack the nahualli's totems; the Loa were out in force and backing the Dirts.

The war below suddenly made sense. The Dirts weren't this smart, they couldn't plan. They didn't strategically corner the Guard or split squads to be dispatched more easily. The Growers were being driven, herded like cattle, manipulated by the Loa heretics.

Precious Feather's church fell behind Akachi, and he flew on. There was nothing he could do to help. As a hawk, he was useless in a fight against peyollotl or nagual. There wasn't enough aldatu in his blood to thin the veil so he might become something more dangerous. If he stopped to fight, he'd have to walk the rest of the way to the Northern Cathedral. Assuming he survived the battle.

Cloud Serpent gave him a mission. Saving a few nahual wouldn't matter if all Bastion died. He had to find the staff. He had to hunt the two Dirt girls. Nothing would distract him from his holy purpose.

Banking to look back, Akachi saw the Precious Feather nahual clubbed senseless from behind, her creations becoming disjointed and ungainly as she wobbled on weak knees. The second blow dropped her to the ground and the leopard and gorilla once again became lifeless wood totems. Was she dead, or unconscious? Filthy Growers swarmed over the beautiful nahual, tearing away their vestments.

I can't help.

Was that who he was?

Was that the kind of man he was?

Would he turn his back on fellow nahual?

No!

About to turn back, it hit him: Everything had changed. They weren't *fellow* nahual. They were priests of a god who competed with Cloud Serpent to become head of the pantheon. The realization took his breath away. The world was different now. He was no longer a nahual of the gods of Bastion. He was the Heart of Cloud Serpent. The priests of every other god would work to impede him. It would be their holy duty to kill him so their own god's Heart might ascend to become Heart's Mirror.

He was alone in a world of enemies, not even Captain Yejide at his side.

I should be praying that nahualli was Precious Feather's Heart, not flying back to save her.

It felt wrong. Guilt hung heavy in his gut. Even if he was right, it felt like an excuse. An excuse for cowardice.

Captain Yejide made me brave.

He wouldn't fail her, wouldn't fail the memory of her.

Were she alive, whose side would she be on now?

Would she stand with Akachi, or kill him for Southern Humming-bird?

Continuing its flight toward the cathedral, the blood-tailed hawk screamed in frustration.

In the last twenty-five thousand years, Bastion had survived count-less changes in leadership among the gods. She would survive this, too. Chaos would not take the Last City!

Akachi flew north. Scenes of horror beyond count passed beneath him. Churches defaced, their nahual sacrificed or tortured. Over and over he saw Dirts bring down squads of Hummingbirds through sheer weight of stinking flesh. The Growers outnumbered all the other rings of Bastion combined. What chance did the Guard have?

A church of Sin Eater burned, having been stuffed full of straw and scraps of wood. The temple priest, a stooped old man, staggered about the ravaged courtyard, his once-pristine robes torn and matted in filth.

Akachi flew on, struggling to ignore the atrocities. Retreating into the hawk's reality helped. The bird cared nothing for the world of men. Yet he could not escape his fears.

What was happening in the heart of Bastion? Had word of the Grower uprising reached the Priests' Ring? It took many days to walk from the core to the outer ring, though there were faster means of communication. Dream messages must have been sent, nagual or peyol-lotl dispatched with reports.

Does father know I am Cloud Serpent's Heart?

Would the Lord of the Hunt inform his High Priest?

Were he not a hawk, Akachi would have grinned. No one was born knowing they were a Heart. In times of peace, Hearts were born and died unaware of their potential and importance. As High Priest, his father might have assumed the role would fall to him.

Does everyone already know of Father Death's demise?

It seemed likely, but the gods often went hundreds, or even thousands of years without uttering a single word to a mortal. It was impossible to know what they thought important.

Akachi considered the task ahead. Would Bishop Zalika await him in the dispensary like the dream promised? The thought of all those narcotics quickened his heart. Not knowing what he'd face, or how long before he'd get the chance to restock, he'd best pack some of everything.

Jainkoei! Aldatu! As much as he could carry!

He swallowed his building hunger.

After Zalika, he'd have to face the street-sorcerer and Mother Death.

I'll need a sizeable quantity of narcotics to hunt and fight her.

A flash of shadow as something passed between Akachi and the smoke-obscured sun. The bird in him reacted instinctively, flinging itself to the side. An eagle screamed past, raking Akachi's wings with vicious talons, banked sharply, and disappeared into the smog.

Pain flared through Akachi like fire.

The bird had been huge but misshapen, its eyes too far apart. The claws were hooked and jagged, as if carved in a rush, the feathers subtly wrong.

Street-sorcerer. It had to be.

Flying in looping serpentine arcs, Akachi tried to watch everything at once. His wounded wing, bleeding profusely and missing several critical flight feathers, hampered his progress. Impenetrable smoke blotted the sky. Had the eagle not made the mistake of passing between Akachi and the sun, he never would have seen it coming. Smaller shapes flitted beyond sight, teasing. He couldn't shake them. No matter how fast he flew, they kept pace.

Turning, he caught sight of two falcons giving chase. With speed and agility on their side, they gained quickly.

Should he try climbing, lose them in the thicker smoke above? Could he breathe up there?

A ragged tearing pain shredded Akachi's thoughts as the eagle crashed into him from above, clawing great wounds in his back, ripping flesh and feathers. Twisting in the air, he managed to strike at the bird with his beak, causing it to release him.

Akachi fell.

NURU - THE FINAL IMMOLATION

Obsidian is the stone of souls. The more souls stored within, the more powerful the stone. Typically, the sacrificial daggers of the nahual are rotated on a monthly basis, returned to the Gods' Ring where they may be drained of souls. The knives used by the Hummingbird Guard might go a year before making the journey to the Gods' Ring and are powerful weapons indeed. The obsidian swords of the Turquoise Serpents go many years, centuries even, and cleave through both stone and bone with ease.

Ancient myths tell of sorcerers battling gods and winning, slaughtering them with blades reeking of death and riven souls.

—The Loa Book of the Invisibles

Gripping Nuru's hand like she meant to tear it off, Efra dragged her back into the street and away from the illusory safety of the abandoned tenements.

They can't search them all.

If they hid in the right one, the rioters and Birds might pass them by. Once things settled down, they could venture out in search of food.

Nuru's stomach rumbled complaint, reminding her she hadn't eaten more than scavenged scraps in days. She couldn't remember her last meal. Was it a crust of hardbread Happy brought back to the basement they hid in?

He always fed the others before taking anything for himself. Nuru stifled a laugh; Efra had called him an idiot when he tried to give her a larger share than his, threatened to kick his balls in if he didn't eat.

She isn't all selfish. Not all the time.

Smoke. Ash. Eyes stinging, Nuru coughed and spat grey sludge. Her nostrils felt clogged with drying mud. Every day of her life had been hot. The stone of the city seemed to soak up the sun and amplify the heat so you cooked from all sides.

Today was hotter.

The world burned.

The sky burned.

It felt like the whole city was on fire, like out beyond the Sand Wall, the red sands of the Bloody Desert burned too.

The final immolation of a world.

At least this street was quiet, the fighting having moved on. Bodies, already gathering a blanket of ash, littered the square. None moved.

Where are we? What district? Nuru had no idea.

"I'm so dry I could shit dust," said Efra, pulling her toward a well.

Nuru didn't recognize it. Though still part of the single piece of stone that was Bastion, this one was shaped differently than the well she knew in the Wheat District. A little taller and more oval, the rim more worn and rounded by countless generations of Growers kneeling to raise the bucket from the depths. Were those imperfections? Had the gods made mistakes, or intentionally fashioned the wells of various districts differently? She couldn't imagine Smoking Mirror or Mother Death putting thought into the shape of individual wells.

Squinting into the well's darkness, Efra said, "Is that water?"

Nuru leaned past to get a better look. In all her life she'd never seen a well so low. The gods brought water up from the ground. No one ever went thirsty. "I can't tell."

Surprisingly, the bucket still hung on its hemp rope. It had been damaged, the wood scarred, but not holed. Nuru stared at the battered object, worn smooth and round like everything in Bastion. Like Bastion herself. How old was this bucket? How many generations of Growers drank from it?

"Keep watch," said Efra, lowering it into the well.

When she hauled it back up, damp ash filled it.

Efra looked close to tears, the scar tugging her lip down, eyes bright. "Fuck. Fuckers."

"Fuckers?" asked Nuru.

Never still for long, never one to wallow in misery, Efra again pulled Nuru into motion. "Fucking Loa," she growled. "They knew." Angry eyes glanced at Nuru. "Burn the fields. Leave the Growers no choice but to move inward."

Was that true? Had the Loa done this on purpose, planned in such detail? How insane would you have to be—how desperate to take power —to risk the extinction of all humanity? Did they know something she did not?

Not hard to know more than an ignorant Dirt.

She couldn't imagine what knowledge they might have that would make this anything less than suicidal madness. Did they think Mother Death would somehow save the city? They couldn't *know*, not for sure. They certainly hadn't known of her return. If they had, they would have been there, ready to give aid. Nuru suspected there'd been no communication between the Loa and their god in all the millennia she stalked the Bloody Desert.

They don't know she's here, or they'd take her from me.

No way the Loa would leave their god with some Dirt street-sorcerer. From what little she'd heard, most of them came from the inner rings. They were nahual of Mother Death. She knew exactly what priests thought of Growers.

Efra herded Nuru into another street. There were more bodies here, fresher. Some still leaked blood, or lay moaning. Efra slowed, searching. She paid no attention to the wounded and dying, ignored their reaching arms, begging eyes, and pleas for aid. Their misery was beneath her notice.

"What will the Loa do to me?" Nuru blurted, stumbling over something buried in the ash. Her bare feet turned black, the stains reached up to her knees. No part of her remained clean. Greasy ashen grit in her hair, on her lips, and in her teeth. She felt like she'd been dumped in mud and rolled in sand.

"Do?" Efra asked, over her shoulder, distracted.

"When they find out I have Mother Death."

"Don't know." She stopped, head cocked, listening. "If they take the carving, can they use it like you did?"

"I don't think so." It wasn't as straight forward as that, but she hesitated to explain it to Efra, Smoking Mirror's Heart.

A sorcerer used totems or fetishes to call allies. Those spirits existed outside of the sorcerer, beyond the veil. It was different with Mother Death. She didn't wait beyond the veil to be summoned. The Queen of the Red Desert was *in* Nuru.

The hematite carving, part gorgeous woman, part hideous spider, was a focus. The carving wasn't Mother Death, it merely helped Nuru envision the god clearly enough to call her forward. She had this terrifying feeling that, with some practice, she might be able to call the god without the carving. Even more scary, she suspected that once The Lady of the Dead regained some of her power, she'd step forward at will.

What will happen to me then?

"Only you can use it?" Efra asked. "That's good. It makes you valuable."

To you, or to the Loa? Nuru winced. *That was unfair.*

"We're going to need every edge and angle," added Efra. "But maybe we hold on to that one until we need it."

Hold on to it? Until we need it?

The sounds of battle grew louder. This whole time Efra had been leading her toward the rioters!

When she tried pull free, tiny scarred Efra gripped her hand so tight Nuru squealed in pain.

Efra hauled her to another corner before finally stopping. "Wait," she said. "Got to find one."

"One?"

"Loa."

The two women huddled at the corner, watching the madness and violence in the street. Birds and Growers clashed, smashing into each other like bulls loosed into the same pen.

Something was different here. The Growers fought like they were possessed by demons. Eyes wide, teeth bared in rictus snarls, they hurled themselves at the Birds with no thought for their own safety. Men and woman, some of them barely teens, clawed and bit, punched and kicked. The Hummingbird Guard, normally expressionless even in their bloodiest moments, fought as if terrified. They cowered behind shields, lashing out at opponents with none of their usual finesse.

"Perfect," said Efra. "All we have to do now is figure out which of the Dirts are Loa. They'll be at the back, not in the fighting."

Nuru scanned the crowd. Seething screaming humanity. Except they didn't look human. Faces twisted in loathing, they looked like rabid animals, feral and vicious.

There, at the rear of the crowd, stood a young man in a filthy thobe. As smeared in ash as any, he still stood out. He was too…round. Not fat, more like the muscled Crafter she and Efra garrotted. Where the Growers were gaunt strips of sun-wizened leather, this man's skin was smooth. He looked healthy and strong unlike any Grower. Happy, who'd been a slab of muscle stuffed into a too-tight thobe, had still been all veins and tendons. Everything about this Grower was wrong. He stood tall and confident, eyes bright and aware. Despite the obvious muscle he looked soft.

"There," said Nuru, pointing him out.

Efra nodded. "Yeah. That's the one."

Still clutching Nuru's hand, she dragged her into motion, pulling her toward the riot.

Nuru resisted. "Are you crazy?"

"Probably," Efra snapped over a shoulder. "But if we don't get out of the ring, we're dead. We need the Loa to get out, and that fat fuck is Loa."

Fat? Nuru let it go. Like Nuru, Efra hadn't eaten in days.

As they approached, Nuru spotted strange twining tattoos hidden beneath the sleeves of his thobe. A tattoo of half a dozen snakes sharing a bulbous central body entwined his exposed forearm. Inked black on mahogany flesh, they writhed with the bulge and flex of muscle as he clutched a chunk of raw flint. The rock wasn't shaped, wasn't even sharpened along one edge. Beyond clubbing people, it was useless as a weapon. Not that he was anywhere near the fighting. Yet he gripped it like it was the most important thing in the world, jaw muscles working in time to the tensing and relaxing of those thick arms. Nuru studied him as they neared, attention darting from the young man to the crowd. Teeth bared, his jaw tightened in anger. Thick chords of ridged muscle stood out in his arms. At the same time, the Grower's frenzy increased in pitch, pulses of rage moving through the mob.

Waves of savage fury.

Rising screams of madness.

Attention on the riot, he failed to see Efra and Nuru approach. When Efra grabbed his sleeve, he twitched, startled, lifting the rock in threat. Noticing Nuru, he hesitated.

He sees us the way nahual see us. We're things, not people.

"Tell us where the nearest Loa church is," demanded Efra.

Seeing her face, focussing on the scar, he retreated a step. "Go away."

"A real Dirt would say 'fuck off.'" Efra shoved him. "Tell us where the church is, and we'll fuck off."

Square jaw working, he glared at the women with a look of intense concentration, muscles tensing as he squeezed the chunk of raw flint. Hate filled his eyes. Disgust. Loathing.

Deep anger grew in Nuru, a building rage only violence could quiet. This wasn't her enemy. Those Birds over there, cowering, were. She needed to charge them, hurl herself into the fray. She wanted to claw out their eyes, vengeance for the centuries of oppression, for all the times she and her friends had been lashed in the public square.

Mother Death stirred, a colossal soul in a fragile body, a monstrous constrictor crammed into a too-small glass jar.

The rage was gone, snuffed like it was nothing.

"Whatever nahualli shit you're *trying* to do," snarled Efra, shoving him back another step, "it's annoying."

"She gets violent when annoyed," added Nuru.

"I know you're Loa," growled Efra. She had that look that usually ended in corpses. "You're all wrong. You stand wrong. You walk wrong. You think you matter. Tell us where the fucking church is, or I'll kill you." She showed that scar-stretching grin, all teeth and murder.

Her outburst earned only a raised eyebrow of curiosity. "You shouldn't have been able to resist the stone," he said.

With a sharp whistle, the Loa called another Grower over. This one didn't move like a Grower either. Straight spine. Purposeful stride. She didn't shuffle like she'd been broken by a life of hard labour. Skin clear and unblemished, she looked like she spent most of her life shaded from the sun's wrath. Even smeared in ash she was cleaner than the real Growers. Like the man, she held a shard of raw flint.

"We need to take this block before moving on to the gate," he told the woman, gesturing at the mob. "Throw them against the Humming-birds."

"We never call them that," said Efra, which earned her an annoyed look.

He studied Nuru and Efra, brows furrowed in thought. "I need to understand how you resisted. Come." He set off with the assured swagger of someone accustomed to being obeyed.

"Later, when he's not useful," muttered Efra, "I'm going to kill him."

Hand in hand, the women followed the Loa priest.

"My name is Kofi," he said, when they caught up.

Walking fast, looking everywhere but at Nuru, he made no attempt to learn their names.

"You were doing something to them," Nuru said, looking back over her shoulder. "Controlling them?"

The Growers' rage had subsided while he talked to Nuru and Efra.

The other woman joined the crowd, flint in hand, and once again they fought at a fevered pitch.

"You're a Loa nahualli," said Nuru.

"We're called tecolotl," he answered, distracted. "Growers are docile by nature. They need a push to get moving. If they don't rebel, the movement will stall."

He spoke as if from rote, like he was spouting something memorized.

"Are we?" asked Efra. "And I suppose you know what *we* need? Going to free all the docile Growers, are you? Understand them, do you?"

Nuru knew that look, that glint. But this handsome young man, confident in his size and muscle and whatever stone sorcery he possessed, didn't understand the danger.

"Yes," said Kofi, stopping to look down an alley. "I've been living among them…you…for the last month, preparing for the Queen's return." He turned, looking down another alley as if lost. "We know what they need. We know what's best. Bastion must be reborn, remade anew, as she intended it to be from the beginning."

"Then," said Efra, sliding closer, "there's something you should know."

He looked down at her. "What?"

Efra grabbed the collar of his thobe, slipped a leg behind him, and put him on the ground with a hard shove. He went down with a yell, landing on his back. Efra kicked him in the side beneath the ribs. Even startled, he reacted fast, rolling away and coming smoothly back to his feet, fists raised and ready for a fight.

Efra stood, arms crossed, hip cocked. "We aren't all docile you fat fucking nahualli idiot.'

"Tecolotl," he corrected.

She ignored him. "You don't understand shit."

Fists clenched, he towered over Efra. "Lay hands on me again, you filthy—"

"I can find us another stupid Loa," growled Efra, hand creeping into her thobe.

"Mother Death sent us," said Nuru, pushing between them.

Kofi glared down at her, brow furrowing in doubt. "Really? Mother Death sent us a couple of Dirt women?"

Nuru didn't back down. "You have to get us out of the ring."

"Out of the— You're kidding, right? Growers don't leave the ring. What would you do?" he asked, waving a hand in bewilderment. "You're wholly ignorant. You don't know anything. What use could you possibly be?"

"We know a fuck lot more than you do, fat boy," barked Efra, leaning past Nuru.

He grunted a laugh. "I seriously doubt that."

Reaching into her thobe, Nuru drew out the hematite carving of Mother Death. She allowed him the briefest glimpse and once again hid it away.

"I... I..." he stuttered. "That—Where did— You stole it!"

"She carved it," said Efra. "Now take us to the church."

He studied Nuru, doubt warring with hope. "Did you? Did you really?"

Looking him straight in the eye, something she never would have dared with a nahual, she nodded.

His breath caught, and he forced calm. "You aren't really Dirts," he said, nodding to himself. "You're from the Priests' Ring."

Nuru lifted a finger before Efra could call him stupid or hit him again. "Take us to a Loa church. We *need* to get out of this ring."

If he wanted to assume they were Loa spies, that was hardly her problem.

"I'll take you to Kuboka."

Somehow, in that way that priests had, he made the simple statement sound like a threat.

AKACHI - KNIFE OF THE MIND

Failing to uphold their promise to Bastion and reneging on their debts, those earning the rank of indentured are stripped of their god-given rights. Indentured are forbidden to own property of any kind. The proceeds of all efforts and labours go to the owner of their debts. Indentured have fallen so far from the grace of the gods they, themselves, have become property. Murder of an indentured is considered theft of valuables, the punishment depending on their value.

Indentured are forbidden to leave their owner's district without written permission. Attempting to escape their debts is punishable by sacrifice.

—The Book of Bastion

Wings wide, fighting to slow his plummeting descent, Akachi fell from the sky. The world spun, a blur of ash and stone and spattered blood. Spotting a nearby tenement, he banked toward it. Pulling his wings in tight, he landed hard, tumbling across the flat stone roof. Feathers tore free, the pain wrenching an avian squawk of agony from him. He came to rest on his back, staring up into the smoke-choked sky. Dark flakes of ash wafted down, swaying and swinging like dancers in the Senators' Ring. He saw nothing of the eagle that attacked him, though shadows flitted above.

Rolling to regain his feet, hawk talons scraping stone, Akachi flexed his wings. The right one hurt, flesh and feathers torn, but he didn't think he broke anything. There were dangers in taking on the shapes and characteristics of animals. The bones of birds were brittle and hollow, easily shattered. Such wounds stayed with the nagual when they retook their own form.

Once again searching the skies for enemies and seeing none, he hopped to the edge of the roof. The streets below were chaos. Birds and Growers fought a pitched battle. Bodies lay scattered, men and women.

No children.

He'd never given much thought to Grower young. Raised by the nahual of Her Skirt is Stars, they lived in crèches, safe from the dangerous stupidity of the Dirts. He looked toward the distant fields. Judging from the smoke surrounding Bastion, damn near everything out there must be on fire. If everything really had burned, the city was doomed. Given over to the running of civilization, the rest of the rings possessed no space for farming, and few of the inhabitants knew anything about raising crops.

His mom maintained a small garden for treats, those few things that rarely survived the trip from the outer ring to the core. Strawberries. Bananas. She even kept a cherry tree in the yard. If every garden in every ring beyond the Growers was turned to growing vegetables, it would feed less than a tenth of the city's population. Though he had no idea where the seeds would come from.

Bastion might already be dead.

In the street below, a gang of Dirts dragged a nahual of Feathered Serpent into the public square. They stripped away his mask of worn bone, dropping it to the stone. One of the Dirts stomped on it, fracturing the skull. Akachi watched, helpless, as they held the nahual, arms and legs spread wide. A woman wearing a cloak of singed owl feathers, strode from the church. The stink polluted Akachi's raptor senses.

A nahual of Father Death?

No. Something wasn't right. The woman carried a chunk of crystalline rock in her left hand, and the cloak looked too carefully burned, each feather singed and curled, the underlying structure undamaged.

The Lord is dead.

The cloak was meant as blasphemous mockery.

Kneeling at the pinned nahual's side, the woman in owl feathers held the shard of pale blue stone against the priest's temple. He screamed, eyes widening in terror, and then slumped, limp.

She stood, brandishing the stone in triumph. "I have him!"

The Feathered Serpent nahual blinked up at her in dull confusion. Fear gone, there was no hint of recognition or intelligence in his eyes. He looked lost, gaping at everything like a newborn seeing the world for the first time.

The mob of Growers followed the cloaked woman into another street, chanting about the Queen of Bastion returning to sweep her house free of snakes. They left the nahual lying in the square. He struggled to move, flopping about like he didn't know how to use his own limbs, a baby trying to roll onto its stomach.

Kyanite, remembered Akachi, *the knife of the mind*. The stone stole memories, robbed its victims of their personality. There was more, but he couldn't recall the details. Something about ancient Loa sorcerers using it to install spies into Bastion's true churches.

Feathered Serpent watch after his soul, Akachi prayed.

The nahual cooed like a frightened child, flinching from every sound, coughing as ash gathered upon him. Utterly helpless. More Dirts would come. They'd see the broken bone skull mask. They'd see him for what he was, a nahual. They'd kill him, and he'd never understand why.

The life of one man means nothing. Bastion is all that matters.

How many times had he told himself that? How many more people would he abandon?

How many is too many?

He wanted to say one, but knew it for a lie.

Faith and obedience. Bastion was everything.

Without her we are doomed.

Turning from the nahual, Akachi studied the streets. At first, he was lost. Everything looked so different, ash blanketing every detail. Here and there he saw signs. An overturned wagon that would have required a team of a dozen oxen. Once used to carry wood from the forests out near the Sand Wall to the Crafters, it was massive. This was a Lumber

District. He remembered passing through here with Captain Yejide and her squad of Hummingbird Guard when he first left the Northern Cathedral. Though it seemed like an eternity had passed, it was only two weeks.

I'm not far from the cathedral.

Stretching his wings, Akachi flexed them experimentally. Painful, but he thought he could fly. Though if that eagle came after him again, he'd be in trouble. In this wounded state, aerial acrobatics were beyond him.

With a pained squawk, Akachi took to the sky. Though the smoke scraped at his throat, he hoped he might lose himself in the thicker smog higher up. He'd have to rely on his sense of direction to keep him from flying in circles. A score of heartbeats later, lungs feeling like they were filled with sand, he realized he couldn't maintain this altitude. Biting down on the pain, he beat powerful wings, clawed his way up, until he burst free into clear blue sky.

He'd never seen anything so beautiful.

Looking toward the distant Sand Wall, he saw the red desert beyond. From this distance, there was no detail. The sun-whitened bones of those thrown from the wall were hidden from sight, the sand, a bloody and indistinct blur, wavering in the heat. Of the Growers' Ring directly below, he saw nothing. The Grey Wall remained occluded, but much of the Crafters' Ring seemed free of smoke. By the Wall of Lords, a vague shape due to the vast distance, Bastion looked as she always had.

Though free of the smog, heat crushed Akachi, baked him dry like clay in a Crafter's kiln. The sun's searing rage burnt a hole in the sky's gentle blue.

The Fifth Sun. Father of the Day. The Lord's murdered brother. All reality wavered and rippled as if seen through warped glass.

Bastion and all her gods seemed small, weak, and helpless in comparison to the dead god's wrath.

He wanted to stay up here forever, escape the stench and pollution of life below. The lure of the allies in the smoke, the purity of existence found in letting go of the self and embracing the essence of a spirit animal, pulled at Akachi.

It was time, he decided, to dive back into the stench and filth.

Whatever it took. Whatever the cost.

The survival of humanity was at stake. To flinch from foul deeds was to fail.

Akachi would not flinch.

Pulling his wings in tight, he dropped into the roiling smoke, returning to the Growers' Ring below.

A scene of madness greeted him.

Bears, jaguars, snakes, birds, creatures of all kinds, battled in the streets, tearing each other apart. It looked like the menageries had been cracked wide. An alligator shook a venomous viper in its jaw before swallowing it whole. A mountain lion clung to the back of a massive grizzly, clawing and biting, while the bear staggered in circles stomping on the two dog-sized lizards worrying at its legs. An eagle downed a falcon on a nearby rooftop and stood over its prey, tearing at the exposed breast with a hooked beak, digging for the tender heart within.

While most must be nahualli, Akachi couldn't tell friend from foe. How many of the animals were street-sorcerers or Loa tecolotl? Some looked less well-formed, more like a child's idea of the animal than the reality. Those would be the Dirts. Most, however, looked indistinguishable from real animals.

There was nothing he could do here to aid his fellow priests. As a hawk, and a wounded one at that, he was useless in such a fight.

It hardly mattered. Bishop Zalika must have called for the Turquoise Serpents by now. Their arrival would end this uprising. Armour of jade stone. Perfect formations. Blood in the streets, running deep in the gutters, flowing to the gods at the heart of the Last City. Obsidian Swords, as long as a man was tall, cutting Growers in half, spilling their guts to the stone. Death on an unimaginable scale. Thousands of corpses choking the streets, piling up in alleys.

Southern Hummingbird's elite were shrouded in myth. Some said they were katle, born soulless, gifts from The Lord to Father War. The

Loa *Book of the Invisibles* claimed the highest ranked among the Turquoise Serpents were survivors of the Last War granted immortality by the gods.

Akachi shook off the vision. There, wreathed in smoke, lay his destination, the Northern Cathedral.

Ignoring his wounded wing, putting aside the pain, he drove himself forward, flitting and diving erratically to throw off potential pursuit.

While Nuru, the Heart of Mother Death, was the obvious threat, it was Efra that Cloud Serpent first showed Akachi. He remembered that first vision, dreaming he stood atop the Grey Wall. It had been his first night in the Wheat District church.

The foul stain that spread to engulf the city.

Turquoise Serpents, marching in flawless formation, entering the outer ring for the first time in millennia.

Efra, standing in the street below, face twisted in a scar-stretching grin.

Hunt the girl, Cloud Serpent commanded.

There'd been no mention of Nuru. Of course, that was before the street-sorcerer brought Mother Death into Bastion.

That's what changed!

Relief flooded Akachi. The apparent discord in messages from his god was purely due to his own ignorance. The danger Efra offered paled before the new threat of Mother Death. The scarred little Dirt might be murderous and violent, but she could never be more dangerous than the street-sorcerer. Nuru called Mother Death through the wards of the Sand Wall, gave her entrance to Bastion. Akachi couldn't imagine such skill and power.

Nuru is the real threat.

The two Dirt women, Hearts of competing gods, would turn on one another. They had to; only one could ascend to be Heart's Mirror.

Clouds of smoke parted as a nightmare dove from the sky to hang over the cathedral. Over sixty paces long, its iridescent green and blue body shimmered as if lit from within. The monster flew on colossal reptilian wings, most of its body swinging, snake-like, beneath it. The tail lashed out, slapping birds from the sky as if in annoyance. A forked tongue, red as fire, flicked out to taste the air. It spat bubbling bile on the church below. Where spit met stone, the eternal rock of Bastion sagged and ran like watery mud.

Akachi slowed, terror threatening to drown his thoughts. This was an impossibility, a creature from the most ancient myths.

They were just stories!

Nahualli could only become real animals. A nagual could only take the shape of creatures they'd studied. Everyone knew that. It was fact, immutable as stone.

A section of wall melted and slumped.

This wasn't possible.

It had to be a god or a demon or something from beyond the Sand Wall. The street-sorcerer must have weakened the wards when she called Mother Death.

Oh gods, what else gained entrance?

How many dead gods wandered Bastion's streets?

The air around the creature shimmered, and Akachi recognized the thinning of the veil. Reality bent beneath the influence of a truly powerful nahualli on a terrifying quantity of narcotics. This was no god or demon.

It's a skyvyrm.

He'd seen pictures, ancient sketches of monsters.

The skyvyrm killed at a terrible rate, spat its stone-devouring bile on everything. It hovered over the cathedral, leathery wings keeping it alight. The cruder creatures flocked to it, fought at its side, and Akachi realized it was either a Loa tecolotl, or a street-sorcerer. Never had he seen so many sorcerers in one place, and they were dying faster than he could count.

Bastion's nahualli were losing. They fought bravely, hurling themselves at this nightmare monster, hawks and eagles clawing at its serpentine body, but there was nothing capable of harming it.

Akachi wanted to flee this madness. He was helpless. Defenceless. Already wounded and bleeding, growing weaker with every beat of his wings.

If this skyvyrm was real, then what else from the ancient texts was true? There were stories of techutli calling souls back from the underworld, raising armies of the dead to do war.

This thing hanging in the sky shattered everything Akachi believed.

Somewhere, a nagual had studied a living skyvyrm. They'd spent enough time with it, they were able to carve it so perfectly it worked as a focus for their sorcery. Skyvyrms were real. There was at least one of these somewhere in Bastion. No, that wasn't right. Somewhere, someone was breeding them, or they'd have died off thousands of years ago.

Dragons. Elephants. Winged lions as big as a Grower tenement. He'd read about all these things over the years. So many stories that were supposed to be just that: stories!

Cursing, Akachi bit down on his fear and dove for the cathedral.

NURU - FRACTURED GHOSTS

Unlike the sorcery of the nahualli, stone sorcery does not require narcotic assist-ance. While the power to affect change in the world lies within the very bones of the earth, it can only be accessed by a skilled practitioner. Every stone stores what is, in effect, an emotional state. To free that emotion, to unleash it with intent, *requires the sorcerer to master that emotion, to be able to call it up at will and feel it in the very depths of their soul.*

Tecolotl, stone sorcerers, tend to peak in power in their late teens and early twen-ties.

—The Loa Book of the Invisibles

Nuru and Efra followed Kofi through the streets. Far beyond the Wheat District she knew, the world was strange. Broken wagons carrying loads of dung lay spilled onto their side. Even through the smoke, she caught the deep animal stink. Where she expected wheat storehouses, there were long rows of barns and the harsh reek of chicken shit. The people looked different, too. Flesh pallid, chests sunken, they looked ill. It was as if a life tending chickens broke them differently than harvesting wheat broke the Growers of her own district.

No, she realized, *broke is wrong. They look drained.*

If anything, Kofi stood out even more. Smooth skin, free of scars and bruises. Back straight and proud. Chest broad, thick with muscle. So much more solid than any Grower.

Like he's more real. Or more sure he's real.

And what, really, was the difference? The Crafters she'd seen were more real than Growers, and Kofi made them look like furtive ghosts.

Do people become more real the closer they live to the gods?

It made a frightening amount of sense. Mad street-preachers claimed reality was nothing more than the drug-induced hallucinations of the gods. No wonder their favourites got the best of everything, felt the deepest emotions, lorded their existence over the lesser dreams.

It explains why being a Grower feels so empty.

Growers faded from Kofi's path. She imagined him walking into someone, walking *through* them.

Hand in hand, she and Efra followed in his wake.

Though there was no fighting here, bodies choked every street and alley. Most were Growers, ashen thobes black with blood. Some were recognizable as priests or Birds.

Kofi moved with a purpose foreign to Nuru.

Better to be invisible. Grower life was a flinch from shadow to shadow.

Looking down an alley, she saw ranks of Birds in red leather armour marching against a mob of Growers. Ebony cudgels lashed out, crushing skulls and shattering bones. Then, with a roar, the Growers swept over them, ants swarming an invading spider.

Kofi didn't so much as glance at the fight. Dying Dirts were nothing to him.

Nuru studied the priest from behind. Where Efra exuded a lithe and coiled strength reminiscent of those scrawny cats that haunted tenement alleys, Kofi reminded her of the squat muscle-bound dogs the nahual used to patrol the crèches.

He's a nahualli.

What was it he said the Loa sorcerers were called? Tecolotl? The words meant nothing to her. Were Loa sorcerers a match for temple-trained nahualli? She'd seen him use stone sorcery, but was he skilled in narcotic-based sorcery as well?

Either way, he was dangerous.

The way he talked about and treated the Growers suggested he grew up in the Priests' Ring. Having only been out of the Growers Ring for that one brief trip to the Crafters, she couldn't imagine what it must be like.

If he was from the inner-most ring, did that mean the Loa had infiltrated the very heart of Bastion?

Not infiltrated, she realized. They were always there, right from the very beginning.

I need to be smart, watchful. If she paid attention, perhaps she might come out of this alive.

Nuru stepped over the corpse of a young woman, her skull caved in, ash gathering in sightless eyes. So many dead. Driven from their homes. Slaughtered in the streets.

The Loa want us to fight their war. The nahual want us to be mindlessly obedient and grow their crops.

Two more ashen corpses, huddled together, limbs broken. On and on. Every street, scenes of brutal violence. An old woman, sunken skin stretched on bone, lay blinking up at the sky. A viscous gash exposed her innards. Fat green flies swarmed the gaping mouth of a youth, no more than a year out of the crèche. The dead were littered everywhere, an afterthought. The Growers were a tool used and tossed carelessly aside.

A smouldering rage grew in Nuru.

Maybe survival wasn't enough.

The Dirts needed someone on their side, someone looking out for their interests. Nuru might not be anything special, but she carried Mother Death within her. That had to be worth something. Somehow, she would bend the god to her purpose.

Efra would be better at this.

The girl was smarter in the right way. She might not be skilled at the subtle manipulation of emotions, but she possessed a raw cleverness and bloody single-mindedness Nuru suspected would see her through even the worst holocaust.

I need her.

Turning into a trash-littered alley, Kofi led them to a tenement. Two

Growers, both too alert, too round with muscle to be real Dirts, lounged at the entrance. They nodded to the Loa spy and studied the two women, noting Efra's scar, attention lingering on Nuru, as they passed. The bulge of hidden weapons distended their awkwardly worn thobes.

The inside was like every tenement Nuru ever saw, sleeping rooms, an eating room and a waste room, and yet it was unlike all of them. People hustled about on unimaginable business. Orders were barked in crisp tones, with none of the Grower slang or slurs she was so used to. Every word was enunciated the way nahual spoke during sermons. Strong people with intense eyes came and went, some sticking their head in the door only long enough to receive a snapped order before ducking back into the street. They were all so young, few older than she and Efra. They were serious and excited. Motivated.

Growers didn't move like this.

Growers slouched from task to task.

Growers cowered in doorways, ducking from sight if a nahual passed by.

Growers stared at the floor. In part because they went everywhere barefoot, but also because meeting the eyes of a priest almost always landed you in trouble.

Growers were bent, edges and angles abraded by sand and wind.

"They're all so fucking *young*," hissed Efra. She spat grit and ash, earning several reproving looks. "And *attractive*." She made it sound like a fault.

"This way," said Kofi, waving them forward. "Come."

He set off toward the stairs, once again assuming they'd meekly follow. With few choices, they did.

If the ground floor was unlike other tenements, the lower level was a different world. Scores of bright candles were jammed into the tops of more glass bottles than Nuru would have thought existed in this ring. The candles were purest white and didn't stink of burning ox fat and hair. With this many people crammed into such a small, sweaty space, the air should have been thick with sweat and the stench of unwashed bodies.

The room smelled more like lavender and honey than anything. Was this some Loa sorcery?

Kofi led them to an older woman who towered over most of the room. Those who stood taller, she dwarfed with her presence. Big-boned and broad-shouldered, she wore her thobe with the sleeves torn off and the rest cut short enough to expose her knees. Nuru stared, awed by the freedom of movement and the sheer brazen sin of such a display.

"Kuboka," called Kofi. "I brought something I think you should see."

Something. Did he mean the carving, assuming Nuru and Efra weren't worth mentioning?

The woman turned. Tattoos covered her arms, brightly coloured sketches writ in mahogany flesh.

Nuru stared, awed at the work. The tattoos moved, scampered about her skin.

Spiders, she realized. Not tattoos at all. The woman wore thousands of spiders of every type. From those harmless little gnat-eating spiders to the big ones that killed mice and nested in the guts of dead Growers left too long to rot.

"Spiders," said Efra. But she wasn't looking at Kuboka. Glancing at the ceiling, the walls, and then down at the floor, she did an awkward shuffling dance. "Fucking spiders."

They were everywhere. Everything moved, a rolling blanket of furry legs and glistening bodies.

A translucent white spider lowered itself by a strand of web and disappeared into Kuboka's hair while another leapt off, landing on the wall where it promptly scampered from sight. They came and went, a constant flow of traffic all centred on this commanding Loa.

Kofi approached, and the big woman pulled him into a careful hug. They stood whispering while Efra and Nuru waited, ignored. Finally, Kuboka looked over the young priest's shoulder and met Nuru's eyes. She nodded, waving them closer.

It was the kind of commanding gesture Nuru had seen so many

times from nahual she reacted without thought, dropping her attention to the floor and approaching. The spiders on the floor flowed around her every footstep, unimpeded. Efra followed.

"My son tells me you have a carving," Kuboka said.

Son? Confused, Nuru nodded. Did she mean that this man was her offspring, or was it like the way the nahual called everyone my son, my child, or my daughter?

Having seen that the Crafters raised their own children, it made sense the inner rings did as well. Or did it? Nahual never seemed like real people. She couldn't imagine them having parents or being children.

If Kofi stood out among the Growers, Kuboka was a viper among the chicks.

The world burns and this woman is excited about what will happen next.

Growers were never excited about tomorrow. However bad things were now, that was as good as you could hope for. How many times had she heard people say, 'Nothing ever gets better'?

Kuboka's attention never stopped roving. She noticed everything. Everyone was seen and measured, their usefulness determined.

Only an idiot would mistake her for a Grower.

"More fucking nahual pretending to be Growers," sneered Efra, scarred lip curling back to expose teeth. "You don't fool anyone. Except maybe other nahual."

Kuboka laughed, rocking back. "Precisely who we need to fool. And I am not pretending to be anything."

"The thobe," said Efra, "both agrees and says you're lying. If you're not pretending, why wear one? And yet you wear it as no Dirt would. You're either a fool, or making no effort." She sniffed. "Or both."

"My garb is a sign of unity, of respect. You know what they say: When in the Senators' Ring…"

Nuru had no idea what that meant. If Growers grew things, and Crafters crafted, what did Senators do?

"Unity?" asked Efra. "Respect? Your thobe is a lie, and not a very convincing one. Your words are lies, and no more convincing." She snorted and spat more ashen sludge. "*You* are a lie."

"Is this the one with the carving?" asked Kuboka.

"No," answered Kofi. "It's, um, the other."

"Ah. The quiet pretty one you keep not looking at."

Kofi flushed and stuttered, glanced at Nuru, and looked away.

"Who are you that we should trust you?" demanded Efra, ignoring the exchange.

"I am Mother Kuboka, tecolotl of Mother Death. I have been sent to aid the Growers and to guide where needed. To offer assistance. I'm here to help you overthrow the nahual who have held you in slavery for tens of thousands of years—"

"Why did you wait so fucking long?"

Kuboka's eyes narrowed in annoyance. This was a woman unaccustomed to being interrupted and questioned.

"How," asked Nuru, "do you plan to do that? Will you train the Growers to fight the Birds?"

Attention again on Nuru, Kuboka examined her. "There is no time for that. Training and teaching will have to wait until we've won. When Mother Death reclaims her throne everything Bastion has ever known will change."

"Promises and threats," said Efra. "Typical nahual."

Kuboka grunted a laugh unlike any Nuru ever heard from a priest. "You aren't wrong, my scarred child."

Teeth clenched, Efra said, "I'm not your child.

Kuboka ignored her. "Now, let's see this carving." She shot Kofi a warning look like she'd better not be disappointed.

Surrounded by Loa nahual, Nuru realized she had little choice. Even without the spiders, there was no chance of escaping the basement. Taking a deep breath, she drew out the carving. Once again, it became her world. That terrible spider body, jagged legs, viciously barbed. The woman, young and beautiful and perfect. Sable hair, long and silken, hung past the bulbous glistening abdomen. Taught curves. Flawless onyx. Except the red eyes, embers of hate and madness.

Kuboka's breath caught, an audible intake of surprise. She leaned close, lips pursed, eyes narrowed as she studied the carving. Hands clasped before her, she made no attempt to touch it.

"The work is phenomenal," Kuboka said, straightening. "This was carved and painted by a master. The quality and choice of paints is perfect." She looked to Nuru. "And it's haematite."

Nuru nodded.

"The tecolotl who made this knew it was The Lady's stone. To carve her in anything else is blasphemy, punishable by sacrifice on the altar."

"The Loa are as quick to bleed Growers as the real fucking priests," grumbled Efra.

"We *are* real fucking priests," said Kofi. "We are the L'Wha, the *first* fucking priests."

Kuboka ignored the exchange. Taking a bowl off a nearby table, she dipped a finger in and rubbed the thick sap onto her lids.

What is that? Nuru had heard of tezcat rubbing etorkizun on their eyelids to catch glimpses of the future, but she saw no blood in this mixture. The colour was all wrong.

Nuru returned the carving to its place in her thobe.

Kuboka stood for a score of heartbeats, eyes closed, before turning to Nuru. "One of my girls is on you."

Understanding, Nuru swallowed. One of this nahualli's allies rode Nuru. In her hair. In her clothes. There were tiny spiders entirely capable of killing. It could be anywhere. Her skin crawled with the scampering of imagined legs. She wanted to scream, to slap at her clothes and crush whatever it was, to tear her thobe off and find it.

Nuru stood motionless.

Efra glared death at the Loa nahual. "If your *girl* hurts her, you'll be dead before she is. I promise"

Kuboka lifted a hand, stalling Kofi's protective outburst.

Ignoring Efra, she stared into Nuru's soul. "She'll know if you lie. She will feel the tremor in your blood. Understand?"

Nuru swallowed, blinked.

Nodding, Kuboka asked, "Who carved the First Mother?"

Nuru had never heard Mother Death called that. "I did," she whispered, afraid to move. "I carved her."

"This is the work of a temple-trained tecolotl."

Somewhere, the Loa had their own churches and temples. They had schools, trained sorcerous priests. Nahualli. Tecolotl. Whatever they were called. Did they exist openly in the inner rings, living alongside the true nahual? She had no way of knowing. Was all this a lie?

When Nuru said nothing more, Kuboka asked, "What ring are you from?"

"I've lived all my life in the Wheat District."

The slightest twitch, almost unnoticeable. Was that doubt? Fear? "Why?"

Unsure what she was being asked, Nuru said nothing.

"Why did you carve the Mother?"

"I had a dream," Nuru answered.

"How did a Grower manage this? How did you get the paints?"

"We went into the Crafters' Ring," said Efra, "and took them."

The room froze, everyone listening.

"Impossible!" said Kofi.

Kuboka's rapt attention finally left Nuru and she turned on Efra. "This was you. *You* took her to the Crafters. I see ruin in you. Chaos. Madness and murder."

"I see the same in you," whispered Nuru.

Kofi hissed in anger and was silenced by a look from Kuboka.

"We are what we need to be to survive," Efra said. She looked the big woman up and down, unafraid. "Isn't that right?"

"Indeed. And you, street-sorcerer, what will you do with that carving now?"

"What will she *do*?" demanded Kofi, incredulous. "She can't keep it!"

"We can't take it," said Kuboka. "We dare not. If…" She hesitated, jaw working like she fought some internal desire. "If the Mother has made a choice, it is not for us to question."

Seeing Kuboka's expression, Kofi bit down on his retort.

Nuru hesitated. Was there really a spider on her that would know if she lied? Was it all an act to fool the stupid Dirts? Would it really kill her?

Efra is right. We do what we must to survive. It didn't feel like enough. *We must be more than cowering Dirts.*

Nuru looked up, forced herself to meet the woman's eyes. "Get the spider off me."

Kuboka nodded, "It's gone. I wouldn't dare hurt—" She darted a look at Efra.

"Mother Death has returned to us," said Nuru, unsure if she did the right thing. "She has once again walked the streets of Bastion. She has tasted blood." Deep in her gut, the god stirred. "She wants more."

A lot more.

Rivers of blood.

Raging torrents of gore.

A feast of souls.

"She will have more," agreed Kuboka. "She will drink her fill, I swear it."

Another well-fed man hurried down the steps, stumbling over the hem of his thobe. "The Hummingbird Guard are coming in strength! There are fifty or more, backed by a squad of Turquoise Serpents. We can't hold them!"

Turquoise Serpents. Jade stone armour. Obsidian knives as long as a man is tall. Butchery. Blood-bathed streets. They were here. Now. In the Growers' Ring. The vision Smoking Mirror showed her was true!

Nuru's chest tightened in terror. She needed to run, to hide. They were all going to die.

Taking Nuru's hand, Efra gave it a reassuring squeeze.

Kuboka cursed in a most un-priest-like manner. "Send word to scatter. We'll regroup later." She faced Nuru, eyes straying to where the statue lay hidden. She hesitated, fists clenched. Need. Desire. Purest envious lust. "I would give anything to cut you open, search your heart."

My heart? For what?

Smoking Mirror's words, when he spoke of Efra: *She is my Heart*

Could the term mean something more literal?

"What is a Heart?" Nuru asked.

Efra looked from Kuboka to Nuru. "Do we have time for this?"

"No," said Kuboka, sagging. Gesturing at the Loa who'd come storming down the steps, she said, "Take Athua with you. Hold the Hummingbirds off as long as you can." A young woman stood, ducked a quick bow to Kuboka, and then sprinted up the steps with the other.

Such energy. The only time Nuru ever saw Growers move that fast was if the Birds were chasing them. Even so, what could these two possibly do?

"We'll talk more when you're safe," said Kuboka. "Kofi." She took the young man by the shoulders. "This woman is your sole priority. Protect her with your life. Do you understand?"

Kofi nodded once. "Yes, mother."

When he looked to Nuru, she saw through his confidence to the scared boy within.

Their eyes met.

"Oh," he said. His lips moved as if he wanted to say more but lost the words.

Efra cleared her throat, eyebrow arched. "Are we leaving now?"

"Follow us," Kuboka ordered. "If anything happens, take them to Subira." To the rest of the room she commanded, "All right, people. Let's move!"

Everyone filed up the shallow steps and into the eating area. Two men, heavy with muscle, stood guard, ebony cudgels clutched in massive fists. Several more stood ready, armed with an assortment of weapons from flint knives to sharpened sticks and jagged chunks of rock. Several held small, useless shards of raw crystal. Blues. Reds. Greens. Some colours and stones Nuru had never seen before. They moved wrong, acted with such defined purpose.

A feeling of surreal distance crept over Nuru. She stood surrounded by Dirts who weren't Dirts, a stranger in an endless desert of alien familiarity.

Gaze darting to the nearest alley, Efra looked like she wanted to run, wanted to bolt for freedom.

The cudgel men went first. The rest followed, Kofi, Efra, and Nuru coming last.

Billowing clouds of smoke rolled through filthy streets. There was no sky. The ring, already a world of grey, lost what little colour it had. Vision was reduced to a score of strides. Here, the bodies had been dragged away.

Screams of agony and the crack of wood on stone echoed like fractured ghosts.

"The smoke is an ally," whispered Efra.

Nuru prayed she was right. While not a narcotic smoke, it might still hide them from sight.

The mob set off and Nuru followed, watching Loa flinch from shadows and distant screams. They shuffled, hunched and huddled.

"Finally," muttered Efra, "they're moving like Dirts."

"Quiet," growled Kofi. "We're going to get you to the gate. Once we're through, we'll take you to the Priests' Ring and find out for sure what—" He cut himself off when Kuboka, a half dozen strides ahead, shot an angry look over her shoulder.

The Priests' Ring.

The Crafters' Ring had been a different world, unlike anything Nuru had ever known. Food beyond stale hardbread, rinds of crusty cheese, wilted vegetables, and tough strips of dried meat.

There had been children everywhere, running in the streets.

Children holding their mother's hand.

Children laughing and playing.

Children.

Nuru's throat tightened at the memory.

"You set the fields on fire, didn't you?" asked Efra, poking Kofi in the ribs.

He slapped at her hand, but she was faster. Scowling, he said, "Not me."

"Your people. You did it to make this happen." Efra waved a hand at a crumpled body lying sprawled on its back, mouth open to the sky and filled with ash.

"It has to happen," said Kofi, speaking in a soft voice, attention darting to alleys and from corpse to corpse. "If it doesn't, nothing changes. Bastion stagnates and dies."

"You don't know that," said Nuru. "Not really. Not for sure."

He slowed and Efra and Nuru slowed too, allowing Kuboka and her people to drift further ahead.

"We do," he said. "We *know*. Every tezcat who has seen far enough into the future says the desert is everywhere, Bastion gone. The world is dying."

Was that true? Was Mother Death the cause or the solution?

"This war," continued Kofi, "is the only way to stop that from happening."

"Has a tezcat ever seen the end?" asked Efra. "Has anyone seen the last day?"

He shook his head. "No one knows for sure when it happens. A thousand tezcat will see the end on a thousand different days."

"That makes no sense," Efra grumbled.

"You don't actually know how it ends?" asked Nuru.

"Well—"

"You could be causing it rather than stopping it," said Efra, poking him.

He tried to bat her hand away and failed again. "We know that if we do nothing, the world dies."

"Really?" sneered Efra. "How many thousands of years have you been planning Mother Death's return? How long have you been plotting the downfall of the nahual? If you all changed your mind, what would the future look like then?"

Kofi opened his mouth, blinked, and closed it again.

"You don't *know*," said Efra.

"We know," he said, defensive. "You wouldn't understand."

"Because we're stupid Dirts? You don't know shit."

"What if you're the cause?" asked Nuru, more gently.

What if I'm *the cause?*

Kofi shook his head. "No. They are hunger, we know that."

"They?"

"The gods hoard and devour; it's their nature."

What did that mean?

"More weird Loa pig shit," grumbled Efra.

Nuru had to agree.

Kofi picked up the pace, and Efra drifted back to walk alongside Nuru.

"He's an idiot," she said. "Too dumb to question."

That, Nuru suspected, was true of most people.

Ahead, the Loa slowed and spread out, weapons and shards of raw stone held at the ready. Nuru, Kofi, and Efra caught up with the main group, the young Loa moving to stand beside Kuboka.

A flash of white, startling for its purity in the ashen world of the Growers, caught Nuru's attention. A single man, bent with age, skin hanging in wattles, gaunt like a sun-sunken corpse, stood before the gathered Loa. Leaning on his cane, he looked too weak, too unsteady to stand unassisted. Even with the sun throttled in clouds of smoke, his robes were blinding; impossibly bright and clean.

This wasn't some filthy street-sorcerer or a rock-clutching Loa blasphemer.

The air around the old man wavered like a black stone in the sun.

He was a nahualli of She Who Devours the Filth, this was a true temple-trained sorcerer.

A lifetime of terror built in Nuru.

Every Grower went to confessional at Sin Eater's church at least once a month. Her nahual knew if you lied. They knew if you hid doubt or blasphemy or if you'd transgressed against the *Book of Bastion*. The Birds might shatter bones or whip you in the public square, but Mother

Sin's nahual were nightmares of fanatical purity.

Leniency, a sin.

Redemption through suffering.

Flay the flesh, free the soul.

"Just a moment," Kofi whispered. "Mother's Osiri will deal with him."

Nuru wanted to scream, 'How can you be so fucking calm?' but she couldn't move, couldn't speak.

A man and a woman in ill-fitting thobes stepped to the front of the crowd. Each held a wedge of raw stone.

Grabbing Nuru's hand, Efra took a step back. "We're fucked."

Knees wobbling like he might collapse at any moment, Sin Eater's priest raised a hand as if to deliver a sermon to a hall of fidgeting Growers. "Blasphemers," he said, voice rattling and weak, pebbles in a jar of sand. "You are sickness. You are disease. You are filth. I cleanse you of your sins."

The woman beside Nuru bent double and puked blood and writhing maggots. Boils broke out across her flesh, skin darkening like rotting cherries, swelling, and then bursting to drool yellow puss. The stench staggered Nuru and she retreated. Half the Loa were down, retching and vomiting. The street ran with gore and bile, all of it twitching and squirming.

The two Loa who approached the nahual lay shuddering as snakes and spiders struggled in a bloody red tangle to escape every orifice. Insects, worms and spiders and glistening beetles, deadly vipers and great constrictors. All these creatures fought free of the Loa, leaving them a torn ruin.

Efra pulled Nuru back, dragging her toward the nearest alley. She said something, but Nuru couldn't hear her. Screaming Loa drowned out thought.

Kofi saw them leaving, and hesitated. He looked to Kuboka, who held a rock gripped in each fist, and then back to Efra and Nuru.

Emotions warred across his face.

He wanted to stand and fight.

He wanted to defend the woman he so obviously worshipped and called *mother*.

He wanted to flee the nahualli's horrible sorcery and hide somewhere far away.

He wanted to obey Kuboka, make her proud.

With a roar of despair, Kofi turned his back on his fellow Loa and chased after Nuru as Efra hauled her away.

AKACHI - ASH AND BLASPHEMY

The stone of souls, obsidian is a mirror to the heart's intent. Through the black glass the gods speak. It is a stone of connections, a path to power, a conduit to divinity. Each god's Heart carries a sliver in their own heart. They are the gods' will given flesh.

—The Book of Bastion

Akachi twisted and turned through the air, ducking and weaving through the madness of sorcerous battle. Hawks, sparrows, and eagles clashed, tearing at each other with hooked talons. Lions, jaguar, bears, and all manner of beasts warred on the ground. Sorcerers who'd lost themselves to their spirit animals stopped to devour fallen foes. He knew that feeling, the raw glory of letting go, the freedom in succumbing to the base need of the beast within.

The skyvyrm did terrible damage. It smashed birds from the sky with no regard for which side they might be on, and spewed stone-melting bile on those below. Akachi stayed well clear. Whatever it was, wherever it came from, there seemed to be nothing here capable of harming it. Until the narcotics wore off, it ruled the sky.

An eagle fell past Akachi, blood and torn feathers raining around it, to land with a flat *smack* in a puff of ash. Avian corpses littered the ground.

Wreathed in smoke, stained in ash and blasphemy, the Northern Cathedral remained a thing of impossibly beauty. Unlike the squat tenements surrounding her, the church soared into the sky and reached deep into the earth. Spires of smooth stone joined by arched bridges of rock that looked too thin to bear their own weight. Though he'd lived there as an acolyte for five years, Akachi had seen little of the church, and never from this angle. Another time, he would have happily stayed here for hours, basking in the perfection of the gods' creation.

Swooping low, the skyvyrm loosed a long vomitus stream upon the cathedral. Akachi watched in horror as a sweeping stone bridge melted and fell upon the tiny figures far beneath it.

Dropping as fast as he dared, Akachi spread his wings to halt his plummeting descent at the last moment. He landed hard, legs buckling as his wounded wing folded beneath him. Staggering to his feet, he bird-hopped to cover. Cowering in the corner of the cathedral courtyard, he struggled to pull himself together, to search out the scattered reality of his soul and once again become Akachi the man. His ally resisted being forced back through the veil, and he fought with it, finally martialling his will and driving it out.

Lying curled on the stone, his red, white, and black robes of Cloud Serpent stained in ash and blood, he cradled his right arm. A long gash cut through the muscle of his shoulder. Had returning to himself been more difficult than usual?

Traces of the narcotics still singing through his blood, reality felt thin and stretched.

The great skyvyrm twisted through the billowing clouds of smoke. It was coiling darkness backlit by a bloody, muted sun.

With a pained groan, Akachi pushed to his feet.

Fierce battle raged at the Northern Cathedral's main entrance. Nahual and nahualli of every sect fought alongside squads of the more organized Hummingbird Guard. Many fought with sticks and stones or empty fists. Their opponents, Dirts and Loa blasphemers, were equally poorly armed.

If the cathedral fell, it would be a great victory for the Loa, doing irrevocable damage to the nahual presence in this quarter. In their ignorance, the Growers would do terrible harm to both themselves and the great church. Relics and artefacts dating back to the very birth of Bastion would be lost. If the Loa had time to solidify their position and access to the stores of narcotics and sorceries in the cathedral, driving them out would cost a great many lives.

This might be Akachi's war, but it wasn't his battle.

Staying close to the wall, he made for the acolyte's entrance at the rear of the cathedral. Throat raw and burning from smoke, stinging eyes bleeding gritty tears, he found three Hummingbird Guard and half a dozen terrified acolytes guarding the back of the building. Seeing him approach, the Guard moved to block him.

"Name?" demanded the Captain, a short woman with a shaved head and tattoos of holy scripture inked in black across her skull.

"Akachi," he answered. "Pastor of the Cloud Serpent church in the Wheat District." He didn't bother mentioning that he was a nominal pastor at best, or that his posting had been temporary. "I'm here to report to Bishop Zalika." A lie, but he needed to get into the church.

The Hummingbird stopped him with a hand hard against his chest. "Any of you know him?" she called to the acolytes. She held a cudgel, low and ready.

Akachi didn't recognize any of the acolytes, and they shook their heads.

The Captain studied him. "Loa spies have infiltrated the Cathedral, have walked among us for years. How can I know you are who you claim?"

"I was assigned a squad of Hummingbird Guard," he answered. "They were led by Captain Yejide." Speaking her name hurt.

The hand on his chest dropped. "Yejide? Where is she? Why are you alone?"

"She's dead," said Akachi, throat tightening.

"Khadija?"

He shook his head.

"Lutalo? Talimba? Njau? Gyasi?" She rattled off the names.

"All dead."

A flash of pure heartbreak and misery crossed the Captain's face and was gone, replaced by cold purpose. "Enter. Report to the Bishop, if you can find her." The Captain stepped aside. "The cathedral will fall. Tomorrow, if not today." She shook her head, suddenly bent by weariness. "We don't have the numbers. The Loa are amassing armies of Dirts, thousands of them, and driving them mad with their blasphemous sorcery. When you go, take these acolytes with you."

"I cannot. They would slow me, and I hunt."

Nodding, she straightened with a show of teeth. "Good hunting, nahual of Cloud Serpent. We will stand to the last."

Bowing to the Captain, Akachi entered the Northern Cathedral.

Inside, the air was better and he could breathe without feeling like his lungs were caked in damp chalk. Smooth walls, not a single seam, this great cathedral was another projection of the single stone that was Bastion.

Most of the candles and torches unlit, the halls were gloomy, wreathed in shadow. Where scores of young acolytes usually sprinted back and forth on business for the nahual of every sect, a strange and oppressive stillness ruled. The few acolytes Akachi saw flinched away, eyes downcast as they shuffled past, looking more lost than busy. He saw no nahual. Were they all out in the courtyard in battle, or did they cower in one of the cathedral's many sub-basements?

Worrying that Zalika may have already left, or been taken somewhere safer, Akachi stopped the next acolyte to pass him. "Is the Bishop still in the Cathedral?"

The acolyte blanched at the sight of his blood-stained robes and bowed. "Yes, nahual. I heard she was in the basement."

"What level?" he asked, realizing he already knew.

The acolyte swallowed. "The dispensary."

Excitement and fear warred.

With so many nahualli battling the Loa, the dispensary may have been emptied.

That would be bad. Without the narcotics of his profession, he'd be unable to properly pursue his prey.

Dismissing the acolyte with a wave, Akachi ran for the nearest stairs. Reaching them, he slowed to a stop, peering into the inky black.

The torches usually lining the steps were gone.

Did Bishop Zalika wait below with the Staff of the Fifth Sun?

His heart slammed in his chest.

I walked these steps before.

They led to Father Death's realm, the underworld.

He remembered the feel of his flesh rotting and sloughing away, the sound of bone feet on stone.

I watched a god die down there.

It wasn't real.

Or it was, and it wasn't.

A reliquary of the divine. The same gods over and over in different forms.

Always bragging of their accomplishments.

Always hungry for blood and souls.

There was a message there, one he couldn't bring himself to understand.

So many of the gods claimed to have birthed mankind or to have gifted humanity with fire or knowledge.

They can't all speak truth.

Could they all speak lies?

Questions are the antithesis of faith, Akachi reminded himself. *Obedience is everything.*

Cloud Serpent did not require him to understand.

Retreating into the hall, Akachi grabbed the nearest lit torch before once again approaching the stairway.

The ancient stone steps were worn concave like shallow bowls. He once read that in one thousand years roughly thirty generations lived and died. That meant these stairs had seen the passage of over seven hundred and fifty generations of nahual and acolytes. How many more would pass until this was a smooth ramp descending into the dank guts of the world?

Torch held high, Akachi descended.

The first floor, the acolyte's library, was dark and silent. With the ever-present candles and the warm scent of melting wax missing, the level smelled strangely damp. The rank redolence of thousands of mouldering scrolls, as if those small flames were all that had held the rot at bay, pushed Akachi onward.

The second basement, the dispensary, also looked abandoned. The first security gates lay open and unattended. Beyond, Akachi saw the flickering of a single lonely flame. Following the light, he found Bishop Zalika. She stood as if waiting. Beside her sat a dusty wine bottle with a candle jammed into the mouth. Melted wax drew white lines along its curved belly. Neat piles of narcotics lay at her feet. Jainkoei. Etorkizun. Aldatu. There was even a heap of Zoriontasuna, a powerful euphoric commonly enjoyed in the Bankers' Ring.

Licking his lips, Akachi pulled his attention from the drugs.

Zalika studied him, her eyes red and glassy, pupils huge and dilated. A lip curled in distaste. Her owl-feather cloak, once grand and impressive, the garment of a High Priest of The Lord, looked tattered and worn. Feathers littered the floor.

"S'you," she slurred. "I dreamt that I gave you the staff."

Not seeing it, he asked, "Then where is it?"

She shook her head as if disappointed in Akachi, as if her cowering down here, skirting the edge of brain-burn on massive doses of gods knew what, was somehow better than being *him*.

"It's all going to burn," she said, wet eyes focussing on the candle.

He hadn't known what to expect, but it hadn't been this. Arguing, perhaps? He'd thought he might have to convince her to give him the staff. He'd even half expected her to be down here waiting, ready to use the staff as a weapon. Though a massive quantity of narcotics swam her blood, she seemed wholly unprepared for battle.

"Bishop," he said tentatively. "Why are you not out there? You are the High Priest, a powerful nahualli of Father Death!"

Her lip twitched. "Don't pretend you came to scold me about my duties."

"You know why I'm here."

"Yes, but I trust not my dreams. Who sent them?"

"Cloud Serpent speaks to me."

She snorted with disdain. "Are you certain?"

He remembered being uncertain if it was a dream of a vision.

"Yes," he said.

"Are we to believe your god spoke to me as well?"

Unlikely as that sounded, Akachi ignored the question. "I need the staff to defeat the Loa."

"Really? What will you do with the heart of a dead god? Do you know what powers it holds? Do you understand the weight of responsibility that comes with such an artefact?" She barked a scornful laugh. "No, boy, you do not."

"My understanding," Akachi said, repeating his earlier thought, "is not required. I obey my god."

"Do you? Are you sure?"

What was she talking about? Did she think something else sent him here for the staff, another god or errant spirit?

The heaped narcotics kept drawing his eye. Had she done that on purpose?

She's trying to distract me. She's trying to fill me with doubt.

"Father Death is fallen," she said abruptly. "An upstart godling, Face Painted by Balls—"

"With Bells," Akachi corrected.

Zalika shrugged, fat earlobes swinging. "She is spawn of the Lady of the House. She holds The Lord's domain, awaiting the Queen's return."

"We can still win!"

"Can we?" Zalika grunted a despairing laugh. A lone tear trickled down her cheek, following the line of her jowl. "My god is dead. I might as well be a Grower, a stinking mud-fucking Dirt. I am less than nothing."

The thought of his god dying, of being stripped of purpose,

slammed Akachi in the gut. There could be nothing worse. Cloud Serpent was his life, the reason for his existence. Only the will of his god mattered.

Zalika glared blearily up at him. "You are a fool to trust the dream."

"Am I a fool to trust my god?"

"You're a fool." She said with damning finality.

"I need the staff," he said. "I will destroy the Loa and save Bastion."

"You?"

Akachi drew the sacrificial dagger she gave him little more than a week ago. "Where is the Staff of the Fifth Sun?"

Eyes locked on the knife, Zalika paled, looking decidedly ill. She swallowed with a grimace. "So many souls. So many dead in here. Too many."

"More now than when you gave it to me," answered Akachi.

She looked away, staring off into the darkness, a look of misery clouding already cloudy eyes. "You should never have carried this. They'll never be reborn."

He blinked. Did she not understand the implicit threat? "They will. We will win. We have to."

"What do I do?" she asked, pleading, as if Akachi and his knife were nothing. "Bastion *needs* a death god. Without one, no souls will be reborn. Bastion will dwindle and die."

"One of the other gods will step forward and take his place. Gods have died before."

"I know the damned Book!" snapped Zalika. "Can you imagine the horror of a mad god like Smoking Mirror claiming death as his own? What of Southern Hummingbird's love for war or Sin Eater's insane need for perfection? What of that whore, Precious Feather? Bastion," she said, mocking, "the Last Brothel of Humanity."

Stunned, Akachi retreated before the blasphemy. There had always been conflict between the gods, between their nahual, but to call Precious Feather a *whore*? "You are in a state of shock."

"Your god, Cloud Serpent, is a murderous maniac. He lives to stalk his hoarded souls. He feeds off their fear and horror. Imagine the Lord of the Hunt ruling the underworld!"

Hoarded souls? Blasphemy. So much blasphemy. It felt like the world shifted beneath him, like reality itself became increasingly unstable the more she spoke. How could she talk like this?

The need to silence her built in him.

"Bastion will survive," he said, voice gentle. "She always does." He breathed deep, searching for calm. "I *need* the staff."

Ignoring him, Bishop Zalika waved at something he couldn't see and said nothing.

"Bastion is all that matters," he added, hoping to convince her, praying she'd see reason. "You must fight the evil of the Loa however you can! You will be reborn."

"Will I, though? What if I oppose Mother Death and she wins?" She glanced up at Akachi. Guilt. Misery. "She's offered The Lord's nahual a place."

Praying he'd misunderstood, Akachi asked, "She has?"

"Every night her Loa invade my dreams. They demand I worship her, sacrifice in her name so she may feed and grow in strength. They promise I will be one of her High Priests. She will give me meaning. She is Rada Loa. The last Rada Loa. She *is* death. True death. The Lord of the House was but a pretender."

And that was the most terrible blasphemy yet. Bishop Zalika quoted the Loa *Book of the Invisibles*.

"If I turn my back on Mother Death," Zalika continued, "they've sworn I'll never be reborn. If I fight her, she will banish my soul to the Bloody Desert." Tears spilled free, and Zalika shook. "My god is dead. Do you fucking understand?" She stared into the candle's flickering flame. "She promises purpose. She promises redemption for my sins." Eyes clouded in a smoky haze of poorly blended narcotics, she struggled to focus on Akachi. "You understand how tempting that is." She gestured at the dagger he held. "I see in you a purpose. You're burned empty with it."

He remembered feeling that as Cloud Serpent healed him of his wounds. Now, that confidence was a fading memory. All of it, torturing the Artist, fighting that gang of Dirts, battling Mother Death, seemed increasingly unreal.

Akachi held up his left hand, wiggled the smooth stumps of his severed fingers.

If not for this, I would doubt everything.

"Give me the staff, and I will stop Mother Death," swore Akachi. "I will kill her Heart."

"The staff," she said, eyes unfocussed. "The Lord was tricked into murdering his brother, manipulated by Old Coyōtl."

"I don't know that god," admitted Akachi. "Is he dead?"

Zalika gave him a withering look. "He is the Father of Lies, the Snake in the Grass."

"I don't know those names."

"He *is* the smoke in the glass," she whispered, as if afraid some long-dead god might overhear. "Don't trust the dreams."

She drew her own sacrificial dagger from within the owl-feather cloak.

Their eyes met and held.

With surprising speed for such a big woman, Zalika leapt forward, thrusting her knife at his heart. Swaying away, Akachi buried his own dagger in her chest. Staggering back, she wobbled on unsteady legs.

"Your father," she said, coughing blood, "sent you here because he was ashamed. You're empty, like katle. Dirts are deeper. I... I just... I need to sit."

Zalika lowered herself gingerly to the floor. "You were supposed to die," she whispered. "Everyone else I sent out there did." Eyes sliding closed, she eased herself back as if to take a nap on the floor.

A last wet bubbling breath.

The Bishop lay dead at Akachi's feet. Blood leaked from her chest, a spreading pool. Stepping out of the way, Akachi watched it flow past. Even down here, gutters lined every wall.

I should feel more.

Such a colossal character in his life as an acolyte, she'd become near god-like. Yet here she lay, cooling meat feeding the gods. Another soul in the stone.

Akachi glanced at his sacrificial dagger. Holding it up, he studied the face reflected in the glass. The eyes. Twisting souls shimmered the black. He remembered how it felt when Zalika first handed it to him. He'd thought then that it tainted him, that it somehow stained him. He'd been at the edge of puking.

Now, it was nothing but cold stone.

He felt none of its death.

I'm not empty like a katle.

He wasn't soulless. He had a mother and a father. He'd been a happy child.

"You are wrong," Akachi said to Zalika's corpse. "My father would be proud. I will be the next Heart's Mirror."

He glanced at the floor. "Shit."

Zalika's spreading blood had engulfed the neat piles of narcotics she'd arranged around her. They were ruined, fouled.

Where would the staff be?

The basements below the Northern Cathedral were labyrinthine. If the Bishop took the time to hide it, he'd never find it.

"It's not down here," he told the corpse. "You weren't thinking straight."

All those terrible things she said, that was the drugs. Her mind was addled, already suffering the effects of brain-burn.

"It's not down here," he repeated, grinning at Zalika. "It's in your chambers."

First, however, he needed to stock up.

The single candle burned steady. Collecting it, Akachi went to see what remained of the cathedral's narcotic stores.

NURU - A LITTLE SADNESS

The Ceremony of Belonging, where a Grower baby is accepted into the arms of the gods to be raised by the nahual of Her Skirt is Stars, is a lesson in power. Every time a Grower mother gives birth, everyone in her district is forced to stand by, helpless, as the nahual claim her child. It's cloaked as the welcoming of a new soul, but it is a reminder: You are nothing. From your first breath to your last, we will control every breath in between. You are powerless.

—The Loa Book of the Invisibles

Retched tearing screams chased Nuru and Efra as they fled. Efra dragged her around the first corner. Slipping in a smear of viscera, Nuru tripped on a corpse, pulling them both to the street. Side by side, they crawled, hands and knees sliding in congealed blood, until the Sin Eater nahual and dying Loa were out of sight. Kofi sprinted around the corner, spilling over the same body, to land beside them in a heap. He looked ill, a froth of vomit caking his lips.

Coughing, he gagged, dashing a terrified look the way they came. "I had no idea." His voice shook.

"Never faced a real nahualli before, have you," growled Efra. "Fucking idiot."

"I was told they sent the outcasts to the outer ring!"

A huge Bird, crimson leather dripping blood, gore painting his face a hell of red, stepped from the smoke. A cudgel hung loose in his meaty fist. Dead eyes studied Nuru, gaze starting at her feet, travelling up her legs, lingering on her chest, and finally making eye contact.

He lifted the cudgel as if displaying it. Fragments of curved bone were embedded in the ebony, clumps of bloody hair clinging to them.

Skulls. He likes smashing Dirt skulls.

Kofi pushed to his feet and the Bird waited, unmoving. No fear. This Grower boy was nothing.

Efra and Nuru also stood, and the Bird grinned in anticipation.

He likes this. He wants us to run, to beg, to fight. He doesn't care. He wants to break us.

The Bird rolled his shoulders, loosening the muscles. "I'm going to —"

Efra stepped in, ducked under the cudgel as it lashed out. The Bird moved like it was nothing, effortless violence, and punched her in the side of the neck. She landed, soggy and boneless, bleeding into the ash.

He stood over her, grinning with his bloody teeth, enjoying this moment, knowing they'd stand and watch him shatter Efra's skull all over the filthy rock of Bastion.

"Look away," whispered Kofi.

Drawing a deep breath, he stepped between Nuru and the Bird. He made no threatening moves, no attempt to attack or defend himself.

That earned a raised eyebrow. "Really?" The big man shrugged as if in good-humoured acceptance. "Fine then. I'll give you first go." He spread his arms, inviting. "You're scared. I can smell it."

"I *am* scared," agreed, the Loa, eyes wide and blinking rapidly. "But emotion is my strength." Kofi opened his left hand to reveal a shard of crystalline stone, bright and clear.

The Bird's mouth opened in an O of recognition and understanding, the cudgel moving. A blinding flash seared the moment in Nuru's retinas. The Bird's eyes burst like rotten grapes crushed in an angry fist as the stone turned to dust.

Black.

Kofi screamed in agony.

The stench of charred flesh.

"Don't move." It was Kofi. He sounded strange, like he was talking through clenched teeth. "I told you to look away!"

Nuru's heart shivered in her chest, building horror. Had her eyes melted too? Was she forever blinded?

A useless Grower was a dead Grower.

"I can't—" She shook so hard she had trouble speaking. "I can't see."

Someone touched her shoulder and she flinched away with a squeal.

"Sorry," said Kofi, voice tight and pained. "It's me. I'll guide you. More will come. That lit the city for blocks."

Nuru nodded, holding out a tentative hand.

Kofi took it, his own palm dry and warm. He pulled her into motion.

"Efra?" she said.

No answer.

Nuru halted, dragging Kofi to a stop.

"Where is she?"

A heartbeat's hesitation. "Dead. We have to go."

"Are you sure she's dead?"

"We have to go! *Now!*"

"Bring her."

Kofi cursed, a spilled rhetoric about ignorance being the death of justice, too fast not to be memorized scripture. "I can't carry her and guide you."

He tried to pull her back into motion. Nuru resisted, blindly flailing at him.

Somewhere, someone screamed over and over. Mindless animal misery.

"We'll hide," she said, remembering the tenements all around them.

"They'll search. They'll find us. We have to go!"

"No!"

"She's dead!" snapped Kofi.

"Fuh," slurred Efra from the ground, voice feeble, terrified. "Dunt livmuh. Fuckinahualcunt."

"I'm not leaving her," she told Kofi. "Run away if you want."

Please don't. Please don't leave us.

She was blind, helpless. After that first outburst, Efra remained silent.

"Run away?" said Kofi, sounding wounded. "Mother said to protect you with my life. I would die to save you."

He sounded so young, so sincere.

So utterly fucking terrified.

"I go nowhere without her," said Nuru. "You want to protect me, you protect her as well."

"I can't—"

"Pick her up," commanded Nuru, interrupting the priest. "I'll hold on to your thobe. Don't go too fast."

"Remember this," snarled Kofi, "when the Hummingbirds are cracking our skulls."

Carrying Efra, Kofi guided Nuru. He whispered directions, warning her of obstacles. She stumbled often, stepping in pools of thick, warm damp, imagining blood and gore squishing up between her toes.

It felt like they wandered in circles, lost. The sounds of fighting and violence echoed madly through stone streets. Efra remained quiet. When Nuru tried to talk to her Kofi hissed for silence.

Nuru's world of perfect black slowly changed, becoming grey, and then showing blurred shapes. Rubbing at her eyes, blinking furiously, she cried when she realized she wasn't forever blind. Light returned, details growing.

Efra hung in Kofi's arms, slumped and unconscious, her head lolling. He staggered, exhausted, struggling under her weight. His left hand closed in a fist, he ground his teeth in pain.

"What happened?" Nuru asked, trying to get a better look.

"Nothing."

"This is far enough," she said.

"I can go further."

"Dropping Efra on her head isn't going to help."

"It might," he said.

Now that her vision was returning, Nuru pulled Kofi toward the nearest tenement entrance, praying it was abandoned. He didn't resist. Inside, she had him lay Efra on the stone table. Her scarred lip twitched, a hand lashing out in feeble defence.

Kofi sagged to the floor, putting his back against the wall. Nuru knelt before him, and he looked away, hiding something. Weakness? Fear? She wasn't sure.

"Let me see it," she said, nodding at his hand.

Kofi tucked it into an armpit. "I'm fine."

Grabbing his wrist, she pulled the hand free. "Open."

With a grimace, he unclenched the fist. The palm was burnt black, charred flesh flaking away in chunks of grey ash. While the stone must have been incredibly hot, the heat hadn't lasted long.

"Mostly a surface burn," said Nuru. Painful, to be sure, but he'd likely regain use of the hand once it healed. "That must hurt," she added.

"Not too bad," he lied, not meeting her eyes.

"How many of those stones do you have?"

He blinked in surprise, finally looking at her. "Are you kidding? That was a diamond! You know what that's worth?"

"Worth? It's a rock." Did they trade rocks like Growers traded food and narcotics? Being a source of power to Loa sorcerers, it made some sense.

Kofi stared at her in confusion. "That rock would feed a family of five for years in the Bankers' Ring."

Family.

She remembered children in the Crafters' Ring, mothers hugging their daughters. Tears stung her eyes.

Tables of prepared food.

A woman lying dead at the bottom of the steps, choked to death by Efra and Nuru.

The murders didn't touch Efra. She'd been confused when Nuru tried to explain that they couldn't keep killing people.

Efra was right. We did what we had to.

Nuru crushed the memory, shoved the surge of emotion deep.

But this man, handsome and strong, young and weirdly innocent, didn't seem so different. He looked at her the same way men always had. At least when he thought she wouldn't notice.

A little lust. A little longing.

A little sadness, though she didn't understand the last.

The nahual weren't so different from the Growers. The same desires drove them. She knew what priests did with Grower women who caught their eye. They wanted what Growers wanted. The only difference was, they had the power to take it.

When Kofi tried to stand, wincing in pain, she pushed him back to the floor. His resistance was a weak show at best. Cradling his burnt hand, trying to hide his pain, he leaned his head back against the stone and closed his eyes.

"I didn't want to leave her," he said. "I really did think she was dead."

Nuru said nothing, unsure if that was an apology, excuse, or explanation.

"There's something wrong with her," he added. "She's dangerous."

You have no idea.

Were the roles reversed, Efra would have left Kofi in a heartbeat.

I would have, too.

But he hadn't left them, hadn't abandoned them. He carried Efra the whole way. Nuru couldn't have managed a tenth of the distance.

"I'm going to make sure the tenement is empty," she said.

He cracked open a single eye, looking up at her. Finally, with a grimace that had nothing to do with pain, he grunted an affirmative and closed the eye.

"I wasn't asking," she said. "I was informing."

A flash of fractured smile. "Sorry."

She stared down at him. Never in all her life had she heard a nahual apologize.

After checking on Efra, Nuru headed into the back where the

sleeping rooms were.

The first was empty, barren stone dusted in red sand. Spiderwebs, thick and ropey, clogged the corners and hung broken from the ceiling. Refuse littered the floor. Scraps of grey cloth, shattered glass rounded with time.

The second room showed signs of recent habitation. A threadbare grey sheet draped the raised stone slab Dirts slept on. A plate of wood bark bore rinds of fruit that didn't look more than a day or two old.

Nuru shivered, tension creeping up her spine. The air felt heavy, oppressive. Like that crushed feeling you got when approaching the towering beehives out in the menageries. That rumbling buzz you felt in your chest that said not to come closer.

Uneven, spiritually unbalanced like something terrible just happened and she'd walked in a moment too late. She stopped, one foot in the room, hesitating.

Something moved in her peripheral vision. When she turned, there was nothing.

Had a mighty street-sorcerer hidden here? She'd heard tales of sorceries so powerful they left traces of their passing, a weakening of the veil that took hours to heal.

Behind her, Kofi headed down into the basement.

Turning to scold him, she found him slumped against the wall, eyes closed, snoring softly. Efra, too, lay where the young nahual deposited her, chest rising and falling with each breath.

I imagined it.

Moving to the top of the steps, she peered into the silent dark.

Still air, the slightest taste of musty damp not yet devoured by the morning's heat. It would be cool down there, pleasant. Though it was nice in here, out of the sun and ash, the basement air would be cleaner. She couldn't imagine taking a breath that didn't smell like burnt garbage.

If she still had Isabis, her viper, she would have sent the snake down into the basement first. No one messed with Isabis, and the snake wouldn't tolerate intruders.

I'm the intruder here.

"Hello?" she called down the steps. "Anyone down there?"

Behind her, Kofi grunted as he shifted position.

No one answered. Taking the first step, she heard nothing, not even the scamper of rats or cockroaches fleeing her approach. Another step and then another.

The strangest feeling, like she'd been here before, faced this same decision: Go into the basement, or return to the kitchen. She knew which choice she made because, somehow, she'd already made it. Almost like it was made for her, except it wasn't.

She would go into the basement to make sure it was safe to stay here because she would make the decision to do so.

She wanted to wake Efra. The girl was more dangerous than the snake.

But I don't do that. I let her sleep.

Down into the dark, as if decisions were a trap, a self-imposed prison.

On bright days tenement basements were murky and dark, places of fear where Growers rarely ventured. Too many deadly spiders. Too many snakes. Too many stories told by wrathful nahual of The Lord's underworld teeming with harvested souls. It was always down, always beneath. She never knew how literally to take the nahual's lectures.

"Hello?" she tried again, keeping her voice low so as not to wake the others.

Another choice. Another step.

There's no one down here. It's empty.

No Grower would stay in a dark basement.

Except maybe when squads of Birds roamed the streets bashing in heads. Loa nahual drove those Growers not hiding to riot, turning their forbidden stone sorcery against those they claimed to protect.

Hiding quietly in a dark basement was the smartest thing a Grower could do right now.

We should be doing that.

Reaching the bottom step, she said, "We're not here to hurt you. We're no threat. A couple of hours and we'll be gone."

A score of candles burst into flame, filling the basement with warm light.

A man stood in the centre of the room, long arterial red robes brushing the floor. Turquoise stones hung about him, woven into the bloody fabric. The green stones, misshapen and shot through with veins of yellow and brown, looked like puss and rot. Like when one of the goats had diarrhoea and shat in the milk bucket. The stones rattled together with every movement, with every breath.

How did I not hear that?

His hands and face, his only exposed flesh, showed terrible burns. He looked like a partially melted candle, skin slumping in folds. A wrinkled mess of ill-healed burn wounds, his bald skull reminded Nuru of a decaying potato.

She didn't recognize the robes, but he was obviously a priest.

A nahualli.

Eyes, bloody and stained yellow, studied her.

She knew that look, had seen it on the old street-sorcerer who first taught her to use her gift. This man was a tezcat on a massive dose of etorkizun.

"I have been waiting," he said.

He shuddered, turquoise stones clicking and clattering. Reality stretched and warped around him. Like looking into obsidian, the way it bent everything it reflected. The veil shredded apart under the weight of narcotics coursing through his blood. His allies lurked beyond, waiting to be called. Impossible creatures, foul nightmares. Not spirit-animals, they were nothing she recognized.

A huge jackal, hunched spine reaching to her shoulder, prowled to the nahualli's right. It had the hands of a monkey instead of paws, wrinkled black flesh glistening. Obsidian spikes jutted from its body at every angle making it look like a jagged stone porcupine. At the priest's left, flew a demonic wraith with the hollowed skull of a man and bat-like wings of fire.

Not just a tezcat, she realized.

Other figures stalked the blurred darkness. Ancient gods, long dead. Primal fears. The thing in the dark cave that dragged away your child. Ignorance and terror, slithering through the blackest depths of murky waters.

The air rippled around the nahualli, the surface of a pond disturbed by a dropped pebble.

The narcotics required to achieve such a state—the skill and will needed to control it—staggered Nuru with awe. This man should have been curled foetal on the floor, hallucinating and mewling like a terrified child, as his brain burned to a charred husk.

But there he stood, eyes calm, allies ready and waiting.

The veil buckled under the strain. Something—some stain of shadow and soul, a snaking wisp of intent—slipped through. It swam the room's perimeter, gauging, before fleeing up the stairs to disappear.

He's damaging the veil.

She couldn't comprehend the power involved. Somehow this nahualli single-handedly weakened Bastion's eternal defences.

This is impossible!

"A Grower," he said, shaking his head in bemused wonder. "Never before has a god chosen a Dirt."

"I—"

"Killing you," he said, speaking over her as nahual always did, "saves Bastion, opens the path for me to become Heart's Mirror."

She'd heard the term used in countless sermons. The Heart's Mirror was the representative of the gods, the one mortal allowed to enter the Gods' Ring.

"I have seen it," he continued, "in the Temple of the Last Day."

She'd heard the name but had no idea what it meant.

"You are the end," he said. "You are the Last Day."

I am the end, the destroyer of worlds. When had she said that?

"I don't understand," Nuru said, stalling. No nahual could resist preaching to an ignorant Dirt.

"I am the Heart of Turquoise Fire," he said as if it explained everything, as if she'd suddenly understand.

She is my Heart, Smoking Mirror had said of Efra. Nuru remembered thinking it sounded like a title.

She understood. The nahual always said that Dirts all looked alike.

He thinks I'm Efra.

"If you live," the nahualli added, "everyone you have ever known and loved will die."

Nuru's fists tightened with anger. "They're already dead."

"Ah," he said with disappointed amusement. "That, then, is why you are so dangerous."

He believed what he said, she saw it in his stone confidence. All nahual were like that, utterly sure of themselves and their place in the world. Who was she to doubt? Just an ignorant Dirt, something to grind to dust and bone in the wheat fields.

So sure was he, she almost believed him. A thousand generations of obedience. A lifetime of unquestioning faith. Be a good Grower and be reborn closer to the gods. Earn your way to something better by dying having spent all you are in service to the city.

Or bleed on the altar. Either way, we feed the gods.

Scarred little Efra terrified the nahual so much they sent this nahualli to kill her. She was Smoking Mirror's Heart, and while Nuru didn't know all of what that meant, she was beginning to get an idea.

Nuru cracked a broken smile, startling the priest. "You got the wrong Dirt."

"I do not."

He was a fool, so sure he couldn't possibly be wrong.

Mother Death, the spider laying obsidian eggs in Nuru's soul, lay dormant. Twenty-five thousand years spent beyond Bastion's walls, existing on the edge of starvation, devouring the ghosts of long forgotten gods, left her weak and likely insane. If sanity were something one could ever attribute to the immortal.

Smoking Mirror claimed that stagnation would end the Last City.

Mother Death wanted to use the Growers to reclaim her place at the head of the pantheon.

This foolish and overconfident nahualli thought Efra had to die to save Bastion.

"What," Nuru asked "is so great about the way things are that it's worth saving?"

AKACHI - STAINED WITH SACRILEGIOUS TRUTH

The Senators' Ring is the outermost ring to be a fully functioning member of Bastion's great and eternal economy. Everyone over the age of seven must contribute to the city and be paid for their efforts.

However, with the opportunity for wealth and advancement comes the possibility of abuse.

Failure to repay debts in a timely manner will earn one the rank of indebted. All indebted are tattooed on their arms to show how much they owe and are forbidden sleeved clothing. Hiding one's failures earns lashes.

As the amount changes, tattoos will be added or removed. Sorcerous in nature, only nahualli of the Lord of the Vanguard can make and alter the tattoos.

Repeated offences will earn the indebted the rank of indentured. When an indebted or indentured dies, their family inherits the debt. Spouses first, children next, in order of age.

—The Book of Bastion

Candle in hand, Akachi stood before the entrance to the dispensary. The ebony doors, always locked, always guarded by Hummingbird nahualli dosed with whatever narcotics they needed to fuel their sorcery, lay open and unattended.

Silence.

None of the chaos of the war above reached down here. The cool air carried hints of ancient paper and the dusty spice of cured leaves and fungi.

It's peaceful.

He could almost believe everything he'd seen was narcotic-induced hallucination. No snaking skyvyrm claimed the skies, puking stone-melting acid on the holy cathedral.

Another boring day as an unassigned priest.

No Wheat District.

Nafari was off chasing girls or chatting up the nahual of Precious Feather.

Captain Yejide… Akachi swallowed a lump of pain.

She was gone, dead.

He barely knew her, but knew he loved her. She…

She what?

They never talked about it. Beyond a rare touch on the shoulder, they had no physical contact. He never held her hand, much less kissed her.

What do you know of love?

Nothing, really. He'd never had a girlfriend.

If you love someone, does it matter what they feel for you?

Whatever she felt, she was gone. All he could do was be true to his memory of her.

And punish the Dirts who murdered her.

A deep rumble tickled at the edge of hearing, and the floor moved beneath his sandals. Dust rained from the ceiling, powdered the matted and tangled braids of his hair. Akachi stood waiting, wondering if the cathedral would fall in, bury him alive. He half hoped it would.

Nothing happened and silence returned.

Entering the dispensary, he discovered long rows of barren shelves, stripped of their stores by the nahualli fighting the Loa. His heart fell, hope sinking.

Nothing.

He'd used the last of his narcotics to come here. If he couldn't find more, he'd likely die here when the Loa took the cathedral. The hunt would die with him.

Desperate, he headed for the far end of the dispensary. Passing through another set of ebony doors, he entered another room of naked shelves.

With nothing else to do, he kept going, leaving behind the rooms he'd accessed as an acolyte.

Akachi smelled the hot tang of fresh blood before he saw the body. At the far end of yet another stripped room, lying before an open doorway, he found the corpse of a Hummingbird Guard. The man lay in a spreading pool, the blood trickling toward the nearest wall where it joined a gutter and flowed sluggishly away.

Even down here the gods get their due.

Crouching at the corpse's side, Akachi found a slim shard of sharpened flint rammed into the base of the man's skull.

Who could take a Hummingbird Guard by surprise?

"Bishop Zalika," Akachi said, remembering the narcotics piled before her.

She must have killed the Guard to gain access to the stores beyond. But why? She was the Bishop. She could have ordered the man away. Unless word had already spread of The Lord's demise. With Father Death no longer head of the pantheon, his priests had lost their pre-eminent rank. The Hummingbird may have refused her.

Stepping over the dead Guard, he entered the room beyond. Everything a nahualli could want lay before him. Shelves and shelves of narcotics. All the tools for preparation, ready and waiting. This must have been the reserves set aside for only the highest ranked nahualli. Perhaps even Bishop Zalika's personal cache.

Collecting narcotics, filling bag after bag of everything he might need, Akachi stopped before the jainkoei. There was enough here to brain-burn a thousand priests.

His breathing quickened, heart banging in his chest. Hunger built in him, a snarling emptiness starting deep in his gut and spreading like a conflagration. That itch at the back of his skull screamed to be scratched, jagged nails of clawing need.

Just a little.

Oh gods, he wanted it. The slightest taste of Cloud Serpent's attention would renew his purpose.

Ausardia, to give him the confidence to face the task at hand.

Foku, to keep him from straying from his holy path.

Kognizioa, so he remembered the feel of his god's love, to heighten his intelligence so he might better serve.

Pizgarri, to keep him sharp and alert.

Too much. Too much. Too much.

He wanted it all. *Needed* it all.

Stuffing the jainkoei into its own pouch, Akachi tucked it behind his banded belt beside the carvings of his spirit animals. Now was not the time. He would be strong. Stronger than any crystal magic.

The floor shook again, and dust fell. The distant, muted thunder of falling stone echoed through the dispensary. The war above continued, but now he was no longer helpless. Now he was a temple-trained nahualli armed with the tools of his trade. He would ingest these narcotics and bring hell down upon the Loa heretics. These were not gods. Unlike Mother Death, they would fall before his holy wrath.

Hunger, subtle and pervasive.

Was this the right thing to do?

Losing a battle was one thing. Losing the war was another.

"If the Northern Cathedral falls," he said aloud, "we will retake it."

In their greed for power, the Loa blasphemers would destroy all Bastion. They had to be stopped.

"I am a nahualli of Cloud Serpent. I hunt."

Taking the stairs two at a time, Akachi returned to the world above.

Where before he found the cathedral largely empty, now nahual and acolytes ran scampering in every direction. If there was order or purpose, he saw none of it.

A priest sprinted past carrying the ornate carving of a nagual in mid-shift, caught between the woman she was and the puma she'd become. It used to sit in the acolyte's dining hall.

They're looting the cathedral!

Other nahual ran by with art, utensils, or draperies. Nothing was sacred.

Horror gripped him when he realized someone might have already ransacked the Bishop's chambers. If the staff was already gone…

Akachi ran.

Dodging around acolytes, sending them scampering from his path with a sharp word, he recalled the oil painting in Zalika's office. It portrayed Mother Death as a beautiful woman with skin black as the space between the stars and the body of a terrible spider. She was being thrown from the Sand Wall by her husband, Father Death, depicted as a giant skeleton with a necklace of eyeballs. A one-of-a-kind work of art. In the inner rings, it would be worth a fortune. Had she brought it with her, or had the painting lived in the Northern Cathedral for thousands of years?

Another acolyte staggered by, bent under the weight of heavy blankets. What did he intend? Was he going to try and barter with the Dirts or the Loa, buy passage out of the Growers' Ring?

They're taking everything!

Akachi ran faster.

He found Zalika's chambers unguarded, the door closed. Letting himself in, he felt a pang of sheepish guilt. Here he was, nahualli and Heart of Cloud Serpent, future Heart's Mirror, pillaging the belongings of woman not half an hour dead.

Entering, he closed the door behind him.

The first room had been untouched, the looters likely terrified of the Bishop's wrath. The painting of Mother Death hung where he remembered it. And there, the colossal tapestry showing the Last Pilgrimage, the remnants of humanity fleeing to Bastion. Looking closer, he saw the ghosted images of the gods floating over the endless stream of people, shepherding them to safety. Some, he could name, but many he didn't recognize. Those who had not survived the march lay littered along the trail. Over each corpse lingered a wisp of soul. Squinting at the depiction of the city, he saw sharp edges and corners. This Bastion carried none of her rounded age. The detail was incredible, a work of mastery unknown today.

All humanity's greatest achievements lay forgotten in a long dead past. All the best tools and devices. All the most skilful works of art. There wasn't a single treasure that wasn't tens of thousands of years old.

We huddle in a dying city surrounded by the ghosts of all the world's dead. Maybe we, too, are ghosts.

An uncomfortable thought. Too close to Loa blasphemies.

Through an open door, Akachi spotted a wall of bookcases. A huge tome, pages opened like a lover spreading her legs, sat on its own stand. His breath caught and with no thought or intent he went to it. He had to. It drew him.

He knew what it was before he read the first word, before he caressed the soft pages with awed reverence.

The Book of Bastion.

Thicker and older than any copy he'd ever laid eyes on.

Akachi turned a page, listened to the sigh of paper on paper, inhaled the dry straw warmth of it. It smelled of history and time, the hopes and dreams of a thousand generations. Desperation and decay. Faith and blood.

He drank the words. Turned another page.

He wanted to take so much gorgoratzen, he'd remember every curve of calligraphy in his next life.

Another page and another. Holy words, written by the first nahual of Bastion. A passage caught his eye and he stopped.

'Katle were first created out of a need for leadership.'

Zalika called him katle. It was purest madness.

I have a soul. I can love. I have friends.

Friend.

Had.

Uncomfortable, Akachi read on.

'Stripped of their souls by The Lord, children were born free of the traits that would weaken them as masters of men. Humanity was dying, and hard choices had to be made. Warriors who would not flinch at atrocity were created. Leaders who would not hesitate, who were not tainted by love and emotion, were born to rule.'

Loa blasphemy, right there in what must be one of the first copies ever written!

Turning more pages, skimming through a blur of words, Akachi discovered a seamless blend of nahual faith and Loa heresy.

He read of how nahualli assassins murdered the first Hearts' Mirror, toppling the Queen of Bastion from her place at the head of the pantheon. When her husband banished her from the city, casting her into the Bloody Desert, her nahual rebelled.

Prior to the rebellion, her priesthood was known as the First Nahual.

They were the L'Wha, servants of the last of the Rada L'Wha.

Foulest blasphemy!

Chest heaving, Akachi turned another page. A single sentence caught his eye: 'The Lord of the House claimed the underworld for his own and dwelled in eternal night.'

Bring the staff to the place of eternal night. Bishop Zalika's words. Was this what she meant? Was he to take the Staff of the Fifth Sun to the underworld? Why? The Lord was dead, defeated by the godling Face Painted with Bells.

More pages. A forgotten history. A past erased.

A word from the darkest myths of nahualli legend caught his attention: Nahuallotl.

Once again skimming, Akachi read how each sect built its own secret menageries beneath the fields of the Life Ring and hid away all the world's most nightmarish creatures. Monsters like dragons and the skyvyrm he'd seen were kept there. They were bred, generation after generation, studied by the nahuallotl, a sorcery closely related to the nagual. He read accounts of mighty nahuallotl soaring the skies, burning rebel Senators or Bankers with dragon fire, stampeding through streets of the Crafters' Ring as unstoppable elephants.

Akachi stopped reading, stood motionless. Were those ancient menageries still out there, hidden beneath fields long left fallow?

I saw a skyvyrm.

Not only were those menageries still there, but the Loa had their own.

Loa. L'Wha. Nahual of the Queen of Bastion, last of the truly ancient gods.

Everything he knew was a lie.

Akachi stared at the book.

I should destroy this blasphemy. Burn it.

Mother Death and her Loa may have once ruled Bastion, but she was overthrown, cast from the city. Her priests were little more than filthy street-sorcerers and vermin, the inbred refuse of a dead sect.

Tears came and he didn't know why. They rolled down his cheeks and fell upon the awful book, staining pages already stained with sacrilegious truth.

Turning his back on what he could no longer face, Akachi searched deeper into Zalika's rooms. He passed through her sleeping chambers, barely sparing them a glance. Her bed sat neat and orderly, creases sharp and tucked tight. Beyond, he found her closets. He tried to imagine her wearing anything other than the owl-feather cloak of her office. He couldn't.

An oak showcase, polished to a lustrous glow, glass doors closed, caught his attention. The glass was smooth, without flaw. He hadn't seen their like since leaving the Priests' Ring. A gnarled oak staff, the top end carved to look like a raptor's talon, sat within. The curled claws clutched a polished red stone shot through with veins of green so dark it was almost black. Leaning close, he studied the stone through the glass.

Father Death murdered his brother, Zalika said in his dream, *cut his heart out*.

The Staff of the Fifth Sun.

As a nahualli of Cloud Serpent, hunting Loa heretics was expected to be one of Akachi's many tasks. Studying Bastion's enemies, learning of their stone sorcery, had been part of his training.

This was heliotrope, a mixture of the opaque green jasper and red hematite. Was it a coincidence that hematite was Mother Death's stone? Was she somehow related to the fallen Fifth Sun?

The combination was called bloodstone.

Akachi had read of ancient sorcerers using bloodstone for everything from weather control to calming unruly mobs. The heart of a dead god, this must be more than simply the bloodstone it appeared to be. Could that be true of all the types of stones the tecolotl used?

So many of the old stories were contradictory. True nahual didn't use stones in sorcery, and yet nahual used obsidian daggers to collect souls. And then there was Smoking Mirror, the Obsidian Lord, a god that some stories claimed was made entirely of black glass. Akachi's teachers taught those ancient tales as fables or parables. There was always some point to the story, something to be learned by a young acolyte. Now, having seen that ancient copy of the Book, Akachi was less sure.

Leaning so close to the glass his breath fogged it, Akachi examined the staff. It looked subtly wrong, strangely grey, as if stained. Opening the door, he reached out to touch it. Cold and hard, it didn't feel at all like wood.

"It's calcified," he said, with dawning awe.

The bloodstone again drew his eye. That eagle's claw had been carved into the wood back when it was still wood. How long did it take timber to turn to stone?

Akachi took the staff. It was heavier than it looked. In the right hands, this thing would cave skulls.

In Captain Yejide's hands.

He swallowed his pain.

Zalika said she dreamed he came for the staff and that she gave it to him. In his own dream, she'd been carrying it, waiting for him. When he found her in the dispensary, however, she had not brought the staff. She said something about not trusting the dream. Who did she think sent it?

She was delusional with the narcotics.

Nothing else made sense.

NURU - TURQUOISE FIRE

There was a time before gods. A time of animal simplicity and innocence. Our nascent sentience, the birth of our ability to truly comprehend—and thus fear—heralded the beginning of the end. The gods feed on fear and blood and worship. Sensing our dawning awareness, they were drawn to it like scavengers to rotting meat.

Life existed here long before there was a death god. Creatures were born and lived and died. The gods inserted themselves in a pre-existing system that didn't need them. Now, many hundreds of thousands of years later, we depend on them.

There was a time when humanity didn't need the gods; that time is long past.

—The Loa Book of the Invisibles

The sorcerer in robes of blood, rotting green stones clacking like dried bones, opened himself to his allies. His back bent, legs shortening, as bright shards of obsidian exploded from his flesh like spears. His hands wrinkled and turned black, glistening claws displacing his fingernails.

Teeth like night, a bright red tongue drooled viscous saliva.

Eyes of madness, jagged nuggets of misshapen coal.

In a heartbeat the sorcerer was gone, his physical form subsumed by his ally. A monstrous jackal, half flesh and patchy fur, half spikes of obsidian, stood hunched before Nuru, pitch hands grasping and twitching as if in expectation of the violence to come.

Ahuizotl, thought Nuru. A distant memory. Some nahual told the children a story about them when she was still in the crèche. Most of the kids had nightmares after. She'd been excited by the idea.

The veil shuddered under the onslaught. The souls beyond threw themselves at it, tearing the wound wider, fighting to gain entrance to the city. For twenty-five thousand years the world's dead warred among themselves, devouring each other for sustenance, battling for supremacy. Only the hardiest, the meanest, and most powerful, remained. Vanquished gods and demons. Powerful nahualli hurled from the wall. Nothing out there maintained its sanity for long. Millennia after millennia of cannibalism, of feeding on the destruction of other souls, broke everything.

The nahualli locked down his control, crushed the dead beneath his will and closed the rip in the veil. Nuru had never seen such an impressive show of strength. Not in a thousand years could she have managed this thing he did with a twitch of thought. He made that Cloud Serpent nahualli who defeated her in the basement of the gang's tenement look like a child.

Ahuizotl. This thing wasn't supposed to exist. Most of the creatures she saw through the tattered veil were myths, stories to scare children. Yet, there they were.

Utterly outclassed. Not a trace of narcotics in her blood. She was helpless.

A sound behind her. Nuru turned, expecting to see Efra but it was Kofi who shuffled down the steps, burnt left hand against his belly. In his right he held something that looked suspiciously like a large rodent turd. For an instant she imagined him throwing it at the ahuizotl and the two of them fleeing back up the stairs while the nahualli recovered from the shock of disgust.

Instead, the young Loa held it out before him as if stench alone would keep the monster at bay. "Nahuallotl of Turquoise Fire," Kofi said. "You are far from the Temple of the Last Day."

The ahuizotl drooled white foaming slather. "To kill a Heart," it said, darting a look at Nuru, "I will tolerate these filthy worms."

"I command you," growled Kofi, through clenched teeth, shoving the turd rock toward the ahuizotl as if that might drive it back.

Black fingers spasming, the ahuizotl looked from the stone to the Loa. "Really?" it said, red tongue lolling, turning its words to a slurred mush. "You would seek to control me?" It laughed, a cruel squealing cackle.

"With the Stone of Domination," barked Kofi, "I command you! You are mine! You obey—"

The ahuizotl pounced, crushing him to the floor. One of its black-clawed hands gripped Kofi's wrist, squeezing until he screamed and dropped the stone. It fell from his fingers, struck the floor, and shattered. The ahuizotl's other hand reached up to encircle the Loa's throat in a choking grip.

"You are nothing," slurred the monster. "Pathetic stone sorcery."

Kofi made a wet gagging sound, eyes bulging.

The creature lifted the young man from the ground with effortless strength. "I will smash your—"

Nuru fled back up the stairs.

With a bellow of rage, the ahuizotl gave chase, tossing Kofi aside.

Reaching the ground floor, Nuru dashed into the kitchen. Sprinting past Efra's motionless form, she ran for the entrance.

You're going to abandon your only friend?

Part of her screamed, *Run! Run, you fucking idiot!* while the rest stabbed her with guilt. Efra could have run when that Bird was killing Nuru. Hell, she should have!

But she didn't.

Nuru slid to a halt, bare feet skidding on stone.

The ahuizotl reached the top of the steps, slowing, when it saw Nuru turning to face it.

It grinned, showing onyx fangs. "So, little street-whore-sorcerer, you have something up your sleeve?" Arms wide, it advanced. "You think your god will save you?" It cackled, sputtering drool.

Runyoustupidwitlessfuck!

A weapon. Anything.

Nuru scanned the room.

A fucking stick. A rock. A god-damned piece of rotten fruit! Nothing.

Reaching Efra, the towering ahuizotl stopped. Head cocked to one side, it examined Nuru. "I know that look. Trapped-rabbit fear." Its red tongue hung wet, swinging and hypnotic. "Little sorcerer. Oh, little sorcerer." Coal eyes lit with fractured glee. "You have nothing."

Run. You can still run.

She couldn't move.

To flee was to leave Efra.

To stay was to die.

Chisulo would stay. He would never abandon a friend.

The ahuizotl looked from Nuru to Efra, and back. "Loyalty, among the Dirts?" It barked a canine laugh. Reaching down it grabbed Efra's wrist. Lifting her so she hung loose and boneless in its grip, the foul creature displayed its trophy. "This scarred Dirt means something to you. A lover?" It studied the limp woman, pondering.

Nuru wanted to laugh, half terror, half humour. This nahualli had the same ignorant superiority all nahual possessed. It held Smoking Mirror's Heart and thought her nothing.

"It matters not," said the nahualli, with a dismissive shrug. "If you flee, I will bleed her, long and slow, into one of your filthy feeding-troughs."

Efra stabbed a flint dagger into the soft underbelly of the ahuizotl's exposed throat. Tearing it out sideways, she jammed it in again, twisting and ripping. Blood haemorrhaged forth in a great spewing fountain, splashing Efra like someone upended a bucket over her head. The monster dropped her, clutching at its throat, desperate to stem the red tide. Landing at its feet, Efra stabbed it again and again in the gut, thrusting and slashing, spilling intestines. She eviscerated the creature, emptied it.

When it finally fell, toppling backward to shrink and once again become the red-robed priest, Efra grinned a feral snarl.

Her scar shone livid through a sheen of gore.

Hair matted with blood.

Thobe soaked and clinging to her slight form.

Ankle deep in effluence.

Rivers of spilled life ran from her, fell upon the stone floor, a sanguinary rain.

She was a goddess, an unstoppable force of death and destruction.

Mother Death chose wrong.

"You stopped," said Efra. "You could have escaped."

"I couldn't leave you."

"Had you fucking well kept running, he would have chased you. The unconscious Dirt he hadn't noticed—until you brought her to his attention—would have been fine."

Nuru stared at her. "Sorry."

Efra snorted a laugh. "Don't think I don't appreciate the thought."

"Chisulo wouldn't have abandoned you."

Efra winced. "And he's dead. We're supposed to learn from our mistakes, right?"

Kofi stumbled up the steps, leaning heavily on the wall. His thobe, now even filthier, hung in tatters. He looked tired and beaten, face bruised, one eye swelling, hair a tangled mess, face drawn.

"He's finally starting to look like a Grower," said Efra. "Couple more beatings and a little more dirt, and he'll fit right in." She tilted her head to one side, looking him up and down. "Still too fat."

He stopped at the top of the stairs, looking like he might tumble back down. "I'm not fat." He blinked in surprise at the corpse of the nahual, taking in the pool of gore and viscera. His gaze darted to Nuru and flinched away.

"I'm sorry," she said, feeling a stab of guilt.

Kofi frowned at the floor. "For what?"

"I left you."

"You left me." He laughed, a rueful cough, eyes wounded. "Protect her with your life. That's what mother said. That nahual…" He shook his head, rubbing at his bruised throat. "I was nothing."

"I know how you feel," said Nuru. "Temple-trained sorcerers are on a different level."

Showing teeth in a grimace, he said, "I *am* temple-trained. Loa sorcerers are a match for any nahualli."

"Clearly," said Efra. "You had him right where you wanted him."

Kofi grunted, shaking his head. "Stone sorcery is about being true to yourself. Nahualli lose themselves to the narcotics. It's an escape. They distance themselves from what they do. We have to feel it." He chanced another tentative glance at Nuru. "The more we feel, the more exposed our vulnerabilities, the stronger we are. It's all about letting your defences down."

"Priests are all the same," said Efra. "So fucking sure of yourselves. So many excuses. So fucking easy to kill." She kicked the corpse. "Who was this?"

"Nahualli of Turquoise Fire."

Nuru and Efra shared a look, both shrugging.

"Is Turquoise Fire a god?" asked Efra.

"Father Flame," said Kofi. "Lord of Time. The Heat in the Night. The Light in the Dark. Turquoise Fire has only one church, the Temple of the Last Day. His nahualli are powerful tezcat, unparalleled diviners."

"He knew we were coming," said Nuru, thinking aloud. "He was waiting—" She caught herself before mentioning that he was waiting for the Heart, for Efra. "He was waiting for us."

"That's possible," said Kofi. "I've never met a tezcat with that kind of accuracy, but I've read stories." He shook his head, awed. "To not only pick the right tenement, but to know you'd go down there alone."

Me? No. The tezcat got that wrong.

Nuru kept the thought to herself. The Turquoise Fire nahualli had been expecting Efra. He must not have foreseen the fight with the Bird before they fled here. Had Efra not been hurt, she would have been the one checking the basement while Nuru tended to Kofi's burnt hand. How different would things have turned out? Could Efra still have killed the priest?

Nuru couldn't imagine anything or anyone capable of killing the girl.

Kofi turned on Efra. "You did that." He gestured at the gutted corpse.

Efra grunted a dismissive affirmative.

"You have a weapon?" he asked.

Drawing the still-bloody flint dagger from where she'd once again hidden it away in the rolls of her thobe, Efra held it up for display.

"Where did you get it?"

"Took it off a dead Loa."

Nuru hadn't seen her do it.

Kofi looked from the stone knife to Efra's face. "Give it to me." He looked to Nuru as if expecting support, and then back to Efra. "I am trained in combat."

Efra cast a pointed glance at the dead priest, cocking a scarred eyebrow.

When she said nothing, he held out his unburnt hand, palm up. "Please. Give it to me."

"No."

"I need it," he said. "I need it to protect *her*."

"So take it," said Efra. Calm. Daring. Almost teasing. "Come, temple-trained knife-fighting nahualli fat-ass. Take this blade."

Shit.

Nuru knew that look. She'd seen it in her boys too many times. Some poor bastard would goad Bomani, not understanding. He'd get this look like too much had been said and there was no turning back now. Omari used to call it Bomani's 'Fuck everything' look, and not even Chisulo got in the way when he had it. The others in the gang realized the best thing they could do was stand at Bomani's side like they were backing him up and hope whoever angered him decided it wasn't worth the fight. Hell, even Chisulo got that looked if pushed enough.

Kofi didn't look ready to back down.

There was something wrong with men at a bone-deep level.

They'd rather suffer a vicious beating than look weak.

Idiots.

Kofi stepped forward in a fighter's crouch. He moved well, Nuru saw. Maybe not as well as the Birds, but he moved with balance and grace. He moved like someone who knew how to fight.

"She'll kill you," Nuru said. "And we'll go on without you."

He stopped, not taking his eyes off Efra. "Tell her to give me the knife."

Like I have any control over Efra. "No. She is more dangerous than you'll ever be."

"It'll be better in my hands."

"How many people have you killed?" Nuru asked.

He blinked, finally glancing at her. "I've used the Stone of Conflict to kill hundreds of Hummingbirds."

Was that the flint he held when he worked the Growers to a violent frenzy?

"With your hands," said Nuru. "How many people have you stabbed to death? How many people have you choked to death? How many times have you bashed someone's head in with a rock?"

His hands dropped, and he looked from Efra to Nuru. "I know how. I'm trained."

"How many?" repeated Nuru.

His shoulders sagged. "None."

He's ashamed he's never murdered anyone.

What did his shame say about Nuru and Efra? Who did he think they were?

She swallowed the uncomfortable thought.

"Efra," she said, "how many people have you killed?"

Startled by the question, Efra's brow furrowed in thought. "I don't know. Who keeps track of things like that?"

Fadil, the leader of the gang that tried to take Chisulo's turf.

That Bird in the street, stabbed through the neck with a sharpened piece of wood.

The two Crafters Nuru and Efra garrotted to get their clothes.

The two they killed in the Crafters' Ring to get paint and tools.

The Bird squad with the Cloud Serpent nahualli.

The Turquoise Fire priest now dead on the floor.

But who's counting?

"She keeps the knife," said Nuru. "Anyway, you swore to protect me with your life. You can't do that if you're dead."

Kofi seemed to cave in on himself, uncertain, defeated. "Fine."

"I should kill him anyway," said Efra. "He stands out like a nahual of Precious Feather in a pig slop."

"No," said Nuru. "We need him."

His look of gratitude was so desperate she didn't finish the thought.

We need him to get out of the Growers' Ring.

"We'll leave when it's dark," said Kofi, trying to regain some control over the situation. "Mother said that if we got separated, I should take you to Subira, in the Senators' Ring. She'll get us to the Priests' Ring."

"The Priests' Ring?" she asked, dreading.

He nodded. "We can't stay here. And this…" He waved a hand at the corpse-littered streets. "I know this seems terrible. It's nothing."

All those Growers out there collecting ash were nothing? How many hundreds of dead had she seen?

"It's going to get a lot worse," Kofi added. "The Turquoise Serpents are in the ring." He glanced at Nuru and then away. "It's important we get you to the centre, where things matter. Out here, you're vulnerable. I can't protect you."

Accustomed to being nothing, she'd assumed the carving was all that mattered, that at some point they'd take it.

Only the person who creates a carving can use it. You *know* that. *They need me.*

Only Nuru could bring their god, Mother Death, into Bastion.

Eyes narrowed with suspicion, Efra looked from Nuru to Kofi. "Why do you want to take her to the Priests' Ring?"

Ignoring Efra, Kofi asked, "Did you really make that carving?"

Nuru considered lying, telling him she found it.

If he thinks he doesn't need you, he'll leave you here to die.

Efra gave Nuru the slightest nod. She knew. She knew the dangers, and she knew what would happen if they stayed in the ring. This Loa nahual was their only chance.

"I carved it," said Nuru.

"Well, then," said Kofi, "you know what that means."

Both women stared at him, waiting.

Nuru's chest tight with terror, a small voice repeated *no, no, no, no* over and over.

Kofi frowned in confusion. "The Queen of Bastion *chose* you."

"For?" asked Efra.

Eyes never leaving Nuru, he shook his head in stunned awe. "You are Mother Death's Heart."

AKACHI - WITH STONE IN MY HEART

Katle, mortals born without a soul, are abominations. While Father Death ensures this never happens, they can be intentionally created. If a pregnant woman is wrapped in the corpses of snakes and buried up to the neck from just after conception until moments before she gives birth, The Lord cannot find the baby to give it a soul.

While katle look no different from other mortals, there is something about them that the particularly observant will note. They possess a deadness in the eyes, an emptiness. They have limited emotional capacity and are capable of any horror. Nothing stops them from committing the most terrible atrocities. Perfect assassins and murderers, they also excel as Bankers and Senators if placed in the right role. Though most are no smarter or stronger than average, every now and then a special katle is born, deeply evil and clever.

—The Book of Bastion

Staff of the Fifth Sun in hand, Akachi exited Bishop Zalika's chambers. The weight of calcified wood felt good, reassuring in its solidity. Whatever the ancient artefact was capable of, he knew he'd made the right decision. The tighter he gripped the staff, the more certain he felt. This was right. He served his god. He would not fail.

He *could* not fail.

Finding the halls empty and silent, Akachi paused, wondering what to do. Should he make use of the narcotics he'd taken from the dispensary, be ready to call upon his allies? With the dregs of his last dose still in his blood, that was dangerous. He needed to eat and sleep before ingesting more drugs. Much as he wanted to rush off after the two Dirt women, he had to be smart.

It shouldn't be too difficult to outwit them. Wherever they go, I'll be waiting.

He breathed, calming his thoughts.

They would leave the ring; of that he was sure. As they'd already made the journey once, clearly possessing the means to pass through the Grey Wall, he had to assume they'd already left. Once in the Crafters' Ring, he would hunt them through sorcerous means. Until then, he was better off letting the last dose leave his system.

The cathedral wasn't far from the Grey Wall. Perhaps he could convince a squad of Hummingbirds to escort him.

Akachi strode the familiar halls of the cathedral. He'd been twelve when father sent him to serve as an acolyte. For five years he ran errands for the nahual. He missed that. There was a simplicity to the ordered life of a priest-in-training. Obedience was everything. Read what the nahual told you to read. Practice what the teachers instructed you to practice. Dress the way a student of Cloud Serpent was supposed to dress. Pray when the drums sounded.

He hadn't heard the drums all day.

Everything had changed. Reality felt tenuous, like the world he knew was falling apart.

Akachi gripped the staff tighter and felt better. A thought slowed his stride.

When do the gods choose their Heart?

Awe at the foresight and planning of the gods filled him with warmth. According to the Book, the Heart of every god was born with the tiniest sliver of obsidian within their own hearts. Being the stone of souls, this allowed the god a spirit-deep connection with their Heart. It allowed them to communicate directly with that mortal without leaving the Gods' Ring.

Perspective changed everything.

I was born with obsidian in my heart. I was born chosen.

All his life he'd been Cloud Serpent's Heart.

How different would things have been had his father known of

Akachi's destiny?

Or had he somehow known? Was that why he was so demanding?

Akachi gripped the staff tight with his right hand.

I don't care. Cloud Serpent cleansed me of doubts, cleansed me of the shallow worries of youth.

Savage heat and the all-pervading stench of death struck Akachi as he exited the cathedral. The setting sun smeared the western sky red and orange, a child finger-painting in blood. In the last hour, the smoke had thinned. Several of the cathedral's taller spires lay shattered, holy stone littering the grounds. Corpses were strewn about the courtyard. Those killed early in the day were mounds of ash. The more recent dead were merely dusted, chalky eyes staring.

He saw no sign of the skyvyrm.

The Hummingbird Guard were gone, fled, slaughtered, or called away. Southern Hummingbird was likely more interested in protecting his own churches than wasting his nahual on a doomed temple.

Nothing moved but wafting smoke.

No cries of the wounded. No staggering victims or hands raised, pleading for help.

Dust and ash and stillness.

Only the dead remained.

He couldn't look away, couldn't pull his eyes from the horror.

Tears came. Such impossible blasphemy, to so damage the sacred stone of Bastion.

What do they think will come of this?

Surely the Loa knew that such carnage could never be repaired. They would destroy the very city that gave humanity life!

I will not allow that.

Staff in hand, Akachi surveyed the ruin. He would hunt them all. Not just the two Dirt girls, but all the mad heretics. He would kill them all, banish their souls to the Bloody Desert. It was past time the sickness of the Loa was carved from the flesh of the Last City.

"When I am Heart's Mirror, I will purify all Bastion. I will tolerate no sin, no blasphemy."

Why the previous Heart's Mirror permitted the Loa's existence, he couldn't imagine. She was dead now, assassinated. Perhaps that was the gods' justice, a condemnation of her methods.

As if of their own will, the stumps of Akachi's severed fingers dug into the pouches behind his belt and clumsily extricated a small amount of gorgoratzen and foku. Studying the fallen tower, bearing mute witness to the destruction, he ate them.

Until his last breath, this sight, the rage snaking his soul and constricting his heart, would stay with him. He locked every fallen stone, every ashen mound, every corpse, into memory.

Let this remind me. When I falter, when doubt grows strong and weakens my will, let this be my strength.

He might not know what power the Staff of the Fifth Sun possessed, but Cloud Serpent sent him here to get it. The heart of a dead god. An ancient artefact long hidden in the Northern Cathedral, no doubt it was a mighty weapon.

Akachi felt like stone.

Father Death was gone, a fallen god. His murderer, Face Painted with Bells, held the underworld, awaiting the return of the Queen of Bastion. Mother Death had somehow managed to crack the city's defences and gain a foothold. Her priests would sacrifice in her name, feed her blood and souls. She would grow in strength. That crack would become a gaping wound. The Loa would tear a hole in Bastion and all the world's dead would flood into the city.

They doom us.

He would stop them.

Akachi. One man.

There was no place for mercy. The very fate of the Last City hinged on Mother Death's defeat.

Movement caught Akachi's attention. Dim shapes, ghosts in the smoke, entered the cathedral courtyard through the smashed gates. They weren't Dirts; he sensed that immediately, saw it in the way they moved.

For a moment he thought they might be Hummingbird Guard, but even that felt wrong.

Turquoise Serpents.

Obsidian swords drawn, they moved with a grace and precision that put even Captain Yejide to shame. Their armour, boiled leather dyed lustrous green, stitched with scales of sorcerously-hardened turquoise and jade, shone with its own light. Ebony shields wrapped in crimson leather hung slung over their backs. Bloodied, the Serpents looked haggard.

Spotting Akachi, they headed toward him.

A squat, middle-aged woman led the squad. Broad shouldered and thick-armed, she looked capable of kicking down the cathedral's towers on her own. Oddly out of place, she wore the tattoo of a delicate emerald butterfly in the centre of her forehead.

They approached Akachi, spreading out, and he suddenly wished he'd eaten every narcotic he found back in the cathedral. Drawing a deep breath, he waited. Running was pointless. If the gods willed it, here he would die.

He felt no fear.

Three others followed the squat woman. A hugely muscled man, his face and bald head covered in tattoos of eyes, walked on her left. Some of the tattooed eyes studied Akachi. To her right walked a short and wiry youth with a wisp of moustache and a weak chin who looked no older than Akachi. The youth seemed out of place with this squad.

Following behind the rest was another woman. Stunningly beautiful, she wore her hair long, tied back in a tight braid. She studied Akachi, a hint of a smirk teasing full lips. With a shock, he realized her eyes were grey, like slate. Never had he seen someone whose eyes weren't some shade of brown.

She's been touched by a god.

The squad stopped before Akachi, ready for violence, but unthreat-ening. Oddly, they looked too human. He hadn't seen Serpents since he was a child in the Priests' Ring. They'd been imposing, men and women carved from granite. Untouchable. These four looked…they looked like people who had seen and done terrible things. Something lurked behind their hard expressions, a knowledge born of horror. An understanding of mortality, of the cost of doing holy work.

Akachi knew the feeling. He first felt it after taking the baby from that Dirt girl, and he'd known it again after killing the Loa assassin.

Nothing touched the woman with the grey eyes. She alone held the pinnacle of godly perfection the Turquoise Serpents were said to embody.

All four wore fetishes of carved bone, sorcerous talismans imbuing them with various strengths and skills. Hints of tattoos peeked from beneath their armour, wards and runes he didn't recognize.

Taking in the state of his robes, the squat woman nodded to Akachi, the barest minimum of respect. "I am Captain Melokuhle. Identify yourself."

Well, they hadn't killed him. Yet.

"Akachi. Until recently, I was an acting-pastor in the Wheat District. Now…" He shrugged, not wanting to say more.

The rest of the tattooed eyes on the big bald man's skull snapped open and turned on Akachi. "Show me your left hand," he said.

Akachi opened his ruined hand, held it up for inspection.

All the bald Serpent's eyes widened when they saw the stumps of the fingers. "He's the one, Captain."

"You're certain?" Captain Melokuhle asked.

"The fingers."

The Captain looked away, stared off into the smoke. "Fuck," she said. "Fucking bloody fucking sand and shit."

The woman with the grey eyes stepped closer, looking Akachi up and down. "As always, Firash, you forgot to mention how cute he was." She sniffed at him. "Though he's in desperate need of a bath."

The bald man shrugged. "Too skinny for me."

"Nahualli Akachi," said Captain Melokuhle, turning back to face him. Her eyes showed the wounds in her soul, pleading he be worth whatever horrors she'd witnessed. She didn't want this, didn't want to be here. "Hunter Akachi," she said, starting again, "we are here to assist you." She darted a look at Firash. "Apparently."

"In any way you need," purred the grey eyed woman. "At least after the bath. And maybe during."

"Omphile," said the Captain, sounding tired and beaten. "Please. Not now."

Omphile grinned at Akachi, the corners of full lips teasing and promising.

They don't know I am Cloud Serpent's Heart.

If they did, they would kill him. It would be their holy duty.

"Who sent you?" he asked, returning his attention to Melokuhle.

"Firash is our tezcat." She nodded at the bald man, whose tattooed eyes had once again closed. "He saw this moment in a divination."

"A version of this moment," corrected Firash. "Sometimes there are more or less of us." The Captain flinched as if struck. "Sometimes he is missing the entire hand. Sometimes he's dead, and not here. Sometimes we find his corpse with the Bishop." Firash grunted. "And there is always room for interpretation."

"You know where we're going?" Akachi asked Firash. Having a tezcat who knew where his prey were headed would be handy indeed. "You know who we hunt, and why?"

One of the tattooed eyes opened and rolled to stare at Omphile, who blew it a kiss. "I do not," said Firash.

"I left the Priests' Ring with a score of Turquoise Serpents," said Captain Melokuhle, that wounded look deepening. "Firash said we had to find you. That if we didn't, Bastion would fall." She saw the unasked question in Akachi's face. "We were attacked by Loa."

"Did you see…" How to ask without sounding delusional or brainburned?

"There was a grootslang," said the scrawny youth, "a colossal snake with the head of an elephant and teeth like the biggest lion." He glanced at his Captain and she nodded. "And there was an impundulu, each wing longer than a tall man. It called lightning from the sky and drank the blood of the fallen."

More creatures of myth. Stories no one took seriously. The Loa had secret menageries. How organized must they be to keep them hidden all these long millennia.

"They were waiting," said the Captain, "expecting us."

"I was out-manoeuvred," admitted Firash. Guilt hung about him like a heavy cloak, bent his broad shoulders. "I did not expect them to have a powerful tezcat of their own."

"Only we four remain," continued Melokuhle. Teeth clenched, she examined Akachi, trying to see in him what might be worth the sacrifice. "Tell me those lives were not wasted. Tell me we are here for a reason."

"We're going to save Bastion," promised Akachi, the staff a comforting weight in his hand. "We're going to save all humanity. We're going to crush the heretics." He took a calming, shuddering breath, swallowing his rage. They blasphemed the cathedral. They damaged the very stone of the city. "We're going to kill them all."

"Cute and murderous," said Omphile. "I like him!" She winked.

Hypnotized by eyes, the likes of which he had never seen, Akachi struggled for focus. If Precious Feather selected the finest, silkiest clay, and crafted the most perfect woman imaginable, Omphile would still be more beautiful.

Some of the rage and hurt bled from Captain Melokuhle. "That's a start." Turning, she introduced what remained of her squad. "Firash, the bald lump, is our tezcat." She gestured at the youth with the wisps of moustache. "This is Lubanzi, our otochin. And the god-touched, here, is Omphile, our assassin."

Omphile dipped a quick and flirtatious curtsey.

"We're going to the Crafters Ring," Akachi announced. "Perhaps further. We'll talk along the way."

"Good," said Lubanzi. "This ring stinks."

NURU - SHE WAS THE NOTHING

*The myriad pantheons battled for supremacy. Gods strode the earth, battle-nahu-
alli at their side, warring with other deities. The world shook. Great sorceries,
forbidden magics, were unleashed. Life teetered on the brink of extinction.*

*The Queen, in her horror, called for a truce, one last attempt at saving both
humanity and the gods.*

This world was dying, riven.

A thousand gods from a thousand pantheons couldn't repair the damage done.

'Quell your hungers,' The Queen commanded. 'For we must learn restraint.'

*And she, The Destroyer of Worlds, did threaten to undo this last reality should
her children not obey. Cowed by her rage, the gods bent before her.*

*But her children hungered, chafed at the rationing of souls, and the Queen was
betrayed.*

—The Loa Book of the Invisibles

Nuru and Efra followed Kofi into the night. With the sudden drop
in temperature, a cool breeze swept much of the smoke away. For the
first time in days, it didn't hurt to breathe. The stars, usually a hard white,
glowed dull red, muted by the lingering haze. Strangely silent after the
day's riotous cacophony, the streets felt oppressive, the city judging.

Kofi set a slow pace, picking his way through and around ash-
covered corpses, staying close to the tenement walls, pausing often to
squint into the dark.

"Do you know where you're going?" whispered Efra, poking the
young Loa from behind.

He shot an annoyed look over his shoulder. "Of course I do."

"The Grey Wall is that huge thing off to our left."

"I knew that." He looked left, squinting into a dark alley. "I *know* that," he corrected.

Nuru felt lost, her mind reeling from Kofi's claim she was Mother Death's Heart. What was it to be the Heart of god? Smoking Mirror said that Efra was his Heart, but she seemed no different.

No, that wasn't true.

Something had changed. Back before Nuru started carving Mother Death, Efra lingered on the edges of the gang. She'd disappear for weeks and come back looking like she lost a fight with a pack of rabid cats. She drifted purposeless, never really doing more than the minimum demanded of her.

Now, Efra moved with purpose.

Focus, damn it!

What did it mean that both she and Efra were the Hearts of gods?

Nuru hesitated to ask Kofi while Efra was around. Maybe, if she got him alone, she could dig for more.

For now, they had to move. They couldn't stay in the Growers' Ring. Plan or no, everything important, everything shaping the fate of Bastion and the Growers, took place in the inner rings.

"Once we're in the Crafters' Ring we'll be safe," said Kofi, "I know people there. We have a church. Supplies. Somewhere to sleep. On a real bed." He dashed a quick look at Nuru and away, suddenly embarrassed. "They'll help us get to Subira in the Senators' Ring."

"Poor boy has it bad," whispered Efra.

Nuru, surprised Efra was aware of someone else's emotions, said nothing.

"It's good though," Efra continued quietly. "Having people care about you..." She looked wistful, eyes distant. "Makes them easy to use."

Ah, that's more like it.

Nuru stepped over another body. Every day for her entire life Bastion had gone on, unchanging. The Eternal City, the nahual called it.

After twenty-five thousand years, Bastion became unrecognizable in less than a week. Blood and corpses. Ankle-deep ash. War in the streets. Open rioting and murder. The stink of rot and death. It even sounded different, muted, small, like it was falling in on itself.

If Bastion changed, was it still eternal?

Nuru and Efra followed the Loa nahual into another street, heading ever closer to the Grey Wall. With the stars muted, smeared embers behind a curtain of haze, it was a slab of black, a hole in reality. Even from here, a few thousand strides away, it towered over everything, a presence like a god.

"I hate being this close to the wall," muttered Efra. "I *hate* feeling small."

Efra being tiny, Nuru wasn't sure if she was joking. She possessed a clenched-fist hardness that made her seem bigger. Of all the people Nuru didn't want to fight, Efra topped the list.

She felt like a twig tossed into one of the rivers out in the fields. Helpless, she went where the current took her.

Mother Death. The Loa. Maybe even Efra. They all had plans for Nuru.

I need a plan. I need control.

The thought felt foolish.

Mortals plan and the gods laugh. Nahual said that so often she wondered if it was in the Book.

She was tired.

Tired of walking. Tired of hiding.

Tired of being hungry.

Tired of being afraid, and tired of feeling powerless. Tired of being used.

So fucking tired.

If only we could banish the gods from Bastion.

She imagined the Last City free of gods, mortals left to choose their own path.

No more nahual. No whippings in the public square for transgressing the Book. No bleeding. No sacrifice.

It was hopeless, the foolish dream of a foolish girl. Bastion needed her gods. They were life. Father Death purified the souls of the dead so they could be reborn to live again. Her Skirt is Stars, also known as Mother Life, oversaw childbirth. Sin Eater devoured the filth and sins of the weak. Feathered Serpent gave knowledge and learning to humanity. Each of the gods was, in some way, critical to the survival of the city.

Yet, the thought lingered.

Kill the gods.

A mob of Growers, brandishing ebony cudgels and flint knives, exited an alley. Nuru tensed to flee, but Kofi raised a hand in greeting, and in moments they were surrounded by Dirts who moved like priests.

An elderly woman, skin like a dried plum, hair a bright shock of white, approached the young Loa. She moved well for her age, careful, but not limping or shuffling. Eyes lost in deep folds of wrinkles, she saw everything.

Nuru had never seen anyone so old.

"These," the woman said, confronting Kofi, and nodding at Nuru and Efra, "are real Growers."

"They are," agreed Kofi.

When he offered no explanation, she examined Nuru the way Nuru studied a chunk of wood before carving it. Was there something useful hidden in there she might discover once the dross was carved away?

"Pretty," said the old woman. "Your mother will be angry if this is all you've been up to."

"Kuboka ordered me to deliver her to Subira," answered Kofi, shrinking beneath those ancient eyes.

"Why?" demanded the old Loa.

Kofi's mouth worked for a moment as he struggled to find a suitable answer. Finally, he managed, "You'd have to ask her that." Though it came out as more of a question.

Eyes narrowing, the old woman nodded grudgingly. "Fair enough."

As if finding his confidence, he straightened. "We need an escort to your home base."

"I can assign—"

"This woman," he said, gesturing at Nuru, "is more important than stirring up Dirts. You will *personally* see us to your base."

Again, those deep-set eyes found Nuru. A heartbeat, and then a stiff nod. "Follow."

More dark streets and more corpses.

The thought of stopping, of being allowed to finally collapse to the floor, drained the strength from Nuru. Stepping close, Efra offered support. Together they staggered after the Loa.

Scouts came and went, reporting to the old lady in hushed whispers. Several times the entire group stopped and hunkered down in the trash to wait. Someone would appear out of the night, there'd be more whispering, and the group would move off in a new direction.

By the time they arrived at their destination Nuru felt like she'd walked the entire way around the outer ring. More Loa dressed as Growers appeared out of the dark and led them into a barley warehouse. A massive stone building, the arched ceilings were so high overhead Nuru couldn't see them. The still air stunk like Bomani's breath after a night of drinking street-swill liquor.

Kofi ushered Nuru and Efra to an area of floor where grey sheets had been laid out. Choosing one, Efra was asleep and snoring in a dozen heartbeats.

Exhausted, Nuru sat on another. Her mind a whirl of blasphemy, she knew she wouldn't sleep.

Kofi sat across from her, a silhouette in the dark. "We've taken about a third of the gates," he said.

Was he making conversation, or would this lead somewhere?

"In this quarter?" Nuru asked.

"In the ring." He cleared his throat, a soft noise, and shuffled, trying to find a way to be comfortable on the stone floor.

Having been born to this, Nuru watched with interest. Blankets. Pillows. Real beds. She'd seen it all in the Crafters' Ring and couldn't imagine what wonders awaited deeper in the city.

"We'll go through in the morning," he added.

He can't sleep either, she realized. *He needs to talk, to distract himself.*

They sat in silence, Kofi fidgeting.

"Do gods have hearts?" she asked, voice low so as not to wake Efra.

"Not in the typical sense, not a muscle that pumps blood, but yes." He paused. "I suppose."

Why couldn't men admit when they hadn't a fucking clue?

"What is a god's *Heart*?" she asked.

His breath caught. "I shouldn't have said anything."

It was, Nuru decided, time to see if Efra was right. "Please," she said, letting him hear her need. "I'm so lost."

Kofi studied her in the dark. "You've heard the term before," he said. "I saw it in your reaction."

"The nahual of Feathered Serpent for the Wheat District talked about it a couple of times. It sounded like a title, like it referred to a person or spirit rather than an actual heart."

He sat in silence, fingers drumming on stone. "I shouldn't—"

"What if I am?" she asked, leaning toward him so she could see his eyes, make out his features. "What if I am?"

"Then you are everything."

"And if I am," she whispered, "I need to know what it means."

"But... But I..."

"Have you been told *not* to saying anything?" she asked.

"Well, no," he admitted.

"What do *you* think?" she said. "Look at me, really look at me. Am I Mother Death's Heart?"

He stared, biting his bottom lip. Perhaps a year or two older than Nuru, he was too young for this task, too easy to read.

He wants me to be Mother Death's Heart.

He wanted to believe in her. He needed her to be something special, something more than an ignorant Dirt. Nuru understood: If she was important, then he was too. It made his existence, his every decision, matter.

He wants that more than anything.

Kofi nodded.

"Tell me," she said.

Taking a deep breath, Kofi said, "Each god has a Heart, someone who represents them. Usually it's the High Priest, though sometimes it's a Bishop in one of the Quarter Cathedrals."

"Quarter Cathedral?"

"North, South, East, West. There's a cathedral at each compass point in every ring. It's the spiritual centre for that quarter. All the priests, no matter what sect they belong to, report there. Each cathedral has a Bishop, a ranked priest of whichever god rules the pantheon. Until recently, all of the Bishops were nahual of Father Death."

Nuru felt like a constrictor sought to crush the air from her. "Until recently?"

"We killed The Lord," he said with pride. "The pantheon is without leadership. The Queen of Bastion shall reclaim her place."

Killed.

Father Death was dead.

I was thinking of killing gods.

It had seemed impossible. But if the Loa had killed a god, particularly one as powerful as The Lord, perhaps it wasn't.

Gods can die.

The holy truth, grilled into her through a life-time of sermons, killed the brief moment of fierce joy.

We still need them.

The loss of Father Death was only manageable because his wife, Mother Death, was there to take his place. The pantheon wouldn't be without a death god for long.

Nuru struggled to fit this into her understanding of the world.

If there was no death god overseeing the underworld, purifying souls so they might be reborn, did that mean there were no babies?

The nahual never talked about such things.

I need to know more.

"And the Hearts," Nuru said, "what role do they play?"

"In times of peace they go unnoticed. Hundreds of generations of Hearts live and die without knowing they were chosen." He reached out a hand like he might put it on her knee, hesitated, and returned it to his lap.

Smoking Mirror promised all-out war among the rings. There would be no peace.

"In times of war?" she asked.

"Before Bastion, the gods fought each other more literally." His voice changed as he recited something memorized. "The damage was terrible. The world died, destroyed by warring deities. To protect the Last City, the gods decided they would no longer directly oppose one another, but work through mortal agents, their Hearts. In times of war, a Heart can change everything."

Nuru wanted that, craved that power.

"The gods war through their mortal Hearts," Kofi continued. "When all the Hearts but one is dead, that last Heart becomes the Heart's Mirror. Their god ascends to the head of the pantheon. We assassinated the previous Heart's Mirror to weaken The Lord. Then we lured him from the Gods' Ring and killed him."

Mind racing, pieces falling together, Nuru knew a dawning horror.

'She is my Heart,' Father Discord told Nuru during the dream that wasn't.

Efra is Smoking Mirror's Heart.

If this Loa was right, Nuru was Mother Death's Heart. She glanced at Kofi, saw no doubt in his eyes.

No. He's wrong. I'm nothing.

She was the nothing who carved Mother Death, the nothing who brought the god into the city.

Nuru glanced at Efra, watched the slow rise and fall of her chest. She tried to imagine the scarred girl ruling over the mortal population of Bastion, being the voice of Smoking Mirror, God of Strife, The Enemy of Both Sides.

How perfectly he chose his Heart.

That constrictor crushed Nuru. She couldn't breathe.

Should she tell Kofi what Efra was?

He'll kill her.

She knew it to be true.

Maybe Efra and I aren't enemies. Nuru sagged with relief, the constrictor loosening its grip. Facing the gods was bad enough. She didn't ever want Efra as an enemy.

Luckily, the girl showed no understanding of what it was to be a Heart. She seemed utterly disinterested when Kofi mentioned it. She gave no sign she'd ever heard the term.

How do I ask?

She couldn't. As long as Efra didn't know, Nuru could trust her. Well, trust her as much as anyone trusted a vicious viper. Which seemed unfair to Isabis.

"Are you all right?" asked Kofi, leaning forward.

"Sorry," said Nuru. "It's a lot to take in."

"Yeah. But don't worry. I'm here to—" He cut himself off, grimacing in embarrassment and looking everywhere but at her. "I'll help." He finally made eye-contact. "Whatever you need. My life is yours."

So easy.

Nuru crushed the pang of guilt. *Be like Efra. Use this young man.*

Would Chisulo do that?

No. Never.

The answer fed Nuru's doubts.

Did Efra ever doubt?

Not a chance.

Don't let doubt make you weak. She could easily imagine Efra saying something like that.

"The previous Heart's Mirror," said Nuru. "The nahual preached that she was ancient, thousands of years old."

"The Heart's Mirror is immortal. They're incredibly difficult to kill."

And yet the Loa managed to do just that.

Nuru struggled to understand, to piece together sermons heard over the years. "The nahual say Mother Death was banished. They say she lived in the Bloody Desert, fed off the souls of those cast from the Sand Wall."

Kofi stared at her, eyes wide in awe.

"What?"

"*Was* banished. *Lived* in the desert."

Nuru saw her mistake. The Loa, for all their confidence and pride, had no idea where their god was. They thought her still trapped beyond the Sand Wall.

"The carving," whispered Kofi. "You… You're a nagual. Somehow, you *used* it." He stared at Nuru, waiting, desperate hope painting his features. "You *are* her Heart."

She saw love and worship there too.

She nodded once. "Can a god possess their Heart, completely take over?"

Kofi blinked. "No. A god can speak through their Heart. But if Mother Death truly possessed a mortal, moved the fullness of herself into the meat of their body, it would kill them."

He kept talking, droning on about the *Book of the Invisibles* and reciting sermons no doubt learned as a child. Nuru wasn't listening.

It gave her hope. The god needed her. She might get what she wanted, and yet not have to wage war against everything she'd ever learned.

But then maybe that war was exactly what Bastion needed, exactly what the Growers needed.

What do I *want?*

A world where the people who grew the food for the entire city were worth something.

A world without public whippings, where no one was bled on the altar.

A world where Grower women raised their own children.

A world without gods.

AKACHI - THE CRACKS IN HER SOUL

Faith alone separates us from the animals. Faith is the mechanism driving birth and rebirth. Through faith mortals gain some small taste of divinity.

Faith is the gateway to immortality.

—The Book of Bastion

Akachi followed the Turquoise Serpents through winding and garbage-strewn streets. Not yet cresting the Sand Wall, the rising sun lit the eastern horizon a deep crimson. The thick clouds of smoke had scattered in the night, leaving only a bloody haze to taint the sky.

Another day, thought Akachi, *and it will be the same blue it has always been.*

As if the world wiped clean all the sins of mankind. Like nothing had happened.

Except it had. The fields were ash, fires lit by heretics bent on destroying Bastion.

Turning into a courtyard, Firash, who had taken the lead, held up a hand and crouched low. Captain Melokuhle crept forward to look. Akachi, curious, followed.

A huge smoking mound, four times the height of a man and fifty strides across, filled much of the public square.

Akachi asked, "What's that?" He smelled roast pork.

"People," said Firash. "Nahual, mostly. A lot of Hummingbirds. Some Dirts."

Akachi stared in horror. How many bodies did it take to make a pile that large?

There some drivel in the *Book of the Invisibles* about fire purifying souls for rebirth. They claimed that humanity used to do it that way before the gods inserted themselves in the natural order. Purest insane blasphemy!

Beyond the square lay the gate to the Crafters' Ring. Both entrances, the massive gates for the wagons, and the smaller pedestrian doors, were closed.

Nothing moved.

"It looks unguarded," said Akachi.

"It's a trap," said Omphile. He hadn't heard her approach. "Step foot in that tunnel, and you're dead. They're watching both sides."

"Are you sure?" Akachi asked. The next gate was hours away.

No one bothered to answer.

"We go around," said Melokuhle.

Firash nodded and led the squad away.

With a weary sigh of acceptance, Akachi followed. He picked up his pace to walk alongside the Captain.

For hours they travelled empty streets. Were the locals dead, fled, or merely hiding from the Turquoise Serpents?

"I've read about the Turquoise Serpents," Akachi blurted, breaking the long silence. "I saw a few when I was a child, in the Priests' Ring, but never met one."

"We train in the Jade Temple," said Melokuhle.

He'd seen it as a child, a cathedral constructed entirely of jade and yet still somehow a seamless part of the single rock that was Bastion.

"We spend our lives there," she continued. "From our first steps, we train for war. We are separate, as we must be. We only leave when called, when troubles grow beyond what the Hummingbird Guard can handle."

"Not entirely true," said Omphile. "Sometimes we sneak out to fuck." Once again, she'd appeared at Akachi's side without him noticing.

Having spent five years among acolytes in the Northern Cathedral, he couldn't imagine an entire life spent in one temple, leaving only to fight, or dispense punishment and justice.

Where the others seemed, if not broken, at least cracked by whatever they'd seen and done on their way to the outer ring, Omphile glowed with contented happiness.

Akachi thought he understood: This was purpose. They might not like their holy task, but at least, unlike a great many, their lives had meaning. He couldn't think of a way of expressing this without sounding naive.

"Our gods tell us what we must do," he said. "We are nahual, the protectors of Bastion. We do not question. We obey."

Omphile grunted a laugh. "Which would be true if the gods actually talked to us. They don't. Some filthy old man who stank like piss sent us out here."

"Nahualli Jaafan is our High Priest," warned Melokuhle.

Omphile ignored her Captain. "He ranted about the end of the last world, threw open the gates of the Jade Temple, and ordered every Serpent old enough to lift a sword to march on the Life Ring. He scattered us in every direction, divided our strength. He's an idiot."

"That's not quite true," said Firash, from in front.

"Pretty fucking accurate," said Omphile.

Lubanzi grunted agreement, and Melokuhle said nothing, looking away. How unlike Captain Yejide she was. She had none of Yejide's confidence, none of her stone strength. Akachi expected more from the Turquoise Serpents.

Grey-eyed, Omphile was god-touched. Did her god not speak to her?

The Book of Bastion said the god-touched were rarely sane, having been damaged by contact with the divine. In the stories, the Touched always died terrible deaths serving their god's purpose.

Melokuhle introduced her as the squad's assassin.

"Firash," said Omphile. "You said we had to find this skinny Cloud Serpent nahualli to save Bastion. Well, we found him, cute ass and all. Now what? What else have you seen?"

"Too much," said Firash, fingering the pommel of his stone sword.

"Not enough. Sometimes he turns on us, betrays us to our death." The tezcat's tattooed eyes opened and focussed on Akachi.

"I would never—"

"But mostly I see him dying terribly." Firash glanced at the assassin. "Sometimes Omphile kills him." He coughed a rueful chuckle. "Pretty often, actually."

"Hey!" barked Omphile, sounding hurt, like she'd been accused of something socially egregious. She looked, however, more excited than wounded. Amused, even. "If it turns out I need to kill him" she said, shooting the tezat an annoyed look, "you've likely just made the job more difficult."

"When have you ever found killing difficult?" asked Melokuhle.

There was a dark undertone there, some tension between the captain and her assassin.

Omphile ignored it.

"Sometimes," Firash added, approaching Akachi so he stood uncomfortably close, "the Loa split your ribs and cut your heart out. Sometimes you're thrown from the Sand Wall. For blasphemy. Mostly, though, you bleed out in an alley, alone and broken."

"Great," said Akachi. "Good to hear."

"The gate is just around the corner," said Firash, turning back to the others.

Tension between the squad members strung every breath tight.

They'd followed their tezcat to the outer ring not knowing why. Now that they knew their purpose, they seemed no happier.

Akachi wanted to grab the sullen Captain and shake her, while screaming, 'This is all there is! Obey the gods! Do your duty!'

She'd probably kill him.

The rising sun crested the Sand Wall. In a score of heartbeats Akachi dripped with gritty sweat.

There was a sun god.

The Fifth Sun, brother to The Lord. The knowledge felt strange, like the memory of a fading dream growing blurrier the longer he was awake.

The day's light showed the true horrors of the night. So many dead. It was hard to believe there were this many Dirts in all the ring. Were any left to work the fields? Was there anything out there for them to work? The frustration of not knowing how bad the damage was gnawed at him.

"Dead," said Omphile, peering around the corner to study the gate. "Lots of dead. Not a trap though."

Accepting Omphile's pronouncement without question, Firash led them to the Grey Wall. A colossus of stone, it towered over them.

A dozen Hummingbird Guard lay dead before the pedestrian door, stripped of armour and weapons, only their sandals remaining. The massive gate for the wagons remained closed.

"Omphile," ordered Captain Melokuhle, "read it."

Dipping a quick nod Akachi suspected contained more than a little insubordination, the beautiful god-touched approached the gates. Examining the scene, she leaned low to sniff at bodies, studying things from different angles.

Akachi watched, mesmerized. The assassin didn't simply *walk*. She strutted, each step a sensual act, somehow seductive despite the armoured leather skirt. Even the bobbing swing of her braid was teasing.

Bending to examine another corpse, she pulled the braid forward. Straightening, she turned back to the group, eyes lingering on Akachi, braid hanging between the curve of armour-hidden breasts.

"They were attacked by Growers first," Omphile reported, "a great mob of Dirts. They would have chased them off but were surprised from behind. Someone came through the gate from the Crafters' Ring. The timing was perfect. Some of the dead bear strange wounds. Melted eyes. Shattered teeth. Loa stone sorcery."

"Where did their attackers go?" asked Melokuhle.

Omphile sauntered back to stand near Akachi. "Some went back through the gate. Some headed into the Life Ring. There isn't much ash on the bodies, so this happened late at night. Not more than a few hours ago."

Leaning close, the assassin whispered to Akachi, "Did you enjoy the show? I saw you watching."

Flustered, he didn't respond.

"We're going through the gate," said Melokuhle. "Firash, you're in front." She winced at the decision, like she wanted to change her mind or regretted having to make decisions at all. "Omphile, stop tongue-fucking the Cloud Serpent nahualli's ear. You're at the back. Eyes open, everyone." She looked away, gazing toward the morning sun. "No one else dies."

When she turned back to the squad, her pain was gone, locked away, showing only through the cracks in her soul.

Her decisions got people killed. Akachi saw it in the way she hesitated before barking orders, in the doubt she tried to hide.

Torches and candles stolen, the tunnel through the wall showed no hint of light.

"The far gate is closed," said Lubanzi. "I was really hoping it would be open so we could see a little."

Firash in the lead, they entered.

"Smells like a fucking grave," said the otochin.

The last time Akachi came through a gate he'd just turned twelve and was riding a wagon on his way to the Northern Cathedral. There'd been torches lining the tunnel and a squad of Hummingbirds at each entrance.

The light at their end didn't reach more than a few strides.

Shuffling forward, Akachi imagined a tunnel filled with waiting Loa sorcerers, monsters from a forgotten age. Snakes. Spiders. Death at every step.

"Lubanzi," said Melokuhle, drawing to a halt, "you got anything that will help us see?"

"No need," said Omphile. "There's nothing more dangerous in here than me."

"In that case," said the otochin. "I have something."

"Save it," said the Captain.

The squad continued, picking their way over corpses and scattered detritus, cursing when they stumbled.

Starting low, barely a whisper, and growing in volume, Omphile sung a droning dirge, voice echoing and haunting in the long tunnel.

No one spoke. The Captain did nothing to silence the assassin.

A mound of piled corpses, stinking and slick, blocked the far gate. Melokuhle ordered Firash to move them, and the squad stood ready as the muscled tezcat worked.

Heaving aside the last body, Firash cracked the door open enough to peer through.

"Looks clear," he said over his shoulder.

Stepping into the sunlight on the far side, Akachi was astounded to see less ash then in the Growers' Ring. No bodies littered the streets. A few Crafters hurried about on early morning business, but most of the tenement doors remained closed.

It seemed a perfectly normal early morning.

"Was there no fighting in this ring?" Akachi asked, surprised. Somehow, he'd assumed the rioting had engulfed all Bastion.

"There was," said Melokuhle, "but confined to a few districts. The Loa concentrated their efforts on the Dirts."

"They hit the weapons manufacturing districts," added Firash. "Cleaned out the warehouses, stole weapons destined for the Humming-birds. They're arming the Growers."

"We came through one of those districts," said Melokuhle, eyes hooded. "They were waiting for us."

Omphile flashed a grin. "It was fun."

Firash closed his eyes, though many of the tattoos snapped open, blinking and looking everywhere. Some watched Akachi, following his every move. "All around the ring," said the tezcat, voice far away, "there are unwatched gates, the guards, dead or fled. Supply wagons are stopped and looted. From this point until the end, little food will make it to the inner rings. Less every day." He sighed, opening his eyes. "I've seen this a thousand times. War. When the true strength of the Turquoise Serpents arrives, it will be a slaughter. Tens of thousands of dead, rotting in the sun. Cannibalism. Desperation. Starvation."

"Sounds exciting," said Omphile with a glint in her eye and no trace of humour.

Again, the Captain ignored her.

Yejide never would have tolerated that attitude.

Akachi swallowed a knot of pain.

"We've been on our feet for three days," said Melokuhle. "We have to get off the street, find somewhere to sleep." She pointed out a dark Crafter home, rounded and fluid-looking after the blunt simplicity of the Grower tenements. "Omphile, make sure it's empty."

The assassin wandered off, hips swinging and seductive.

"She's killing me," muttered Lubanzi.

Melokuhle shot him an annoyed look, and he shrugged. "Like you don't want that."

How could these legendary Turquoise Serpents be so disappointing after Yejide's squad? Was it the Captain that made the difference? Did Yejide define her people? Was Melokuhle to blame for their shoddy attitude?

Omphile disappeared into the tenement only to return a few score heartbeats later. "It's safe!" she called.

"Omphile," said the Captain. "First watch."

The rest of the squad entered the home, Melokuhle heading straight to a back room.

Exhausted as he was, Akachi realized he couldn't sleep. He needed to prepare his narcotics. Finding a corner, he sank to the floor, back against the wall, and laid out the tools he'd need. Attention on the task at hand, he was only nominally aware of the others. They chatted briefly, a background murmur, and were asleep in moments.

Omphile wandered the tenement, checking windows, and then sauntered over to sit beside Akachi, their shoulders touching. With the sun risen, everyone stank of sweat. The Serpents, in their leather and stone armour, smelled worse than most.

In Omphile, that scent was somehow enticing. Like she exuded desire.

Glancing up from his work, Akachi saw a glistening bead of sweat trickle down her neck and into her armour. He wanted to lick it. To kiss the hollow of her throat. To peel away the layers of boiled stone-scaled leather and strip off whatever lay hidden beneath. He wanted to—

Yejïde! I love Yejïde!

Love battled the lust of youth. He had a lot of experience with one, and little with the other.

She's dead.

He was going to bring her back. Once in the Priests' Ring, he would deliver the dagger to be emptied of souls.

When Yejïde's soul was purified, she'd forget all about him. She'd be reborn a different person.

If I can never see her again, can never have her, what am I saving myself for?

"That song you sang in the tunnel," said Akachi, to break the uncomfortable silence, "it was beautiful."

Omphile shuffled closer, leaned her weight against him. "It was for Captain Melokuhle. She needed it. She needs to grieve."

Did she? The Captain seemed no happier for it.

Omphile lay her head on Akachi's shoulder. "She tries to be like me but fails. You have to know who you are, *what* you are. Otherwise, you're lying to yourself."

"That was real," Akachi said. "You feel the loss too."

"No."

"Maybe you're lying to yourself."

She snorted in amusement. "I can list off the names of the dead and how they died. But it doesn't touch me. I don't care. They aren't why I'm here. They were never my purpose."

Turning her head so she could look up at him, a smile played about her lips. Grey eyes. Slate cold. God-touched. So close. So alive and warm.

"To sing with such emotion," he said, "you must feel it."

"I mimic. It's nothing. These are the skills of an assassin. I can be whatever I need to be to get close to my target." She squirmed against him. "Though you are pleasantly easy to be close to."

"I... uh..."

"You said we're going to save Bastion. You said we'd save the world."

Akachi nodded.

"How do you know?"

He looked into grey shards of smoky diamond. "Cloud Serpent told me."

Her eyes widened with awe. "What's it like to have purpose?"

"You're god-touched. Surely you have purpose."

She laughed through her nose with soft breaths. Her warmth felt good, so real. "Everyone says grey eyes means god-touched. They assume it was Southern Hummingbird."

"It wasn't?" Akachi asked, startled.

Omphile shrugged, snuggling against him as if they were long-time lovers. "How would I know? It's frustrating. But you...you know exactly what your god wants from you."

He considered the dream, Zalika and the staff. "Things are a little less clear than that."

"Really? Hunt your enemies. Kill them."

"I could fail. According to your tezcat, I probably will."

Grey eyes studied him. "Maybe. Maybe not. What if Cloud Serpent touched me and not Southern Hummingbird? With me at your side, nothing could stop you." She placed a warm hand on his thigh. "Even among the Serpents I am special. Do you think I'm something special? Yes," she said, not waiting for an answer. "Of course you do. Touched. Special. Beautiful. You want me."

Not a hint of humility or self-mockery. She wielded confidence like a weapon, wore it like her impenetrable jade armour. He wanted to lift her hand from his leg, be true to Yejide. But this woman was gorgeous and alive, vibrant in a way so utterly different from Yejide.

"Nothing and no one kills like me," said Omphile. "The nahual who taught me said I was the perfect murderer."

He'd read something about perfect murderers recently but was too distracted to chase the memory.

Calling herself a murderer doesn't affect her.

Most people cloaked such things in excuses and justifications.

"I am supposed to be with you," she said. "Tell me this doesn't feel destined."

Hooking a hand behind his head, the assassin pulled him into a hot kiss, all warm and questing tongue. Slippery like silk. She was deceptively strong for her size.

Finally pulling away, Omphile gazed into his eyes with a look of devotion, heart-breaking worship, and need. "I've fucked Cloud Serpent priests before, but never a nahualli. At least not that I know of. I am going to fuck you." She winked. "Someday."

In a blink of an eye the love and devotion disappeared, replaced with mocking humour.

"Wouldn't that make killing me harder?" Akachi asked.

"It would make some of you harder."

He ignored the joke. "Wouldn't it make it more difficult?"

"Why?" she asked with genuine curiosity. "If anything, it would be easier."

Rising smoothly to her feet, she sauntered away.

Was this all a game, a joke? Did she believe any of what she said?

She's toying with you.

Omphile and Yejide shared a strength and confidence he appreciated, and a dangerous edge he found deeply appealing. Yet they could not be more different. If anything, this deadly woman reminded him more of the Loa assassin with the bright eyes, the one who killed Father Death and ascended to become Face Painted with Bells.

He watched her ignore him. Sighing, he returned to his work grinding and blending narcotics. Not once did she sneak a glance to see if he watched her. He knew this because he had so much trouble taking his eyes off her.

NURU - AN ANCIENT HUNGER

The end of the fifth sun was a cataclysm beyond mortal understanding. The blood of billions, baked dry by the sun's anger, became the endless red desert surrounding the Last City.

As every tecuhtli knows, there is great power in death. Many forms of energy are released when the meat surrenders the soul. The bones of the earth became receptacles for the dreams, emotions, nightmares, and mental states torn from the dying.

Different kinds of rock are more susceptible to different emotions. Some store rage or despair. Others store love or the hunger to belong. This, at root, is the strength of the tecolotl.

—The Loa Book of the Invisibles

Nuru woke to find herself back in her room in the gang's tenement. Pushing aside the single grey sheet, she sat up, naked. Swinging her legs over the edge of the stone platform, she stood. Already warm, the air stank of wheat dust.

Wrong. Wrong.

"Hello?" she called.

No answer. The boys were gone, probably off to meet Omari's contact. The gang's Finger knew a Grower who had an erlaxatu plot hidden in a corn field.

Home, alone.

She luxuriated in the rare moment of privacy.

Breathing.

The sharp grit-feel of stone beneath bare feet.

Naked.

A spider.

Long flanks of flawless black skin. Inhuman beauty. Red eyes like blood, holes torn in night, embers of madness. Curves and hunger. Perfect like only a god can be.

It's you, said Efra.

Nuru blinked, lost the thought.

Alone.

Spotting Isabis coiled in a corner, Nuru collected the snake and draped it about her neck, enjoying the feel of scales on skin.

If the boys were out in the fields, collecting the week's supply of erlaxatu, they wouldn't be back for ages. Bomani would bully them into stopping for a drink on the way home. They'd come back stumbling and slurring and Chisulo would look at her in that way he only did when drunk. He'd keep almost saying something, and then he'd go to bed.

It was a nice look. Maybe her favourite, if she was honest.

Smashed chest crushed ribs and blood leaking from his nose. Shattered.

Descending into the basement, she found everything as she left it. Her precious glass jars. Her few pages of paper. Three half-finished wood carvings.

Spiders.

Savage glee.

Blood and souls.

Down here the stone was cool, felt nice on her feet. Isabis hung heavy, a comforting weight.

There, in the centre of the floor, sat a woman's severed head. Blood leaked from the tattered flesh around the neck. She was beautiful, skin smooth like a polished stone. Too bright to be tattoos, she wore a glowing yellow disk painted on each cheek.

The eyes opened. They shone bright as the purest candle, lighting the basement. For the first time, Nuru realized how filthy it was down here. Dust and cobwebs and red sand. The hollowed husks of countless scorpions and beetles.

Eyes glowing as if lit from within, the dead woman studied Nuru, looking her up and down, eyes lingering, making no attempt to conceal her appreciation.

Covering herself with her hands, Nuru waited, suddenly self-conscious.

"I understand now," said the woman, "why she chose you."

Spiders and death. Rage and destruction. Betrayal.

"Who?" asked Nuru, dreading the answer.

"The Lady of the Dead. The Queen of Bastion. The Falcon. The Great Mother. Nephthys. Nebthet. Mother of the Universe. Kālarātri. The Black One. The Destroyer of Worlds. The Lady of the House." She smiled the most beautiful smile Nuru ever saw. "Mother Death."

"Did she choose me," said Nuru, "or was I the only sorcerer dumb enough to listen to the dreams?"

"She chose."

I don't believe you. "I'm nothing."

"Aren't we all?"

Dreaming. I'm dreaming.

Was this woman a pactonal, a nahualli skilled in dream-walking?

Like that Cloud Serpent nahualli, this woman's skill dwarfed Nuru's.

"Who are you?"

"I hold the underworld until Mother Death returns."

Did Mother Death send this creature?

Nuru's heart slammed in her chest. Her boys. They weren't here because they were dead. "My friends—"

"This is not then," said the woman, bright eyes staring up at Nuru, blood drooling from the tattered wound of her neck. "What you desire is beyond me."

Nuru's heart cracked open, bled despair.

"There is something you and I must do," said the severed head.

Was this a godling visiting her in her dreams?

The nahual preached of the terrors a skilled pactonal was capable of, shattering minds, even killing someone in their dreams. What could a god do?

"I am Face Painted with Bells."

Nuru studied the bright disks painted on the face. "What's a bell?"

The godling laughed, a sweet ringing shimmer of sound. "I have no idea. The Queen of Bastion named me. Come now, you must kill a god."

Nuru stood in a field of flowers more beautiful than anything she'd ever seen. So many colours. Green so deep she felt it in her soul. The sun shone overhead, but it wasn't the sun she knew. More yellow, less red rage. She felt none of its anger, none of its hateful desire to burn everything to ash. This sun was warm. It was life.

Bees, fat and wobbling, flitted from flower to flower. Clover. Endless fields of soft lavender.

Face Painted with Bells stood at her side, whole now, body decorated like her face, so beautiful she hurt to look at. Still naked, Nuru was reminded of her own flaws, the awkward angles of her, the countless imperfections.

The godling caught Nuru's hands as she tried to once again hide herself away. "Be stronger."

"I..." Nuru took a breath. "Standing beside you, it's difficult not to hide. I'm all flaws."

How many times had she said that? All her life. All flaws.

"We're *all* flaws," said Face Painted with Bells. "So be your flaws."

Easy for her to say, she has none.

The godling glowed with a confidence Nuru admired and hated. She wore her nakedness like it made her strong rather than vulnerable.

What Nuru first took to be painted decorations were stones sunk into the woman's smooth flesh. They were beautiful. Not wounds, each stone and pebble seemed a natural part of her. Catching the sun, they lit the woman in a rainbow of refracted light. A garnet glowed between her full breasts. She was, Nuru realized, missing one hand, the wrist a raw wound dripping blood. White bone, splintered and jagged, jutted from the stump. It looked like an animal had gnawed the hand off.

How did I miss that?

The godling grew in detail, becoming more real with each breath.

Face Painted with Bells noticed her attention. Holding up the bloody stump she said, "Sometimes we make sacrifices to get what we want."

Strange yet achingly familiar sounds grew in volume.

The din of youngsters, running and playing in the fields.

Children dashed everywhere, chasing each other, singing and dancing in clover. Clothed in flowing robes of a thousand colours, they looked like tiny nahual of some unknown god.

Hundreds of them.

Thousands.

Even back in the crèche where she grew up there'd never been this many.

"Not real," whispered Nuru, reminding herself. "Not real."

But she wanted it to be. More than anything she wanted there to be a place like this, filled with children.

"Just wait," said the godling.

Seeing the two naked women, the youngsters came to investigate. Curious and innocent, they surrounded Nuru, touching and sniffing at her with an utter lack of fear, babbling incomprehensible gibberish.

A girl of seven stood before Nuru, staring up like she'd never seen anyone so freakishly tall. She said something, a rolling stumble of syllables ending in an interrogative.

Reaching out, Nuru touched her head, felt the softness of her hair.

The girl allowed the contact as if it were expected.

Too much.

Too much innocence.

None of the children were scarred or wounded. Fresh-faced, they were without blemish.

No bruises or cuts.

No one had ever whipped them for playing in the mud.

How many times had Bomani suffered the lash as a boy? He was constantly healing, constantly bearing fresh 'lessons' on his back and arms.

Nuru broke, her soul cracking like shale.

Her knees folding, she found herself among the flowers, crying great racking sobs. Her body shook, convulsions of heartbreak and loss for a sight no adult Grower had ever seen

Children.

Gathered around her, they cooed comfort, stroked her hair, sang gentle songs.

Innocent concern. They wore her hurt as if they were trying to draw it from her, help her carry her burden.

She cried harder.

Face Painted with Bells put a hand on Nuru's shoulder. "Each of the gods rules their own domain. Father Death ruled the underworld. This one belongs to Her Skirt is Stars."

Nuru wanted to laugh, to scream, to tear her hair out and claw great wounds in her flesh. Anything to ease the pain in her heart. The god whose nahual ran the crèches where Grower children were raised also kept this... whatever it was.

Why were we treated so differently?

"It's a menagerie of souls," said the godling, squeezing Nuru's shoulder to comfort her. "Each of the gods has one. By the oldest rules, those set down by the Queen, such hoarding is forbidden. But unlike his wife, Father Death turns a blind eye."

Fighting tears, fists clenched so tight her nails dug grooves in her palms, Nuru said, "They're beautiful."

"They're doomed. Her Skirt is Stars has trapped them here forever. They will never be reborn. They will never live full lives. They will never grow up. They will never get to test their abilities or reach their potential. They will never have their own children or learn what it is to love someone more than you love yourself."

Cold rage replaced Nuru's hurt. "Growers don't get to raise their children."

"That's why we're here. Mother Death will change that. Forever."

"Everyone makes promises," snapped Nuru. "I promise to protect you. I promise I will never leave you. Trust me," she added, mocking.

"The nahual of Her Skirt is Stars run the crèches" said the godling. "They raise the children. They indoctrinate them with the *Book of Bastion* before they can even speak. From your earliest memory you've been infected with the way things are *supposed* to be. Growers obey. Growers are meek. Work hard and be reborn closer to the gods. They write it in your blood, pound it into your soul like a Grower shoving seeds into damp earth. Those who transgress are whipped and beaten, starved and punished in cruel and subtle ways."

Even now, listening to this blasphemy, Nuru felt like a sinner. "I remember."

Face Painted with Bells released Nuru's shoulder. "These souls must be freed." Her voice shook. "It's the only way they can be reborn. I'm... I'm sorry."

Sorry?

"Bastion needs more souls," said the godling, "or she'll die."

All those empty tenements.

Far out near the Sand Wall where no one went, forests and fields ran wild. There were abandoned menageries, the animals long fled. She'd heard stories of haunted districts, overgrown by jungle or half buried in sand, that hadn't been used in thousands of years. Could there ever have been so many people in Bastion that all those empty tenements were filled?

"The gods hoard souls and Bastion dies a slow, choking death," said the godling. "We must free them."

"We must free them," Nuru agreed.

"We must free them all."

"Yes!"

"We will return Bastion to its former glory! It will once again be a city of life!"

Nuru rose to her feet, turned to the godling. "How?"

Lifting the stump of her wrist, Face Painted with Bells asked, "What will you sacrifice to save humanity?"

She wants my hand?

Nuru retreated.

The godling, head cocked to one side, eyes glowing impossibly bright, waited.

"You're not telling me everything," accused Nuru.

"Freeing these souls will bring Her Skirt is Stars."

"And then?"

"You will kill her. Her priests will be robbed of their god. The crèches will fall. Growers will once again raise their own children."

Was any of this true? Was this even real?

"Mother Death makes you this promise in blood and souls," swore the godling.

Grower women free to raise their children. Mother. Daughter. Son. Words she knew but had never used. "I want that."

"There is only one way to free these souls," said Face Painted with Bells, "and it is terrible."

Sinking horror as comprehension dawned.

Children gathered around, touching her as if to confirm her reality, cooing in that soft babble.

Nuru shook her head. "No."

"If we don't, they remain here forever, playthings of Her Skirt is Stars. The Grandmother guards them jealously."

Like all the gods, Her Skirt is Stars had many names. Mother Life. Skirt of Snakes. Goddess of the Stars. Grandmother. Nuru hadn't heard that last one since she was small. Like so many words the nahual used, she had only the barest understanding of what it meant.

"These children are a source of pure faith, unstained by even the chance of doubt," continued the godling. "The gods are ravenous, never satisfied. They hoard more and more, and every year there are fewer souls in Bastion. The city is dying."

"No!"

The children flinched at her outburst but didn't flee.

This was too much, too terrible a price.

"They will be reborn," argued Face Painted with Bells. "Killing them weakens Grandmother. It's the only way we can kill her. Once she's dead, the evil of the crèches will die. Mother Death forbid it, that's why Her Skirt is Stars turned on her with the other gods. Kill Grandmother, and free the Grower children for all time."

"No!" screamed Nuru, again startling the children.

Face Painted with Bells crossed her arms, tucking the ragged stump into an armpit. "Make a sacrifice or do nothing. Your choice." She cocked her head to one side, studying Nuru. "We can leave now if you want. The nahual win. Things go on as they are until Bastion dies."

Nuru shook her head, unable to speak for the horror.

"You have a mother," said the godling. "You've never known her, and she's never known you. Wouldn't you like to know your daughter?"

Nuru shook her head in mute horror. Children. Innocent souls.

"You don't understand," said the godling. "The gods don't just feed on blood and worship; they feed on souls." Words poured out of her. Words and pain. "Her Skirt is Stars will grow bored of this batch. She'll harvest a few. She'll *devour* them. Then she'll claim more. She is an ancient hunger, endlessly ravenous. She'll hoard and feed and hoard and feed until this last world is dead. Like all the others."

Last world.

Like all the others.

"Kill them to save them," said the godling.

Sobbing, Nuru nodded.

AKACHI - LIKE A SNAKE THROUGH WATER

Faced with extinction, difficult choices had to be made. The old world died, its few survivors forced to learn from the ashes of its mistakes. The survival of humanity depended on the understanding of two truths, the second born of the first.

The few cannot dependably control the many for any length of time. Thus, the many must be convinced to control themselves. From this axiom comes the second truth. There are two means of convincing a population to police itself: Religion, and Economy.

Faith and greed.

With the failures of the age of progress, it was time to return religion to its proper place, at the top of the power pyramid.

As greed has always been humanity's second religion, economy must come second to the church.

While civilization begins with a system of laws, those laws must be shaped and directed by the cornerstones of control and thus come third.

Priests.

Bankers.

Senators.

—The Book of Bastion

Two hours later, the Turquoise Serpents were up and bustling about as if they'd enjoyed a full night's sleep. The sun, balanced precariously at the pinnacle of the sky, screamed at the world, desperate to burn away this last stubborn crust of life.

The Fifth Sun.

The last sun.

Shading his eyes, Akachi searched the skies. Gone were the flocks of warring raptors. He saw no sign of the skyvyrm. The morning haze cleared, columns of roiling smoke climbed the distant horizon, the last smouldering remnants of the fires that burned the fields.

Unlike the Growers' Ring, only a thin blanket of ash besmirched Bastion's perfect stone.

Crafters hustled about their tasks, brown and orange clothes stained and filthy, smeared in grey. It looked like the ring he remembered, but a current of tension lurked beneath everything. Suspicious glances and nervous eyes, people crossing the street to avoid squads of Hummingbird Guards. There were fewer Crafters than Akachi remembered, but then he had passed quickly through this ring on his way to the cathedral.

It was one thing to know that the population of the outer ring was greater than all the others combined, but the Crafters' was the second most populated, and it seemed empty. Were they hiding, fearing the spread of riots? Or were there more Dirts than anyone realized? The last census he'd seen was thousands of years old. No one bothered anymore.

Time to renew the hunt.

Where were the two Dirt girls now? Were they still in the outer ring, or had they got here first?

They'd hide. They'd flee like filthy rats. Tracking them in their dreams would likely be impossible. They could be anywhere, and proximity mattered. There was no way to know which gate they used to access this ring. If they passed through the gate in the Wheat District, that was a full day's travel around the ring from here.

He might not be able to track them, but he wasn't without options.

"Firash," said Akachi, catching the tezcat's attention. "How is your supply of etorkizun?"

"I was wondering when you were going to ask."

"Ignore him," said Lubanzi. "He's faking, always pretending he's seen every last detail of everything."

"Are you sure you want to see the future?" asked the tezcat.

Something in his voice caught Akachi's attention. *He's seen this.*

"I need to know which gate the Growers I'm chasing will use to flee into the Senator's Ring," said Akachi. "I want to be waiting for them."

Firash studied him, eyes narrowed. Finally, nodding, he said, "I make no promises. You know how twisted the future is. It's a lot like the past. We want it to be set in stone, but our emotions colour everything. We see what we want to see."

"How often have you looked into the future just to see me naked?" asked Omphile, appearing at Akachi's side.

"Every night, I bet," said Lubanzi, looking wistful.

"Never, girl," said Firash. "I'm old enough to know that beautiful as you are on the outside, you're diseased within."

Smacking Firash on the shoulder, she laughed. "You say the nicest things!"

Firash turned to Akachi. "I take it you have no talent as a tezcat?"

"Minimal. My teacher said I was too caught up in the now." He left out the rest. Akachi's teacher said he was too desperate to please his father, too worried what other priests thought.

"The future *is* emotion," said Firash. "It's all desires and plans, goals and doubts and fears. It's what we hope to achieve. It's the consequences that terrify us. It's the things we dare not reach for."

"So," said Omphile, "it's like my ass."

Though Firash ignored her, several of the tattooed eyes opened to watch the assassin. "The future is the things we know we shouldn't do, but will anyway."

"Still talking about my ass."

The slightest frown of annoyance wrinkled the bald priest's forehead. "The gods might shape it—"

Omphile wiggled her shapely butt. "Definitely my ass."

"—but even they can't control it."

"My ass *is* out of control."

"We'll try—"

"My ass?"

"—but I make no promises."

"That's where my ass differs" admitted the assassin. "It makes a lot of promises and keeps them all."

"I think I need to be alone for a moment," mumbled Lubanzi.

Studying Akachi, Firash ignored them both. "You have some talent as a pactonal."

"I do."

"I bet I walk in your dreams," said Omphile, reaching out the touch Akachi's chest with a fingertip.

"Omphile!" barked Melokuhle, touching the butterfly tattoo on her forehead like it might give her strength. "Be silent."

With a sultry smirk, the assassin wandered away, hips swinging.

Lubanzi watched with undisguised hunger. "She's killing me," he whispered to himself.

"Come," said Firash. "Sit with me while I prepare the blend. I will attempt to see the future but will do so in a deep trance. You must dream-walk alongside me. You need to see what I see."

The two men sat facing each other. Akachi lay the Staff of the Fifth Sun, a comforting weight, across his lap.

Firash bent to preparing his mixture. Removing a wood bowl so shallow it was almost flat from within his armour, the tezcat set it on the floor. Digging out a leather skin, he let a dozen drops of etorkizun fall into the bowl. After adding a healthy dose of ameslari, he cleared a hand-length of his sword from its scabbard and nicked his arm. Adding two droplets of blood to the etorkizun and ameslari, he stirred the ingredients.

Glancing up, Firash nodded at Akachi.

Retrieving his own narcotics from behind his belt, Akachi set about grinding pure ameslari. The etorkizun was tempting, but his teacher made it clear he lacked the needed mental-state to be a tezcat. Still, just a little, blended with the ameslari, might have interesting results.

And then you'll want to stir in some foku, gorgoratzen, and jainkoei.

He couldn't do it. They were all watching. They'd think he'd lost control, fallen prey to the lure of the allies in the smoke.

"Once we enter the dream-world," Firash said, when Akachi was ready, "you must stay with me. Do not allow yourself to be distracted. Your mind will try and take you elsewhere."

Confident in his skill as a pactonal, Akachi said, "I shall remain with you."

"We are like shards of stone," continued the tezcat, "fragments. But we are not *one* stone. Each of us is made of many parts. Love and healing. Destruction. Self-destruction." He glanced at Akachi. "Emptiness that can never be filled. Hate and murder." He looked to Omphile. "Some of us have more of one shard than the others."

Firash finished preparing his etorkizun. One at a time, he rubbed the milky smear on his eyelids. When he nodded at Akachi, it ran from the corners like bloody tears.

Akachi chewed his ground fungus. Dry and gritty, it tasted like clay.

Closing his eyes, Firash dropped into a deep trance.

I could never manage it that fast.

Every time Akachi tried to enter a tezcat trance, it took an hour or more. Sometimes his teacher gave up, angry at him for fidgeting.

He eyed Firash's bowl. Etorkizun, ameslari, and blood puddled at the bottom.

Wipe it on your eyes. Do it.

No. He knew better. Nahualli only used their own blood, though he didn't know why. It was one of those many lessons the teachers hammered into him without ever explaining the reasons.

Understanding is a distraction, his teachers said. *Obedience is critical.*

Ameslari slid through Akachi's thoughts like a snake through water. The world changed, became brighter, crisper. Colours deepened until they were archetypes of themselves, pure beyond the comprehension of mere mortals. A swirl of Firash's blood, so perfectly red as to be blinding, coiled through the milky sap of the etorkizun. It still moved, spiralling, from the motion of the tezcat's final stir.

The future is shot with blood.

The Heart of Cloud Serpent, Lord of the Hunt.

Future Heart's Mirror.

What were the rules of stodgy old nahual to Akachi now?

Dipping his finger into the bowl, Akachi changed the direction of the rotation.

I am in control.

He stared at his damp finger.

Closing his eyes, Akachi wiped a thick smear of sap and blood across his lids. It stung, his eyes burning like he'd doused them with lemon juice. The blend mixed with real tears and ran down his cheeks.

The world fell away, became thin and unreal.

So many veils.

Reality, he saw, was nothing more than a construct held up by the walls of faith.

The veil between Bastion and the Red Desert.

The veil between this reality and those myriad existences of the smoke allies and animal spirits.

The veil between people.

And finally, the veil separating now from the future and the past.

They were all so thin, so easily snapped. Just the slightest pressure.

A shadow fell across Akachi. Someone stood between him and the light.

Has the sun come up?

Unable to remember the time, he tried to open his eyes. Hardened sap glued them closed. He knew a moment of fear.

Where am I?

Was he still in that abandoned Crafter home? Had the narcotics taken him somewhere else? This could be anyone. A Crafter might be about to crush his skull with a stolen Hummingbird cudgel. It could be another Loa assassin!

His skull shattered. A spray of grey and red and fragments of bone painted the wall. It spelled something, teased with hints of portent.

A possible future. He knew it to be true. So close, almost real.

If someone made a slightly different choice…

"Oh, you're crying." A soft voice, feminine.

Akachi recognized it but lost the name.

The smell of a woman's sweat.

A gentle caress, a warm hand on his cheek, a feather of contact.

Yejide?

Was he hallucinating the Captain?

A hard kiss, tongue pushing into his mouth, hands gripping the back of his head.

Not Yejide.

"You poor thing. Tears of blood."

He recognized the voice, the taste of her lips.

Omphile.

Did she just decide not to kill me?

The Turquoise Serpent wasn't alone. Another voice spoke at the same time, mirrored her words in grating chaotic discord.

"Just a boy," purred Omphile. "Just a stupid boy."

Akachi heard the soul-deep sadness and knew it was feigned.

All an act.

"So many stupid boys," she said, "willing to give their lives for stupid shit they don't understand. So many stupid boys ready to die for a cause. Any cause. So desperate to mean something."

That second voice speaking beneath Omphile's, presaging her words by a fraction of a heartbeat, twisted Akachi's bones until they snapped and splintered like green twigs.

Mute agony.

He tried to talk, tried to make any sound, and failed.

His heart slowed, each beat a sluggish shuddering contraction squeezing mud-like blood through his veins.

"It's a shame," said Omphile, lips tickling Akachi's ear. "A real shame, what he wants me to do. You're cute. Perhaps I can play both sides, do as he commands, and still get what I want. Would he appreciate the irony?"

Akachi couldn't breathe. Air too thick, each inhalation felt like sucking water into his lungs.

"I could love you," she said. "I really could. Maybe I even do." He couldn't tell if she lied. "I'll enjoy what comes first. But what comes later, in the end…" She licked his ear and laughed, hot breath on his neck. "Oh, I'll enjoy that too."

He couldn't move, couldn't twitch a finger or draw a sip of breath.

Drug-locked. That's what his nahualli teachers called it.

Precursor to brain-burn.

Cold hands turned his face and Omphile licked the blood, tears, and etorkizun sap from his eyelids.

Was this real, or his drug-addled mind hallucinating his desires?

Too much an adolescent fantasy, it couldn't be real.

She kissed him, licking and sucking his tongue. She tasted sweet and salty, slippery and sticky.

Oh fuck!

'Never,' said his tezcat teacher, 'never *ever* ingest etorkizun.'

Omphile licked his cheeks clean and kissed him again. He tasted blood and sap on her silken tongue.

What happens when you ingest it?

Was it poisonous?

Too scattered. Too much ameslari.

Oh gods he wished he had some foku to help centre him.

This can't be real!

The narcotics took him away.

Akachi stood in the Crafters' Ring, the sun overhead giving light but no heat. Each exhalation hung before him in a fog. Tools lay scattered on massive oaken tables, axes and chisels of finely shaped flint.

A jagged obelisk of jade, tall as a man, core shot-through with cracks and deep stains of brown rot, stood before him.

NURU - WOMB AND TOMB

The Temple of Shei Baal Ba has stood empty for ten thousand years. If it belonged to a god, all memory of that being has passed. In the deepest basement of the abandoned temple lies a place of nightmares and a thousand, thousand doors. While most are of a simple wooden construction, some doors are ornate, carved from different kinds of stone. These lead to a thousand dead worlds, entire realities stripped of life by the endless hunger of the gods.

—The Loa Book of the Invisibles

Face Painted with Bells held an obsidian dagger, one end wrapped in frayed leather. She raised it in offering.

Nuru had no idea where it came from. The godling had one hand and was stark naked.

Looking from knife to godling, Nuru shook her head. "Me?"

"The gods must not war directly. If I strike against Her Skirt is Stars, the pact will be broken."

More children came to see what drew the others. Thousands gathered, pressed in close, reaching and touching, babbling incomprehensible sounds.

So many eyes, wide and dark, focussed on Nuru.

"I can't."

"The Grandmother will come," said Face Painted with Bells. "When she does, you must be ready." She placed the stone knife, cold and empty, in Nuru's hand. "The dagger must be filled."

The smoke is the souls. That's what the nahual always said.

The nahual forced Growers to witness sacrifices in the churches and public squares. So many times she watched as throats were cut, or wrists slashed for a slower bleed. Sometimes she'd been near the front, close enough to smell the blood. Too often she felt the sacrificial dagger's foul weight in her heart. They weren't all bad; sometimes she sensed nothing but stone. Sometimes the black glass exuded death and rot and it infected the very air, made every breath taste like corpses smell.

She sensed nothing from this one, the black smooth and glossy. Studying the stone, she saw her eyes reflected in its polished surface.

Smoking Mirror spoke in smoke and stone.

His words were all cutting edges and stolen souls; she understood that now.

She wants me to fill this dagger with the souls of these children.

It made sense, she supposed. With the souls in the stone, they could be carried away from this reality, returned to Bastion.

"Killing them will bring Her Skirt is Stars," said Nuru, struggling to piece it together. "But you can't fight the god yourself."

"The more souls in the stone," said the godling, "the more powerful it is. You will make, for yourself, a god-killer."

A world without gods. The thought returned. Was this the first step? Had Mother Death unwittingly given Nuru the answer?

Kill these children.

Face Painted with Bells waited.

"This is a dream," said Nuru. "You're a pactonal. It isn't real."

The godling said nothing.

"You're trying to tell me something, to teach me something. It's a test." Words spilled out and she fought for understanding. "This is a metaphor! Sacrifices will have to be made to save Bastion. It will cost me a part of myself. I will have to do things I cannot do. Mother Death is trying to prepare me for what is to come."

Giving Nuru an odd look, Face Painted with Bells said, "You need to do this *now*."

If this wasn't real, nothing she did here mattered.

But what if it was? What if Nuru could make a weapon capable of killing gods? She'd still be able to free the trapped souls after.

Gripping the dagger tight, Nuru stabbed the first child.

The boy stood, blinking in surprise, staring at the wound in his chest. Reaching up a small hand, he touched fingers to blood, and crumpled to the ground.

All around, children babbled in their high-pitched voices. They sounded shocked and confused, concerned, but not scared.

Nuru killed another.

Run! Run away!

Gathering closer, the children gestured at the two dead. Brows furrowed, they turned on her as if to say, 'Why?'

She killed another, stabbing a little girl in the heart.

The gritty feel of obsidian on bone. The hiss of parting flesh.

Blood.

The dagger felt heavier. Her hand shook. Hot nausea crawled up her arm.

"Run!" she yelled. "Fucking run!"

Startled, the children retreated a step and she followed.

She killed another, stabbing him through the throat. The boy fell gagging, clawing at the torn flesh, sputtering blood.

The crowd watched until he stilled.

"The heart is faster," said the godling. "Less painful."

Nuru killed another.

And another.

She broke.

Screaming denials and pleading with the children to flee, she killed another.

Wretched soul-deep horror. This was not possible. She would never commit such atrocity. Not if it was real.

She had cried when she saw Crafter children.

She could never—

Hearing the commotion, more children came to investigate.

She killed them.

Cutting and stabbing, slashing and screaming and pleading, Nuru killed them.

Not real.

The dagger caught in tough tendon, she ripped it free with a splash of blood. She felt the impact when the blade struck bone.

Not real.

She couldn't stop, couldn't contain the horror.

Nuru screamed and murdered children who refused to flee.

Fucking wake up!

The dagger grew heavy and foul, evil seeping into her blood, staining her bones black with rot.

Nuru killed and killed.

With each harvested soul it cut more easily though flesh and bone.

She killed until the terrible dagger bled death into her heart. The world warped and twisted, bent around the knife in her fist, writhed in sundered agony.

She lost herself to the horror.

Bodies everywhere.

Small bodies.

Contorted.

Flesh torn.

Gutted and bled.

Corpses piled high.

Nuru stood surrounded by death, the dagger in her hand pulsating the soul-churning horror of countless thousands of brutal murders into her blood. The stone, once bright and glossy, looked leaden and smoky.

"I'm sorry," said Face Painted with Bells, standing at her side. "It had to be done."

Had to be. Save Bastion.

What a fucking laugh.

Not real.

She sacrificed thousands of children and wasn't breathing hard.

She needed to wake up.

Wake up, and all this would be gone, would fade like night faded before the rising sun.

"Are you ready?" asked the godling.

"Ready?"

"I can't help you. The gods cannot war directly."

All the evil in the world festered in the dagger.

"She's coming," said the godling. "Kill her."

"No. No more."

The Grandmother came.

Serpent Skirt. Mother Life. Goddess of the Stars. Skirt of Snakes. Grandmother. Koatlkwe. Teteoh Innan. On and on, forever, through time. Older than life, more ancient than the sky.

Womb and tomb, she was all.

Mother Life came to her world and saw the horror wrought there.

Once, long ago, it had thrived, a universe populated by untold trillions. She fed, gorged herself on blood and souls. She grew strong. Other realities bordered on her own, ruled by other gods. She devoured them too, growing and spreading. She was life and death, and all must worship.

Reality after reality, she bled them dry, leaving barren landscapes in her wake. She subjugated worlds, left entire universes stripped of souls.

Her Skirt is Stars, wearing a long thobe of writhing vipers and a necklace of skulls and beating hearts, stood before Nuru. Bent with age, her naked breasts hung flaccid and wrinkled.

"What have you done?" the god demanded, stalking forward, waving a hand, fingers hooked like talons. "My precious souls! My beautiful children! My perfect—"

"Kill her," said Face Painted with Bells. "Kill her with the dagger of her sins. She broke the Queen's law and must be punished."

The Grandmother turned ancient eyes, wet with jaundiced milk, on Nuru. "I remember you. Long legs running in the field with those boys. Always in trouble. Always causing trouble." The vipers in the skirt hissed at Nuru, stretched toward her, flickering forked tongues tasting. "You never suffered for your sins. Always...Always...what were their names?" She grinned cracked grey teeth, gums receded so each one hung separate from the others. "Bomani and...Chisulo. That one, he loved you even then. Did you ever?" A pale pink tongue slid out to lick thin lips. "No. Of course not. Always afraid. And so now he is dead."

Nuru lifted the dagger, held it out before her like it might fend off the god.

The old lady grunted a damp laugh that turned into a wheezing cough. "I watch you all. All my children. I know you. This..." Bone fingers fluttered at Nuru. "This pretty shell, you wear it well. But you're still the same terrified little girl. Afraid to be powerless. Afraid to use the power you have." The god spat saliva, gritty with red sand. "You killed my darlings. And so you shall give me more."

Nuru couldn't speak, couldn't move.

"You shall be mother to ten thousand. You shall be the conduit for souls." She cackled, the cracked sound of splintering wood. "You want to be a mother. A real mother. So. You. Shall."

Mother.

Mother Death. Mother Life. Mother of Stars. Mother of Flowers. Mother Sin. Mother Purity. The Great Mother. Mother of the Universe.

So many gods used the word, and none of them understood what it meant.

"Ah," said Face Painted with Bells. "There she is. There is the woman Mother Death chose."

Skirt of Snakes was right. Nuru was afraid. She was terrified of being powerless.

This god who called herself Mother and Grandmother played her part in ensuring the Growers stayed weak and powerless.

Obsidian dagger in hand, the sickness of it filling her heart, foul death and rot coming off it in reality-bending waves, Nuru approached the god. A snake lashed out, and she took its head with a careless flick of the blade.

And another.

Eyes wide, Grandmother retreated. "Child. You can be a mother to thousands. I see the need in you."

Insane, the god couldn't possibly understand what Nuru wanted.

They're all like this. All driven by their own sick needs and hungers.

Mouths gaping, finger-length fangs dropping into place, snakes struck at Nuru.

She was faster. The souls in the knife gave her strength and speed.

Heads fell, littered the already blood-soaked grass. In a score of heartbeats Mother Life's skirt of snakes hung limp and dead. The hearts on her necklace beat fast, throbbing and pulsating with terror.

"Promise me!" screamed Nuru, advancing. "Promise me you'll never again hoard souls!"

The Grandmother retreated before her wrath. "I kept them safe! I kept them pure!"

She lied. Nuru saw it in the convulsions of the hearts, in the way those mad milky eyes darted toward the littered corpses with undisguised hunger.

Driving the dagger into the Grandmother's chest, Nuru killed the god.

The sacrificial dagger claimed one of the most ancient souls in existence. Smoke wafted off it in thick waves, fouling the sky, collapsing this pocket reality, sucking all existence in toward it with devouring hunger. It was death.

Stained to the marrow, her own soul riddled with worms of rot, Nuru became death, a destroyer of worlds.

She wanted to scream for the horror of it.

She wanted to carve away the meat of her and dig out the infection.

Nuru's flesh became black like nothing, black like the gaping wounds in reality between the bright sparks of the night sky.

Flawless black. Unblemished. Perfectly smooth.

Black, like Mother Death.

There is power in blood.

There is power in death and souls.

Having killed a god, that power now resided in Nuru's dagger.

For the first time in her entire existence, she had nothing to fear.

She revelled in it.

She wanted more.

There were gods out there dwarfing Her Skirt is Stars, gods so ancient and powerful that the Grandmother bowed and grovelled before them.

I need to be stronger.

"All of the gods hoard souls," Face Painted with Bells reminded Nuru. "All of them. The Grandmother's collection was nothing."

Small bodies everywhere, contorted in death.

Blood.

"Mother Death forbid it," said the godling, "and they turned on her."

Nuru only half listened. Power. Right there in her hand.

"We have to free them all," said the godling.

The power to kill gods.

"Every hoarded soul," continued Face Painted with Bells. "It's the only way to save humanity. To save the gods."

To save the gods?

Why would I save the fucking parasites who did this to us?

More souls. So many more souls. Sacrifice every soul hoarded in every reality, killing god after god until she could cut down Mother Death herself. Then, when every god was dead, she would break the dagger, repopulate Bastion as she was in her earliest days.

Nuru woke on the floor of a massive and empty warehouse in a Barley District. It stunk.

Efra and Kofi lay sleeping, each curled in a ratty grey blanket.

A dream.

Numb death crept up her right arm from the dagger clutched in her first.

Nuru stared at it. Tendrils of smoke wafted from the blade. It bent light and life.

How many souls were trapped in there?

She remembered killing. Eyes closed, screaming, hacking at the gathered children, cutting them down.

Smash the stone and free the souls trapped within to be reborn, or keep a weapon capable of killing gods.

The choice should have been difficult.

The dagger throbbed with power.

Nuru touched the blade to the floor and left a groove in the stone. Guilt stabbed her.

You defaced Bastion!

But the signs of wear and tear were all around. Hairline cracks in the stone, every edge rounded smooth by wind and sand and shuffling feet. Bastion wore her years. Everything looked sunken and shrunk.

Colossal as the Last City was, nothing lasted forever.

The gods killed our world.

She knew it to be true.

The Grandmother hoarded souls like a starving Grower hid crusts of hardbread.

Kill them. Kill them all.

It was the only way to be free.

Her thoughts skittered and jumped, struggling to contain the scale.

What started as an errant thought—humanity will only be free once the gods are gone—had somehow grown into an increasingly real plan: Kill the gods.

Efra, curled in her blanket, drew Nuru's attention. The scarred woman wouldn't so much as flinch at the thought.

I need her. I can't do this alone.

AKACHI - A RIVER OF WHITE BONE

Finesse, rather than brute force, is of essence in dream-world battle. Any skilled pactonal can define that world's laws, but once a law is set, once it is defined by a practitioner, further alteration is extremely difficult. To change a defined law, one must first understand exactly how it was defined. Warfare within dream-worlds often becomes a race of definitions and workarounds as pactonal wrestle to trap their opponents within parameters set by two competing parties. Among masters, this is a war of puzzles, layers within layers, rules within rules, building toward a final trap from which one's enemy cannot escape.

—The Book of Bastion

The jagged obelisk of rotten jade shuddered and became a man.

"Firash?" asked Akachi, blinking in surprise.

"I thought I'd lost you already," said the tezcat. Reality coughed and stuttered around the nahualli and he once again became a pillar of stained jade. "Are you all right? You look a little ill."

Dream-world, Akachi reminded himself.

But was this manifestation of Firash a creation of Akachi's?

Or is this my skill as a huateteo showing me something of his true nature?

"Sorry," said Akachi. "I…" Should he tell Firash about what happened with Omphile? Was it real, or some juvenile aspect of Akachi's youthful lust for the woman? Standing in this empty street with a speaking shard of jade, everything seemed unreal. "I'm fine," he finished.

A man once again, Firash studied him, hesitating.

"Yes?" asked Akachi.

Eyes feverish, the tezcat said, "Does your god speak to you? Do you *know* what he wants? Have you seen him?"

"He speaks to me. I have seen him." He hesitated to share the experience. It was too personal, to jealously guarded.

"All my life I have served Southern Hummingbird," said Firash. "Never have I felt even a hint of his presence. I doubt my god knows I exist."

"I'm sure he knows," said Akachi, offering comfort and wondering if he lied. "You are a talented tezcat and huateteo."

Firash turned into a shard of jade and a new crack appeared, cleaving into the heart of him. Brown decay followed the crevice like an infection, oozed foul puss. "I fail in my role as spirit guide for this squad. Captain Melokuhle is broken inside. She lost two thirds of her squad to assassins and riots. The things we did. The things she had to do. The men and women we left behind because we had to."

The cracks in Firash weren't random. Someone was breaking him, chipping away at his soul, undermining his faith. Intentional, the work of a master craftsman, they told a story of misery and trauma, guilt and pain.

"She is strong," said Akachi, thinking of Yejide. "There is an inner strength—"

"We train. Every day. All our lives. But training and practising differ from the reality of cutting a woman in half because she's attacking you with a blunt rock. Nothing prepares you for holding someone you've known your entire life as they scream with a shit-covered stick jammed in their belly."

The Turquoise Serpent stared at the ground, stuttering back and forth between being a man and cracked jade.

He's too human.

Too frail. They all were.

All except Omphile.

Efra, that scarred little Dirt, was harder and meaner than any of them. Except maybe the assassin.

For a heartbeat Firash was a jade statue of a man, his pulsing heart yellow and cancerous. "Do you know how long it takes to die from a gut wound?" he asked. "Days, sometimes. And a shit-covered stick? There's no recovering from that. We had to kill our own people. That, or leave them to be fucking skinned alive by the Loa. We killed friends we'd trained with our entire lives." He looked away, baring teeth in a grimace. "It was a mercy." He stared at nothing, became jagged jade again, cracks deeper, darker. "It was a mercy."

"The Loa are to blame," said Akachi.

Firash ignored his words. "Captain Melokuhle is brittle. I see it in her."

She's not the only one. The tezcat looked like he might shatter and splinter apart at the slightest touch.

"We war," said Akachi, "because we must. We fight for the survival of the Last City. If we fail, humanity dies."

Firash grunted his doubt.

"We will save the city, carve out the rot that is the Loa."

Though the Loa heresies were there, in the first copies of the Book of Bastion.

There can be no justice where there is inequality. That line was in both the *Book of the Invisibles*, and the copy in Zalika's chambers. Why was that cut from the version he knew?

More mindless Loa rhetoric, he decided, *designed to confuse*.

Firash shattered, crumbling to dust. A gust of wind blew the street clean.

The man was gone. In his place a giant snake, banded in red, white, and black, moved in hypnotic knotted coils.

Falling to his knees, Akachi felt the jolt of stone as he prostrated himself before his god.

"The war has begun." Cloud Serpent spoke in scales on sand.

Purest blinding joy broke Akachi's skull wide, screamed purifying light into the darkest pit of his soul. His god saw him. His god found him worthy. Lightning pleasure like a thousand orgasms smashed all thought, left him twitching in glorious agony on the stone.

"The Heart of Mother Death murdered Her Skirt is Stars," said the god.

Akachi's blood boiled.

"She will be the death of Bastion."

Awash in divine joy, Akachi couldn't piece enough of himself together to form cohesive thought.

Akachi orgasmed over and over, screaming in pain and gratitude. He wanted to tell his god he'd done as commanded and acquired the Staff of the Fifth Sun, but speech was beyond him.

"Hunt the Hearts!" The god's rage was the roar of an inferno, shuddering conflagration of burning worlds.

Akachi's bones burned to dust.

Searing white light blasted him empty.

From somewhere beyond, intent pressed into Akachi, wormed through his thoughts like a glistening black snake. Nuru would journey to the underworld. Once there, she'd call her god. The Lady of the Dead would once again take the mantle of Death as her own. If she succeeded, the god might be impossible to banish again.

You have to stop her. The grinding glass voice in his skull sounded nothing like the sand and scales of Cloud Serpent. *Take the Staff of the Fifth Sun to the place of eternal night.*

This was his chance! Instead of pursuing Nuru through the rings, he would be there, waiting!

He would end her. There, in the land of the dead, Akachi would be the saviour of all humanity.

The last time they fought, she called upon the might of her god. This time would be different. This time, Akachi carried the Staff of the Fifth Sun.

"The Heart of the Lord of the Root is near," said the Lord of the Hunt, startling Akachi. "Find Darakai. Kill him in his dreams."

Confused at the sudden change, Akachi said, "I shall hunt—"

The massive snake coiled about Akachi, crushing him until his ribs shattered, shards of bone tearing through papery lungs, chest collapsing.

Sword-length fangs, sank into his ruined body and the god fed.

Glorious agony.

Giving.

Anything.

Everything.

Akachi lay curled in the street. His knees bled from the impact, further staining the white band of his robes. His heart kicked and twitched, struggling to rediscover its natural rhythm. Tremors ran through him, shaking his body, rattling his clenched teeth.

All was silent except his ragged breathing.

He saw me. He saw me. He saw me. He saw me. He saw me. He saw me. He saw me.

When sanity returned, he struggled to piece the vision together, to make it once again real. He *needed* it. That attention, that gaze.

A chance to defeat Mother Death, to kill her Heart!

There were two voices.

That wasn't possible. Cloud Serpent was perfect. The god wrote its plans in Akachi's blood, but the proximity to such colossal divinity left his thoughts a chaotic maelstrom.

Darakai, Heart of The Lord of the Root. For now, nothing else mattered.

The war of the Hearts was the true battle, and this struggle would go on until only one remained.

Kill him in his dreams.

Holy purpose filled Akachi. Cloud Serpent worked through unexpected subjects. Akachi hadn't thought to prepare for a sorcerous battle, but here he was, dosed with ameslari and, thanks to Omphile, a sizeable quantity of etorkizun. Joy at the perfection of his god filled him and he laughed aloud, hearing the slap-echo of his voice careening off stone.

He would be careful. The Lord of the Root's Heart, while likely unprepared for such an attack, would be a powerful nahualli.

For years his teachers berated Akachi's lack of talent as a tezcat, belittling his ability to separate himself—his desires—from the task at hand. All he needed was a true purpose. Etorkizun coursing through his blood, Akachi hunted through countless futures, looking for the one where he found the Healer's Heart. Possibilities spread out before him like the fanned pages of a book, skimming past too fast for more than the briefest glimpse. In some futures Akachi ran afoul of a Loa nahualli and was killed. In others, someone murdered his body back in that Crafter home and he died, his soul wandering the streets of Bastion until a slave-sorcerer in the Bankers' Ring bound him to create a fetish.

He sifted through the futures, searching for the right one. In so many he saw his death.

Efra cut his throat. Nuru tore him apart, littering his limbs across some broad esplanade in the Bankers' Ring.

She makes it that far?

No. Just a possible future. He'd catch her in the underworld, end her there.

Time after time he watched himself brain-burn, die choking on vomit in some dark alley.

Glimpses of a near godless world, the entire pantheon except one, dead. Efra and Nuru struggling atop the Sand Wall. He saw the scarred girl push her friend from the wall and stand watching the street-sorcerer's tumbling descent to the Bloody Desert.

Doomed city.

Dead city.

He found it, a string of random chances and choices leading to the Lord of the Root's Heart.

Walking the path of dreams, Akachi followed fate to his prey.

The elderly nahualli stood waiting in The Lord of the Root's local church. He looked kind, eyes gentle.

Darakai, thought Akachi. *His name is Darakai.*

"I've felt you searching for me." said the old man. "You are clumsy in the arts of the pactonal."

"I am not unskilled," said Akachi, pride wounded by the dismissive tone.

"Not unskilled is not the same as mastery. This, young nahualli of Cloud Serpent, is not a fight you can win. I beg you, return to your body. Do not die out here."

"I am the Heart of Cloud Serpent," said Akachi.

"Ah." Darakai sighed. The old man looked tired, though not scared. "Mine is a god of healing, not murder."

"I…" Akachi neither wanted nor expected to converse with his enemy. Better to have this done fast so he might seek out Mother Death's Heart. "I have no choice." He winced at how pathetic he sounded.

"We always have a choice. That is why they war through us." Eyes filled with sadness, the old man shook his head. "I think it makes it more interesting for them."

Something was wrong.

This felt too familiar.

"I have to do this," Akachi said to the Artist, standing among the detritus of the man's work. Drawings littered the floor. The charcoal sketch of Efra with the scar that should have defined her. Lean and hard, wound tight like rope, she was beautiful in her strength. Not like the other woman, Nuru, but still striking.

"No, it's a choice, the Artist answered.

The frustrating man couldn't see that to serve a god was to surrender choice, set aside one's own desires.

"Obedience lies at the heart of faith," said Akachi, quoting the Book.

"And faith lies at the heart of control," said the Artist. "You really should try to remember the entire line."

That wasn't in the book, was it? The infuriating man probably made it up.

"I didn't want to torture you," Akachi explained to the Artist.

It was the only way to find Efra.

Except she'd come strolling along the street moments after the Artist died.

"Educated," the Artist said, "is different than intelligent."

The man was a fool. He had no understanding of what it was to be a nahual.

Akachi swept the vision aside. "Simplistic and crude," he said.

The pactonal shrugged, unconcerned.

This, he realized, would not be as easy as wrestling control of a dream-world from a talented but unskilled street-sorcerer.

"I did what had to be done," he told the old priest, feeling the strangest need to explain himself.

"Did you?"

"There is no abstaining from a war such as this."

"Of course there is."

"The last Heart remaining becomes Heart's Mirror. There cannot be two. Either you will be the last, or someone will kill you to be the last."

"That someone won't be you, boy."

Darakai altered their shared reality and the two nahualli stood in the red sands of the Bloody Desert. The great Sand Wall towered over them, one hundred times the height of a man, its outer surface carved with ancient runes and wards. Pitted and gouged, the stone showed the wear of twenty-five thousand years of wind-driven sand. The protections, once cut deep, were little more than shallow indentations.

Another thousand years and they'll be gone.

Maybe less.

The Last City would be vulnerable to all the demons and damned souls haunting the endless desert.

One war at a time.

When he was Heart's Mirror, he would send nahualli to strengthen the wards.

Or did it even look like this? How real was this vision?

Pulling his attention from the wall, Akachi realized he was surrounded by sun-bleached bones. Starting at the base of the wall, they reached out a score of strides.

Human bones, all of them.

The damned, those cast from the Sand Wall as punishment.

This close, he detected no curve to the great stone edifice. It was too big, stretched from horizon to horizon. With it, a river of white bone as far as the eye could see.

So many dead.

Herein lay the core of one of the Loa's foulest, most vexing blasphemies: If the number of souls is finite, how can we afford to throw any from the wall?

The nahual response was simple: Some souls cannot be saved, are beyond even The Lord's ability to purify. Such irredeemables must be cast out for the good of the city.

Akachi hadn't seen his first penance wagon until he'd been at the Northern Cathedral for two years. By his fifth year, they were a daily occurrence.

Twenty-five thousand years of banishing souls from Bastion's light. How many times were each of these people reborn before they were deemed beyond redemption?

"It's a lot of dead, isn't it?" said Darakai. The nahualli stood a dozen strides distant, surrounded by bones. "Did you never think to ask why more and more were thrown from the wall every year?"

"Obedience—"

Darakai waved him to silence. "Think about it. Really think about it."

After twenty-five thousand years, what turned these souls from the light of the gods?

Akachi remembered his visit to the menageries as an acolyte, watching the Dirt in charge of feeding the jaguars toss chunks of meat over the fence.

"They're feeding something," said Akachi. "Something beyond the wall."

"What are they feeding?" asked Darakai.

The answer, so obvious, horrified him. "Mother Death."

That was impossible. To suggest this was some insidious Loa plot was to claim the heretics had completely infiltrated the true nahual.

He's trying to make me doubt, to weaken my faith.

"I know what you're doing," said Akachi. "Building the battle-ground, filling it with these details and doubts. The more I contemplate its meanings, the more real it is in my mind."

"You understand but a fraction of my intent."

"Not everyone can be saved," said Akachi, cringing at parroting the words of his teachers.

"Perhaps. But the Lord of the Root is a god of healing. He condones no murder that does not give the soul in question the opportunity of redemption."

"Some are beyond redemption." Again he spewed words hammered into him in countless sermons.

"You don't know that," said Darakai. The nahual was too confident, too smug in his age-earned wisdom.

He thinks that because I'm young, I'm foolish, naive.

But age, wisdom, and that annoying need old people had to educate the young, could be a weakness.

Ameslari in his blood, Akachi turned his will to subtly bending their shared reality. Nothing visible. Nothing obvious. Instead, he rewrote some of its rules.

His earlier conversation with Bishop Zalika gave him an idea.

In the stone reality of Bastion, a nagual could only become some-thing they'd studied exhaustively, and meticulously carved in wood, every detail perfect. Without the right blend of narcotics in their blood, and the figurine to focus on, they were helpless, unable to shape-change.

But this was not that reality.

This was the dream-world and subject to dream logic. Every temple-trained pactonal learned how to control their dreams, how to shape their reality as if writing a story.

Akachi told the story he needed to tell. Every narcotic he'd ever experienced pumped through his veins. He knew exactly how each felt, their effects. He made it real.

Here, in this fluid smoke-reality, there was no need for dangerous interactions, and so he wrote that out of his rules. He could, if he wanted, reach into his belt and pull out the carvings he kept there. But that was the action of an unimaginative novice.

Or an old man stuck in his ways, accustomed to the rigid rules of reality.

Instead, Akachi built in his mind something Darakai would never have witnessed, could never have studied.

Akachi became a colossal skyvyrm.

NURU - BLESSED IGNORANCE

Four gods, each in turn, rose to claim the sun as their own. Their deaths heralded ages of apocalypse, the undoing of worlds.

Mountainheart was first to claim the sun. Smoking Mirror dragged him from the sky, murdered him with foulest deceit, and devoured the god, taking on many of his qualities. For one thousand years terrible storms wracked the world.

The Lord of the Wind took the sun as his own, sweeping away ancient nations. His worshipers built great cities of stepped stone pyramids and spilled blood in daily sacrifices. Jealous of his power and rank, the Enemy of Both Sides betrayed the god. The resulting cataclysm saw winds lay waste to the world.

The Rain of Flint Blades, once a weather god, was third to lay claim. Father Discord cast him down, drown him in lies. Centuries of rain flooded the world, toppled civilizations.

Loved by all, She Who Shines Like Jade was the fourth god to call the sun her own. The Obsidian Lord betrayed her in the night, fed her heart to his jaguar nagual.

And so began the Fifth Age.

—The Loa Book of the Invisibles

Nuru sat waiting for Efra and Kofi to awaken. Efra slept facing the young nahualli, while Kofi slept with his back to the Grower.

Though Nuru had been in similar warehouses in the Wheat District, this one felt different. Everything sounded strange. Of the Loa she'd seen the night before, there was no sign. They left while she slept. The ancient building, robbed of its purpose, breathed sighs of abandoned disappointment. The air stank of the ghosts of thousands of years of barley bales and dung. She imagined huge wagons, drawn by teams of six oxen, groaning their way in to be loaded. The beasts crapped everywhere, uncaring that they shat on holy stone. The cursing and sweating of Growers bent under the weight of bales, their skin scratched red and raw from dried barley. After, once the barley wagons were gone, the dung wagons arrived. The exhausted Growers scraped up the shit with bare hands and loaded it into the wagons. A daring few might steal some to be dried and later burned for heat at night. There were always nahual willing to turn a blind eye.

For a price.

How many times had Nuru watched young Grower men and women march off to entertain the priest while the rest grabbed as much dung as they could carry? That was back before the Birds guarded every wagon no matter what it carried.

Nothing is so worthless Dirts can be allowed to have it.

Efra woke first, stretching with a loud groan. Rising, she stood for a long moment glaring at the sleeping Loa nahualli. She rubbed at the ridge of scar cutting her lower lip. Nuru knew that measuring look, but doubted she understood its meaning.

She looked at Chisulo like that.

Like she was either thinking about fucking or killing him.

As if sensing the attention, Kofi woke with a twitch. Blinking, he peered blearily at the two women.

"Get up, fat boy," said Efra. "We've been waiting hours for you."

Shooting her an annoyed look, he rose to his feet. He stretched, thick muscle and the hard plane of his belly exposed as his thobe fell open.

Nuru looked away.

"Sleeping on stone every night is murdering my back," he complained.

"Fucking idiot," said Efra.

Understanding lit his face like dawn on the Grey Wall. "Sorry. I didn't mean—" Kofi stopped, brow furrowed as he tried to figure out how to extricate himself. "I know Growers sleep on stone—"

"Put your floppy tits away," snapped Efra. "Let's get moving."

Noticing Nuru for the first time, he turned away, stuttering something while he pulled his thobe back into place, wrestling awkwardly with the sweeping folds and layers.

"Sorry," he said again, finally turning back.

"Hey fat boy," said Efra, snapping her fingers to get his attention. "All the Loa churches in the Growers' Ring are hidden in the basements of tenements. Do you have real churches in the Crafters' Ring, or do you skulk around like rats there too?"

"We don't skulk. But yeah." He darted another embarrassed look at Nuru. "The churches are hidden. The nahual hunt us. The one we're going to is in the basement of a tannery. The Hummingbird Guard rarely patrol that neighbourhood because of the stench."

"Cowering rats," said Efra.

"We're the Invisibles."

"Too fat to be invisible."

"The term means—"

"Anyway," interrupted Efra. "I'm pretty sure it was originally meant to refer to the Growers, the people invisibly supporting all Bastion."

Startled, he blinked, mouth working as he thought it through and began to doubt.

"We should get moving," Nuru said to distract the two from yet another argument.

Her neck and shoulders itched with the feel of watching eyes. She carried some shred of Mother Death in her soul. The nahual of Bastion would not rest until she was dead.

After a few crusts of hardbread and a rind of dried melon that barely touched Nuru's hunger, Kofi led them from the warehouse.

"Shouldn't there be more Loa rats with us?" asked Efra. "In case we run into trouble?"

"Called away," said Kofi. "The Guard took back several gates, and there are squads of Turquoise Serpents in the ring. All the tecolotl were summoned to deal with them."

Ankle-deep in ash and littered with sun-bloated corpses, the ground looked like a rolling landscape.

They walked in silence for an hour. At each intersection Kofi waved them to a stop and went ahead to check the corners. The world felt dead, abandoned. No faces peered from dark doorways.

Efra, becoming increasingly twitchy with each passing block, asked Kofi, "What happens to the souls of the dead now that The Lord is gone?"

It was an odd question. Was she worried about the souls of their friends, or did she have some deeper reason for asking? Curious, Nuru listened.

"They still make the journey to the underworld," answered Kofi with typical nahual confidence. "But they'll be trapped there until a new death god rises. Face Painted with Bells holds the underworld for Mother Death, but she does not have the power to purge souls."

"Once your god returns," said Efra, glancing at the Loa, "can she bring back the dead?"

He nodded. "Mother Death is the greatest of the gods." He darted a look at Nuru.

Kofi directed them to turn into the next alley with a wave of his hand. "I've never met Growers like you two before," he blurted. Embarrassed, he added, "You're not what I expected. Either of you."

"Nah," said Efra. "We're just a couple of stupid Dirt girls."

Kofi shot Nuru a raised eyebrow but said nothing.

After being waved forward by Kofi at yet another intersection, Nuru saw that someone had been at work clearing the corpses from the street. Much of the ash had been swept to the side and piled in gutters. Those perfect troughs, lining every street, funnelling blood to the gods, were blocked with refuse. Nothing felt real, like she and Efra were the last two Growers in the city.

They're hiding. They're waiting.

Once the Loa sorcerers stopped driving them against the Birds, everyone must have fled back to their tenements. With no nahual around to tell them what to do, they'd stay hidden. At least until hunger drove them out.

At the next turn, Kofi waved at them to stop. Ignoring his frantic gestures, Nuru and Efra crept forward to look.

"I told you to stay back," he hissed.

Both women ignored him.

Clothed in armour of green stone, swords held at the ready, a squad of six Turquoise Serpents guarded the gate. Each carried a shield of hard-boiled leather stretched over a frame of ebony. A short and wiry woman, hair hanging in long braids, barked orders. She looked like she'd been carved from oak.

The corpses of well-fed Growers littered the ground, bent, broken, and shattered. One had been nailed to an upright of wood and tortured. She'd been stripped naked first, and carefully beaten. Swollen bruises covered every part of her. She must have held out at least that long because the Serpents hadn't stopped there. Shallow cuts told an excruciating story. Head hanging forward, long hair dripping blood, only the slight movement of her chest said she wasn't dead.

"They must have retaken the gate in the night," whispered Kofi, pulling back from the corner.

Efra and Nuru retreated with him.

"She's still alive," said Efra.

Nuru turned on the girl. Was she insane? "We can't rescue her."

"Rescue?" Efra gave her a confused look. "She's still alive. That means she hasn't told them anything. Yet. But she will." She turned on Kofi. "Do you know her? Does she know anything about us?"

"I…" Kofi dashed a quick look around the corner. "I don't think so."

"Good," said Efra. "Then we can go through another gate." She set off, stopping when no one followed.

Seeing the Loa nahualli's face, Nuru said, "We can't save her."

"I know. But the church—" He growled in quiet frustration. "The church is right near this gate. Going through another means walking for hours. Even then, it might be in Serpent hands. This was the one gate I knew for sure we'd taken."

"You Loa are fucking useless," said Efra.

"If they hold the next gate," argued Kofi, "we could be walking for days."

Efra shrugged. "So, we walk for days. Work a bit of that fat off you."

He was silent for a dozen heartbeats, jaw working. "They'll torture that woman until she tells them everything she knows about our plans."

"So?" demanded Efra. "We'll be gone."

"This is bigger than just us."

"Is it?" Efra nodded at Nuru. "Killing that woman before she spills whatever she knows is more important than her?"

He winced. "We can go through this gate."

Efra stared at him in mock wonder. "Are you deranged, or stupid? Those are Turquoise Serpents."

"Most of what you've heard is lies and propaganda," he said. "They're just people."

Nuru, having seen them in the Smoking Mirror's vision knew otherwise. "We go around."

"No," said Kofi. "I can do this."

Efra snorted. "You'll get us all killed."

"You underestimate me."

"You overestimate you."

"And anyway," he growled, "this isn't a discussion. *I* decide what happens." He turned on Nuru. "You're my responsibility. That carving is too important to be wandering around the Growers' Ring."

"Just the carving, eh?" asked Efra. "Your showing off is going to get us killed."

He flashed her an angry look. "We go through."

Retreating from the corner, Kofi fished about in his thobe until he found two chunks of stone. The first was a thumb-sized length of flint. Dull and unshaped, it was useless as a weapon. The second, a jagged black stone Nuru didn't recognize, was larger.

"What's that?" asked Efra.

"Skystone," he answered, distracted. "Now shut up."

The Loa using their stone sorcery to drive the Growers against the Birds had all been clutching flint. Nuru looked around, saw empty streets. Could he use the flint to turn the Serpents against each other? If he could do that, why had the other Loa used the Growers?

"What's the skystone do?" demanded Efra.

"It's a magnifier."

"What's a magnifier?"

Eyes still closed, he said, "It makes things bigger, more powerful."

Head swivelling back and forth, Nuru watched the two.

Efra scowled at him. "What are you making bigger?"

With a groan, Kofi opened his eyes. "Are you going to let me—"

"No."

He sighed. "It increases the potency of other stones. It makes our sorcery more powerful. It's incredibly rare, incredibly valuable."

Ah. Only with the skystone can he turn the Serpents against each other.

The Loa she'd seen working the Dirts to a murderous frenzy hadn't had that rock.

Efra squinted, nose wrinkled in doubt. "Rocks come from the ground. Why is it called skystone?"

"Because," he said, exasperated, "it falls out of the fucking sky."

Efra looked up at the endless bowl of blue. "Really? When?"

"This isn't the time—"

"When?"

Kofi gave up. "You know those streaks of light you see in the night sky after dark?"

"Dirts aren't allowed out after dark." She flashed a scar-stretching grin. "But yeah."

"Those are falling chunks of rock. They mostly land out in the desert, beyond our reach. But sometimes one lands in the city. After that, it's a race to see who finds it first."

"The nahual don't use stone," said Nuru. "What do they do with it?"

"Mostly keep it from us." He studied them both. "Are we done? Can I get on with this?"

Efra and Nuru nodded.

"Good. Now stay close. If you get too far away, you'll feel the effects."

Once again closing his eyes, Kofi held the two stones in his fists.

"Ever notice how much he sweats?" whispered Efra too loud for Kofi not to hear. "He's not used to being out in the sun."

This day, like all the others in recent memory, was sweltering.

"How can he sweat so much and still be fat?"

"Please," said Kofi. "Please shut up."

Teeth bared in a snarl, eyes clenched closed, a growl built deep in his throat. Like the low rumble of distant thunder, it grew in volume. Pure animal fear and rage.

She watched the young man work himself up, fists clenching and unclenching, muttered curses. He spat anger, sometimes directed outward, but often muttering at his own weaknesses and failures. She'd seen similar behaviour before. Chisulo, Omari, and Happy had done it before street fights.

As if calm, rational thought is an impediment to violence.

Bomani never had to. He was always ready, always willing. He walked through each day with so much pent rage there was no need.

So much blood had been spilled since his death. Did ash now cover his brutally beaten corpse? Had his blood fed the gods? Had he been purified and reborn before Father Death was murdered?

Kofi made a high-pitched keening sound of loss and terror and hate.

Emotion, Kofi had explained, was the basis of Loa sorcery.

They use it like the nahualli use narcotics.

She recalled the hate and madness in the eyes of the sorcerers driving the Growers against the Birds.

Efra watched, eyes wide and bright.

Something crept closer, stalking Nuru. Spiders. A deadly viper. One of the huge hunting cats that liked to eat people's guts while they still kicked and struggled. She couldn't see it, but knew it was close.

Nuru felt cornered, trapped.

A man stumbled out of a nearby tenement, a Bird's ebony cudgel gripped in a shaking fist. Eyes wide with terror, he twitched, flinching from unseen enemies.

Then another.

Two women exited a tenement, sticks raised, ready for a fight.

Danger thickened the air, choking Nuru. Every stone emanated threat. All the world sought to do her harm. Nowhere to hide. Nowhere safe.

Find the threat and kill it. Certainty filled her.

Kill.

Kofi's snarl scaled upward, a tortured scream.

Sorcery. It's his sorcery.

This was what those Loa did to the Growers. This was how they threw them against the Birds.

He wasn't going to turn the Serpents against one another. He was going to smash Growers against them until sheer numbers won out.

Knowing what was happening didn't help. Reason was dust in the tornado winds of soul-clenching terror.

The threat grew more defined. She knew where it was. Around the corner, right near her! Fists bunched, Nuru took a step toward the corner. Efra stopped her.

Though smaller, the scarred girl physically dragged her back.

Nuru tried to pull away. "We have to kill it!" Rage and fear flooded her. The only way to free herself from this threat was to utterly crush it. Bash it with a rock, over and over.

Efra slapped Nuru, snapped her head around.

Nuru lashed out, trying to claw the woman's eyes, trying to tear her flesh, and was slapped again. Her face stung, eyes watering.

Efra's face remained a mask of calm, emotionless and empty.

Something stirred deep in Nuru's belly. Spasms of flawless black.

Eight legs, barbs sharper than freshly knapped obsidian. Ancient as time. Older than suns.

The rage and fear died, brushed away by Mother Death.

"What happened?" asked Efra. "You looked like you were about to charge in with the rest of those idiots."

More and more Growers streamed from dark doorways, came screaming from the basements where they hid. In moments, the street filled with raging men and women, some brandishing makeshift weapons, most unarmed.

Face burning from the slap, Nuru said, "Didn't you feel it?"

"Just for a heartbeat. And then it was gone."

Aware of Mother Death's intervention, Nuru thought she understood. *Smoking Mirror protects Efra.*

The sounds of fighting drew Nuru to the corner. Peeking around, she saw the Growers and Turquoise Serpents in a pitched battle. Fighting in a tight formation, the Serpents stayed low, behind their shields. Obsidian swords licked out to sever limbs or disembowel. Screams echoed up and down the street. Wounded Growers lay sprawled on the ground, one or both legs missing at the knee. A woman staggered away, entrails spilling over her hands, splashing at her feet. Black stone lashed out in a blur, and took the top of a man's skull off, just above the ears. He stood staring at the bowl of bone spinning on the ground before him, the grey of his brain. Grabbing at the edge of a shield, a woman struggled to open a gap and lost both hands at the wrists. She fell back, fountaining blood.

Kofi screamed and screamed, ground the edges of the clutched stones against his forearms until he drew blood. More Growers came. Shoulder to shoulder, packed tight, they fought each other to get at the Serpents.

I saw this.

The street ran deep with gore. The gutters funnelling blood under the wall overflowed.

A sword stabbed out from between shields, entered a man's belly, swept up to pass effortlessly out the top of his head.

Growers poured from dark tenements, sprinted from every alley.

Growers died.

Not a single Serpent fell.

"They're butchering them," said Nuru, numb from horror.

Eye closed, Kofi roared louder, voice cracking. Face purpling from strain, stretched in a rage of madness, sweat poured off him.

More Growers filled the streets. If they could hear his voice, they answered the call.

They came to kill.

They came to die.

They fought without finesse or skill, with no thought to defence or self-preservation.

The Serpents, behind their wall of shields, killed dozens. Scores. Corpses piled around them, hampering the Growers. Limbs littered the street.

They're going to kill them all.

And why? So Nuru, Efra and Kofi didn't have to walk to another gate?

Nuru screamed at Kofi to stop but he heard nothing, didn't react.

Not knowing what else to do, she turned to face Efra. "Stop him!"

With a curt nod, Efra stepped behind Kofi, slid an arm around his neck, and jumped to wrap her legs around his waist. Her weight driving Kofi forward, he staggered and fell. Forearm under his chin, she growled, tightening her grip, until he stopped moving. She continued to squeeze with all her strength.

The sounds of battle changed, became the terrified screams of people suddenly returning to their senses. Growers fled in every direction in a mad exodus of the limping and wounded.

"You can stop," said Nuru.

Efra ignored her.

"Stop, or you're going to kill him."

Efra looked up, eyes cold. "Fucking right."

AKACHI - THE HEART OF A DEAD GOD

Knowing they could no longer afford open war, each of the gods shaved a sliver from their heart and chose a soul to wrap around that shard of divinity. Each Heart carries obsidian buried in their own heart, linking them to their god.

When a god's Heart dies, that god reclaims the sliver and chooses a new soul from the pool of dead. During times of war a god's Heart cannot be reborn until a new leader of the pantheon has been chosen. When a god's Heart dies, that god no longer competes to become head of the pantheon.

—The Book of Bastion

Akachi bent his nagual power to becoming a great skyvyrm. Here, in this created reality, it didn't matter that he had never studied one in a menagerie. It didn't matter that he had not painstakingly carved a figurine to work as a focus, or that none of the right drugs pumped through in his veins. This was a game of wits and imagination, and this old man had no comprehension of what he was up against.

Darakai studied the colossal skyvyrm, and then thinned the air to the point both men could barely breathe. He increased the pull of the earth.

His vast wings suddenly useless, Akachi plummeted to the ground, crashing into the sands and shattering bones. He squirmed, trying to writhe through the desert to reach the old man, but the skyvyrm's body weighed too much. Flopping and twitching in the sand, gasping for air, he became a poisonous viper. Though he still felt the pull of gravity, it became less crushing.

Darakai was gone.

He's invisible.

Akachi laughed at the pitiful attempt and tested the air with his tongue.

Nothing.

No heat of life beyond a surprising number of insects hiding in the sands.

Was that true? Akachi always imagined the Bloody Desert a place of endless death. Did insects live out there, feeding off one another, much as dead gods and demons fed off banished souls?

Surely not!

He's doing this. He added life to the desert for some reason.

To hide. That had to be it. Darakai must be one of these many insects and spiders Akachi sensed.

Akachi the viper lifted its head above the sands. The desert, it turned out, teemed with life. He felt movement through the scales of his body, heard it through the bones of his jaw. A larger than normal spider dug a hole near where he had last seen the Heart of the Lord of the Root.

Akachi knew that type of spider. It was one commonly studied by nagual due to its size and deadly poison.

Unimaginative.

Normally, Akachi would have turned into a bird and snatched the spider from above, holding it helpless. Between the thin air and the pull of gravity Darakai had written into this reality, nothing could fly.

Thinking of Bihotz Blindatua, his pangolin spirit-animal, Akachi changed the rules, turning his scales into overlapping plates of impenetrable armour. Still wearing the shape of the viper, he approached the buried spider. Something tickled, along the length of his spine. Looking back the length of his serpentine body, Akachi saw several spiders had climbed aboard, as if they sought to ride him. He slowed, frowning. Had he been mistaken about which spider was Darakai?

More spiders scampered onto his back, hairy legs pulling at the plates of his armour. The spiders grew, became stronger, and fought to lever him open.

Startled, Akachi further armoured himself, turning the length of his body to stone so no opening existed. Thousands of spiders scampered onto his back and, for a moment, he laughed at the futility of their struggles. They grew heavier, pinning him helpless beneath their weight.

Too late, Akachi saw his mistake. The spiders were *all* Darakai. He lay trapped beneath the pactonal. While he was safe for now, armoured in unbending stone, he was also helpless. The spiders became huge amorphous slugs, growing in density and weight.

He couldn't move, couldn't escape.

If I change into something less armoured, I'll die crushed beneath them.

The air further thinned, the taste of it changing, and Akachi writhed and gasped, drowning. Did slugs breathe? He didn't know. Fat damp bodies pinned him to the sand. The stone of his armour groaned and creaked as the pressure built.

He needed to change! He needed to be something stronger than stone, something that didn't breathe!

Akachi gasped, twitching.

Nothing was stronger than stone! Everything breathed!

He'd failed. This old pactonal bested him easily. He failed his god. His father was right. He was nothing. He was endless disappointment. Cloud Serpent sent him to fetch the Staff of the Fifth Sun so he might kill the Heart of Mother Death in the underworld, and Akachi failed before even *trying* to reach that realm.

The staff.

He'd left it lying upon his lap as he sat across from Firash.

What had Zalika said about the staff in his dream? It was formed of a dead god's heart. The god of the sun.

Weather control.

Akachi changed the rules of this shared reality so those items he had contact with back in the stone world of Bastion were here with him now. He felt a startled gelatinous twitch run through the weight of slugs as the staff appeared alongside him, touching his stone body.

Akachi laughed and again rewrote the laws. He became stone, through and through.

He called a storm.

Clouds, unlike anything he'd ever seen, foreign to his life of endless blue sky and raging sun, blanketed the world. Cold winds whipped up, spinning sanguine sands into a bloody dance. Lightning cracked far above.

Cackling with glee, Akachi screamed for more.

Darakai may have written thin air into this reality, but the gods cared nothing for the whims of man. The Staff of the Fifth Sun was something beyond. It existed both within and without this dream-world. Blood-stone, the heart of a dead god, pulsed with life.

More! screamed Akachi.

Twisting whips of lightning lashed Bastion's Sand Wall, charring stone, leaving bright lines of cherry-red heat.

He had an idea.

Akachi summoned lightning. He commanded it. He owned it. The weather of this false reality was his plaything, the staff's divine power leaving Darakai helpless.

Akachi drew crackling bolts to himself, gloried in the chaos of it as it cracked the sky over and over. In moments his stone body glowed with heat, traceries of fire dancing the length of him. The staff protected its wielder. No act of sun or weather could harm him. He could call the very fire of the sun itself down to scorch the desert to glass and remain unharmed.

The damp slugs burned and crisped and smoked. They charred and fell away.

Darakai, Heart of the Lord of the Root, died in that dream-world, blasted to nothing. No longer did the Healer vie for control of the pantheon.

Once again himself, Akachi stood surrounded by endless sun-bleached bone. The sky above roiled and twisted to his desire and he wrote his rage upon the heavens. The power of a god filled him, coursed through his blood, a thousand times more addictive than the best narcotic.

Call the storm.

Smash Bastion to dust and ruin.

Akachi screamed with joy as he flailed at the Last City with coiling snakes of lightning.

He understood.

He understood what it was to be a god.

He understood why mortals never understood.

We are nothing.

A god explaining its plans to a man was like a man explaining to a chicken why he was about to slaughter it.

The gods weren't contradictory, they were unknowable. Everything Akachi believed, everything every mortal thought they knew, was a shadow of the truth.

We are—

His body twitched.

He couldn't breathe.

Akachi called the winds until red sand tore long gashes in the stone, erasing wards carved twenty-five thousand years ago.

And still he couldn't breathe.

Had he misjudged? Had Darakai tricked him?

Akachi's heart kicked in terror, sight collapsing into a buzzing black tunnel, all light fading to nothing.

As he died.

NURU - I AM BLASPHEMY

Enlil, Lord Wind, rose to domination during the fourth age. Often referred to as The Bright Age, this was humanity's pinnacle of civilization, never again to be achieved. Dedicated to the pursuit of equality, Father Justice forbid the building of temples, dismantled the concept of competition, and fostered an era of cooperation.

Sickened by millennium of progress, disgusted by the very concept of equality, a mismatched cabal of gods banded together and murdered Enlil. The nahual of Cloud Serpent hunted and killed the Keepers of Law, Lord Wind's priesthood. Southern Hummingbird's nahual took on the role of law-enforcement, bringing militant practices to the task. Sin Eater's priests redefined sin, becoming the arbiters of blasphemy.

The dark hand behind the coup, the Lord of the Near and Far, laid claim to dominance of the night winds.

Enlil was the last god of justice, the very concept forever murdered.

—The Loa Book of the Invisibles

Efra's thin arm, corded with ropes of hard muscle, locked tight around Kofi's throat.

The Loa sorcerer's eyes rolled back, and his body slumped limp.

"Stop," said Nuru.

Teeth gritted with effort, Efra growled an angry, "Why?" Veins stood out on her neck, her face purpling with effort.

"We need him," said Nuru.

"We don't. Just another fucking nahual. Killing Dirts. Thinks we're nothing."

She wasn't wrong.

Nuru hesitated. This young man used Growers like they were tools one might bend to any purpose. He threw them at the Turquoise Serpents rather than walk farther than he wanted. Maybe he was right. Maybe the next gate would also be held by the Guard. Maybe they all were. Maybe the only way through was killing, but he hadn't tried anything else. He saw a means of achieving his goal and grabbed at it without thought for the cost.

I should let her kill him.

In a half-dozen heartbeats, the sky darkened as the air grew thick. Clouds formed out of nothing, curling and growing, as the temperature plummeted.

Blinking up at the sky, Efra released her grip on Kofi. The Loa slumped to the ground, drawing a ragged sucking intake of breath.

Ignoring the gasping nahual, as if almost choking him to death was nothing, Efra stood at Nuru's side. The two women watched coalescing clouds blacken the sky.

Efra blinked in confusion. "It's not smoke."

All their lives the sky had been a dome of blue. That only changed when the fields burned. Now, just days later, they once again witnessed something new. But this was different. The air felt syrupy, tasted like a tenement basement on the coldest night. The hairs on Nuru's arms stood, and her skin tingled. The world teetered on edge, like it might snap beneath the strain.

With no narcotics in her blood, she couldn't sense the veil. Was this the result of some colossal sorcery? Had the curtain between realities been so sundered that one world now leaked into another?

With a blinding flash, forked bolts of actinic light stabbed down at Bastion, struck over and over at something in the Crafters' Ring just the other side of the Grey Wall. The sun blotted, the world fell to gloom, night in the middle of day, the streets lit only by the stuttering staccato of lightning.

"We should run," said Efra.

Neither woman moved.

Such a sight. The gods raged, flailing their anger at someone or something in the next ring. It was too directed to be anything else.

"It's going to…" Nuru couldn't remember the word. Water from the sky. The nahual used it in some of the sermons when talking about the world before it died.

"Rain," said Kofi, sitting up and rubbing his neck. He gawked up at the sky in wonder.

It ended as fast as it began, clouds scuttling away, scattering like frightened mice. By the time the Loa priest made it to his feet, the sun was back, the temperature climbing.

The streets were empty, everyone having fled the sudden storm.

"What happened?" asked Kofi. "Did I win?"

"Win?" Nuru turned on the young man. "Did you fucking *win*?"

He retreated before her wrath.

Efra stood, head cocked to one side, watching. A small smile played about her lips, the scar twisting it to something vicious.

"No," said Nuru. "You didn't fucking win. You killed scores of Growers and you achieved nothing."

"The Serpents still hold the gate?" He looked like he didn't believe her, like he wanted to go check.

"Can I kill him now?" asked Efra.

"If he uses the rock like that again," said Nuru, "yes."

"You don't understand," Kofi protested, voice climbing in anger.

He stood tall, towered over her. So much bigger and stronger than either of them. He might be Loa, but he was still a nahual, still owned that stone certainty. Nuru wanted to cower before his wrath, apologize for… She didn't know what. For being Mother Death's Heart. For being here. For being alive. She wanted to apologize for everything! It was all her fault!

"This isn't some *squabble*," roared Kofi. "This is war! The lives of a few Growers, even a few hundred Growers—"

Something in Nuru cracked. "Are what?" she demanded, getting in his face.

She shoved him in the chest and followed when he stepped back.

"Insignificant?" she barked, pushing him again. "How many of us can you kill before it matters?"

She hit him, punched him in the chest. It hurt her hand, and the pain made her angrier. She hit him again. She slapped him, the palm of her hand stinging, his cheek red after the blow. She hit him again and again and he stood there, taking it. He didn't strike back, made no attempt to defend himself.

When tears leaked from his closed eyes, she stopped, glaring at him. Waiting.

"I'm sorry," he said.

"You throw away one more Grower life," said Nuru, "and I'm done. Heart or no, I don't care."

He nodded, eyes downcast, miserable.

"We'll try the next gate," said Nuru, spinning away and setting a fast pace. She didn't look back to see if Kofi followed.

Efra jogged to catch up. "You know he did that to impress you." When Nuru looked at her, confused, she added, "The sorcery. He was trying to show you how strong he is." She shrugged. "Boys are dumb as fuck."

Nuru thought of all the stupid shit she'd seen her boys do over the years. Efra, she decided, wasn't wrong.

They walked for half a day, keeping to the smaller alleys, and avoiding the main streets. After the storm, the sun returned with a vengeance as if angered by the interruption of its attempt to bake the world to dust. Thobe soaked in the sweat, Kofi silently following, they approached the next gate. When Nuru and Efra stopped, he lifted his head, looking around as if surprised. Seeing where they were, he approached the corner.

"They're Loa," he said over his shoulder, after checking who held the gate. "I recognize them. They're Chikelu's people."

Retreating from the corner, he gnawed on his lower lip.

"What's wrong, fat boy?" asked Efra. "These are your people. Let's go!"

"Chikelu is a Loa bishop. He must be at the tannery."

"So?" asked Efra.

"I'm not sure why he's here," said Kofi, darting a nervous glance at Nuru.

Efra raised an eyebrow. "You seem less than thrilled about this Chikelu."

"Mother doesn't like him. She says he's too full of himself. He thinks the revolution is all about him."

"Should we keep going?" asked Nuru. Hunger hollowed her. The thought of walking to another gate left her wanting to lie down and wait for the world to end.

"No," answered Kofi. "We need to rest."

"We need food," said Efra.

"And water," agreed Nuru.

"Our church isn't far from this gate." Even with all his muscle and a lifetime of eating whatever it was they ate in the Priests' Ring that made them grow so big, Kofi looked exhausted. "Chikelu will look for an angle, some way to turn all this to his advantage." He looked to Nuru. "He won't let us into the Senators' Ring until he knows who and what you are."

"So?" asked Efra. "She's your Heart thing, right? She's important."

"I'm afraid he might try to take the carving," admitted Kofi.

The thought of someone else touching her carving left a cold anger festering deep in Nuru's gut. Another fucking nahual who knew better than all the stupid Dirts. Another man who would see the shell and then look through her, wonder how he might bend her to whatever purpose drove him.

"Mother believes in you," said Kofi. He hesitated, darting an embarrassed glance at Efra. "I believe in you," he added, quieter. "Chikelu can't be allowed to take it. No matter what he says or believes, he isn't the Heart."

"You have an idea," said Efra. "You're afraid it's a dumb idea, and you're probably right. But I'm tired and hungry and thirsty. So fucking spill it before I cut it out of you."

Kofi pulled a pouch of narcotics from within his thobe. He offered them to Nuru. "I think you should be prepared."

"He's a temple-trained nahualli," said Nuru.

"Tecolotl. But yes."

"I can't beat a temple-trained nahualli."

"You're Mother Death's Heart," he said, as if that answered her concerns. "If he tries to take it…" He hung his head in shame. "I don't think I can stop him on my own."

"Oh, that must have hurt to say," said Efra.

Nuru took the offered narcotics and shoved them into her mouth. She chewed fast and swallowed. "We'd better move before I start hallucinating."

The Loa at the gate recognized Kofi. Nuru and Efra were examined with doubtful eyes.

"Kuboka instructed me to deliver them to Subira, in the Senators' Ring."

The man in charge, his bald head dented and scarred like someone had tried to reshape it with a chunk of rock, pulled his lingering attention from Nuru. "Chikelu will want to see them first." A necklace of scorpion figurines carved in stone hung about his neck.

Already the first hints of swirling smoke seeped up from Nuru's belly to kiss her heart. Her allies, feeling the veil thin, gathered, ready. Mother Death, slumbering deep in Nuru's gut, twitched with the first twinges of alertness.

"This is not Chikelu's concern," said Kofi, though his voice lacked confidence.

"You pass through his district with two pretty Dirt girls on your way to the turncoat," said the bald Loa. "It's his business."

"I am delivering—"

Fingering the scorpion figurines, the man cut him off with a wave. Gesturing at three other Loa, he said, "Come. Chikelu will decide."

Sagging, Kofi said nothing.

Two Loa in front, two following along behind, they were led to the gate. It didn't feel like an honour guard. It didn't feel like they were being protected. Nuru felt like a prisoner, a lamb being led to the slaughter.

Crude torches, flickering and guttering and spewing oily smoke, lined the long hall. Another group of Loa, dressed as Hummingbird Guard, awaited them at the far end. They nodded to the bald man as he passed.

Nuru, who never expected to see the Crafters' Ring in all her life, once again passed through the Grey Wall.

Led by a pair of Loa men dressed as Crafters, Nuru and Efra were ushered into what Kofi explained in hushed tones was a Tannery District. The air stank of rancid fur. Swarms of flies followed them, trying to crawl into their mouths and eyes. Crafters, dressed in orange and brown, hurried about their tasks, ignoring the flies like it was something one became accustomed to.

Brought to a low building with no windows and a flat roof, they entered. A tingling ran through Nuru and she realized they'd left the flies outside. A cloud of them buzzed about the entrance, apparently unable to enter.

The Loa led them through rooms of stretched hides, into twisting hallways, and down worn steps. In the Growers' Ring, the basement of every tenement was a single large space. Since Growers rarely dared venture down, she wasn't sure why the gods bothered. Here, beneath this tannery, warrens of passages wended away in every direction.

A rat's maze. Efra was right.

Guiding the group to a hall the size of many churches, they were brought before a stunningly handsome man. Square-jawed and tall, all hard lines and flat slabs of muscle, he was beautiful. Kind eyes, bright and intelligent, warm and sensitive, watched everything.

"Bishop Chikelu," said the bald Loa, nodding in greeting. "This boy," he waved a dismissive hand at Kofi, "was trying to smuggle these two women into the ring."

"I wasn't—"

Chikelu silenced Kofi with a look. This man understood power. He oozed confidence.

"Curiously," continued the bald man, "he seemed to want to avoid reporting to you. Even after being informed this district was yours."

Chikelu turned his attention on Efra. Looking her over, he said, "I think I'll stay out of arm's reach of that one. Don't much feeling like getting stabbed today."

Efra grinned. "Ask nice, and you could do the stabbing."

He laughed, utterly comfortable in the knowledge that of *course* women wanted him. "And you," he said, turning to Nuru. His eyes narrowed. "Are you smoky?"

Before she could answer, Kofi stepped between her and Chikelu. "We are passing through, Bishop. My mother, Kuboka, instructed me to deliver these two to Subira."

Glistening black. A twisted sky, clouds roiling as they burned, oceans red with blood.

Oceans?

Nuru saw endless water, colossal crashing waves, stained with the lives of millions.

"Why these two?" asked Chikelu, still watching her with concern.

Nuru fought for balance, strove to control the gut-churning spiral of reality. Nothing was real. It was all an illusion. The permanence of stone was a lie. Chaos lay at the heart of all existence. Fear gripped her.

I am blasphemy!

She felt smoky to the core of her soul, tenuous and unreal.

"It doesn't matter," said Kofi. "They're just...they're Dirts. Mother said—"

"I don't give a shit what Kuboka wanted." snapped Chikelu. "She's dead. They're all dead, her whole coterie."

Kofi stood rooted in shock. "No." He looked to Nuru, looked away. Found a corner of wall and stared at it, blinking, fighting back tears. "No."

"They ran into Turquoise Serpents. I'm sorry, son," said Chikelu, sounding not at all apologetic. "Whatever authority you *thought* you had died with her." He approached Kofi, stood over him, forced him to make eye contact through sheer dominating force of will. "I know it hurts, but her death will make you stronger. She was loved and respected. Her death will unite the Loa." He put a hand on Kofi's shoulder. "Bottle it up, save it. Let it fuel your sorcery. Use it against our enemy."

Anger flared in Nuru. *Fucking idiot men and their need to hide their pain. Oh, I lost someone so now I'm stronger. As long as I don't feel anything* now.

Kofi had bragged about how Loa sorcery was better because they channelled their emotions instead of relying on narcotics. It was an excuse not to feel when it mattered the most, a reason to hide away one's emotions until they could be useful.

"Fucking cowards," said Nuru.

The room stopped, all eyes on her.

"Feel your pain," she said. "Own it. Only then can you start to heal. You're all greedy power-hungry fuckers. None of you deserve to rule."

Chikelu raised an eyebrow. "Interesting." Turning back to Kofi, he said, "Why are you taking them to a tecuhtli?"

Tecuhtli? Did he mean this Subira?

Red eyed, Kofi looked from Nuru to the bishop. "She is Mother Death's Heart."

Chikelu blinked, barked a hard cough of sputtering laughter. "The beautiful smoky one with the mouth?"

"Her name is Nuru," said Kofi.

"The Queen of Bastion chose a *Dirt*?" Turning away from Kofi, Chikelu shook his head, grinning at the others as if sharing some joke.

The gathered Loa laughed dutifully.

"She's a street-sorcerer," added Kofi.

"Oh, no doubt. No doubt this Dirt whore is a force to be reckoned with! Gods," he uttered a rueful chuckle. "I understand *you* falling for this ridiculous lie. You're young, and no doubt she's fucked you blind and stupid. But Kuboka? Tell me your mother didn't fall for this shit."

Kofi's eyes hardened; his breathing slowed. He stood straight. "She is Mother Death's Heart. You'd be well to—"

"She'd fuck a goat for a loaf of softbread. Don't fool yourself."

"I am blasphemy," whispered Nuru.

"Well," said Chikelu, "you certainly have the body for it."

"Show him the carving," said Kofi. "It's the only way."

Smoky and lost, the world spinning around her, the veil so thin that spirit animals and allies prowled in the smoke, Nuru fumbled for the carving. Finally, she managed to retrieve it, lifting the stone spider for all to see.

Chickelu's breath caught, his eyes widening.

Above the jagged and barbed legs of a hunting spider sat the curved form of a young woman. Naked, and unafraid, unashamed. Proud. Powerful.

Chikelu held out a hand, demanding. "Give it to me. Your true purpose is served. You have delivered the Queen to where she should be." He studied Nuru. "She knows she isn't the Heart. The Queen's Heart would never doubt, never quiver in terror at what must be done. The Queens Heart would be strong." He flexed bulging muscles. "The Queen's Heart would be brave, and confident. The Great War is coming. The Last Great War."

The Last War. She'd heard the words a thousand times in nahual sermons.

"I thought humanity fought its last war twenty-five thousand years ago," said Nuru.

Chikelu laughed again, mocking "Hardly. How can someone with a Dirt's knowledge of history lead humanity? Tell us, girl, what do you know of politics?"

"What are politics?" Nuru asked.

"What do you know of economies?" demanded the bishop.

"What are economies?"

"What do you know of leadership?"

Nuru stared up at this incredibly handsome and confident man. "I know people who are afraid follow the loudest man. Even if he's an idiot."

Chikelu's eyes narrowed. "You can't be the Heart. You're nothing."

"I agree," said Nuru. *I am the nothing.*

She lifted the carving, held it before Chikelu's greedy eyes. He couldn't look away. Everything he ever wanted sat in the palm of her hand. Right there. So close.

"Take it," said Nuru. "You're right. I'm just a Dirt."

The veil pulsated around her, a great throbbing wound in reality.

Slick black boiled in her gut. The carving seemed to stare at her, waiting. Ember eyes. Flawless midnight flesh. Curved perfection, more beautiful than Nuru could imagine.

The world stepped back, retreated.

Fled.

Somewhere, Kofi was yelling. Several Loa had grabbed him, pinning his arms behind his back. Efra stood mute, watching with that crooked scarred smile.

"Give me the carving." A voice, deep and melodious. Calm and commanding.

A man's hand, reaching to take, to claim. To possess.

Nuru closed her hand on the statue.

Stone, cold and dead in her fist.

"I have an idea," she said. "How about we let Mother Death decide."

AKACHI - A LIFE OF WAR

Separating church from economy from state, skilled labour from the uneducated masses, Bastion's walls are the pillars upon which civilization is built.

Out beyond the Sand Wall lies the past. There is no gate in that wall because there is no going back. The gods, at the heart, are the future.

Like the ox wears blinders to keep it from straying, to save it from distractions, the walls focus our faith.

—The Book of Bastion

Akachi's eyes snapped open. He lay on the floor of some abandoned Crafter tenement. Omphile knelt at his side, one hand pinching his nose closed, the other clamped over his mouth. She grinned down at him, grey eyes bright with glee.

Body kicking and twitching with the desperate need for air, he grabbed her wrists, tried to pull them away. For the first time he understood some small part of what it was to be a Turquoise Serpent. All his life he'd studied, read ancient texts, learned the nuances of blending and preparing narcotics. He spent days sitting motionless in contemplation of some minutia pertaining to the gods, or Bastion, or the veil. Not Omphile. She spent her whole life training and fighting. Her arms were carved from ebony, cords of rigid muscle.

His, a life of complacency and ease.

Hers, a life of war.

Omphile grinned harder at his feeble struggles.

Vision fading, lungs sucking at nothing, he heard the bass rumble of thunder over the pounding roar of his heart. Through the window he saw a sky of coal-blackened granite lit by the sudden stabbing flash of lightning. Melokuhle and Lubanzi stood, backs to him, staring out in awe.

The dream had followed him.

The Staff of the Fifth Sun brought storm clouds to Bastion.

A high-pitched whine built in his skull as sight faded to black. He sank away, drowning in nothing.

Releasing her grip on his mouth, Omphile leaned in and pressed her lips to his. He drew a desperate inhalation from her lungs. She inhaled, pulling his breath back into her.

Lifting her head just enough to speak, she said, "You breathed my soul." Her lips brushed his, feather light. "You know me now. We are forever one. One breath. One heart. One life."

She kissed him, hard and fierce. Breaking off, she whispered into his ear. "Firash said that when the skies broke, and lightning licked the stone of Bastion, I would know my purpose. I thought he was full of shit. I see it now." She licked an earlobe. "He was right. I am yours. Forever. I will serve and protect. You will be a god and I will stand at your side."

A god.

Staring up at her, Akachi saw no guile in those grey eyes.

Does she know I am Cloud Serpent's Heart?

How could she?

God-touched, anything was possible.

Already the storm outside was fading, clouds breaking up and scattering in the dry desert wind. No more lightning broke the sky.

Omphile stood in one smooth and effortless motion, looking down at him fondly as if she hadn't just tried to kill him.

Or had she? His body's need for air was what woke him from the dream.

She saved me. She saved me from damaging Bastion.

"You did that," whispered Omphile, studying him with awe and worship. "You brought the storm."

Captain Melokuhle turned from the window. "I thought, for a

moment, it might actually rain." She darted a half expectant glance over her shoulder like she feared to miss it. "Can you imagine? Rain? Like the Book said it did before the world died?"

"What *was* that?" asked Lubanzi. "It was centred on this tenement block. Were we under attack?"

Melokuhle shook her head in denial. "The tecolotl can't be that so powerful." She sounded doubtful.

"I was attacked by a pactonal who sought to kill me in my dreams," said Akachi. "I was forced to defend myself with powerful sorcery." He was careful not to mention the staff.

The heat returned with a vengeance. All thought of rain dried up and withered to nothing.

In less than one hundred heartbeats the sky was clear again, as if nothing had happened.

The Serpents accepted his word without question.

The staff controls the weather.

He knew it to be true. And not just in the dream-world. The staff could call storms and lightning. He felt confident that, if he wanted to, he could make it rain.

I could put out the fires in the Growers' Ring!

He could soak the fields in rain. Life would return to the Life Ring. Growers might return to the fields!

He imagined all Bastion celebrating as war between the rings was averted.

Except that was not what his god commanded him to do.

Mother Death would attempt to reclaim the underworld. That would be his chance to kill her Heart. Doing so might cast the god once again from the city. At the least, with her Heart dead, she would be in no position to rule the pantheon. He had no idea what would happen after. His god gave him a task, and he would obey.

Climbing to his feet, Akachi went to the window. Out there, far beyond the reach of his eyes, were the fields of the Growers' Ring. Even at this distance the columns of churning smoke were visible. How big must they be that he saw them from the Crafters' Ring.

Brow crinkled in concern, Lubanzi knelt at Firash's side. The tezcat hadn't awoke.

Some of the tattooed eyes followed Lubanzi. Some focussed on the Captain. Most watched Omphile, blinking, and rolling to keep her in sight.

Lubanzi touched the bald man's cheek. "Oh," he said. "He's dead."

"Impossible," said Akachi. "He was there, in the dream-world, with me."

"Perhaps," said Captain Melokuhle, resting a hand on the pommel of her sword, "you'd better tell us exactly what happened."

NURU - HOLLOWED HOPES

Dead gods beyond count populate the Bloody Desert. Most died long before the last war began.

Since then, however, the death of every fallen god can be laid at the feet of one. Even his name is a lie, for he is the enemy of all sides.

Obsidian Butterfly. Mother of Birds and Butterflies. Seven Serpent. Mother Harvest, god of the Life Ring, Protector of the Growers. Grandfather Coyote, Lord of Tricksters. Loviatar, Mother Disease. Áltsé hashké, Father Cunning. Eingana, Mother Snake.

On and on, the list continues.

—The Loa Book of the Invisibles

Last time Nuru called Mother Death, she knelt on the street in the Growers' Ring as her friends battled the Hummingbird Guard. She'd panicked, terrified of failure. Focussing on the carving had been difficult, her attention continually drawn to the violence not a dozen strides away.

Things had changed since then.

Nuru was a crack in the ancient wards of Bastion. She was a conduit, a tear in the weakened veil protecting the Last City from the death and dead beyond. It wasn't much, but it was enough. In churches all through Bastion, the Loa sacrificed in the Queen's name and she fed. In the Growers' Ring, the Loa jammed refuse into the blood gutters, redirecting the sluggish flow into their own hidden temples. They wrote ancient words in long dead languages, payers and incantations barely understood.

And she fed.

Though nowhere near her true might, this was no longer the starved husk of a god that Nuru first called. This was a voracious force, a hunger older than time, a devourer of worlds.

Cooling blood, thick and largely robbed of its power, was one thing.

A sacrifice, combined with the proper rituals, was something else entirely.

Fresh murder, the slaughter of fleeing souls, the screams as comprehension dawned and they understood the sudden finality of true mortality, was a feast.

Horror and fear were a kind of worship.

Nuru called, and Mother Death came in a rage.

Chickelu, self-proclaimed bishop in *her* church, was nothing. A gnat of a life, annoying in its attempts to insert itself into her plans.

The Queen of Bastion stood before her worshippers, obsidian-tipped legs, barbed and vicious, skittering on stone in a nausea-inducing dance. Bulbous and glistening, her abdomen swung low, mesmerizing. Her top half, a beautiful woman, soft and full, curved with youth, skin gleaming like the blackest oil. A silken waterfall of sable hair hung to her hips, swaying in time with the dance, concealing, and teasing.

The mortals in the room fell to their knees, prostrated themselves before their god. Nuru gloried in the power, basked in the worship.

Chikelu dared to look up from his place on the floor, and Mother Death drove a barbed leg through his skull, lifting the dangling and twitching ruin of his body. She held the corpse aloft, effortless power, and devoured its fleeing soul. With a flick of a leg, she tossed it aside. Chikelu spun, boneless and wet, into the wall. Leaving a crimson smear, he slid to the floor.

The sweet scent of blood and souls filled her, but fewer than there should have been. Her city, crammed with teaming life when last she stood within its walls, stank of gutted stagnation. Her foolish children broke the laws she lay down for them, the restrictions on harvesting and hoarding souls. They would be punished. There were, she realized, no longer enough mortals within Bastion to feed even the ragged remnants of her pantheon. The gods would have to be culled if any were to survive.

That was for later. First, she must feed.

Someone squealed in terror as spattered blood rained upon them. The Queen reared onto her hind legs, punching two forelegs through the woman's gut and hoisted her into the air. This time, she was careful not to snuff the pathetic existence too quickly. Pinioned, it writhed and screamed. Mother Death lifted the woman high, and Nuru leaned back to drink the spill of red life. Hot blood coated her, and she shone, slicked in gore, midnight hair clinging seductively to every curve.

Mother Death inhaled the soul and discarded the empty carcass.

Blood and souls and worship.

A roomful of Loa knelt before their god and the Queen fed off their fear and devotion.

She killed them.

She killed all of them.

Every tiny mortal spark that dared impede her Heart in even the slightest. She made them suffer, each and every one. She tortured them, tearing apart their dreams and ambitions, shredding their sense of self before finally gutting them. The deepest cleanest joy imaginable filled Nuru until she felt like her heart would burst. When the dead lay heaped and scattered, torn limbs littering the floor, she bent to drink from the gutters.

Sated, if just for the moment, Mother Death took in her surroundings. This was a sad, pathetic excuse for a church. There wasn't even a real sacrificial altar. The place stunk of old death and pitiful animal souls not worth her time.

Two sparks remained, one kneeling, forehead pressed to cold stone, waiting. The other stood watching, smirking, scar stretched in wry amusement at what she'd seen.

Mother Death studied the kneeling boy. He meant nothing. Hollowed hopes and dreams, the typical distractions of a life empty of meaning beyond service to the divine. She could snuff that flawed soul, and it would mean nothing.

He's useful, Nuru told the Queen.

Mother Death looked within the boy, peeled away his delusions of self, and saw the raw meat of truth within. He worshipped her Heart. He would sacrifice himself for her without hesitation.

Yes, said Mother Death. *Useful.*

Unlike most, this boy understood the pointless futility of mortal existence and found purpose in service. He lived in terror of never being given the opportunity to die for something that truly mattered.

She would give him that opportunity.

There was more. That strange emotion that mortals carried like it was precious, cradled and protected as if it was somehow special, like it fucking mattered. It lurked beneath his worship.

No, she saw, that wasn't quite right. It wasn't beneath. Rather, it supported that worship. It was the *reason.*

He loved her Heart.

Grunting disgust, Mother Death turned on the scarred girl.

Caught somewhere between divinity and mortality, between the nothing Nuru existence and the eternity of the Mother of the Universe, she hesitated.

The god saw that Efra, a brief gnat spark of will and drive, was unlike the others.

Efra held none of their soft delusions. She *knew.* She understood futility and didn't care. Efra saw impermanence and was unmoved. She could die today, or years from now and none of it meant anything.

The girl held something, waved it at Mother Death, threatening.

"Give me my friend back," said Efra, "or I'll fucking gut you."

Seeing Efra pulled Nuru closer to the surface. For the first time, she sensed something other than ravenous rage and hunger from the Queen: fondness. This god, this soul-devouring monster, *liked* Efra.

She doesn't know what I know.

If Mother Death discovered Efra was Smoking Mirror's Heart, she'd snuff her without hesitation. One thought, one word, and the girl would be gone, Father Discord removed from contention.

"You remind me of better days." Mother Death spoke in silk and venom. "Back in the first centuries of Bastion, we broke souls. Katle, men and women capable of anything." She laughed at the memories. "They became greedy and turned on us. They plotted, thinking they could hide their intentions."

No longer threatening, Efra studied the god with narrowed eyes, one hand rubbing at where the scar crossed her lips.

"Little Efra," said the god, "is hiding things too. I smell deceit. I taste the lies in you." The god shrugged, blood running in rivers, following the curves of her, to fall to the floor. Gore knotted her sodden hair, dripped from her chin. "Mortal emotions are such sad and fleeting things, shorter, even, than your pathetic lives." Ignoring the knife, Mother Death leaned close to sniff at Efra. "Little katle. You will serve my Heart well. But learn the lessons of those long dead, or suffer their fate."

She trusts you, Mother Death told Nuru. *She understands the holes in her. She knows she can't know. She trusts you to know for her.*

Nuru knew another truth: Efra was not as simple as the god thought.

AKACHI - BROKEN IN THE RIGHT WAY

Some tecolotl stones can be used over and over and have been passed down for generations. Others shatter or crack after the first use. Such stones are incredibly valuable.

For twenty-five thousand years the nahual have collected those stones useful in sorcery and hidden them away in the Vault of Baetylus. Now, the Loa scrounge for scraps.

A time will come when there are so few stones in circulation that rebellion will be impossible.

—The Book of Bastion

"What happened in the dream-walk?" demanded Captain Melokuhle. She stood poised, perfectly balanced, ready for violence.

Needing time to think, to process everything he'd seen and learned, Akachi said, "I have no idea."

He recalled the obelisk of jade, shot through with cracks and rot. A skilled huateteo would have known exactly what it meant, but Akachi was left to guess. It could have been anything. Perhaps a manifestation of some deep psychological wound the tezcat bore. Or maybe it had more to do with Akachi than Firash. Had his disappointment in the Turquoise Serpents coloured his dream-world?

Firash shattered just before Cloud Serpent's arrival.

The god may have unintentionally killed the nahual with his arrival. The tezcat might have been the innocent victim of bad timing, brushed aside by a god who desired to speak to his Heart.

Melokuhle advanced. "How did he die?"

"I… I don't know," said Akachi, retreating before her wrath.

She lost another member of her squad. She carried the wound deep. If Firash appeared as cracked and rotting jade, what would the captain's soul look like?

All the dead tezcat's tattooed eyes locked on Omphile and she blew a kiss to the corpse.

Melokuhle ceased her advance, confused.

"The Cloud Serpent nahual didn't kill him," said the assassin, coming to Akachi's defence. "You can see it plainly in his surprise."

"Thank you."

"He's not smart enough to be a good liar," she added.

Lubanzi pushed past his captain, grabbed Akachi by the collar. Not a big man, he still had the years of strength and training of a Turquoise Serpent. "You killed him! He showed you something in the future and you killed him for it! Captain, we can't trust him."

Eyes narrowed in doubt, Melokuhle looked from Omphile to the dead tezcat.

Akachi's thoughts raced. If he told them about Cloud Serpent's arrival, they'd wonder why the Lord of the Hunt visited a lowly nahualli. They might begin to suspect what he was. If they figured it out, they'd kill him. They'd have to.

He struggled to find something to say. "Firash showed me—"

Lubanzi lifted Akachi off his feet like it was nothing, and Akachi realized the youth was only skinny and weak looking in comparison to the other Serpents.

"He saw you betray us," Lubanzi snarled. "He saw your true purpose."

Omphile snorted. "Don't be ridiculous. None of the other nahualli get the same level of training as the Serpents. In the dream-world, Akachi would be no match for Firash."

Swallowing the urge to argue or defend himself, Akachi remained silent.

"Then he ambushed him," said Lubanzi, releasing Akachi and turning on his fellow Serpent. "Caught him by surprise. Like those fucking Loa that got us! Firash made mistakes!"

"Lubanzi," said Melokuhle, voice tired, hand falling from her sword, "stop. Firash led us here. For whatever reason, he brought us to Akachi." She looked down at the corpse, eyes bleeding pain. "We have to trust him."

She's cracking. They're all cracking.

"You saw the way he was, near the end," said Melokuhle. "I think he foresaw this."

"I very much doubt that," muttered Omphile.

Except her. She alone embodies what it is to be a Turquoise Serpent.

Only Omphile wasn't a disappointment to his expectations.

The Captain shot Omphile an annoyed look. "He knew exactly how the night would end and went through with it anyway." She sounded confident in the statement, but her eyes betrayed her.

It suddenly occurred to Akachi that this could work to his advantage. The man who led these Serpents to Akachi, the only one who knew why, was dead.

"Firash showed me Mother Death," said Akachi. "She is coming. She seeks to claim the underworld for her own." His heart slammed in his chest with excitement. Such a beautiful plan, and Firash's death made it all possible. *Cloud Serpent, I am humbled by your prescience!* "Only we can stop her. He showed me that."

All eyes were on Akachi, expectant.

"He's lying," said Lubanzi. "Fuck this shit. Let's go home."

"We were *sent,*" said Melokuhle. "We are the Turquoise Serpents, chosen of Southern Hummingbird. Nahual of Father War, we fight at his side in this life and the next."

"And the next," repeated the assassin.

"Nothing will stop us," concluded Captain Melokuhle.

"Not even death," added Omphile, standing at the Captain's side and sneering disgust at the otochin.

"Not even death," agreed Melokuhle, standing taller, as if the idea of dying for something made everything better. "Good people died bringing us to this moment. If we give up now, we've failed them. We've failed a lifetime of training. We've failed Southern Hummingbird."

"My friends are dead," growled Lubanzi. "Fuck Southern Hummingbird."

"Omphile," said Melokuhle, "if Lubanzi blasphemes again, kill him."

Omphile's sword slid soundlessly from its scabbard. Grey eyes. God-touched. Assassin of Father War. A smile teased the corners of her lips.

She wants *to kill him.*

If Lubanzi said one wrong word, made one wrong move, Omphile, who'd grown up with him, trained beside him her entire life, would murder him without hesitation.

Fists clenched, shoulders hunched, Lubanzi looked from Omphile to his Captain and back to the assassin. The fight went out of him, shoulders sagging in defeat. "You don't... We could... Fuck." Shaking his head as if disappointed, he strode from the room.

Returning his attention to Melokuhle, Akachi said, "We can defeat Mother Death. We can banish her once again. But we must do it in the underworld. Firash showed me that."

"How?" asked the Captain. "How can we possibly fight a god?"

Unwilling to mention the staff, Akachi said, "We don't have to fight the god. All we have to do is kill one little Dirt girl: her Heart."

"If she's the Queen's Heart," said Omphile, "then I seriously doubt she's just 'one little Dirt girl.'"

"She is a street-sorcerer," admitted Akachi. "I bested her once already, before she brought Mother Death into Bastion."

They stared at him in horror.

"Mother Death is returned?" asked Melokuhle. "She has breached the wards and is within the city?"

Akachi nodded. "I almost managed to banish her but was defeated. I misjudged, didn't understand what I battled." So many aspects of that encounter he kept to himself. The stone of self-destruction. All the badly blended narcotics in his system. "This time it will be different."

"How?" demanded the Captain.

"For Mother Death to reclaim the underworld, her Heart will have to be there to call her. We will be there first, waiting. When the Heart comes, we will kill her. The Queen's foothold in Bastion will be severed, and she'll once again be banished." Akachi took a deep breath, thoughts whirling in a mad dance of possibilities and potentials. Inspiration. "Firash said I died in almost every future he saw. But if I die defeating Mother Death, if I die saving Bastion, my death will at least have meant something."

It would never come to that. Akachi knew in his blood he was destined to be the next Heart's Mirror.

Captain Melokuhle's gaze hardened. "We have to make the trip to the underworld."

Akachi hadn't had time to think it through, but it made sense. "I agree."

"The only way to do that," said Omphile, grey eyes glinting with excitement, "is to die."

Melokuhle ignored her. "Where can we find a powerful tecuhtli?"

"I don't know this ring at all," Akachi admitted.

"We'll visit the nearest church of Father Death and ask. If we get lucky, the nahual will be useful." Melokuhle glanced after Lubanzi. "I'll see if he's done skulking."

Shoulders bent under the strain, she left.

So unlike Yejide. In his ignorance, Akachi had assumed all Hummingbird captains would be cut from the same cloth, and the legendary Turquoise Serpents would be cut from stone.

They weren't. If anything, their lives of rigid training left them fragile.

"If I die defeating Mother Death," said Omphile, doing a surprisingly good imitation of Akachi's deeper voice, "my death will at least have meant something." She snorted. "Great speech. I think the Captain believed you. You're broken in exactly the way Bastion needs her hero to be broken."

Too close to Zalika's cutting opinion, the words stung. "I'm not broken." The stumps of the fingers of his left hand drew his eye.

"Of course you are. That's why we're so good together."

"We're not. I'm not."

"Yes, we are. And yes, you are. Look." She pursed her lips in thought, looking for the right words. "You think broken is bad. It isn't. Not when you have to do the things we're going to have to do."

"Just because I'm dedicated—"

She snorted a mocking laugh. "You'll do anything to save the Last City, no matter the cost." She raised an eyebrow. "Tell me I'm wrong."

He couldn't. "Nothing else matters," said Akachi.

"Normal people would hesitate. Normal people would be appalled at the cost."

How many times had he already turned his back on people in need because his task was bigger than saving a single life? Or scores of lives. Or thousands.

"They'd give up," Omphile added. "They'd *fail*." Grabbing his ruined hand, she kissed the palm. "You think normal *whole* people can be heroes?" She snorted in mockery. "You have to be broken to risk everything to save the world. That's the truth. Heroes are broken. You're a hero."

Uncomfortable as her assessment made Akachi, he couldn't argue.

Movement caught his attention. Firash's tattooed eyes still followed the assassin.

"Why do the eyes watch you?"

"Because I killed him," answered Omphile with a careless shrug. "Slipped a needle of hardened bone through his ear as he sat there, help-less." She sighed, a soft and wistful sound. "Watching him die, bit by bit, as his thoughts fell apart, was something new. I've never done it that way before." She glanced at Akachi. "You know how it is. You study the books. You know how. But when it comes time to actually do it…"

Thinking of his first sacrifice, Akachi said, "It's more difficult than you think."

"What? No. It was easy. So easy."

Firash's tattooed eyes slid closed, as if her admission of guilt was all they'd been waiting for.

"Why?" he asked. "Why kill him. He was one of you."

"There's only one of me." She touched Akachi's arm, a tentative caress. "Anyway, he had to die. We couldn't chance him seeing the right future."

The *right* future? What did she think would happen?

Omphile smiled fondly at the corpse. "It's funny, you know. He saw so many futures that he never really took any of them seriously. But I did."

"What do you mean?"

"He once said he saw a future where I killed him. We laughed about it. He said that was the darkest future, the one in which humanity murdered the gods."

A fist squeezed Akachi's heart tight.

Cloud Serpent said the Heart of Mother Death killed Her Skirt is Stars.

The pantheon hadn't changed in twenty thousand years, and now two gods had been killed in less than a week.

Wiggling the stumps of his fingers, Akachi considered the insane risks he'd taken, the massive quantities of narcotics, the number of times he'd skirted brain-burn.

Maybe Omphile wasn't completely wrong.

But if he was going to save the last of humanity, then surely the ends justified any means.

"Broken," he whispered. "In the right way."

NURU - STONE AND STORM

Dead gods and dead names.
She Who is Black.
She Who is Death.
She is the embodiment of the endless hunger of time.
She is the Mother, and yet she devours all.

—The Loa Book of the Invisibles

Mother Death retreated, left Nuru drowning in a murky swamp of narcotics.

Nuru clawed for reality, tried to return to the worn stone certainty of Bastion, and lost her grip. She slipped away, sinking ever deeper.

She stood in obsidian caves, every surface sharp enough to cut deep. The earth breathed, the slow inhalations of stone and storm. In black glass reflections she saw thousands of herself, repeated forever, shards of a soul trapped in smoke.

A man stood before her, raw and glistening with blood, his flesh having been carefully cut away. Lidless, his eyes were huge, gleaming white like polished stones, pupils dilated with black madness.

The Flayed One.

Smoking Mirror spoke in clashing discord and grinding glass. His words, beyond hearing, beyond the comprehension of mortal minds, wrote images in time.

War.

There can be no Last *War,* he said, speaking in her thoughts, using the voice of her mind.

Or had *she* thought that?

Impossible to know.

Was it true? Could there be no last war? Would there always be one more?

Yes. Until the last god is gone.

Nuru stood in a world of night.

The underworld lay sprawled before her, rivers of blood, great fields of marching corpses. The manner of their deaths remained evident. The dead wore their wounds. Crushed skulls. Severed limbs. Some crawled along behind the main force, yet still they came.

The armies stretched out forever, from horizon to horizon.

More dead here, than living in all Bastion.

Battalions of the Hummingbird Guard, endless ranks of Turquoise Serpents. Behind them towered Father War. A blue-green helm like the skull of a hummingbird crowned his coal-black head. In his right hand he held a staff that was sometimes wood, sometimes a writhing viper. In his left he clutched a slab of obsidian polished to a mirror-like finish.

"For twenty-five thousand years," said Smoking Mirror, voice wet and clipped with the absence of lips, "Father Terror hoarded the souls of his favourite warriors. He has planned this day for a very long time."

Father Terror. Father War. The Left Hand.

Southern Hummingbird.

Across the blasted ruin of the underworld, a reality of perpetual night and pain, stood Face Painted with Bells. Taller than one hundred men, smooth stones sunk into her flawless flesh, she was a goddess of beauty marred only by the ragged bleeding stump of her missing hand. Her own legions of dead, pathetic and ragged in comparison to Father War's, stood arrayed about her.

"She is not a true god," said Smoking Mirror. "She does not *own* the souls."

Like the way the nahual owned everything. The way the Growers owned nothing.

Nuru swallowed her rage. Father Discord's choice of words betrayed him. Like all the gods, he thought of humanity as a possession. At best, he played at being on the Growers' side. That, she knew, would only last while they were useful.

I don't know how, but I'll kill you too.

The armies of corpses clashed, butchered each other. The Hummingbird Guard and Turquoise Serpents bore stone weapons, wore leather and jade armour.

"How do they still have their gear?" asked Nuru.

"Ancient rites, older than Bastion. That which you are buried with you retain in the underworld." He laughed, a cracked cackle. "Not that such things would help the Growers."

Dirt dead were taken by the nahual. Nuru didn't know what the priests did with them. Even if a Grower convinced their friends bury them out in some field, what would they take?

Bury me with my favourite stick, Nuru imagined some nameless Dirt asking. *Bury me with this clod of ox shit so I might burn it for warmth in the underworld.*

Efra, of course, would want to be buried with a weapon. Somehow, she always managed to have one.

Nuru watched the dead die once again, butchered in this war. The corpses of corpses littered the battlefield.

"What happens if you die in the underworld?" she asked the god.

"Your soul comes apart," he answered. "True death, forever. Beyond rebirth." Glistening eyes studied her. "Bastion cannot afford this war."

Ahh. Was it the city, or this god that couldn't afford a war?

Nuru watched the surge of battle. "What are they fighting for?"

"Southern Hummingbird seeks to wrestle the underworld from Face Painted with Bells."

"And you?" asked Nuru. "Where is your army?"

"I am the god of the small fight. If I am to be the enemy of both sides, I must not be capable of conquering either." Shoulders flayed of flesh, red ropes of muscle sliding and slick, shrugged. "I have no great armies."

He has Efra.

"If the underworld falls to Father War," continued the god, "he will claim the mantle of Death. Without control of the underworld, the Queen shall be defeated. Without her, the Last City will die." Smoking Mirror waved a peeled hand at the battle raging before them. "Only you can win this war."

"Me?"

Did he know about the dagger, the god-killer? How could he?

"How?" Nuru asked.

The god grinned, a horrific sight without skin and lips. "If you come to the underworld, you can call her. This is *her* realm. Even Father Death was but a pretender. Return her to her place of power, and she shall once again become the Queen of the Dead."

Nuru couldn't decide if this helped or hindered her own plans.

Cursing her ignorance, she asked, "How do I bring her to the under-world?"

"Easy!" The god grinned, exposed facial muscles writhing, teeth drawing her eye. "You die!"

"Of course."

Mother Death can't come to the underworld unless I use the carving and call her.

Nuru locked that information deep, kept her expression flat.

Could gods read the expressions of mortals?

Smoking Mirror was a mystery. Sometimes he was ancient and unknowable, so far beyond Nuru she couldn't hope to understand his intentions. Sometimes he was just another man, and a flawed one at that.

"Once you're there," he said, "you will call her as you do."

There, he'd said, not *here*. This was a dream. She wasn't really in the underworld. At the least it saved her from asking why she'd have to die if he could bring her here any time he wanted.

Turning from the god, Nuru studied Southern Hummingbird.

The chance to kill one more god.

How many times had she seen Birds crack skulls, smash joints to dust? Every time a nahual wanted to cut a throat or bleed a Dirt or throw someone from the Sand Wall, there was the Guard, hauling the prisoners, strapping them to the altar.

For thousands of years the Growers suffered at the hands of the Birds.

I'm going to kill their god.

"You don't have much time," said Smoking Mirror.

Returning her attention to the Flayed One, she studied those huge eyes. Shed of flesh, open to the world, he seemed strangely exposed, incapable of deceit. Veins throbbed, pumped blood. Muscles moved and slid, a nest of bloody snakes. Pale bone peeked out at the joints as if shy.

"Perhaps," said the Enemy of Both Side, "in serving you, I might earn her forgiveness."

I don't trust you for a fucking instant.

But she wanted what he had accidentally offered. If she somehow crossed through into the underworld, her dagger would come with her. She'd have the opportunity to kill another god.

She blinked up at the waiting god.

He doesn't know!

She was so used to thinking of the gods as all-knowing, she hadn't seen the truth.

He doesn't know about the god-killer. He has no idea what I plan.

Would he care if he did?

Nuru bowed low, meek and cowardly. "It will be as you command," she lied, playing to the god's vanity.

"Little street-sorcerer," said the Enemy of Both Sides, "together we shall return the Queen to her throne." The god spoke in ash and bones. "Together we will save Bastion from the stagnation of the nahual, from the rot of the mad gods staining the heart of the Last City."

I wear the god-killer hidden in my thobe.

This was her dream, not the god's.

A dangerous blend of narcotics already coursing through her blood, Nuru used her pactonal power to make it real. She felt the weight of the dagger.

Should she try and kill him now?

No. He's still useful, still playing at helping me.

Smoking Mirror could wait. She knew this god, understood his flawed need to meddle.

Patience. She'd see him again.

I'm going to kill you in my dreams, Father Discord.

AKACHI - THE TERRIBLE EMPTINESS

Faith does not compel the gods to forgive us our transgressions and blasphemies.

Faith in no way empowers the faithful; it bends not the gods to our will.

Our faith is their due, payment for our salvation.

Faith is acknowledging our dependence on the gods.

Faith is the understanding that without their divine intervention, humanity would have ceased to exist.

—The Book of Bastion

Staff in hand, Akachi strode through the streets of the Crafters' Ring. Captain Melokuhle walked at his left, two paces ahead. She moved like a prowling puma, balanced and alert, gaze roving for prey. Given purpose, the cracks in her soul seemed to heal somewhat.

We all seek distraction.

The thought gave him pause. From the lowest Grower to the highest nahual, life was responsibility. Everyone had things they *had* to do. From the dullest Dirt to the hardest Turquoise Serpent, they all sought escape. The need to step beyond, to get out of one's own head, was universal. Growers smoked erlaxatu grown in hidden plots out in the fields. Crafters drank their crude ale until they could barely walk. Senators drank fermented fruit wines. Bankers smoked zoriontasuna until they lay, hallucinating and dreaming, numb to the world.

And priests?

If everyone else needed the same escapes, was it so bad that he too sometimes needed to get out of himself? He was the Heart of a god.

Upon him fell the task of saving Bastion and all humanity. He bore more responsibilities than most.

Lubanzi roved ahead, checking down alleys and making sure no ambush lay waiting for them. Since leaving the lightning-blasted tenement, he'd refused to look at or talk to Akachi. He made no secret of blaming the nahualli for Firash's death.

Why don't I tell them it was Omphile?

Why would they believe him? Given the choice between the nahual of another god, and one of their own, he wouldn't blame them for taking the assassin's side. Though, if he was honest, that wasn't why he remained silent.

Now, under the searing light of the seething sun, it was too late.

Omphile was god-touched. Perhaps Cloud Serpent turned her eyes grey. Akachi could easily believe his god planned all this before either of them was born.

She was right about the tezcat being dangerous.

If Firash saw the real future, that moment when Akachi entered the Gods' Ring and became Heart's Mirror, he could have ruined everything. As nahual of Southern Hummingbird, it would be the Serpent's holy duty to kill Akachi.

Akachi glanced over his right shoulder. Omphile followed two paces behind. For the first dozen blocks after leaving the Crafter tenement, she made quiet comments about the 'taught curve' of his ass and how she thought, given the opportunity, she could bounce figs off it. After that, she moved on to his calves, making low animal growling noises deep in her throat. Did women find calf muscles attractive? He couldn't imagine. Finally, the day's heat wore even the assassin to silence. She still looked fresher than the rest.

Akachi breathed deep. The Crafters' Ring tasted of sawdust and sand and the stink of hard labour. Long tables, usually covered in the raw ingredients the Crafters would turn into actual food, lay empty. How old were those oak tables, faded and cracked, every corner worn smooth?

Akachi studied the streets, trying to figure out what was missing.

"Where are the ox and wagons?" he asked no one in particular.

"The Guard have orders to round them all up," said Melokuhle, shading her eyes from the harsh sun to peer down an alley.

Akachi looked, saw nothing. Shading his own eyes with the ruin of his left hand, Akachi squinted up at the sky. The raging sun burned it white, bleached the colour from it like old bones.

The air rippled. Stone, already worn smooth and round, looked ready to slump in defeat.

Ahead, Lubanzi lifted a hand. The Serpents slowed.

Scores of Hummingbird Guard filled the next street. A mob of Crafters, a slur of earth-tones, stood nearby. Hunched shoulders and clenched fists spoke their rage.

The Guard dragged a family of Crafters, a man and woman and their three children, from their tenement. One of the Hummingbirds shoved the woman when she slowed to check on a child, and the father barked in anger, grabbing at the man who pushed his wife.

The Guard reacted like flame put to dry grass. In a heartbeat, the father was down, twitching on the street, the back of his skull leaking blood. One of the Hummingbirds pinned him, a knee on his neck, though he made no attempt to rise. Two others set about smashing his ankles and wrists with their cudgels. The woman and her offspring were sent away, pushed in the same direction as the rest of the Crafters.

The Guard do not go lightly. Captain Yejide said that after they'd been ambushed. Did breaking one or two people, setting an example, and showing their willingness to harm, save them from having to hurt more?

There is a cold logic to terror.

"The Birds are evicting them," said Omphile, closer than Akachi realized. "They're staying in this ring until enough arrive to mount an offensive on the Growers."

The evicted Crafters took in the woman and children. They raged at the Guard from a safe distance, shaking fists, and were ignored.

Dirts were dumb animals. They didn't understand the concept of property. Toss one from their hovel, and they'd shuffle lazily across the street to the next tenement and live there. The Crafters weren't like the Growers. They were, at least nominally, functioning members of Bastion's economy. They *owned* their homes. They worked to earn the money to purchase food. Crafters who worked harder, and learned more valuable skills, earned more than those working simple mindless tasks.

"There are so many abandoned tenements," said Akachi. "Why not take those?"

"Well," said Omphile, "they're abandoned, for one thing. No furniture. No beds. Inhabited by snakes and spiders." Lips pursed, she watched the Guard drag more Crafters from another home and send them away. "And supplies are already scarce. No doubt they're going tenement to tenement confiscating foodstuffs."

Lubanzi and Melokuhle waited with Akachi as Omphile went to ask after the nearest church of Father Death. The Hummingbirds, dominant and in charge when dealing with the Crafters, were suddenly meek and obedient when confronted with a Turquoise Serpent.

A score of Hummingbirds broke up the gathered Crafters and sent them scampering in every direction.

Omphile returned with a smug grin, like she possessed some titillating secret. "I have directions to the nearest church of The Lord. The pastor is a tecuhtli, but no one knows if he's still there."

Receiving directions from Omphile, Lubanzi took the lead.

At every turn Akachi witnessed scenes of Crafters tossed from their homes, their possessions confiscated. It was, he realized, their bad luck for living so close to the Grey Wall. No doubt those living further into the ring suffered no such hardships. Understanding didn't help. The growing tension was unmistakable. The Guard's rough treatment of the Crafters left them angry. They didn't care if it was for the good of Bastion. This being the second most populated ring, conflict here would be serious trouble indeed. Worse, if they decided they had more in common with the Growers and sided with the Loa. The Crafters had the potential to arm the outer ring. Should that happen, the inner rings wouldn't stand a chance.

He wasn't sure they did anyway.

"We've been complacent for too long," said Melokuhle, watching a squad of Hummingbird Guard push their way into a butchery and claim everything from the smallest hunk of dried meat to the stone knives of the butchers. "This is not well-planned. They're making things worse."

"You think that *isn't* part of the plan?" asked Omphile.

The Captain shot her a confused look. "Who would want that? All-out war between the rings. Chaos. Destruction. At best, things will go back to the way they were, but with a lot of people dead."

"The gods are hungry," said Omphile. "We haven't had a war in thousands of years. Blood in streets sounds exactly like something they might want." She nodded at Melokuhle. "You see chaos, but I see careful planning. We pretend otherwise, but humanity serves one purpose: feed the gods."

Over and over they saw Crafters ejected from their homes and places of business. On the one hand, it was an impressive military display. Streets filled with rank upon rank of marching Hummingbirds. On the other, when they finally moved on the Growers' Ring, they might be leaving an enemy behind them.

Akachi realized none of the supplies being confiscated were being loaded onto wagons and sent inward. He had no idea how much food was stored in each ring. Thinking back to his childhood, he remembered fresh food every day. Bastion was too hot to keep anything for long.

"Two days," said Omphile, as if reading his mind. "Maybe four, if everyone in the inner rings starts rationing immediately."

"They won't," said Melokuhle. She made a noise that might have been a laugh. "Can you imagine a banker rationing?"

Akachi remembered waddling men and woman swaddled in bright robes. "Why is none of the food being sent inward?" he asked.

"Southern Hummingbird's nahual aren't Dirts," answered the Captain. "We don't farm. Out in the fields they might scavenge, but most of the fighting will take place in the streets, door to door. If the Grey Wall falls, the Dirts will rape and pillage the inner rings, with nothing to stop them. They're animals, savages."

Though Akachi had only been among the Growers for a couple of weeks, back in the Northern Cathedral he'd heard from pastors who spent years preaching the Book. Most of the Dirts really were animals, cow-like and placid, dull and desperate to be told what to do. They were so dim-witted it was almost impossible to have an intelligent conversation with one. They needed guidance for even the simplest tasks.

Not all of them.

Farther from the Grey Wall, the streets were quieter. Even here there were signs of discontent. The shelves of butchers and grocers were empty, stripped clean by the Hummingbird Guard as they passed through. Dark stains, brown and swarming with flies, carried the memory of violence.

Up ahead, Lubanzi slowed to a stop. There, beyond the otochin, lay a church of Father Death. Too small to hold a congregation, it looked like more like a child's model of a church, a curved stone spire at each corner. The Lord's churches were often located underground, closer, at least in the minds of the parishioners, to the underworld.

The spires had once been acanthophis snakes, reaching for the sky, mouths open in threat. Hints of the creature's scales remained, imperfections in otherwise smooth stone. Long vanished, snapped off, or victims of the sand and wind, only rounded nubs remained of the fangs.

Inside, a long set of shallow steps disappeared down into the dark. Damp rot, worms and mud, death and bones, teased Akachi's nose.

"Lubanzi," said Melokuhle, "can you help us see down there?"

Grunting, the otochin handed out fetishes, wooden housecats the size of a thumbnail carved in exquisite detail. He refused to make eye-contact with Akachi.

"We should get inside, out of the light," said Lubanzi.

The four descended the steps until shadow leached the colour from the world.

Studying the fetish, Akachi marvelled at the whiskers, fur, and feline facial features. Lubanzi was a master. Not with all the narcotics in Bastion could Akachi carve something so perfect. Perhaps the Serpents really were better trained than other nahualli.

Drawing a finger-length flint blade, Lubanzi went from person to person, nicking each just enough to draw blood. The Serpents, Akachi realized, bore many identical scars, pale lines lacing the dark flesh of their arms.

Reaching Akachi, the otochin hesitated. Spinning the knife in nimble fingers, he offered the leather-wrapped handle. "You'd better do this. If I have to, I'll take the arm." No hint of humour.

Accepting the blade, Akachi cut himself. "I didn't kill Firash," he said, returning the knife.

Sheathing the dagger, Lubanzi turned away without a word.

Everyone squeezed a drop onto their fetish and placed the figurine beneath their tongue. It tasted of blood and bihurtu-infused wood.

"These should give us an hour of dark-sight," mumbled Lubanzi over the carving, esses sloppy and slurred.

Glancing back up the steps toward the light of day, Akachi cursed at the searing light.

"Idiot," growled Lubanzi. "Why do you think I had us move into the dark?"

"Wasn't thinking," muttered Akachi.

"I carved the irises wide open," said the otochin, "like a cat's eyes on the darkest night. Yours won't react now as they normally would. The fetish decides their shape."

Embarrassed he hadn't noticed, Akachi said nothing.

As the bihurtu soaked into his tongue, his world changed. What colour existed down here in the twilight dark of the stairs, faded. His focus narrowed, peripheral vision collapsing to that of a predator. Everything close and directly in front of him became crisp. Beyond a half a dozen strides, the world was an indistinct blur. He felt trapped, claustrophobic.

Where Akachi twitched, constantly checking that nothing lurked beyond his now non-existent peripheral vision, the Serpents seemed comfortable and relaxed. They trained for this.

"Omphile," ordered Captain Melokuhle, "you take the lead."

Reaching the bottom, the assassin said, "We might be out of luck, here."

The hot scent of spilled blood grew as Akachi descended. He took two splashing steps into the church's prayer hall, a room large enough for two hundred standing Crafters. Pews and such comforts only existed in the Senators' Ring and inward. Feet sodden and warm, he stood in ankle-deep blood.

Scores and scores of corpses littered the floor. Piled around the altar, he saw they'd all been cut and bled by a nahual experienced in the sacrificial ritual. Among the dead lay a few acolytes, nahual in training.

"No sign of a struggle," said Omphile, studying the scene. "Did they line up and await their turn?" She bent to dip a finger into the blood. "This is recent. Hour or two at most."

Three swords hissed from scabbards.

Moving into the hall, splashing with each step, Melokuhle asked, "Any sign of the pastor?"

"No," answered Omphile. "Someone plugged the gutters to keep the blood in here."

The runnels exiting the hall had all been blocked, stuffed with wadded rags.

Akachi felt the tingling crackle of sorcery. With this much death, this much blood, what could a powerful tecuhtli manage? Unskilled in the art, Akachi had no idea.

"We'll check the rest of the church," said Melokuhle. "See if the pastor still lives." Sweeping her gaze back and forth, she added, "We need to know what happened here. This might be Loa treachery."

Omphile led the way into the chambers beyond the hall.

In the kitchen and dining room, they discovered the remains of a great feast, a meal served on long oak tables. There were enough plates to feed all the dead.

Lubanzi's brow furrowed as he took in the room. "They came for a meal and then wandered out to be slaughtered?"

Spotting the kind of jar nahualli used to store narcotics sitting on the kitchen counter, Akachi went to investigate. Lifting it, he sniffed, tentatively. He caught the faint scent of cucumber.

"This is bizitza izoztuak," he said. "It leaves you conscious and alert, but immobilized. Totally helpless."

"Sounds like a nightmare," said Omphile.

"It is," Akachi agreed.

In an attempt to help him focus, one of his teachers had dosed Akachi. The memory of those hours, incapable of any movement, unable to do anything but think, haunted him. When he could once again move, he spent hours curled foetal, screaming at the terrible emptiness he found within himself.

'Some people are better on the outside,' the old nahualli had said.

At the time Akachi thought he meant that some lives were best left unexamined. Now, after learning the truth of himself, he knew he had not yet been filled with the will of his god. It only made sense. Even then, he was Cloud Serpent's Heart.

My emptiness served a purpose

The shattered remains of a chunk of obsidian sat near the jar. Someone had beaten it to dust. Had it been a dagger? He'd seen no sign of a sacrificial knife near the altar.

The stone of souls.

But why break it?

It might free the souls, he supposed. But then what?

Akachi looked back toward the dead. Even had all those souls been collected in this stone, it still would have paled in power compared to either his sacrificial dagger, or the swords of the Turquoise Serpents. He struggled to understand.

"They were poisoned here," said Captain Melokuhle, "and then dragged to the altar for sacrifice."

Omphile froze, lifting a hand for silence.

For a moment, Akachi heard nothing. Then, under the slow *drip drip* of thickening blood, he heard quiet, agonized sobbing coming from deeper in the church.

The assassin again in the lead, they followed the sound.

They found the pastor on his bed, arms and legs spread wide as if chained. Nothing held him, and there was no sign there'd ever been restraints. The nahualli had been skilfully flayed, not a single major vein or artery so much a scratched. Opened with surgical precision, his internal organs had been pulled free and laid about him, still attached. His guts throbbed and pulsed, belly digesting, bowels squirming like snakes as they moved shit and piss. Akachi stared, frozen in shock, watching the pastor's pink lungs inflate and deflate with each breath. The heart kicked arrhythmically as if confused by the feel of open air.

Stones of every colour and size filled the pastor's hollowed torso.

"We have to die to get to the underworld," muttered Lubanzi, glaring at Akachi. "Let's go to the nearest tecuhtli to see if they can help with that." He shook his head. "Fucking great."

Pulling his attention from the displayed intestines, Akachi saw the pastor's eyes had been pulled free and lay dangling on his cheeks. His closed lids were misshapen, protruding.

The nahualli opened his eyes, dragging lids across raw stone. Nested in each socket sat a blood-red stone, polished and smooth.

Carnelian, thought Akachi, mute with horror. *Gives the sorcerer command of the dead.*

Shattered obsidian. Carnelian.

"Stone sorcery," he managed. "A tecolotl did this."

Obsidian to capture the souls of the sacrificed.

Carnelian to—

Twitching in their sockets, the stone eyes seemed to focus on Akachi. The pastor's mouth opened with grinding effort, agony tearing the sobbed intake of breath.

"Trap," whispered the nahual of Father Death.

NURU - COLD STONE SILENCE

The Life Ring is the lifeblood of Bastion. Without it, the city starves.
Destroy the Priests' Ring, kill every nahual, and life will go on.
The Growers are the true power.

—The Loa Book of the Invisibles

Nuru woke to cold stone silence.

Rolling her head to one side, she recognized nothing. Shelves, crammed with books, sunk into the walls. Armoires of intricately detailed ebony, and a massive desk of oak, the legs carved to look like creeping vines.

The room looked suspiciously like the personal chambers of a nahual. She didn't want to think about that.

We left the Growers' Ring.

Memories crept back.

Bishop Chikelu wanted to take her carving.

Loa church. Hidden under a tannery in the Crafters' Ring.

Screams and panic, Mother Death killing, killing.

There was none of that now.

On a bed of soft fabrics, she lay floating in impossible comfort.

I could stay here, forever.

"Lazy bitch is awake," said Efra. "Typical Dirt, eh Kofi? Lounging around like there's nothing to do."

Kofi and Efra stood on the far side of the bed.

"If you're done sleeping," said Efra, "we need to move."

"What happened?" asked Nuru, knowing the answer.

"The Queen returned to us," said Kofi, eyes lit with awe and adoration. "She devoured those who would stand in your way." Kneeling on the floor, arms spread before him in supplication, he said, "I am yours to command, High Priest. Until my last breath, I am yours."

Mother Death thought Kofi lived in terror of missing the opportunity to die for something important, as if that were the only way he might find meaning. Nuru was less sure. The gods had a strange blindness when it came to understanding mortals.

Head tilted to one side, Efra eyed Nuru as she rose from bed. "Does looking like that make things easier, or more difficult?"

Nuru blinked in confusion. "What do you mean?"

"You should make an appearance before the remaining Loa," suggested Kofi, eyes on the floor.

Nuru allowed herself to be led from the room. Brow furrowed, Efra followed.

In the room where she called Mother Death, Nuru found sloppily mopped blood stains, brown and stinking. The corpses were gone. The surviving Loa bowed low as she entered, terrified of making eye-contact. Three Birds knelt on the floor, stripped to their underclothes, wrists tied behind their back. Two women and a man, they were lean and hard, chiselled from granite, pale scars writing stories of pain across mahogany flesh.

When Nuru didn't murder everyone and tear their souls out to be devoured, a middle-aged woman, face framed in a shock of white hair, straightened. Gaze still averted, eyes on the floor, she said, "Mother, we have collected these sacrifices so you may feed."

"So that she may feed on someone other than more Loa, you mean," said Efra.

The woman's gaze darted from Efra to Nuru and back to the floor. "We were unprepared for your return," she said. "We have more prisoners below." Again she looked up, the quickest flick of her eyes, attempting to judge Nuru's reaction.

Blood and souls. Endless hunger. Ravenous rage reaching back through impossible thousands of millennia.

Mother Death stirred.

"Call her again," begged the white-haired Loa, "and we shall bathe her in blood!"

One of the Bird women on the floor glared at Nuru. "Change your clothes, but I still see the *Dirt*." She spat the last word.

"Good," said Nuru, turning to the Loa. "No sacrifices." Seeing their surprise, she added, "Not yet."

She wanted to tell them there would never be sacrifices again, that the practice was barbaric and evil, that the gods could no longer feed on humanity like puma on chickens. They wouldn't understand. They'd turn on her even though she fought to save them.

"Later," Nuru said. "When the time is right."

Confused, they grudgingly agreed, and hustled the prisoners away.

They listened! I commanded, and they obeyed!

A thrill ran through Nuru. Power. Real power. Power like the nahual had.

"No longer will you use the Growers to fight your war," Nuru told the gathered Loa. *Shit.* "Our war," she corrected. Remembering something she'd heard once in a Loa church hidden in a tenement basement, she said, "The Growers are the lifeblood of Bastion. They farm the fields. They raise the animals. Without the Growers, the city dies." She thought of all those sun-bloated bodies in the streets of the Growers' Ring. "You treat them like they're nothing! Do you have any fucking idea how many you've killed throwing them at the Birds just to take a single gate?" she demanded.

Kofi hung his head in shame and confusion. Emotion warred across his features. Shame, at disappointing Nuru. The desire to defend his actions and choices.

"Killing Growers," said Nuru, "is a crime against Bastion. From now on, anyone doing so will be bled on the altar."

"And this," whispered Efra, "is how it starts. So easy."

Was this a shot at Nuru's willingness to sacrifice those who would kill their own kind? She couldn't imagine Efra hesitating. The girl seemed neither angry, nor upset. If anything, she seemed to enjoy watching the Loa cringe.

There had to be rules. She had to save the Growers, she had to make the Loa stop.

"Without the Growers," said the white-haired woman, "we'll lose the gates we hold. Without their numbers, the outer ring will fall to the nahual."

"The Growers will fight," Nuru said, praying she was right. "They'll fight by choice. But you must train them. You must arm them. This is their cause too."

The Loa woman struggled with her doubt. "They're too simple to train, too meek to fight."

They need to see they're wrong.

But how?

Nuru glanced at Efra, nodded.

Efra slashed her flint blade across the woman's throat in one smooth motion, so fast, so lacking in hesitation, no one saw it coming.

Eyes wide in shock, the white-haired woman tried to stanch the wound. Blood pulsed past desperate fingers with each kick of her heart. Wet, retched gagging, the sound of exhaled air escaping through a gaping wound. Almost graceful, her knees folded and she sank to sit on her haunches.

No one moved.

Sputtering blood, she blinked slower and slower, before finally collapsing forward. Tremors ran through the body, one foot kicking like a dreaming dog.

Stillness.

Nuru stared down at the corpse. Blood leaked from the neck, pooled about her bare feet, trickled hot between her toes. She couldn't speak, couldn't open her mouth. She'd expected Efra to punch someone, maybe put them on the ground like she had Kofi. There, beneath the horror, lurked other emotions.

Hunger.

Rage at the wasted soul.

"*We* are Growers," said Efra, bending to wipe the flint dagger on the dead woman's shirt. "Your precious Heart," she nodded at Nuru, "is a Dirt."

"Forget everything you think you know about Growers," managed Nuru, finding her voice. "We are not so different."

Even with a dead woman, throat slashed at their feet, they still looked doubtful.

"Should I kill another," said Efra, "so they understand?"

Everyone back away.

"No," said Nuru. She turned on the Loa. "You must convince the Growers you're on their side."

"Actually," said Efra, gesturing at Nuru, "you're going to have to convince Nuru that you're on *her* side."

All eyes were on Nuru. No one looked surprised. No one looked shocked.

Efra just spoke aloud something they all knew. Nuru understood. *That wasn't for their benefit, it was for mine.*

Why was it so easy to underestimate the woman?

"The fields are burning," said Nuru. "Put out the fires or Bastion dies."

The Loa shuffled and fidgeted, clearly wanting to say something.

"You," said Nuru, pointing out a man shifting uncomfortably in his Crafter clothes. "What is it you want to say."

He glanced at Efra.

"I won't kill you," she said, scar stretched in a grin, "unless you say something unbelievably stupid."

Returning his attention to Nuru, he said, "There aren't enough of us to defeat the Guard and the Serpents. Not even close. If we divide in purpose, we will lose." He took a deep breath. "Particularly without the Growers. We need them."

"Well," drawled Efra, "he isn't wrong."

Everyone stared at Nuru, awaiting her decision.

Fight the Birds.

Put out the fires.

Take control of the gates.

Work whatever remained of the fields, so Bastion didn't starve.

Hopeless frustration built in her. This was a war with too many fronts.

A sinking horror filled Nuru. She'd been negligent.

I killed Her Skirt is Stars!

What were the nahual who ran the crèches doing? With their god dead, would they stay and care for the children? Thinking back to how Grower kids were treated, she thought not. She'd been so accustomed to not thinking about children, she'd never considered what would happen to them.

Not that there was much she could have done.

Things have changed.

"Her Skirt is Stars is dead," said Nuru. "Your priority is the children."

All fear forgotten, questions were suddenly shouted at her. How? When? What happened?

A field of little bodies, thousands of murdered children, their souls collected so they may one day be freed.

Nuru swallowed the pain. "I killed her."

Silence returned, stunned faces, waiting. Only Efra looked unsurprised.

Addressing the man fidgeting in his Crafter clothes, Nuru said, "Send people to all the crèches in the Growers' Ring. Save the children."

He blinked. "*All* the crèches?"

"Did she fucking stutter?" asked Efra.

He glanced from Efra to Nuru. "It will be done."

Nuru stared at him. He didn't move. "Now," she said. "Right fucking now. And place the kids with Growers who will take them in. If there's any way of finding their real parents, do it."

"Growers can't raise children!" he blurted.

"Efra?" said Nuru.

"Yep. Going to gut the next person who says anything that stupid."

Struggling to set aside a lifetime of subservient obedience, Nuru put a hand on the man's shoulder.

He swallowed, stared at the floor like a cowed Dirt.

"This is *your* task," she said. "Yours." With a finger under his chin, she lifted his face to make eye contact. "Take whoever and whatever you need. Do not fail me."

Watching the sudden mad scramble of Loa nahual, she understood.

I am the voice of god.

She felt weak, her knees threatening to give.

"Everyone, get the fuck out," barked Efra. "Now. Not you, fat boy," she added, turning on Kofi. "You stay."

In a dozen heartbeats the room was empty.

Kofi approached, concern writ deep, crumpling his face. "What's wrong?"

"You selfish fat fuck," said Efra. "She hasn't eaten in days. And the week before that we lived off scraps. She needs food and she needs sleep. Move your fucking fat ass."

Kofi bowed low to Nuru. "Sorry." And was gone.

"What do we do now?" asked Efra, standing at her side.

Do I tell her my insane plan?

Exhausted, terrified of both the decisions she would have to make, and the ones already made, she saw no alternative.

I need her.

No matter what the Loa believed, she was still just Nuru the Dirt girl.

"I'm going to kill the gods," said Nuru.

Efra raised an eyebrow, said nothing.

"I'm going to kill all of them."

"About fucking time," said Efra, scar stretched tight in a feral grin.

AKACHI - DEAD WEIGHT OF FLESH

A nahualli is an empty mirror. That emptiness doesn't reflect his life, it reflects the gods.

Filled with divine purpose, a nahualli possesses no inner turmoil, no assertions of the self.

A nahualli awaits the will of the gods.

A nahualli takes nothing for granted.

Like Bastion, the elegant sorcerer shows no seams, is a pure and perfect extension of divinity.

—The Book of Bastion

"Oh fuck," said Omphile. "We need to leave."

The whisper of passing ghosts.

A hot wind through a field of sun-burnt corn.

Out in the prayer hall, the dead rose. They faced the kitchen, stood motionless and emotionless. Beyond the sluggish dripping of cooling blood, perfect silence.

Dead-eyed, the corpses stared at the living. No movement. Not the hint of drawn breath or rustling fabric.

"There are sixty or more out there," whispered Lubanzi.

Sixty. Fucking sixty. No. Can't.

Armies of corpses. So many stories, so many myths in the *Book of Bastion*. He'd read them all.

Can't kill the dead.

They felt no pain, knew no fear. They were unhindered by anything less than the most grievous of wounds.

No matter how deadly, three Serpents could never hope to defeat sixty. Even if their foes lacked all martial skill, they would be overwhelmed.

Akachi imagined clawed fingers locking in his robes, dragging him down, burying him. Pinned under a crush of corpses. Can't breathe.

Severed fingers fumbling at his belt, he spilled a measure of erlaxatu onto the bloody floor and cursed.

You're at war.

Once again, he was going into battle unprepared, not even a trace of narcotics in his blood.

Can't be dosed all the time.

Brain-burn. Death.

He remembered the way Captain Yejide looked at him as he stumbled about the church in a narcotic fog. Pity. Maybe disgust.

"Can't—" Akachi swallowed. "Stabbing is useless."

"We know," said Omphile. "Stay behind me."

"We cut through," said Captain Melokuhle, voice calm, unhurried.

She stood straight, every fibre of muscle and sinew poised for war. Only now, faced with certain death, did Akachi see a captain of the Turquoise Serpents.

As one, the Serpents raised their swords in salute.

The dead came.

Thousands of pounds of cooling meat, driven by some unknown will, poured into the dining room. The first few fell apart, limbs spinning away, as the Serpents cut them down.

Bloodless.

Silent.

The corpses cared nothing for wounds. Hacked, stabbed, missing limbs, they kept pushing. Those without arms threw themselves bodily at their enemies. Those without legs dragged themselves across the floor, pawing at exposed boots, trying to climb their opponents.

For a moment, the Serpents held, but the dead weight of flesh drove them back, step by step, until more could pour past them into the room.

A corpse grabbed one of Omphile's arms. When she turned to hack it in half, another darted past, lunging for Akachi. Retreating, he smashed its skull with the Staff of the Fifth Sun. Head dented in, one eye bulging wet in its socket, the thing tackled Akachi. He shoved it off, using the staff as leverage. Another corpse tackled him, driving its shoulder into his gut. The impact forced a wheeze from him and sent the wood fetish spinning from under his tongue. Reeling and off balance, he tripped over the fallen dead and landed hard. The other corpse fell atop him.

Fetish gone, the underground room became perfect black.

No hint of light.

Milling bodies, and the wet slap of flesh.

Luke-warm blood, thick and clinging, splashed his face, stung his eyes.

Grunts of effort, the grit sound of stone scything through bone. The hiss of parting flesh.

Black.

Akachi struggled, trying to wrestle the corpse off him.

Someone grabbed the wrist of his ruined hand and pulled his arm straight. The staff was ripped from his grip and he lashed out, punching wildly. Over and over he struck unyielding flesh to no effect. More dead piled atop him, crushing.

Couldn't breathe.

Suffocating.

A weight fell across his legs, pinning them.

Helpless, one hand free.

Cold fingers found that hand, pulled that arm straight too.

More bodies on his legs. Arms pinned.

Another corpse landed upon his chest, crushing out the last of his air.

Cold fingers found his face, tattered nails scraping at the flesh of his cheek like it meant to dig its way through to his brain.

Panic.

Mindless, crushing terror.

Akachi wriggled, tried to throw his weight, fought savagely to do anything to dislodge his attackers. He couldn't move.

He screamed and a bloody hand jammed into his mouth, choking him to silence.

Biting down hard, Akachi tasted raw meat and blood, felt his teeth grind against bone.

There was no reaction, no bellow of pain.

Filthy fingers on his tongue, gripping.

He gagged, retching, jaw forced wider.

Hands gripped his hair, immobilized his head. He couldn't scream, couldn't move.

Whatever clawed at his face moved higher, caught his cheekbone, dragged the lower lid of his left eye wide.

Questing purpose.

"He'll replace your vision with one of his own," a corpse breathed into his ear.

Akachi clenched his eyes closed, as fingers clawed at his lids.

Pitch black. The image of the nahual with his eyes torn out, stones jammed into the sockets, haunted his thoughts.

"He'll replace your vision with one of his own."

The whistling sound of swords cutting air.

The wet crunch of stone cleaving bone.

Clawed fingers, hard as granite, found his eye.

Akachi screamed in muffled terror and writhed and couldn't move.

Fingers digging. Fingers searching and slipping, pushing into the socket, distending his eyeball, sending purple slashes across the black.

Groping.

Seeking.

Pulling.

Already broken, already ruined, Akachi moaned prayers to his god past the hand jammed wrist-deep in his mouth.

NURU - OBSIDIAN GRIN

Red Smoking Mirror walked the earth clad in the flesh of a flayed mortal. Known as the Flayed One, he brought agriculture to humanity, taught them how to tend crops to maximize each harvest. In the last years before the death of the world, he was betrayed by a lesser trickster god who stabbed him in the head with a smoking obsidian dagger, claiming many of his aspects for himself.

A hollowed ghost, Red Smoking Mirror haunts the Bloody Desert, dreaming of past lives.

—The Loa Book of the Invisibles

Nuru told Efra everything.

She told her how Face Painted with Bells killed Father Death, and how she herself killed Her Skirt is Stars. She told her about murdering fields of children, and the god-killer and how she would use it to collect the hoarded souls of every god.

"God-killer," mused Efra, rubbing at the scar.

"When the last god is dead," Nuru finished, "I'll shatter the dagger, freeing the souls."

"Will they be reborn even though there will be no god in the underworld?" Efra asked.

"I don't know if there will be an underworld anymore," admitted Nuru. "I think those realms only exist because of the gods."

"You *think?*"

Nuru shrugged, helpless. "Bits and pieces picked up from nahual and Loa sermons over the years." She struggled to articulate her thoughts. "I think maybe the gods inserted themselves into our existence."

"Maybe," said Efra.

"Once the gods are gone, things will go back to the way they were before."

"Before there were gods."

"Yeah." Nuru laughed, shaking her head. She knew nothing. All her plans rested on assumptions based on the slimmest hopes. "I could be dooming humanity," she admitted. "Luckily, the odds of me succeeding are so slim we'll likely never find out."

Efra grunted amusement. "Here's how I see it. Whether or not we need the gods, they did this to us. They killed the world. They made the city, and the laws, and forced the Growers to work the outer ring." Her eyes lit with rage. "They lashed us, bled our friends, cut our hearts out and threw us from the wall." She stopped, staring hard at nothing, scar curling the top of her lip. "It doesn't matter if humanity needs them. We're dying. The city is dying. We kill them. We kill them all." Looking up, she met Nuru's eyes with a cutting grin. "We have nothing to lose."

So simple.

For Efra, that was decision made. Nothing would move her. Doubt was worthless.

"Show me the dagger," said Efra. "The god-killer, I want to see it."

The moment of truth.

Would she take it? If she tried, could Nuru stop her?

Not fucking likely.

Nuru retrieved the dagger from her thobe, held it balanced in her palm. The air twisted around it, rippled by the soul-staining taint of rot and death. Numbness crept up her arm. She wanted to scream, to vomit, to hurl it away and cower in a dark corner.

Efra leaned close, gaze fixed on the black stone. Tension hunched her shoulders, her jaw working, lips twitching between a scowl and a snarl.

Take it.

If anyone could murder an entire pantheon of gods, it was Efra.

Efra looked up from the dagger. "Don't ever give this to me. *Ever.*" She sat back, relaxed. "You understand that you are now the Loa High Priest, right? You are their highest ranking nahual. So…" She grinned mischief. "What do you want for breakfast?"

Heaping plates of food, moist dates, softbread, a selection of increasingly strange cheeses, and glass jugs of clear water were brought before Nuru had a chance to ask. The Loa were deferential, bowing, and falling all over themselves to serve.

"I walked around a bit while you were sleeping," said Efra, spitting a date pit onto the floor. "They don't know what to do with me. I'm clearly important, but I'm also clearly just a stupid Dirt."

She's talking. Efra rarely said anything without there being some point.

Efra did a half shrug, one shoulder twitching. "I may have played up the ignorant Dirt a bit. It's always best when your enemy underestimates you."

She's right. If the Loa work for the return of Mother Death, and we plot the end of all gods, they are our enemy.

So obvious, and yet it took Efra to see it.

"It's you and me against all Bastion," said Nuru.

"Bastion doesn't stand a fucking chance."

No smile. No hint of mockery or humour.

"While the Loa were busy ignoring me," said Efra, "I listened. They don't believe you're a Dirt. The leading theory seems to be that you were somehow taken from the Priests' Ring at a young age." Picking at where the scar crossed her lips, she added, "It's acceptable if you grew up among the filthy, ignorant, and lazy, but you can't be one of them. You can't have Dirt blood. One of them said that, 'Dirt blood.' Even our blood is inferior."

"It's good enough for the gods," said Nuru.

Even though Nuru spent her life trying to avoid working the fields, she missed them now. The dry sigh of wind through endless wheat. Dark soil between your toes. The crèches were out there. She had to trust the

Loa were doing as commanded, but she wanted to go herself.

Someone coughed beyond the curtain separating Nuru's chambers from the rest of the church. It was easy to forget they were still hidden beneath a tannery.

Efra glanced at Nuru, shrugged.

They waited.

Again, the small cough, someone pretending to clear their throat.

"Kofi," said Efra, "why are you making that noise in the hall?"

He pushed past the curtain, flushing with embarrassment. "It's only polite."

"Polite?" asked Nuru.

"It would be rude to barge into your room!"

With no doors or curtains, Growers did that all the time. No one walked around faking a cough. The Birds never coughed before entering a tenement and bashing heads. The priests didn't clear their throat before striding into your home and declaring you sinful and in need of lashes or being opened before the gods.

Privacy was something only nahual possessed.

"What's the plan? Where to next?" Kofi asked.

I can't tell him.

She struggled to quash the pang of guilt. He knew the Loa. He knew the city beyond the Growers' Ring. Without him, she would be utterly lost.

The nahual have been using us for twenty-five thousand years. It's our turn.

It was a justification.

Kofi could never know the truth, not until it was too late. Seeing how he looked at her, the love and worship, she had no doubt he would die to protect her.

Like Chisulo.

Nuru tried not to think about the coming betrayal, how hurt Kofi would be.

"Southern Hummingbird is going to try and claim the underworld for his own," Nuru announced. "He will launch an attack against Face

Painted with Bells. We don't have much time."

"How do you know?" Kofi asked in shock.

"She's the Queen's Heart, fat boy," said Efra.

Kofi accepted the explanation.

"I can stop Father War," said Nuru, not wanting to go into detail.

"Few of the Loa are trained in the foul narcotic sorcery of the nahualli," Kofi said, rubbing his chin in thought. "We practice a purer art. The nahualli are cowards, they flee reality, go to outside forces. The narcotics change them, hollow them. Old nahualli are all mumbling idiots, brains singed, if not burned."

It sounded like an old rant and Nuru kept her doubts to herself. She'd seen enough elderly nahualli to know they were often quite sharp.

When he looked ready to continue the rhetoric, she silenced him with an eyebrow.

Amazing how that works.

One of the perks of power, she guessed. Though come to think of it, it often worked on Chisulo as well.

"How do I get to the underworld?" she asked.

"Subira," Kofi answered without hesitation. "Mother must have known this was coming; that's why she told me to take you to her."

"Who is this Subira?" Efra asked. "Someone called her a 'turncoat.'"

"She is a nahual of Father Death, and a talented tecuhtli. She's a pastor in the Senator's Ring." Seeing Nuru and Efra's confusion, he added, "Seeing the injustices of the indentured system, she joined our struggle."

"Indentured system?" Nuru asked.

"The indentured and indebted," he said as if that explained anything. "Slavery is an abomination."

Why do the Loa never use the term slavery when talking about the Growers?

"I used to think it was just Chisulo and the boys who were idiots," said Efra. "I think maybe it's all men."

Though she didn't disagree, Nuru ignored the comment. "We have to go. Now."

Kofi looked away, embarrassed. "My store of stones is low. I'm not sure I can protect you."

Was he trying to tell her that she should choose someone else to lead her into the Senators' Ring?

"You have to be the one to protect her," said Efra surprising both Nuru and Kofi. "Your mother gave you this task." She spoke like it was nothing, like she merely commented on the heat.

"How do you get more stones?" Nuru asked.

"The quality of the stones available depends on your rank. With mother gone, I'm not sure where I stand. She was always the power."

"Nonsense," said Efra. "You are the Heart's personal bodyguard. Nothing is more important than Nuru, and no one's task more important than yours." She tilted her head to one side in thought, though Nuru was sure the woman already knew exactly what she would say. "You are the second highest ranked Loa in all Bastion."

"Tell them," Nuru said, "that I command them to give you anything and everything you need."

Bowing low, grinning ear to ear, Kofi dashed from the room.

Nuru turned to Efra. "That was unexpected, you coming to his defence."

Efra flashed that scar twisting grin, though this time with a hint of humour instead of her more typical rage. "Fat boy is dumb as ox shit, and he's in love with you. He'll be easy to manipulate." She studied Nuru. "Though, if you're willing to fuck him, that'll make things even easier."

Not sure how to answer, Nuru said nothing. He was a good-looking man, strong-armed, and broad-shouldered. And the way he looked at her was nice. She had no doubt he'd be willing. But there was something scary there, an unnerving level of worship. In his mind, he wouldn't be with Nuru, the Dirt, he'd be with the Heart of Mother Death.

And Chisulo. He was always in her thoughts.

Efra does nothing without a reason.

Nuru considered the way Efra always poked at Kofi, insulting him. She remembered how, back in the crèche, some girls had strange ways of expressing emotions. Boys too, for that matter. As a child, Bomani used to throw clods of dirt at girls he liked.

Did Efra have feelings for the Loa sorcerer beyond lust?

This is Efra, Nuru reminded herself.

Most likely, the simplest explanation was correct.

She'd fuck him because she felt like it, and to make him easy to manipulate.

AKACHI - NEVER

How terrible were the last moments of the world that the screams of the dying were forever trapped in stone? Every pebble bears memories of torture. Every shard of stone carries the last emotion of a burnt soul. Each grain of red sand in the Bloody Desert is a moment of pain.

—The Loa Book of the Invisibles

Groping fingers scraped across Akachi's eyeball sending slashes through his vision.

Probing. Pushing.

His muffled screams, shoved back down his throat by a dead man's fist, filled his skull.

Helpless. Kicking.

His left eye saw a splash of red and purple stars.

Then white.

Then nothing.

Someone whispered, "He'll replace your vision with one of his own."

Fire stabbed through his skull, searing agony, hot coals shoved into his brain, thoughts burning and smoking.

Fingers returned, scraping at his forehead. Blood trickled into his ear. A thumb dug into his right eye, pushing.

Akachi screamed past the hand, begging for salvation, damning his god. *Where are you?*

Where the fuck was Cloud Serpent?

Save me! Save me! Save me save me save me save me!

"He'll replace your vision with one of his own."

Crushing dead weight smothering him. Couldn't breathe. No room for air.

What strength he had faded, a terrible new darkness replacing the lightless black of the church.

"He'll replace your vision with one of his own."

Akachi cursed his endless stupidity. Dosed, he could become a jaguar, claw these dead apart. He could be a bear and rip them limb from limb. As a pangolin, he could shelter in his armour, untouchable.

Instead, he was nothing. A terrified boy. Helpless. So fucking stupid.

"He'll replace your vision with one of his own."

Air! The slightest sip.

Torn from his mouth, the hand left shreds of flesh in his teeth. Akachi drew a great, sucking breath. The fingers in his right eye fell away and cool blood, thick and sticky, splashed his face.

Hands in his robes lifted him.

Grunting.

Stone on bone.

The damp slap of bodies striking the floor.

Akachi screamed.

Robbed of balance, he couldn't find his feet. The world was chaos, up and down were meaningless in the dark.

They were dragging him!

They're stealing me away!

Struggling, Akachi screamed again.

"Stop fighting me!" snapped Omphile, past the fetish in her mouth.

She hauled him bodily up the steps, his heels striking stone. The world grew in brightness until she pulled him into the sun and spat out the figurine. When she released her grip on his robes, he collapsed to his knees, exhausted and beaten. Everything was wrong, crooked. The world bent to one side, pitching him to the ground. He scraped his hands trying to catch himself, and still slammed a shoulder into stone.

Rolling over onto his back, Akachi stared at the sky.

Wrong. Wrong. Something was wrong.

Omphile and Melokuhle stood over him talking about Lubanzi.

Ignoring them, he closed his right eye.

"They got him," said Omphile. "I was too busy trying to get to Akachi. I couldn't save both."

Darkness.

Captain Melokuhle said something.

Panic rose from Akachi's belly like bile, a rushing explosion of vomitus terror.

No!

Opening his eyes, he lifted his left hand. He couldn't see it until it crested the bridge of his nose.

"My eye," he croaked.

Fingers clawing. The scrape of rough flesh across his delicate pupil.

He blinked and a tear ran down his right cheek.

Melokuhle cursed and spat rage, said something about Lubanzi being a kid. Vehement denial.

"They pulled him down," said Omphile. "They broke him. Pulled his jaw open until it snapped. Popped bones from joints until every limb flopped loose." Omphile looked toward the church. "He was still alive when we left." She caught Melokuhle's shoulder when the captain turned to head back toward the stairs. "It's too late," said the assassin. "Even if he isn't dead, he's ruined."

"We have to try." The Captain's voice cracked with despair.

"We have a more important mission," Omphile reminded her. "We are Turquoise Serpents. I'm sorry, Captain. We have to trust Firash brought us here for a reason."

Lying on his back, endless blue sky above, Akachi waved his left hand back and forth before his face, watching it appear and disappear. Closing his right eye again, covering it with his right hand, he searched for some hint of light. He looked left and right, trying to feel the movement in the muscles of his eyes. Everything felt wrong.

It's a gaping wound. It's a hole in your skull. Brain exposed. Insects and spiders and snakes and—

"No!" Akachi shouted.

Head lolling to one side he saw the two women. Lost in conversation, they seemed unaware of him.

"I had to make a choice," said Omphile, voice twisted in pain. "I couldn't save—"

"Fuck the damned Cloud Serpent nahual!" yelled Melokuhle, spinning to grab Omphile.

The assassin stood loose, relaxed and unworried. "Firash—"

"I don't give a shit! Lubanzi was one of us!" Lips pulled back in rage, tears streamed down her face.

"Help," Akachi said.

Locked in their own world, they ignored him.

I can do this.

It was just a wound. The retina had been scratched or something. Maybe the beating he took swelled the eye closed. He'd seen that before, when indentured fought in the Bankers' Ring to entertain their owners.

With his ruined hand, Akachi touched his cheek, just below his left eye.

Left hand. Left eye.

No. No. He'd be fine.

A little higher. Make sure the eye is still there.

It would heal. He always healed.

Not the hand. Not the fingers Mother Death severed.

He couldn't move the hand. Much as he needed to know, it refused to obey.

He imagined glistening white maggots filling his skull. Writhing, they tumbled, clumped and wet like soggy grains of rice, from the gaping hole.

No. No.

Akachi pushed himself into a sitting position, legs out straight before him.

Dizzy.

"Firash brought us here," soothed Omphile. "He knew what was going to happen and *still* he led us to this."

Half listening, Akachi thought, *She doesn't believe that.*

"Firash was a powerful tezcat," said the assassin. "He knew he would die. He knew Lubanzi would die. Maybe we're going to die too." She gently disengaged Meloluhle's hands from her armoured vest. "It doesn't matter. It doesn't matter because we are the Turquoise Serpents, and not even gods can stop us."

"You could have—"

Omphile shook her head. "No. I had to get to Akachi before they tore his other eye out."

She kept talking.

Tore his *other* eye out.

They took my fucking eye!

Left hand. Left eye. Too much. This was too much! His god took too much. Akachi offered everything and Bastion ripped it from him!

He stared at his ruined hand, wiggled the blunt stumps of his fingers.

How much must I give?

What was enough? When could he say, 'No more, I must retain some self'?

Too close. The thought touched something terrifying, like maybe somewhere along the way he'd lost who he was. Or lost who he wanted to be.

Akachi's stomach kicked and he puked all over his legs.

When did saving all humanity become not worth the cost?

"Never," said Akachi. "Never."

He couldn't see.

Everything was nothing.

"A nahualli is an empty mirror," whispered Akachi, quoting the Book. "That emptiness doesn't reflect his life, it reflects the gods."

Lies.

He was a lie.

His bravery. His willingness to sacrifice everything to save the Last

City.

All lies.

He couldn't breathe.

"Oh shit," said a distant voice. "He's going into shock."

NURU - THE MOST BEAUTIFUL MOMENT

In the first few thousand years after the creation of Bastion each ring was required to offer up one percent of its population for sacrifice to the gods. Weakened by the massive undertaking of raising the stone from the desert, the gods were near death and required sustenance.

In time, the wealthier inner rings grew to resent the demanded sacrifices. Tasked with running every critical aspect of the city's daily life, they argued that their lives were too important to waste on simple bloodletting. And so those who wrote the laws and rules wrote new laws and rules. No longer would sacrifices be selected from each ring. Instead, those who blasphemed against Bastion's sacred laws would be offered up to the gods.

The gods fed well.

—The Loa Book of the Invisibles

Kofi returned to report to Nuru that Loa had been dispatched to the Growers' Ring to care for the children. Seeing the worry and doubt in his eyes, she wondered if she'd made a mistake.

"You disagree with my choice?" she asked.

Kofi bowed. "No, High Priest."

"Don't call me that," she said. "And don't lie."

He swallowed, glancing at Efra like he worried she might suddenly slash his throat. And, fair enough, it wasn't a baseless concern.

"Sending so many to the outer ring leaves us weak here," he said, looking everywhere but at Nuru.

"Gods he's thick," said Efra. She gestured at Nuru. "She's Mother

Death's Heart, right?"

Kofi nodded.

"If she dies, what happens to Mother Death?"

"I'm not sure," Kofi admitted.

"Fine," said Efra. "What happens if she survives?"

"If Nuru is the last Heart, she will ascend to become Heart's Mirror."

"Heart's Mirror is the voice of the gods, right?" said Efra. "And what does that mean?"

Nuru's heart kicked in fear.

Efra must have been awake when Kofi explained everything to Nuru in the barley warehouse.

Kofi's eyes widened as he understood. "Mother Death will rule the pantheon, and Nuru will rule Bastion. She will be the single highest ranked priest in all the city."

"Tell me exactly," said Efra, "what getting Dirts killed will achieve that Nuru can't do once she's Heart's Mirror."

"Nothing," said Kofi.

"Right," agreed Efra. "So do as you're fucking told and leave the thinking to the women."

She was right. This wasn't a war of soldiers at all. The Hummingbird Guard. The Turquoise Serpents. All the dead Growers rotting in the sun. It didn't matter who controlled the outer ring once a new Heart's Mirror ascended. It was all a distraction.

Not quite.

It did serve one purpose.

It feeds the gods.

"How do we get into the Senators' Ring to see this turncoat, Subira?" asked Nuru, saving the young Loa from further embarrassment.

Grateful for the rescue, Kofi answered, "The Hummingbird Guard hold all the gates in the Wall of Lords."

The Senators' Ring. How many thousands of years had it been since a lowly Dirt walked among the city's lawmakers? If they caught her, they'd throw her from the Sand Wall.

Nuru swallowed a laugh. She was well past such punishments. Being here, in the Crafters' Ring, was already an unforgivable sin.

"How do we get through?" she asked.

"Too many people travelling together will draw attention," Kofi answered. "It'll be best if it's just the three of us. You two will be Senators. I will be your bodyguard."

When Nuru agreed to the plan, Kofi left to fetch someone he said could help. He returned soon after with a middle-aged woman in loose and comfortable looking Crafter's clothes.

"This is Mbali," said Kofi, introducing the woman. "She'll make you look like Senators."

Looking them up and down, tutting at their filthy feet, Mbali said, "Come along, girls." Unlike the other Loa, her voice carried no hint of deference.

Nuru and Efra followed as she led them through the underground church. Mbali said nothing, made no attempt to converse, and seemed utterly comfortable with the silence.

Entering a room with a bath sunk into the stone floor large enough to fit half a dozen, she gestured at it and stood waiting. Rose petals floated on the surface, steam rising from the water. Scores of pure white candles lined the walls, giving the room a golden glow.

With a careless shrug, Efra shed her thobe and strode into the tub. Lean and hard, scrapes and scars decorated her torso, a history of violence written in flesh. Though the swollen eye and lip had gone down, her face showed the last fading bruises from the beating she suffered when they killed the two Crafter men for their clothes. Most of the wounds were older, long healed. Nuru had no idea how she earned them.

Gods, I wouldn't get out of bed if that was me.

Efra sank into the water until only her head remained exposed. "It's hot," she said in wonder. "Really hot." With a grin she sank below the surface.

"You next, dear" said Mbali.

Keeping her back turned, Nuru shrugged off her own stinking and stained thobe. Once naked, she dashed into the water as if chased.

Efra surfaced. Seeing Mbali collecting their clothes, she said, "No! Leave them."

Studying the filthy pile, Mbali shrugged and departed.

"Can't have her finding the god-killer," Efra explained. "Or stealing my flint dagger," she added, before once again sinking beneath the water.

Nuru ran fingers through what remained of her own hair. She missed it, the long braids, the gentle rattle of snake bones and rat skulls.

We made garottes with it and murdered people.

Efra's idea, of course.

The heat undid knots in Nuru's back and shoulders she'd carried for so long she hadn't known they were there. A lifetime of tension and fear. Two decades of living hunched, waiting for the whip or the stick.

Nuru exhaled, closed her eyes. "Has any Dirt ever been so relaxed?" she asked.

Efra loosed a long sigh of pleasure. "I'm never leaving."

Mbali returned with thick yellow wedges of what looked like wax. Standing at the side of the bath, she offered one to each of the women.

Nuru leaned close to sniff at it. "Smells like flowers," she said.

Efra took one and bit into it. Spitting into the tub, she scowled in disgust. "Tastes terrible."

Mbali straightened. "It's soap."

Nuru looked at Efra, who shrugged, and back to Mbali. "And?"

The Loa woman mimed scrubbing her armpits. "Wash with it."

Once she was sure they understood, she again left them alone.

"Is this what it's like to be a nahual?" Efra asked. "I could get used to this."

"We're being prepared to enter the Senators' Ring," said Nuru. "I think maybe this is how everyone lives."

The two women bathed, the water changing colour around them.

"That's it," it said Efra. "We are never going back. Fuck the gods. Fuck saving the world. I want to be clean."

Mbali returned with blankets of soft fabric she called 'towels.' Hustling the two women out of the tub, Efra groaning in complaint, she set about brusquely drying them off like they couldn't do it themselves. In the Wheat District baths, Growers climbed from the brown water straight into their filthy thobes. The transition between dripping wet and soaked in sweat was so short as to be non-existent.

Where Nuru covered herself with her arms, uncomfortable with the attention, Efra ignored Mbali as she worked.

Wrapping them in a second set of fresh towels, Mbali said, "This way, please."

Collecting their thobes from the floor, careful to keep the weapons hidden, they followed her to another set of chambers. Assorted tools of unknown purpose sat waiting on one table, lengths of fabric laid out on display. More white candles lit the room.

Directing Efra and Nuru to two chairs, Mbali said, "Sit."

Efra stopped, stood rooted, staring. "Fadil had a chair."

When Chisulo and the gang showed up to rescue Efra, they'd found the gang leader already dead, throat a ragged wound, sitting in a chair much like these. Nuru remembered her awe. Fadil had a chair! A real chair! Such wealth had been unimaginable.

Here she was, a week later, the unwilling High Priest of the Loa, and invited to sit in a chair like it was nothing.

Moving first, Efra eased herself into one of the chairs. "Oh," she said, eyes closing. "It's even better than I thought."

Nuru sat. Polished wood, the seat was perfectly smooth.

"I've never sat on anything that didn't feel like it was stabbing me in the ass," she said.

"Sometimes," said Efra, "I don't mind being stabbed in the—"

"Girls!" scolded Mbali. "Please! Now, if you'll leave those rags on the floor, we'll get you ready."

The Loa woman fussed over them, brushing out their hair with combs of jade, the teeth so fine they were translucent. When satisfied with her work, she set about applying powder to their cheeks and painting long curved lines of glistening black under their eyes. Once finished, she had them shed their towels, and stand naked while she walked circles, studying them from every angle. Nodding, she went to the stock of fabric and selected silk robes of shimmering black for Nuru. Efra's were the red of arterial blood. Draping the silks about their shoulders, Mbali created sweeping curves and plunging lines, strategically tying them with delicate ropes finer than anything Nuru had ever seen. The material hugged every curve, displayed every flaw.

Nuru crossed her arms again. She felt naked without her course grey thobe. The silk weighed nothing, felt like she wore a morning breeze.

"You're a Senator," scolded Mbali. "Stop hiding behind your arms."

She then helped the two women into delicate slippers, muttering at the condition of their toenails as if that was something they had control of.

Nuru shuffled about, afraid to take normal steps lest the slippers fall off.

Huffing, Mbali showing her how to walk with dainty little steps instead of dragging her feet everywhere.

"What if we need to run?" demanded Efra, doing her own awkward shuffle.

"Senators," said Mblai, "don't run."

Efra's eyes narrowed in disbelief. "And what if we need to fight?"

The woman laughed as if Efra had made a joke.

Shrugging, Efra studied Nuru, looking her up and down. "If I didn't kind of prefer men, I would definitely fuck you."

Mbali's eyes widened, but she said nothing.

Turning to Efra, Nuru felt like she was seeing her for the first time. Despite her diminutive stature, she was regal, commanding. Where Nuru hid behind crossed arms, Efra stood with utter confidence.

You're jealous.

The scar drew Nuru's attention from Efra's frighteningly intense gaze to her quirked lips.

"If you didn't scare the shit out of me," said Nuru, "I'd fuck you too."

Efra grunted a laugh. "Liar." She scowled, picking at the thin fabric as if searching for something. "How do I carry stuff?" she asked. "I can see my damned nipples. No way I can hide a weapon in this."

"I…you don't…Pardon?" said Mbali.

"Where do I keep a weapon?" enunciated Efra.

Approaching the table, Mbali selected a dark green fold of fabric with a loop of fine rope attached. "I think the colour will balance the red of—"

"What is that?" demanded Efra.

"A purse." Mbali handed Efra the tiny bag, showing her how to open it. There was just enough room for Efra's dagger.

Efra glared at the purse. "If I'm walking around in this see-through sack—"

"It's called a dress," said Mbali.

"—and carrying this purse-thing, isn't it the first place someone will look for a weapon?"

"No one," chuffed Mbali, "searches Senators. And certainly no one checks their purses for weapons."

"That seems stupid." Efra slung the loop of rope over her head and hung the purse from one hip. The rope crossed her chest between her breasts, making the already filmy fabric even more revealing.

"Oh my gods no," said Mblai, looking ready to faint. "Hang it from one shoulder."

"But it might fall off. I'd rather have a pocket or a pouch in the dress."

"It would ruin the lines," explained Mbali.

"I don't give a fuck about the lines."

Kofi, standing at the door, pretended to clear his throat.

"I think fat boy has a cold," said Efra.

Dressed like a Bird, red leather armour fitted tight, showing off every bulge of muscle, ebony cudgel hanging at his slim hips, Kofi strode into the room. With a quick bow to Nuru, Mbali left.

Efra studied the Loa with undisguised appreciation and loosed a low, throaty growl.

"We need to get moving," he said, ignoring her, "if we're—" He noticed Nuru. "I…If we're… The gate. Today." He swallowed. "We should go."

While Efra collected her flint dagger, placing it in her purse with an annoyed shake of her head, Nuru did the same with the god-killer and the carving of Mother Death. She kept her back turned so Kofi wouldn't see the knife.

When they were ready, he led them through the church, up into the tannery. Nuru did her best not to shuffle in the slippers.

Seeing only a couple of Loa, she asked, "Where is everybody?"

"Obeying your commands," he answered, eyes straight ahead. "Those who haven't left for the fields and crèches are spreading the word."

"Which word?" asked Efra.

"Mother Death has returned. Her Heart lives. For hundreds of generations we have prepared for a war no one believed would come. I see it now. Chikelu thought he mattered more than you." He glanced at Nuru. "He didn't *really* believe in the Queen's return." He waved a hand at the empty halls. "All this was for his own gain."

Exiting the church, Nuru blinked in the morning light. Fat flies, still drowsy from the night's chill, buzzed in lazy circles. Down there, in the tannery basement, time ceased to have any meaning. She could have been there hours, or days.

Four men jogged up the street toward them pulling an enclosed four-wheeled wagon as if they were oxen. Carved in intaglio, every surface depicted scenes from the *Book of Bastion*. It reminded Nuru of the wagons the Birds used to cart Dirts out to the Sand Wall, though much prettier. Slowing, they stopped in front of Kofi. They wore shirts and pants of grey, their arms tattooed in finger-length black dashes. They waited in silence, eyes averted.

Kofi opened a door gilded in worked oak. Peering past him, Nuru saw a cushioned bench on each side. Lace curtains adorned the windows to give the occupants privacy. He gestured for the two women to enter the carriage. When it was Nuru's turn, he stared off up the street like there might be something incredibly interesting in the next block. Once she was seated, he closed the door.

"Aren't you coming?" she asked, suddenly terrified of being abandoned.

She knew nothing of the Crafters. In comparison, the Senators might as well be gods.

"Guards don't ride," he answered.

At a word from Kofi, the men pulling the carriage obediently set off at a jog.

For a long moment, Nuru and Efra stared at each other, swaying with the gentle movement. They moved effortlessly through the streets of the Crafters' Ring. With the curtains pushed aside, the open windows allowed a breeze to pass through.

"Does it feel like we should be going the other way?" asked Efra. "The only time I ever thought I might ride in something like this was if they were taking me out to the Sand Wall."

Nuru nodded without answering.

Streets blurred past. Crafter homes with their odd shapes and blatant decorations. Children here and there, clinging to their mother's skirts, stared with wide eyes. Everyone watched them. Every Crafter slowed to a stop, and stood, eyes locked on the carriage until they were out of sight. Nuru knew that look. Seething anger. Helpless rage. It was exactly the way the Dirts watched the Birds and the nahual.

So many colours and sights, strange buildings—some even with wooden doors barring people from entering!

They passed through an open public square. There were four equally spaced wells where there would have been one in the Growers' Ring. The usual sacrificial altar, worn round, and stained brown from use, sat in the centre.

Efra touched Nuru's arm. "Look," she said, pointing to the far end of the square.

A wood framework stood like the bones of some colossal beast. From it hung scores of corpses, nailed there by wooden spikes driven between the bones in their forearms. Most were long dead, but some few still twitched and cried out. Dried blood stained the ankles of the corpses, showing where arteries had been clipped to bleed them dry. Troughs in the stone beneath them funnelled away the spillage.

"Why?" asked Nuru. "There's nothing like that in the Growers' Ring."

"I guess some people are worth killing slowly," answered Efra, "but not so awful you need to cart them out to the Sand Wall."

Crafters, a mob of orange and brown, scattered from the carriage's path, narrowed eyes following them.

"They think we're Senators," Efra reminded Nuru. "They hate us because they think we have more."

Turning a corner, they passed into a street of tenements nicer than those they'd previously seen. Some were easily two or three times larger than the homes on the other streets. Fresh paint adorned stone. Bright curtains hung in many windows. Though everyone still wore the same orange and brown, the fabrics were noticeably superior.

Were some Crafters better off than others? Why? Not in all her life had Nuru seen a difference between one Dirt and another. Except for, maybe, those serving the nahual's desires.

A woman sat on the stone steps before her home, enjoying the sun, a tiny newborn on her breast.

So small.

So fragile.

Eyes wide, Nuru stared.

"A baby," she whispered, thoughts reeling.

Efra ignored her.

While Nuru knew nothing of children, nothing of caring for them, she'd seen babies at the Ceremony of Belonging, when a Grower's baby was taken by the nahual to be raised in a crèche. This child had that raw look, eyes and fists clenched, flesh wrinkled.

"Funny," said Efra. "Babies look like old Dirts."

"How old do you think that is?" Nuru asked.

Efra squinted through the window as they passed. "A day? Maybe two?"

Nuru agreed.

Two days, at most.

Face Painted with Bells killed Father Death a week ago.

"Kofi!" barked Nuru. "Stop! Stop this thing!"

Without hesitation, he ordered the men pulling the carriage to halt.

Nuru leapt out before it came to a complete stop.

Ignoring everyone, she approached the woman. Startled, the Crafter flushed with embarrassment, lifted the baby, adjusting her brown shawl to cover herself.

Nuru couldn't understand. It had been a beautiful moment, the most beautiful moment she'd ever seen.

Rising to her feet, the woman did a strange thing where she bent her knees a little and bowed.

Confused, Nuru slowed her approach. She hadn't thought this through, had no idea what to say.

"Your baby," she started. "I…"

The Crafter woman shook, tears falling free. She clutched the child close, like Nuru might take it.

"Beautiful," Nuru managed. "It's beautiful. What's its name?"

"Her name is Tapiwa," said the Crafter.

"She's beautiful." Nuru's heart slammed in her chest. Everything about this encounter felt wrong. "How old is she?"

"She was born last night," answered the woman.

Last night.

Nuru staggered away, barely noticing Kofi as he helped her back into the carriage.

Movement, the sound of wood wheels clattering on stone.

"What was that about?" Efra asked.

Checking that Kofi was too far away to hear, Nuru whispered, "Father Death has been dead for days."

"So?"

"That baby was born yesterday. Even though there's no god puri- fying souls and doing whatever The Lord did to make rebirth possible, babies are still being born."

Efra stared at her with dawning comprehension. "We don't need them."

"If that was a lie," said Nuru, "if life goes on without Father Death, what else was a lie?"

"All of it." Efra grinned, mad and evil, terrifying. "The gods need us more than we need them."

"You know what this means?" Nuru asked.

"Fucking right. We're going to kill them all."

The rest of the Crafters' Ring was a blur. Streets of huge homes and fat Crafters led to trash-littered alleys of small unadorned tenements. They passed through another public square with its corpse-decorated scaffolding. She saw anger everywhere, a quiet rage. Having been here once before, she recognized the areas where the Crafters went to get food. The huge tables were barren except for a few sad-looking scraps. None of it looked so bad that a Dirt would comment or hesitate to wolf it down.

They're angry that they have to eat the way we've eaten for thousands of years.

Arriving at the gate, Kofi leaned in the window and said, "Look bored and annoyed," as he went forward to talk to the Birds on guard.

"I am!" Efra shouted after him as he departed.

The squad of Hummingbirds working the pedestrian gate asked a few terse questions, and waved the carriage through without so much as glancing at the women.

Lit by flickering torches, air thick with smoke, the tunnel through the Wall of Lords was half the length of the one through the Grey Wall. They exited the far side, blinking in the sun.

This was a new world, as different again from the Crafters' Ring as that was from the Growers'.

No two buildings were the same, each an intricate work of art. Ornate twists of stone adorned every surface, decorated every doorway. Many towered three, sometimes four stories into the air. Though Nuru had heard the Quarter Cathedrals were impossibly tall and had towers and bridges of stone, she never saw one. The Northern Cathedral, the closest to the Wheat District, was still a full day's travel around the ring.

Men and women, riding in carved carriages that were themselves works of art, were hustled around the streets, darting through knots of pedestrians with careless abandon. People scattered from their path, often yelled at, or cursed by those pulling the carriages. The main streets were clean. Teams of people, all wearing threadbare vests, their exposed arms tattooed in black hash marks, swept and scoured everything.

They passed wood stalls offering foods Nuru had never before seen. Slices of plum and peach coated with what looked like grains of white sand. Intricate rolls of twisted bread filled the air with savoury aromas. Tiny morsels of meat were offered on carved sticks. Tall wood cups full of squeezed fruit juice stood ready and waiting.

Nuru's stomach growled.

Some transaction took place each time food or drink was acquired, but the carriage went by too fast for Nuru to be sure what traded hands.

Down dark alleys she caught sight of yet another world. Scraps of paper, so precious in the Growers' Ring she'd never owned more than a couple of sheets, lay in filthy heaps. The people sweeping the main streets brushed everything into the closest lane, and then left it there. Gusts of wind blew half of it back out moments later. Slumped forms sat or lay sprawled in the shadows. She couldn't tell if they were asleep or dead. Those she saw clearly were emaciated beyond even the worn scrawniness of the Growers. Everyone who bustled past their carriage smelled of flowers and fruit, but each time her carriage passed an alley, she caught the scents of rot and decay, puke and shit.

Even Dirts don't live like that.

How could someone live in a reality of so much, and have so little?

The silk dresses Nuru and Efra wore suddenly seemed dull. Many wore robes with so many clashing colours they hurt to look at. Strange headgear wobbled precariously as people went about incomprehensible tasks.

"Everyone is rushing everywhere," said Efra, "but no one is actually *doing* anything."

Nuru understood. With a few exceptions—those in street gangs, the whores at the gates, and those who served the whims of the nahual—Growers had few choices: work in the fields or menageries, or work in the warehouses loading wagons. Work and sleep, that was life. The Crafters worked too, making things. They prepared foods, built tools.

Nuru studied a passing man, a sheaf of papers tucked under one arm. Though the flowing robes hid it somewhat, he sported a distended belly, as if pregnant. His arms and legs were thin and weak, flabby.

A day harvesting wheat in the sun would kill him.

Efra was right. Nowhere did Nuru see a single person working at a task that would create something.

Efra touched Nuru's arm, jolting her from her thoughts. The carriage tilted as it headed up an incline. Leaning to look out the window, Nuru saw they passed over a bridge of stone. Below, dark blue water swirled by. Strangely shaped wood carvings, painted in reds and greens, rode the currents. She longed to touch them, to have access to such paints and carving tools.

Those were made by Crafters, she realized, knowing it was true. No one here painted or carved. No one worked or sweated or laboured.

Ever alert, Kofi stayed by Nuru's window. A child, a boy of maybe ten years, scampered toward them, a score of black lines inked into his arms. One of the men pulling the carriage sent the child fleeing with a swift kick.

Men and woman dressed in dull clothes, their tanned arms black with tattooed lines, pulled carriages. In a world of fat and soft people, these beasts of burden were uniformly skinny and exhausted. People lined the street, kneeling on the hot stone, crude wood bowls held out before them. Gaunt and malnourished, teeth rotting, arms black with tattoos, they looked worse than Growers. Though few were scarred, they possessed none of a Dirt's lean muscle.

"What do the tattoos mean?" Nuru asked Kofi.

"Indebted and indentured," he answered. Realizing she didn't understand, he continued. "Sometimes people borrow too much and get themselves into trouble. Sometimes they make bad decisions and wind up in debt."

"Borrow too much what?" Efra demanded over Nuru's shoulder.

"Scrip." Seeing their blank looks, he sighed. "The gods back the currency. Each unit of scrip is worth one hour of labour. Work for an hour, and you earn one scrip. You can then use it to buy food and rent a home."

Not knowing what rent was, Nuru ignored that part. "If everyone gets paid the same for an hour of work, why are some people starving."

"Well, some hours are worth more than others. An hour of a High Senate member's time is easily worth two hundred hours of someone who sells food by the road."

"Why?" asked Efra. "People need food."

"It's a question of importance, and skill. Anyone can sell a cake. Few people have the wisdom to make just and lasting laws."

"The High Senators are wise above all others?" said Nuru.

Kofi winced. "That might be an exaggeration."

One hand on Nuru's shoulder, Efra asked, "Why don't these 'just and wise' laws apply to the Dirts?"

"They do!"

"The way Growers live is just?" asked Nuru.

"Well, no, but it's a matter of perspective. You have to see the bigger picture."

"No," said Nuru. "You have to see the smaller picture."

A pained look crossed his features. "Outside of the Growers' Ring everything has a price. Every bite of food. Every sip of water. Clothes. Homes. All the luxuries in life."

For a Dirt, working under the shade of a tree was a luxury. What was a luxury to people who had everything and did nothing?

"Luxuries?" Nuru asked.

"Books and perfume and sweets and nice clothes and a bigger house and servants."

Efra leaned past Nuru again. "Servants? People can own people?"

"Of course! Money is just a way of assigning a value on your time. You get paid to do your job. If you spend more money than you earn, you're spending time you haven't yet been paid for. If you spend too much, you can spend all your time. Whoever paid you the money is owed, and your time—your life, if it comes to that—is how you repay them."

"Growers don't pay for food. We don't own our tenements," said Nuru "Why would the inner rings not get the same?"

"This is why most people see the life of the Growers as idyllic and simple. They have no concerns. They do simple tasks, work the fields, raise the animals—"

"You've clearly never shovelled shit or bailed wheat," snapped Efra.

Ignoring her, Kofi continued. "Growers don't have to worry about debt or whether they'll be able to afford to feed their families."

"We're not allowed to have families," Nuru pointed out.

He winced. "Right. Sorry. But you must admit, your lives are simple compared to this."

He waved a hand at the mad crush of carriages jockeying to make it into the next street. Guards shoved pedestrians out of the way, clubbing those too slow to move. Children, skin stretched on bone, ran everywhere, begging. Sometimes people handed them scraps of paper or crumbs of food, but mostly they were ignored.

"I've never seen a Senator in the Growers' Ring," said Efra. "Why do they think our lives are so fucking great?"

"That's what the nahual tell them," explained Kofi.

Efra rubbed at her scar, watching the passing crowd. "Just like they tell everyone we're all stupid and ignorant and docile."

Kofi looked away, pretending to be alert for trouble. "Yes," he finally admitted.

Ahead, the jam of carriages cleared, and they were once again moving, Kofi walking alongside.

"When we've killed the last god," Efra whispered to Nuru, "we start on the Senators."

And then the Bankers after that?

A fat woman, jiggling like even the most buxom Growers never could, stepped over a scrawny child sleeping in the street. Though maybe it was dead. Nuru couldn't tell. It didn't move, showed no sign of life.

"Kofi," she said. "Is that child alive?"

He shrugged. "Don't know."

When he made no sign of moving, she said, "Go check."

"We don't have time for this. You can't save everyone."

"Not being able to save everyone doesn't mean I can't save *one*."

He turned on her in frustration. "This isn't how Senators act."

"I'm not a Senator."

"It'll draw attention!"

Seeing her expression, Kofi went to check on the child. The crowd parted around him, angry at the inconvenience, as he knelt beside it. He touched its shoulder and then returned to the carriage.

Lips cutting a hard line, he shook his head. "Cold. Dead." Wincing, he added, "Sorry."

The carriage lurched back into motion and life in the Senators' Ring continued as if there weren't a dead child lying in the street.

Numb, Nuru sat in silence.

And they think we're *animals.*

Unfortunate deaths happened in the Growers' Ring all the time, but each one made a mark. If someone died working the fields, pitching dead for some unknown reason, killed by the heat, or dragged off by one of the many feral animals that had escaped the menageries over the years, everyone knew. Corpses weren't left in the streets. Or, they hadn't been. Now, there were so many sun-bloated dead, covered in ash, she couldn't imagine anyone was left to collect them.

Peering from the window, Nuru looked up and down the street. No ash. No swelling bodies. Not even the red sand that dusted everything in the Wheat District. Fat soft people everywhere. There were no signs of violence, and yet people stepped blithely over the corpses of children.

Retreating from the view, she sat back, eyes closed, trying to lose herself in the swaying of the carriage.

"You're wondering if it's worth saving," said Efra.

"Is it?"

"No."

Eyes still closed, she heard Efra moving on the bench, trying to get comfortable in these strange clothes.

"*This* is not worth saving," continued Efra. "The Senators aren't worth saving. I haven't seen them yet, but I'm betting the Bankers aren't worth saving either." She grunted a harsh laugh. "The nahual *definitely* aren't worth saving."

"So?" asked Nuru. "What are we doing? Why bother?"

"You have to strip these people of their possessions. You have to strip them of their titles and excuses. Reduce them to what they were; people."

Efra talking like she cares about people?

Nuru waited.

"We aren't saving Growers or Crafters or Bankers or nahual. We're saving people. The gods built this city. They built the rings and they decided some people would be slaves while others got to be fat. We kill the gods. We kill their world. We make something new."

She makes it sound so easy.

Turning another corner, she stared up at a twisted colossus of stone. Towers and spires curled so far into the sky she could barely see their tops. Windows followed the spirals up. The thought of looking down from such a height turned her stomach. The nearest wall, shaped by the gods, looked like the owl-feather cloak of a nahual of The Lord.

"We're here," said Kofi.

The carriage slowed, entering the shadow of the church. Though the temperature hadn't changed, a shiver ran through Nuru. She felt small here, weak and pathetic.

The gods built this, all of it. Anyone who thought they could challenge them was a fool.

As high as ten men standing on top of each other, the main building towered over all the other structures.

"Why men?" asked Nuru, to distract herself. "Why do we always think of how high a thing is based on the number of men standing on each other?"

"Women are too smart to stand on top of each other just to see how tall some dumb building is," said Efra. "But men…you know they'll try."

Back in the tannery, Efra said that if Nuru was the last Heart, she would ascend to become Heart's Mirror. 'Heart's Mirror is the voice of the gods,' Efra had said. 'And what does that mean?'

But the question was rhetorical. She knew the answer.

"Come," said Kofi, opening the carriage door. "Let's pray Subira is still here,"

Let's pray.

Nuru looked to Efra and the scarred girl nodded.

Fuck your doubts. Fuck your fears. Do what you can. What happens after will be the problem of those who survive.

Efra took her hand.

The gods didn't stand a fucking chance.

AKACHI - SHE IS POISON

Faith with certainty isn't faith at all. True faith can only be found at the bottom, in the hollowed-out gutted depths of a ravaged soul. There are a thousand parables about faith, but do any sing the praises of the untested?

No.

True faith is what remains when the gods have taken everything.

—The Book of Bastion

Akachi woke to a crushing headache, the feel of rough stone on his spine, and the stench of sweat and terror. With a groan, he pushed himself upright. Soaked through, his robes clung to him, the red, white, and black bands stained with blood and filth. His wrists, all bone, poked out from his sleeves. He looked sunken, caved in. Never a large man, he'd lost weight. He couldn't remember his last meal.

He didn't think so. The thought of food turned his stomach.

Reaching up, he touched the cloth wrapping his head and covering his left eye with the stump-fingers of his left hand.

They tore my eye out.

"I think I missed my calling," said Omphile.

"What?" Turning, Akachi realized she stood on his blind side.

"I should have been a nahual of the Lord of the Root," she said. "That's some damned fine bandaging."

Left hand. Left eye. It felt like he'd lost half himself. He was half a man living in half a world.

You can't hunt like this, nahualli of Cloud Serpent.

He was broken, ruined. He served his god, and it cost him everything.

I have nothing left to give.

Hollowed.

He couldn't do this. What if he lost his other eye?

A shiver of fear ran through him. He felt strangely vulnerable now.

The less there is of you, the more you have to lose.

Bastion's enemies were destroying him, bit by bit, piece by piece.

First, his fingers. Now, his eye.

Something else was missing too, but he couldn't put a word to it. Some piece of *him* had been cracked off, like knapped flint. The detritus of his soul lay scattered in the dark basement.

Had it been gone when he woke on the altar, healed by his god?

"Fucking—" He couldn't say more. Sobs shook him as he mourned what was lost. His past. His future. Everything gone. Stolen. No hope. He was a failure. The forces of evil had won. This was too much for one man. His god—his father—they asked too much. He wanted to go home. Everything was wrong. He should never have come here, never have left the comfort of the Priests' Ring. He could have stayed there forever, lived in father's shadow. He'd be nothing, and no one, and happy like he was as a child.

How many parables had he read about the gods testing the faithful?

They were horseshit! No one ever bent in those stories, no one ever broke. Saying that a man could stand against such torture was a lie! Take all he is, and he cracks! Everyone breaks! Even Bastion, eternal Bastion, showed wear and tear! Towers of the Northern Cathedral lay sprawled and shattered across the church's courtyard. Stone melted.

Everything breaks. Everything fails.

Fucking *Book of Bastion*.

Fucking parables. Fucking lies and shit.

No one ever said, 'I can't do this.' No one screamed 'You ask too much!' at their god.

They never just laid down and died.

Akachi lay back on the stone, closed his eye. "I'm done."

Tears ran free and he didn't care, felt no shame. Compared to failing his father and his god, disappointing a couple of Serpents was nothing.

Shadow fell across his right eye.

"Get up," said Omphile. She stood over him, the Staff of the Fifth Sun held in one hand.

"Fuck off."

Reaching down with her free hand, she gripped the collar of his robes and hauled him effortlessly to his feet.

He blinked at her in surprise.

"You're strong," he said, stupidly.

"You have no idea."

"Doesn't matter how strong you are. I'm done. We're done."

Captain Melokuhle sat a dozen strides away on a raised curb of stone, her head in her hands. She ignored them.

"You want the good news first, or the bad?" Omphile asked. She spun the staff, rolling it across the back of her hand like a baton. An ancient artefact of immeasurable worth, the heart of a dead god, and she played with it.

She's insane.

She killed Firash, and now Lubanzi was dead. They fucking tore out Akachi's eye, and here she was, joking.

"Neither," Akachi said, not caring.

"The good it is! You're not dead."

"Great. Just fucking fantastic. What's the bad news?"

"Oh. You're going to wish you were dead before the end."

"How do you know?"

Leaning close so she could whisper in his ear, she said, "I was fucking Firash. He told me everything. I know *exactly* how this ends. Why do you think I am so unconcerned?" She spun the staff with effortless precision, always in perfect control. "Everything turns out just fine."

"It does?" Akachi touched the bandage over his eye.

"For me. Less fine for you. But there's more good news!"

"Yeah?"

She grinned, leering. "I'm going to fuck you before all this is over."

"Oh."

He was right. Everyone broke. Omphile hid behind her own wall, but she was as shattered as anyone. Whatever god touched her and gave her those grey eyes, cracked her wide.

"Can I tell you a secret?" asked Omphile, tossing the staff up in a lazy arc and catching it with the other hand.

"Sure."

"I killed Lubanzi. Fucker was always staring at my ass, yanking it at night thinking about me."

Akachi looked to Melokuhle, but she remained head in hands, muttering to herself. "That's why you killed him?"

"What? No. I'm not crazy. I killed him because each time one of the squad dies, the good captain breaks a little more." She spun the staff from one hand to the other and back, continuous smooth motion. "She's far too emotionally invested in her people to be good at this. That's why she's such a shitty killer."

In the dream-world, Firash had looked like rotten jade, cancerous cracks cutting through him.

Omphile did that. She's an infection.

She nudged Akachi's arm with the head of the staff. Even though he'd given up, even though all he wanted was to go home, he hated seeing it in her hands.

It's mine.

He wanted to hold it again. Gods he missed the feel of it, the confident weight of calcified stone.

"You know," mused the assassin, "what's really amazing to me is that you're still going to let me fuck you. It's kind of sad, really."

Focussed on the staff, her words slid off him and she looked annoyed.

"Firash was a tezcat," said Akachi.

"He was a fool."

"You're assuming he didn't lie to you," he continued. "You think you're safe, but he told you what he wanted you to hear."

"What he wanted me to—" Omphile studied Akachi with narrowed grey eyes. "Maybe not so dumb."

"I could tell the Captain," said Akachi, wondering if this would be the moment she killed him.

"You don't," she said. "Don't know why. Maybe because then I'd kill her."

Captain Melokuhle rose from where she sat. Shoulders bent, eyes hollowed with guilt, she looked frail, defeated.

"I've decided," said the Captain. "We'll return to the Priests' Ring to be reassigned or punished for our failures." Her voice lacked all authority. It sounded like she offered suggestions rather than gave orders.

Home.

Akachi wanted to see his mom again. He wanted to curl up in his bed and sleep until Bastion returned to the sand. Even facing his father was better than this.

"They took my eye," he said, as if that explained anything.

"Captain," said Omphile, ignoring him, "We haven't failed yet. The Cloud Serpent nahualli is still alive." She placed a comforting hand on Melokuhle's shoulder. "Sure, there's a little less of him than what we started with, but all the important bits are still there." She winked at Akachi.

The Captain turned to Akachi. "We can't do this with just the two of us." Explaining. Rationalizing. Apologizing.

He didn't care. Going home, saving what little remained of him, was all that mattered.

"We can, if one of them is me," answered Omphile.

With a deep breath, Captain Melokuhle nodded. Akachi saw no fight in her. She didn't agree, she gave in.

"What do we do now?" Melokuhle asked.

Akachi opened his mouth to argue, to demand they see him home, when Omphile handed him the staff. Surprised, he clung to it. His eyes locked on the bloodstone.

The heart of a dead god.

In the hands of a god's Heart.

This was not some trifle to be toyed with. This was an ancient arte-fact. With the Staff of the Fifth Sun, he would kill Mother Death's Heart, banish the god forever! Nothing could stop him!

"We still need a tecuhtli," he said, surprising himself.

"That's better! See Captain? Even half-blind and totally useless, the boy stands ready to do his duty!"

Gripping the staff tight, fingers aching from squeezing so hard, he realized he was. *I can do this.*

He would do whatever was required of him.

"Can we do any less?" the assassin asked her captain.

Melokuhle shook her head, sagging in defeat.

Frowning, Omphile turned a complete circle as if getting her bear-ings. "Ah! We're near the Wall of Lords. There's a church of Father Death not far from here, in the Senators' Ring."

Akachi recalled her smug grin when she returned with the directions leading them to the church they'd just escaped. She'd looked pleased with herself, like she was party to some small whimsy.

Had Firash warned her what awaited them?

Stop, Akachi chided himself. Contemplating the plans of tezcat was a short path to madness. Theirs was a chaotic art, prone to misunderstand-ings and confusion. Firash could never have been so accurate.

Pushing his doubts aside, Akachi gripped the staff tighter. No point in worrying himself over impossible possibilities.

Walking with only one eye proved trickier than expected. Even constantly moving his head, swivelling from side to side, he tripped often, stumbling over the tiniest imperfections in the stone.

Akachi and the Turquoise Serpents passed through the gate into the Wall of Lords without issue. The Birds on guard waved them through without question. Walking the length of the tunnel, the calcified Staff of the Fifth Sun ringing off the floor with each stride, Akachi felt increasingly better. Confidence grew in him. He bore a weapon of gods. He was the Heart of Cloud Serpent and would someday enter the Gods' Ring and ascend to be Heart's Mirror.

Stepping into the Senators' Ring, Akachi bared teeth at raging sun in a victorious snarl. Nothing could stop him! As long as he held the staff, he was the will of the Cloud Serpent writ in flesh and bone. He placed the ruin of his half-hand over his heart. Obsidian lay in there, a direct connection to his god.

How could I have doubted?

Though he remembered his fears, they seemed foolish now.

He gripped the staff tighter, grinning until his face ached.

"Feel better?" asked Omphile.

He nodded.

"Then come."

She led them through the Senators' Ring. Better than the Crafters', and a thousand times more civilized than the animal filth of the Growers', it still paled before the beauty of home. Someday, he would return, triumphant.

Akachi shook his head in wonder. Waking to realize his eye was gone, that it wasn't a terrible dream, had been crushing. Though muted, the loss still bothered him. Lying defeated in the road, he'd understood how much he'd lost, he'd known that if he kept on this path, he'd lose even more. He remembered thinking that he'd lost more than an eye and some fingers. What had Omphile called him? Broken. She said he was broken the way a hero needed to be. And now he was even more broken. He laughed at the sun's heat, felt more ready to be the hero than ever before.

A willingness to do anything, to commit any atrocity to achieve the desired end, was a horrible thing. He knew it in his blood. People should have doubts, they should question. They should question both their own motives, and the motives of others.

Akachi had no need for questions, no use for doubt. He did the work of the gods; he was the will and fist of Cloud Serpent. As long as he had this staff, he was invincible.

Akachi stopped and Omphile and Melokuhle halted with him.

"Omphile," said Akachi.

He didn't trust her. She was insane, god-touched and grey-eyed. But she'd handed over the Staff of the Fifth Sun without hesitation. Maybe she was on his side.

The assassin waited, head cocked.

He held out the staff. "Take this for a moment."

With a shrug she accepted it.

Akachi gasped, his knees buckling.

Understanding savaged him, a jaguar with a baby rabbit in its jaws.

His losses weren't nothing.

His god took everything and would demand more.

Cloud Serpent wanted him to kill Mother Death's Heart in the underworld, maybe even battle the god herself. There was no way Akachi would come out of this unscathed.

His eye was gone, a gaping wound in his skull, a hole torn clear through his soul!

More than anything, Akachi wanted to flee his destiny. He wanted to curl up on the road and cry or run home to his mother. He wanted to beg forgiveness for all the terrible things he'd done, for all the worse things he knew he would do.

"Give—" Akachi's voice cracked. He reached out his right hand, fingers spasming in need. "Give me the staff."

Omphile hesitated and Akachi wanted to scream. And then his fingers touched it and it was in his hand and his doubts fell away, the pitiful fears of a little boy.

Faith was everything.

Using the staff as a crutch, Akachi rose to his feet.

"May we continue now?" asked the assassin. "If we keep moving, we might make it before nightfall."

Akachi nodded, and they set off.

Leaving behind the dull dreariness of the Growers and Crafters helped. The Senators' Ring might not possess the fulsome beauty of the Priests' Ring, but it gave him at least a taste of home. The other rings aspired to achieve the perfection found at Bastion's Heart.

I can't let Mother Death and her Dirt Heart ruin that.

It was impossible to understand what drove the street-sorcerer. She was blind to the fact her efforts could only lead to the destruction of the Last City. She doomed humanity. Was she so deranged, so evil to the core of her soul that she *desired* that result?

Or does she think she's doing the right thing?

The ignorance of Dirts was stunning. To give one such power was an unforgivable sin. That Mother Death had done so was a sign of how desperate the god was.

'The Destroyer seeks the end of all,' Zalika had said during the dream that was more than a dream. 'The final blasphemy, the murder of an entire pantheon.'

Mother Death is insane if she thinks she can replace the other gods.

He remembered thinking something similar before. The memory seemed unreal, tenuous.

No. His god mentioned that Nuru had killed Her Skirt is Stars but said nothing more.

Her intentions are obvious.

But he couldn't quite remember how he'd pieced it together. It felt like the answer had somehow been handed to him. A voice in his thoughts. Broken glass.

I figured it out.

Akachi gripped the staff tighter, knew he was right.

Questions are the antithesis of faith.

The Book said so.

The street-sorcerer was the weak point. Kill her, and Mother Death's plans would crumble.

She is the end. He knew it to be true, knew it in his heart, right to the very core of his existence. Only one man could stop the street-sorcerer. The fate of all the world, every living soul in Bastion, rested on his shoulders. He would not fail. He could not.

Akachi realized he was once again grinning. His hand ached, he clutched the staff so tight, tendons standing tight in his forearm. Calm strength and certainty crept up his arm, infused his heart with holy joy, lit his soul on fire like a beacon to call the worthy to prayer.

It felt like lying in the shadow of a building and being slowly exposed to the heat of the sun as it rose. In moments its warmth filled him, and he was again confident in his destiny.

I can do this. I will not fail.

Akachi understood. Cloud Serpent knew his Heart's doubts, saw his weakness.

That's why he sent me for the staff.

The dream of Zalika in the cathedral was different than when Cloud Serpent came to him as he lay dying on the altar, or when the Lord of the Hunt told him to kill Darakai. Those experiences were etched in Akachi's blood.

It's the drugs.

The dream must feel less real due to the lack of jainkoei.

Omphile leading the way, Senators parted before the jade armour of a Turquoise Serpent. Where the assassin strode with a confident strut, head held high, grey eyes seeing everything, the captain followed like a beaten dog. She looked at nothing, saw only the ground before her feet.

Akachi wanted to hand her the staff so she could feel better but couldn't bear the thought of parting with it.

What if she didn't give it back?

NURU - PARASITIC DIVINITY

A working economy is part of a working civilization.

Civilization falls apart when people begin to believe that the economy is *the civilization.*

In the earliest edition of the Book of Bastion, *the Hour was given as the only monetary denomination. Work one hour and get paid for one hour. Each piece of scrip represented an hour of labour, no matter what that labour was. A Banker's hour was worth the same as a Grower's hour.*

Unfortunately, there will always be people who believe their hour—or what they're doing during their hour—is more valuable than the hours of others.

How can the hour of someone who creates nothing be worth more than an hour of someone who feeds the city?

How can the hour of someone who creates nothing be worth more than that of one who crafts the tools that keep Bastion functioning?

Once the Hour standard was broken, it didn't take long for Bankers and Senators to make many hundreds of Hours for each hour they worked.

—The Loa Book of the Invisibles

The tecuhtli, a thick-set woman of indeterminate age with grey hair and laugh-lines crinkling the corners of her eyes, met them at the church's entrance. All white, her owl feather cloak stopped just shy of touching the floor behind her. Her deep, caring eyes passed over Kofi and Efra, and locked onto Nuru. She looked her up and down, but not the way most people did. Nuru saw no hint of lust or hunger or judgement.

"You three are a long way from home," said the woman.

Nuru's chest tightened in fear.

She knows. She sees through these disguises.

They should run. This was a nahualli of Father Death! She could rip their souls from their bodies, damn them to an eternity of hell!

"Nahualli Subira?" Kofi asked.

She waved him to silence with a flutter of fingers.

"Why would we trust a nahual who betrayed her own kind?" demanded Efra with her usual tact.

"This is not a conversation for the street," said Subira. "Come!"

Turning on her heel, she set off into the church. Nuru, Efra, and Kofi followed.

"When I was an acolyte," said Subira as she walked, "I found a copy of the very first *Book of Bastion*. Things were different then, in the first millennia. Before the great schism, the nahual and tecolotl—that's the old name for stone sorcerers—were one. We call her The Lady of the House because she made Bastion. She was our Queen, and we betrayed her. We cast her out. She saved humanity and the few surviving gods, and we repaid her by banishing her."

In the Growers' Ring, churches of The Lord were stone shacks with nothing but an unadorned set of stairs leading into a damp dark that stank of salt and decay. The prayer halls were stone boxes, Dirts crammed in shoulder to shoulder, as the nahual droned on about souls and rebirth. The altar was a raised slab of stone, stained with generations of spilled blood. Subira's temple, in the Senators' Ring, was nothing like that. The front entrance led to a grand hall, arched ceiling towering far above. Columns of worked stone depicting souls being dragged down from the skies, stood every twenty paces.

"I realized," continued Subira, "that much of what we learned as acolytes were, in fact, lies. If you read your histories…" She glanced at Nuru and Efra. "Sorry, I know you can't read. But if you could, you'd see Bastion has been dying since that day. Every generation is smaller than the last. The more I thought about it, the more I realized there could be but one answer: Father Death hoards and devours souls."

"They all do," said Nuru.

"Ah," said Subira, "the pretty one speaks. Blood and worship are not enough. The gods hunger for souls. The oldest copy of the Book says Mother Death forced rules upon the gods. She culled their numbers to something manageable. She forbade the hoarding of souls and enforced strict rationing."

Only half listening, Nuru's breath caught as disparate pieces of information, fragments of remembered sermons, came together.

Face Painted with Bells didn't rule the underworld. A godling, she merely held it for Mother Death.

There is no death god purifying souls. Nuru thought it through. *That means the souls of new-born babies aren't coming from the underworld.*

At least not at the moment.

New souls were either being created or coming from some unknown source. If the gods could purify souls for rebirth and new souls were available, why, then, was Bastion dying?

The answer was so horrific she shied from admitting it. Even with new souls being created and old souls reborn, the gods still managed to devastate the population. All those empty tenements. All those fields gone wild. She'd heard stories of ruined menageries grown over by rampant forests, the animals long escaped.

The gods feed on worship and blood and souls.

The underworld was a means of allowing people to live and worship and bleed on the altar over and over. It was a system of recycling. And still, Bastion died.

Nuru dared not speak any of this aloud.

Reaching the far end of the hall, Subira led them down a long, winding staircase. Even here, in the stunning wealth of the Senators' Ring, the steps were sunken and shallow, worn smooth. The walls were shaped to look like skeletons trying to claw their way free of some thick swamp. Flickering candles lined the wall, mounted in ancient wax-encrusted candelabrum, themselves extensions of Bastion's stone.

The gods made the Growers' Ring an eternity of endless grey, every tenement the same, every district the same, but took the time to shape these walls.

"When I understood that Bastion was dying," continued the tecuhtli, "I realized there was only one way to save the city: The Lady must return." Reaching the bottom of the stairs, she led them into a long hall lined with more candelabrum and ebony doors cracked with age. "Mother Death," she said over her shoulder, "is the only one who can force her children to behave."

Nuru wanted to tell this kindly old woman that there was another way.

The gods are ravenous, all of them.

Returning Mother Death to the head of the pantheon achieved nothing more than trading one predator for another. The Queen might ration the gods, force them to devour human souls at a more sustainable rate, but she wouldn't stop it. They'd still feed.

Blasphemous almost beyond comprehension, Nuru couldn't speak the words.

"Won't the gods cast Mother Death out again?" Efra asked Subira. "They did it once."

"Things have changed," said Subira. "When she first raised Bastion from the sands, there were more gods. The pantheon was much larger. Time has taken its toll on them as it has on all of us. Some grew out of favour, their worshippers turning to other gods. Those faded to nothing. Or almost nothing. Ghosts of gods haunt the Priests' Ring. Some…" She flashed a glance at Nuru. "Some fell to violence and plotting. Only a handful remain. If Mother Death reclaims the underworld, they won't have the power to remove her."

Nuru found herself wanting to like this blunt woman despite her owl-feather robes. Dedicated to the city and her people, Subira was what all priests should be. The tecuhtli hadn't so much as blinked at Efra's casual blasphemy. She saw people for what they were, rather than what someone else told her they should be. She talked to lowly Dirts like they were humans and not animals. She saw the wrongs inherent in Bastions' gods—in her own god—and took action to make things right. Maybe not the right action, but at least she tried. That was more than Nuru could say for any of the other nahual she'd seen. Most were perfectly happy to lash people in the public square or open their veins upon the altar. Where other nahual blindly followed hallowed scripture, Subira carved her own path.

She was…

She's what I imagine a mother to be.

"Do you have children?" Nuru asked.

Subira stopped, turned to put her hands on Nuru's shoulders. "I'm so sorry," she said. "What the nahual did was terrible. I read about the changes they made in the Life Ring and cried tears of helpless rage."

Subira pulled Nuru into a hug, holding her tight, Nuru's face in her neck.

For a moment Nuru stood stiff. Never had a nahual touched her like this. Feelings she couldn't understand bubbled to the surface.

This gesture was nothing sexual. It was an offering of comfort, the sharing of pain.

Nuru remembered a nahual of Her Skirt is Stars screaming at her in the crèche. A girl of maybe eight years, she'd cowered before his rage. Though she couldn't remember what she'd done, she recalled the helpless fear. More than anything, she'd wanted someone to hold her.

This embrace was what an adult should offer a scared child.

This was the concern and shelter of a mother.

Nuru fought tears. She swallowed pain.

Subira stroked her hair and the two women cried for generations of loss and abuse.

"We'll change things," the nahualli whispered in Nuru's ear. "Ancient wrong can still be mended."

Kofi pretended to clear his throat.

"That boy really must learn patience," whispered Subira. Releasing Nuru, she turned on the young man. "What?"

"We need your help."

"You didn't come for my cooking?"

"We need to get to the underworld," he said.

"Easy," said the tecuhtli. "Cut your wrists. You hardly need me."

Efra grunted a laugh. "If we get rid of fat boy, can we keep her?"

"We need to survive the journey," said Kofi, ignoring Efra.

For the first time, Subira gave him her full attention. "Why?"

He nodded at Nuru. "She can explain better than I."

Attention again on Nuru, Subira said, "You're not just a street-sorcerer."

Even though she wanted to argue, Nuru shook her head.

"What then?" asked the nahualli.

Silence, no one willing to answer.

Much as Nuru wanted to tell this woman everything, share the crushing burden of her insane plan, she said nothing. It was too much to hope that a powerful sorcerer, a true temple-trained nahualli, might take up her cause.

"You're here," said Subira, looking from Kofi to Nuru. "You came because you need the help of a tecuhtli and I'm probably the only one the Loa know."

She's not Loa, Nuru realized. *Not really.*

The Loa called her the 'turncoat.' That wasn't a sign of respect. They might be willing to use her, but they didn't consider Subira one of them.

He brought us here, but he hesitates to tell her who I am.

"We have others," said Kofi, defensive. "They're far away though," he added when Subira shot him a look.

"There's going to be a war," said Nuru. "Face Painted with Bells holds the underworld." Subira showed no hint of surprise, which, Nuru guessed, made sense for a nahual of Father Death. "Southern Humming-bird's army of hoarded souls, generations of dead Hummingbird Guard and Turquoise Serpents, marches on the underworld."

"The godling will never hold against Father War," said Subira. "How can you stop him?"

"She's a powerful street-sorcerer," offered Kofi.

"No doubt," said the tecuhtli, eyes never leaving Nuru. "I'm a temple-trained nahualli of Father Death, and I couldn't change the outcome."

Kofi swallowed, and said, "Nuru is the Heart of Mother Death."

"You are such a fucking idiot," said Efra. "She's your High Priest. She's the Heart of your god, and yet did you leave the decision to share that to her? No. Why? Because you still think she's a stupid, helpless Dirt."

Kofi flinched as if struck. He stared, blinking, at the floor. "Sorry."

Subira grunted a wry laugh. "Well, the damage is done and it's not the end of the world. Though you're lucky I'm a friend."

"You're just going to have to trust that we can handle this," said Efra.

Subira nodded to herself. Decision made, she said, "Getting to the underworld without dying is no easy task. It requires a doorway. Gods can make them. Some very few sorcerers. There are rumours of tecolotl using rare stones to thin the veil between worlds so someone might step through, rather than calling something to our world."

"I have no stones that can achieve this," said Kofi.

"Not to worry," said Subira. "I should be able to bring you to the edge of death, so close your soul takes the first steps into the under-world."

"I'm going too," blurted Kofi.

"But know," said Subira, giving him a hard eye, "that this is dangerous. A single mistake, and you will die forever. Nothing, no god nor sorcerer, will be able to return you to life. Mother Death will once again be banished to the desert."

"We have no choice," said Nuru.

It wasn't lie, but it was a half-truth at best.

If I fail, Mother Death will be one less god feeding off Bastion.

At the bottom of the stairs, Subira opened a heavy oak door, ushering them into a dark room. Grabbing the nearest candle, she followed them in. The room smelled of damp stone and still air. The walls glistened with moisture, and Nuru caught flashes of movement as insects fled the intruding light. Six evenly spaced raised altars stood waiting. Blood runnels, clogged with mud, lined the floor. Bowls sunk in the stone beneath each altar, awaited the spilling of life. There were no straps to hold a sacrifice helpless. Who had the church sacrificed down here, hidden away from the public eye? Other nahual?

This room hasn't been used in a long time. The thought made her feel marginally better.

This nahualli wasn't bringing her here to open her veins and feed the gods. This was merely an out of the way place to do the things that Subira's fellow nahual would no doubt damn her for. That she had lived in both worlds—that of the priests, and that of the Loa—for so long spoke well of her discretion.

Subira raised the candle and studied Efra. "Formidable as you might be—and I see great strength in you—you carry no great magic. You are neither sorcerer nor tecolotl. Will you go with your friend?"

"Her war is my war," said Efra.

A pleased smile played about the nahualli's lips. "I expected no less." She touched Efra's shoulder with unexpected fondness. "You have a warrior's soul."

Approaching one of the altars, the tecuhtli drew pouch after pouch of narcotics from within her robes, laying each on the stone. Nuru recognized the jainkoei and aldatu, though she'd never seen so much in one place. More drugs followed, many that Nuru didn't recognize.

Placing the last pouch, Subira straightened. "Each of you lie down on an altar, please."

Nuru froze. This nahualli wanted her to voluntarily lay herself on an altar? The politeness of the request didn't help. How many times had she woken from nightmares of dying, strapped down and helpless, wrists open? It was the one nightmare every Dirt shared.

Kofi and Efra selected altars without hesitation.

Subira touched Nuru's arm. "It's your choice, dear. I can't force you and wouldn't even if I could." She snorted a soft laugh and said too quiet for the others to hear, "You're right to be scared. This is terribly dangerous."

Kill the gods.

This was her chance to murder one of the most ancient and powerful members of the pantheon.

You'll never get another chance like this.

Teeth clenched, she climbed onto the altar.

Seeing Efra place the purse bearing her flint dagger on her belly, Nuru did the same with hers. Tucking the carving of Mother Death alongside the knife, she prayed the god-killer would make the journey to the underworld.

The stone's cold imperfections felt strangely reassuring through the silk dress. An uncomfortable connection with reality, still appreciated.

Subira stood over her. "Ready?" she asked.

No.

Unable to speak, Nuru nodded.

"This blend includes everything you might need to work your nagual sorcery."

Grateful someone thought this through for her, she offered a shaky smile. Gods, she'd almost made the journey to the underworld with no narcotics in her blood! She would have been helpless! While she had no intention of calling Mother Death, there were other uses. And it didn't hurt to have access to the god in case everything went terribly wrong. Though she shuddered to think how bad things would have to be before she was willing to call the Lady of the Dead back to her realm.

The tecuhtli fed her a strange mix of narcotics. It tasted of stale seeds, raw liver, and oily soot. Time slowed as the drugs took effect. A tingling cold, starting in her toes, crept up her legs.

Eyes closed, Nuru saw fat flakes of greasy ash falling from the sky in the Growers' Ring. Bastion's future burned. Corpses. Open eyes filling like pools. Gaping mouths brimming with cinder.

Subira pushed more drugs into Nuru's mouth, and she choked down grit.

"This isn't going to be pleasant," said Subira, a cool hand on Nuru's forehead. "There's no easy way to die."

"Whurk?" She couldn't form words.

Limbs growing heavy and leaden, her heart slowed to a sluggish throb, weakening with each beat. Each breath came shorter, shallower, her world fading. It was like drowning in nothing, lungs simply unwilling to work.

I'm dying.

She knew it to be true.

Someone in the room made a desperate noise of wet terror. She couldn't tell who, couldn't open her eyes or turn her head to look. Had Subira just cut someone?

Nuru tried to wiggle a finger, to move anything.

Couldn't.

No fingers to move.

No body to breath.

No heart to beat.

Fear stabbed her.

Even knowing she was dying, a new horror took root. Her soul would travel to the underworld, but would the god-killer?

I had it in the dream with Smoking Mirror!

But that was a dream, something maybe even created by Father Discord himself. What if it had all been a trick to lure Nuru, and through her Mother Death, to the underworld?

Father Discord.

The Obsidian Lord.

The Enemy of Both Sides.

Why had she listened? Why had she thought she could outsmart a god?

Stupid fucking ignorant Dirt!

No! Smoking Mirror hadn't known about the dagger. Face Painted with Bells gave it to Nuru in the realm of Her Skirt is Stars.

I woke in Bastion with it.

The underworld was no different. It would be there.

Please let it be there. Please don't let me die for nothing.

She didn't know who she prayed to. The gods she planned on murdering?

She'd laugh if she could.

Nuru's heart gave one last sad kick and stilled.

Her final breath hissed out in a long sigh, left her empty.

AKACHI - THE SICK VENOM OF FAITH

Order is temporary, a fleeting delusion.
Decay is the one constant.
In time, only time can win.
Discord is the natural state of reality.

—The Book of Bastion

Civilization starts with the Senators.

That's what everyone said. Half joke, half axiom.

The Growers were ignorant animals. The Crafters, marginally better, were at least trainable animals.

The Senators' Ring was where things began to matter. They upheld one of the three pillars of society.

Law.

Economy.

Church.

Always in that order. Remove one pillar, and the structure tilted and fell. That's what Akachi's teachers said.

It was good to be back among real people, among the civilized.

And yet, even here, even in the third ring, Akachi saw the unmistakable signs of Bastion's age. Everything rounded by millennia of wind and sand, she looked oddly pillowy. In the Growers' Ring, where everything was dull and lifeless, such imperfections were easy to ignore. Who cared if the Dirts lived amid squalor and decay? It wasn't like they had the wit to appreciate anything better. But here, surrounded by life and colour, it was different. The flaws stood out. Cracks in stone screamed for attention. Gutted windows, their panes of glass long gone, gaped like open wounds.

Does no one make glass anymore?

He'd never seen it made in the Crafters' Ring, had no idea what was involved. Come to think of it, even in the Priests' Ring glass was treated with reverence. A broken window was a crime punishable by flaying. He couldn't remember anyone ever replacing a broken window.

Off in the distance the House of the Senate for this quarter rose above the other buildings. After the squat filth of the Dirts, it was glorious.

He couldn't enjoy it.

While the main streets might be clean, swept free of sand, the alleys were clogged with detritus. Each citizen was responsible for maintaining the streets and walkways around their homes, but that clearly wasn't happening. Broken furniture. Discarded belongings. Some alleys were so packed with trash they were impassable. Indentured and indebted sifted through the junk, looking for anything they might sell. Many lay sprawled in dark doorways, sleeping or dead.

An edge of desperation lurked beneath the veneer of civilization. Like the façade was cracking, and, though everyone saw it, no one was yet willing to admit its existence.

Passing a vegetable stall, Akachi heard raised voices, bitter complaints at the sudden increase in prices. What stock the shopkeeper did have, looked as bad as the food in the outer ring. Someone shoved the shopkeeper, who shoved back. In a heartbeat, fists flew, desperate hands grabbing sunken fruit. None of the mob saw the Hummingbirds until it was too late. The sound of cracking bones and screams of pain were a reminder that what began in the outer ring would eventually devour all Bastion.

The brawl spread fast as people realized this was not a lone event, that none of the stalls in the market would be refilled anytime soon. Other shopkeepers joined the fray, swinging makeshift clubs, as more senators poured into the square. Turning away, Staff off the Fifth Sun held tight, Akachi followed Omphile down another street.

"By the end of next week," said Omphile, "the Guard will be fighting a war on two fronts with no way to retreat. They need to pacify one ring at a time."

Captain Melokuhle quickened her pace to catch up. "It's the life ring. All the food, animals, and things we use to craft everything Bastion needs to survive, comes from there. If it falls to the Loa, they win."

Akachi understood her concern. He too had shared similar thoughts. "It doesn't matter. None of this matters." He gestured back toward the warring mob. "This is the war on the surface. It's the war beneath the war that we need to win."

The war beneath. Fitting, he decided. The war for the underworld. The realm of Father Death was perhaps the greatest prize, no doubt coveted by all the pantheon. Whoever held it would be counted among the greatest of gods.

The Staff of the Fifth Sun filled Akachi with the searing heat of certainty.

"I will kill Mother Death's Heart," he said. "With their god gone, the Loa will crumble."

"For the last twenty-five thousand years," said Omphile, "their god has been banished to the Bloody Desert. Didn't seem to slow them much."

She was right, but what if he could do more than kill the Heart? Killing one Dirt girl seemed such a petty goal. What if he killed the god too? The staff was no trinket. This was a mighty artefact from another age!

The thought felt right, like maybe it had always secretly been his plan. Or his god's plan.

"I'm not going to banish the Queen. I'm going to kill her." He had no idea how, but knew it was true. The ruin of his left hand clenched into a partial fist. "We will crush the Dirts back into obedience. They must know their place. All will be as the gods decreed!"

He wanted to scream with joy, unshakable faith crashing through his blood. Biting down hard until his face hurt and his teeth felt like they'd explode, he fought the mad grin.

Omphile once again took point. She led them through a maze of streets and alleys cluttered with refuse and those too lazy to earn their way. Not once did she pause to get her bearings or look lost. The Captain walked at Akachi's side now, head down, barely paying attention.

"Do the Serpents spend much time in the Senator's Ring?" asked Akachi.

"Never been here before," she grunted, without raising her head.

The church of The Lord, while a drab and sad temple in comparison to the Northern Cathedral, at least looked like a real church. An elderly woman in a cloak of white owl feathers sat on the front step, watching the city go by.

Her god is dead, and yet she remains at her post.

Akachi wasn't sure if he should be impressed or depressed. Seeing them heading toward her, she brushed grey hair from her face and stood. A couple of years ago, she would have been a real beauty, coal eyes bright with humour and intelligence. What she'd lost with the passing of youth, she more than made up for with the mature confidence he'd come to recognize in certain powerful women. Captain Yejide. Bishop Zalika. Omphile.

Maybe that scarred Dirt, Efra, that the Artist captured so well in his charcoal sketch.

The nahual smiled warm welcome when she spotted Omphile. "Om! My dearest child! I haven't seen you since you were this high!" She held her hand out at waist height.

Om?

Akachi couldn't imagine the assassin as a child.

Omphile hugged the nahual like someone seeing their mother for the first time in years.

Could it be? Akachi saw no familial resemblance.

"Subira," said Omphile, face serious, "we need your help."

"Of course, child. Anything. But first, who are your friends?"

"This is Akachi," said the assassin, gesturing at him. "He's the reason we're here. He pursues dangerous prey."

Subira bowed low. "These are troubled times, but a Cloud Serpent nahualli on the hunt is always welcome."

"This," continued Omphile, nodding to Melokuhle, "is my Captain."

Subira bowed again. "To host a Captain of the Turquoise Serpents is a rare honour."

"Friends," said Omphile, "meet tecuhtli Subira, pastor for this district."

Melokuhle gave the nahualli a numb look.

"Not anymore," said Subira, with a sad shake of her head. "As you no doubt know, The Lord has fallen."

"You remain at your post," said Akachi. "You do your duty."

"It would be impossible for me to do otherwise," answered Subira, leading them into the church.

Akachi followed, the calcified Staff of the Fifth Sun ringing off the stone floor with every stride. Inside, the church was clean and orderly, exactly as he'd expected.

"Who do you hunt?" asked Subira, blunt and to the point.

"Two women," he answered. "One is the Heart of Mother Death."

Subira showed no hint of surprise. "The other?"

"The Heart of Smoking Mirror."

She stumbled in shock, catching herself. "Are you certain?"

"Yes."

"But…" Lost in thought, no doubt following the implications, her eye glazed. "Two Hearts travelling together?"

"Either their gods are in cooperation," said Akachi, "which means Father Discord plots the return of the Queen, or one or both of the women don't know who the other is."

"How could they not know?" Subira cut herself off. "Ah." She gestured at Akachi's stained robes. "Ash and blood. You've come from the Life Ring. One of them is a Dirt." She watched for Akachi's reaction.

"Both?" she asked, incredulous. "Impossible!"

"And yet true," said Akachi.

"These truly are the end times," she mused with wry humour. "Well, you must be exhausted. And hungry! Come," she said, waving them to follow. "I'll have a meal prepared."

Though he hadn't eaten much in days, Akachi felt no hunger. The need to move built in him, a crushing pressure. "We need your help," he said, making no move to follow her. "I must journey to the underworld."

The nahualli stopped. "Explain."

"The Queen is returned," he said. "Mother Death has manifested within Bastion. She seeks to reclaim the underworld." Staff in hand, righteous fury filled him, the sure knowledge his did his god's will. "I must meet her in battle." Killing the Heart wouldn't be enough.

Subira's attention slid to the staff and back to Akachi. "I can offer only one path to the underworld."

"Then I shall walk that path."

"And you wish to do so now."

Akachi's face threatened to stretch into that mad grin and he fought it. "There can be no delay. This is the only chance we'll have to stop Mother Death."

Bowing, she said, "Follow."

Subira led them up a set of winding stairs, the sun streaming in through regularly spaced windows. On the second floor, she showed Akachi and the two Serpents to what looked to be quarters for the guards of visiting guests. Cots, all neatly made, sheets tucked tight at the corners like his mother used to do, lined the walls with military precision.

"Make yourself comfortable," instructed the tecuhtli, as she laid out narcotics drawn from within her robes.

Selecting a cot, Akachi sat cross-legged upon it, the staff laid across his thighs. Omphile and Captain Melokuhle also chose cots and sat.

Noting his attention, Melokuhle said, "We see this through to the end. For Firash."

"I just thought it would be more entertaining than sitting here awaiting your return," said Omphile. "But sure."

As Subira prepared the narcotics for her tecuhtli sorcery, Akachi laid out his own supply. Not knowing what he'd face, he prepared some of everything he might need.

He ate aldatu mushrooms, to thin the veil in case he should need to access his nagual power. The dried petals of the epelak flower he crushed in the fist of his right hand and devoured. His third eye would be open wide, should he need to see obscured truths. Cracking the wax seal and popping the cork on a tiny glass vial, he let two drops of bihurtu fall onto his tongue. A poisonous residue collected from the backs of deadly frogs, it would connect Akachi to the reality of his animal spirits. He took gorgoratzen to ensure he never forgot a moment of his coming victory.

More than anything that had gone before, what happened next would be his first true step toward becoming Heart's Mirror. He would kill the Heart of a god. He would kill or banish Mother Death, forever cleansing Bastion of her stain.

Akachi's face hurt, but his hands were steady.

Shoving a fistful of foku seeds into his mouth, he chewed and swallowed, realizing the mad grin had returned as he worked. He didn't care. It was just the narcotics.

He took arrazoia to keep his thoughts clear, to stop the dangerous blend from leaving him a hallucinating blubbering mess.

Akachi eyed the ausardia on the bed before him. It would make him brave, fill him with the confidence of the gods. He rested the useless ruin of his left hand on the Staff of the Fifth Sun.

I don't need it.

Replacing the ausardia in its pouch, he returned it to his belt.

Pizagarri would keep him sharp and alert, focussed on what must be done.

Jainkoei.

The last time he took a sizeable dose he'd been dying on the altar in his own church. Cloud Serpent came to him, sank fangs deep into his flesh and filled him with the sick venom of faith.

Venom? Blasphemy!

Blaming the errant thought on the narcotics snaking through his blood, Akachi devoured the last of his jainkoei.

Reality swirled around him.

A rock in a sluggish river.

The veil thinned and stretched. He pulled it apart with the merest flick of will. His allies in the smoke circled, awaiting his call.

Dead worlds.

Dead realities.

The ghosts of countless billions.

War upon war.

Death unending.

Until one remained.

"Ready?" asked Subira, standing at his side.

Akachi opened his eyes to discover Omphile and Melokuhle sprawled boneless and supine upon their cots. Melokuhle lay perfectly still, eyes closed.

Omphile rolled her eyes to see him. "Can't move," she mumbled. Managing a slipping grin, she added, "Quick. Take advantage of me."

Ignoring her, the tecuhtli held out a foul-smelling blend of narcotics in offering. "Eat."

He stared at the balled clump sitting in her palm. The narcotics already in him snapped the world into focus so sharp, so harsh, it hurt. Closing his eyes, he accepted the drugs, and ate them. With no idea what she'd included in the mix, he couldn't begin to guess how it would react with what he'd already taken.

"This will bring you to the brink of death," explained Subira. She raised an eyebrow at the remains of the narcotics piled before him. "And likely to the edge of brain-burn."

Unworried, Akachi lay back, adjusting the staff so it lay alongside his body.

Her narcotics worked quickly, stealing the strength from his limbs.

The constant painful smile loosened its grip. His face hung so slack it felt like the skin might slide from his skull.

"Akachi," slurred Omphile. "how many times did Firash see you die?"

"Many."

Had the tezcat mistaken this journey to the underworld for true death?

The assassin's eyes glazed and she stared, unmoving and unblinking, at the ceiling.

Surrounded by so many realities, Akachi hardly noticed when his slipped away. He felt himself sink down through the cot, through the floor beneath, soul drawn to the underworld. Drowning in stone.

I don't have to come back.

It was an oddly comforting thought, the idea of never returning, of letting Bastion care for itself while his soul went off to whatever awaited.

His responsibilities and concerns drowned with him.

He wanted that, to die. To be rid of the expectations of father and god. To be blessed nothing.

He couldn't blink, couldn't draw breath. The Staff of the Fifth Sun lay at his side, a comforting weight.

Subira moved to stand over him. A wraith. A shadow.

Opening his eyes was an act of colossal will.

The tecuhtli looked different now that he was dying. Cold and hard, all warmth and care gone. The woman she'd been fell away, a mask no longer needed.

She placed a polished stone on his forehead, a cold weight between his eyes.

It looked familiar.

"Amethyst," she said. "The stone of self-destruction. You already reek of it, but I must be sure."

Helpless, he watched as she placed another stone, a shard of flint, over his heart.

"The stone of conflict," she said. "It will drive you to war with yourself. It will push you to a rage and violence your meek soul is incapable of reaching alone."

Her casual dismissal enraged him.

I am not meek! I will kill a god! I will be the Heart's Mirror!

Subira placed a polished pink stone over his groin. "Kunzite."

Stones.

This… He couldn't…

Stone sorcery.

Muddled by a colossal dose of narcotics, he finally understood: She practiced both the art of the nahualli, and the tecolotl.

Stone sorcerer. The ancient enemy of the true nahual.

The Loa must have got to her after The Lord fell. It was the only thing that made sense. Omphile never would have brought him to the enemy.

They knew each other.

He lost the thought to the maelstrom of narcotic interactions.

Akachi's heart gave one last weak kick.

The world fell in, icy water washing over him, pulling him into the deepest black.

Subira's voice followed him down. "No doubt you think I'm a Loa infiltrator. Stupid, really, how nahualli refuse to make use of stone sorcery. As if smashing one's brain with narcotics is somehow purer than accessing our own inner strengths and emotional states and channelling them through the very bones of the earth." Her laugh echoed through his skull. "Nahual. Loa. You're all fools. Bones of the earth. Mother Death isn't the only god to make use of stone."

Father Discord.

God of storms.

God of Strife.

Lord of the Night Sky

Enemy of Both Sides.

Lord of the Near and Far.

Father of the Night Wind.

Lord of the Tenth Day.

The Flayed One.

The Jaguar God.

Smoking Mirror, the Obsidian Lord

Akachi died.

NURU - FAMILY

The nahual preach salvation. They will smash the bones with ebony, lash the meat with whips, flay the flesh with flint, hack through ribs with obsidian, and tear free the heart.

All to save the soul.

The Bankers preach economy. They will work the bones until they break, drive the meat until it fails, ink the flesh with the sins of debt, and break the heart if it means a profit. They care not for the soul for it has no intrinsic value.

—The Loa Book of the Invisibles

Nuru stood in a mud field stretching from horizon to horizon.

Something grew here once. Maybe corn. All that remained were splintered stalks jutting from the earth like shattered bones. Stars glinted bright, savaging the perfect black of the night sky. Kofi and Efra stood with her, the Loa still dressed as a Bird, Efra in her clinging silk dress. They were ghosts, leached of life and colour.

"Flawless diamonds," said Kofi, head tilted back.

"I'm not sure what I expected from death," said Efra, pulling one foot from the muck with a wet sucking sound, "but I'm disappointed." She held the purse up, testing its weight. "At least this came too."

Nuru realized she still held her own purse, the god-killer and carving of Mother Death tucked within.

It worked!

A small victory, it was better than nothing.

The black dress offered no warmth. Huddling her arms about her, she shivered.

The Growers' Ring seemed vibrant in comparison.

The nahual loved preaching about the underworld, about the unlife after death. They spoke of paradise, rivers of blood, fields of unending harvest, tortured souls nailed to trees with wooden spikes, and beautiful young men and women servicing one's every need. Heavens and hells. She couldn't remember one of them ever mentioning this.

"They've never been here," Nuru said.

"Hmm?" asked Kofi, pulling his attention from the cold ice shard stars of the sky.

"The nahual," said Nuru. "They're alive. They've never been to the underworld, yet they keep telling us what it's like. I used to think it was either contradictions, or many different realities. They don't *know*."

"Fucking typical," said Efra.

Nuru turned a complete circle. Nothing differentiated one bit of horizon from another. Which way should she go? She saw no signs of war, no titanic struggle of the gods.

Smoking Mirror tricked me. I walked to my own death like a stupid fucking cow.

"We should get moving," said Efra.

Nuru raised an arm, let it fall. "Where?"

"I doubt it matters," said Efra. "But we're here." She glanced at Kofi. "Now we do what we came to do."

And how would they do that? Southern Hummingbird and his armies were nowhere to be seen. A twinge of guilt stabbed Nuru. She'd lied to Kofi about why they were coming. He was so trusting, he never thought to ask.

"This way," said Efra, pointing in what looked to be a random direction.

"Why that way?" asked Kofi. He looked terrified, as if maybe dying on an altar in a church of Father Death might not have been such a great idea.

Without answering, Efra shoved Nuru and Kofi until they grudgingly moved.

They walked.

Crossing an eternal field of mud was exhausting. With each step they sank to their ankles, the muck reluctant to release them. Sometimes sharp stones, hidden in the earth, cut their feet.

They walked forever, limping, getting nowhere. The stars never moved, and no part of the horizon showed any hint of light.

"Is there a sun in the underworld?" asked Efra.

Kofi shook his head.

They walked, the slurp-suck of mud following each stride.

Nuru's feet bled. The flimsy Senators' slippers were useless as protection, quickly becoming sodden and heavy. Removing them, she tossed them into the mud.

Efra did the same and limped on, Nuru and Kofi following.

Mud and stiff muscles. Cold pulled the strength from Nuru's bones.

Legs aching, she stopped.

"Why are you stopping?" asked Efra.

Not bothering to answer, Nuru sat in the mud, wincing when something sharp stabbed her in an ass-cheek. Shifting, digging in the muck, she found a curve of rib cage. Shuffling, she dug again in the mud. More bones. She pawed in the clay muck, exposing a human skull clogged with damp earth. Again and again she dug, each time uncovering bones. She crawled and dug. More bones. Moved somewhere else. More human bones.

Nuru gave up. "We're going to die here." She laughed, a sob of self-mockery and pain. "Stupid. Stupid. We're already dead."

She pulled an arm bone from the earth.

At least they're resting.

More than anything, she wanted to lie down, sink into the clinging mud. Surrender.

"Get up," said Efra.

Nuru looked up at her, the scar a white line cutting across midnight flesh leached of colour. She looked as tired as Nuru felt. "Sit," she said.

"Just for a bit. We'll rest, and then keep going."

Hands on hips, Efra said, "Get the fuck up."

"Too tired."

Kofi watched the exchange. "We could rest," he offered.

"We have to keep moving or they win," said Efra.

"In a moment," agreed Nuru. "Just going lie down for a bit." She lay back. The ground was soft, inviting.

Bending to lift a skull from the muck, Efra said, "All these people under the mud, they stopped to rest."

Nuru closed her eyes. "Sounds good. They seem peaceful."

"Get up." For the first time, since that Bird dislocated her shoulder, Efra sounded scared.

"Why? We can't win."

"So fucking what?" said Efra. "If you think *anything* matters, you're an idiot. Everything is pointless. But if nothing matters, then we get to decide what's important to us. We get to pick the one fucking thing that matters more than anything else. You did it. You picked the thing. You gave us purpose." She knelt in the mud, leaning low so she could whisper in Nuru's ear. "We're going to kill the gods."

"You do it." Nuru held out the purse in offering.

Efra's hand clamped on her wrist, grip crushing. "Get up or I'll bury you here. You can finally be the dirt you think you are."

"Get up," said Kofi. "Please."

Opening her eyes, she stared up at him, saw his desperate longing. He believed in her. He had more faith in Nuru than he had in his own god.

Kofi isn't here for Mother Death, he's here for you.

She'd seen that look before. There'd been another man willing to die for her.

No. Not again.

If she gave up, if she lay here until the mud took her, until she joined the bones, she'd be letting him down. She'd be letting them both down.

Chisulo.

She couldn't do that, couldn't betray his memory. He would never accept defeat. He would never lie down in the mud to die. If a friend needed him, he would fight to the end.

Kofi needed her. Even Efra needed her, though she pretended otherwise.

If you can't get up to try and save Bastion, at least get up to help your friends. Don't betray their trust now.

Eventually, Kofi would learn the truth of what Nuru planned.

In the end, you'll betray him anyway.

Maybe it wouldn't come to that. The idea of killing a god with a little dagger was insane.

Nuru lifted a hand, and Kofi and Efra pulled her back to her feet.

On the horizon, she saw three familiar shapes crossing the endless mud toward her.

She stood watching, unable to speak, unwilling to voice her hope lest the disappointment crush her.

They're dead.

But then, so was she.

Noticing her attention, Efra turned to look. "I don't fucking believe it."

Omari's hunched gait, like he half-expected someone to lash out and hit him. Bomani, back straight, fists clenched in an anger that knew no limits.

And Chisulo. Unbent. Striding through the mud like it was nothing.

"Who—"

Efra waved Kofi to silence.

"We've been looking for you," said Chisulo, stopping to stand before Nuru. He reached out like he might touch her or take her hand in his, blinked at her dress in surprise, and let it drop.

"The hell happened?" demanded Bomani. Damp with mud, the silk clung to her worse than it had before. "You become a nahual of Precious Feather while we were gone?"

"Idiots," said Efra.

Chisulo grinned at the scarred woman. "I've missed you."

Efra looked away, muttered, "Idiot."

Chisulo. Bomani. Omari. A sick sinking feeling filled Nuru's belly. "Where's Happy?"

Chisulo shook his head. "That nahual killed him with an obsidian dagger. His soul is in there."

Nuru cried like she'd lost him all over again. Her boys gathered around in awkward silence. Bomani, the meanest most vicious Dirt she'd ever met—Efra being the one exception—cried too.

"How did you find us?" she asked, wiping away tears and smearing her face with mud.

For all their walking, the fields hadn't changed. They could have been exactly where they started. Maybe they were.

"You had to find yourself first," said Omari. "Once you remembered who you were, it was obvious where you'd be."

Nuru frowned at his carefree grin. "Where am I?"

The Finger waved at an eternity of mud. "Here!"

"Death did nothing for this lot," said Efra.

Chisulo grunted agreement. "She's not wrong."

"Why," said Bomani stepping close to Kofi, "are you travelling with a fucking Bird?"

The Loa stood a hand-span taller and carried a lot more muscle, but Bomani, chin stuck out, got right in his face. Even dead he had no fear in him, no hesitation.

"Leave him alone," said Efra.

Bomani made a show of looking him up and down. "I don't like Birds." He spat. "Let's kill him."

"We need him," said Nuru.

"Nah," said Bomani. "We don't."

Chisulo and Omari surrounded Kofi, cutting off his retreat. They might not be looking for a fight, but they always backed up their friends. Nuru would have laughed from happiness, were it not so stupid.

"He's Loa," said Efra, looking unconcerned.

That slowed the boys.

"So?" demanded Bomani. "Still just a fucking priest."

"Yeah," agreed Efra, "but he's also a nahualli."

"Tecolotl," Kofi corrected.

"I saw him boil a Bird's eyes," she added. Seeing them still undecided, Efra gave them one more reason to leave Kofi alone. "If you touch him, I'll kill you."

Bomani, blood up, glared at her for a score of heartbeats. Finally, he shrugged. "You probably could have led with that." He stood loose and relaxed as if he hadn't been about to beat someone to death.

"Why were you waiting for me?" asked Nuru, desperate to distract the boys from violence.

Chisulo darted Kofi one last distrustful look. "I…Well…"

"You knew I was coming?"

Looking embarrassed, he said, "Eventually."

Eventually? Had he been planning on wandering the underworld until she died of old age?

"We don't know why," admitted Omari. "But we knew it was the right thing to do."

"You were always the best of us," added Bomani.

"You brought us together," said Omari. "We all tried to be better because of you."

"All that shit Bomani did was him trying to be better?" asked Efra. "Imagine if he'd been his full asshole self."

Bomani flashed Efra a grin, unhurt by her words. "Gods girl, you look fine."

"Fuck off."

Chisulo frowned in that way he did when he was trying to say something important. "We could have been anything, but none of it good. We could have been violent. We could have been murderers or farmers. We weren't. We were a family. You made us a family."

"No," said Nuru. "It was you."

"It wasn't," he said. "When we were alive, I could never tell you. I was scared it would break up the family. I was never good enough. You deserved better than some stupid Dirt who could barely hold two corners of turf. I love you. I always have, and always will."

Nuru froze, her thoughts bogging down like a wagon in the mud. How long had she waited for him to say something? How many nights had she lain awake, dreaming about this moment? Though, admittedly, there was never a crowd of people staring at her in the dreams.

She blinked and tears ran free. She couldn't stop them.

Chisulo winced and studied the muck at his feet. "Sorry. I know my timing isn't great."

"Not great?" said Efra. "You waited until you were dead before telling her you loved her."

He closed one eye, mouth twisting, like he was trying to see it from another angle. "Yeah."

"Men," said Efra. "Well don't just stand there, hug her you great fucking oaf!"

And Nuru was in Chisulo's arms, face pressed against the hard muscle of his chest, sobbing into his neck as he held her.

"I want some," said Bomani, stepping in to wrap both Nuru and Chisulo in his arms.

"Me too," said Omari, circling to hug them from the other side.

Eyes closed, Nuru basked in the love of her boys. She'd never dreamed she might see them again. If nothing else came of her mad plan, this made everything worth it.

Mumbling and muttering, they finally separated, and Nuru realized Efra and Kofi had remained on the outside.

Why didn't she take part?

Efra's narrowed eyes followed Chisulo. Love and lust, or adoration and anger? Impossible to tell. Nuru thought she understood.

She's more afraid of weakness—of being vulnerable—than she is of being alone.

Chisulo, gaze locked on Nuru, didn't notice the attention. She wanted to slap him for ignoring Efra and she wanted him to never stop looking at her like that. Bomani, on the other hand, looked like he'd seen

Efra for the first time.

The dresses.

Give the Senators credit for one thing, they knew how to make a dress that caught a man's attention.

Crafters made these, not Senators.

It was so strange to think that the Crafters made all the marvels she'd seen in the Senators' Ring and sent it inward. They kept almost nothing for themselves. No wonder they were angry. Unlike the Growers, they knew what they were missing.

"The underworld is a disaster," said Chisulo. "No one is in control. The dead are splitting off into factions."

"We've come to fight with you one last time," Bomani added.

One last time.

Nuru's heart soared and shattered. Smoking Mirror told her that those who died in the underworld were forever lost, their souls beyond rebirth.

She couldn't lose them, not again. Words spilled out, a panic of fear and loss. "No! You can't help me. If you die again, that's it. Gone. No rebirth. I couldn't stand that!"

"You think we're going to walk away from a fight?" demanded Bomani.

"We stand with you to the end," said Chisulo. "You know that."

"Though it'd be real sweet if that end involved being reborn as a nahual or a Banker," added Omari.

"I always wanted to be reborn as a bird," said Bomani, to everyone's surprise. "Not a Bird," he clarified, "a bird." He fluttered fingers like wings.

"An eagle?" asked Omari.

"No. One of those little ones. They always seemed so free, so happy."

For a moment everyone stood in silence.

"What's the plan?" Chisulo finally asked.

"Nuru is going to topple the nahual from power," said Efra. "She's going to conquer all Bastion and right the wrongs and injustices of twenty-five thousand years."

"Oh good," said Chisulo. "I was worried it might be something dangerous."

AKACHI - DISCORD MADE FLESH

And on that, the very first day of Bastion, the Obsidian Lord did set in motion his plans. The changes he made to the Eternal City were small, beneath notice, but he knew the long-term effects would be colossal. For the behaviour of any complex dynamical system is exquisitely sensitive. The most infinitesimal changes made in the earliest state will result in ever larger changes over time.

All the gods feed off worship and blood and souls, but only one god feeds off chaos.

—The Book of Bastion

Akachi stood in desolation.

The night sky, an endless bowl of stars, curved overhead. Deep cold sank into the marrow of his bones. The burnt husks of ancient trees surrounded him, a forest graveyard. They must have been truly huge when alive. Even now, blackened and denuded of branches and leaves, they stabbed into the air like the fire-hardened spears of gods. The charred and rigid corpses of people and animals littered the ground.

Nothing moved.

Nothing lived.

Where am I?

The trees stood in perfectly straight lines. Judging by how thick the trunks were, they must have been many hundreds of years old. This great forest had been planted long ago, cared for by generations of Growers all for the day when its wood was needed.

Each chilled breath tasted like scorched wood.

I died. I'm in the underworld.

The Staff of the Fifth Sun hung loose in his hand. The bloodstone, a dead god's heart, sat dull in the calcified carving of an eagle's talons. His head hurt, a throbbing behind his eyes.

"You look tired," said Omphile, plucking the staff from his grip and tossing it aside. She was as he remembered, dressed in the jade and leather of a Turquoise Serpent, sword hanging at her hip.

Exhaustion seeped into his bones with the cold.

"This was a terrible mistake," she said.

He felt failure gel in his gut like the congealed fat in stew.

She touched his shoulder. It was supposed to be supportive, a gesture of shared misery, but it felt like a crack through his soul.

Jagged faults in jade, cancerous and yellow.

The cracks weren't random. Intentional. Someone wrote a story of misery and trauma, guilt and pain, in the jade of… of… someone's soul. Akachi couldn't remember who. His entire existence seemed so distant, so unimportant. Everything he'd ever done had led him here. This moment was the culmination of countless failures.

Omphile drew his eye. She was beautiful, a goddess. The only pure light in this dull world. Hips and breasts. Grey eyes. He wanted to hold her, to kiss her, to bury his face in the heat of her flesh. She studied him, eyes roving like he was everything she ever wanted.

Akachi shifted, confused, and uncomfortable in his robes.

God-touched, Omphile was the perfect companion for the Heart's Mirror.

Or she would be if he hadn't already failed.

Akachi felt cold pressure between his eyes, over his heart, and over his groin.

Memories of a life spent in the pursuit of pleasing others.

His father.

His church.

His god.

I had no choice. I fought to save Bastion.

Or had he embraced that task as an excuse to abdicate responsibility? As if taking on an impossible task gave him free rein to do commit any sin. Was that yet another failure, a flaw running through him like cracks in jade.

Memories of a life lost.

Not lost. You gave it away.

"Subira betrayed us," he said, remembering. "She killed us. She…" He couldn't bring himself to admit the depths of his failure.

Melokuhle, the Turquoise Serpent captain who should have been carved from stone but was such a crushing disappointment with her flawed humanity, sagged in defeat. She was nothing. "The Loa turned her?" she said.

Though the captain still wore the armour of a Serpent, her scabbard hung empty. Had Subira taken the sword? If they were already dead, why disarm her?

"No," said Akachi. "She betrayed the Loa as she betrayed the true-nahual. She is a servant of Smoking Mirror. The Enemy of Both Sides."

Though he stood and drew breath, Akachi's heart lay still, a dead weight in his chest.

It's rotting inside me.

Subira lied about having sorcerous means to send his soul to the underworld; she'd simply killed him, murdered him as he lay on a sacrificial altar.

She sacrificed me to her god.

Back the land of the living, in the basement of Subira's church, his corpse lay cooling. Decomposition would set in. Soon, he'd come apart like a dead pig left in the sun. Milky putrescence, brains running like puss, leaking from his nose. Creeping rot would devour him.

Meat. Not a man.

"That's it, then," said Omphile. "Firash was right, I killed you. I brought you to Subira. It's all my fault." She cried, tears rolling down flawless cheeks, perfect lips bent in misery.

So painfully beautiful.

Gods he wanted her. To kiss her. To lick her. Even rotting from the inside, he wanted her more than anything in all the world. Last chance. Sex before his manhood shrivelled with decay and fell off.

She was always too confident.

Firash, a pillar of jade, had been run-through with cancerous fault-lines. Captain Melokuhle seemed broken from the moment Akachi met her in the courtyard of the Northern Cathedral. Her own failures, the loss of her squad, the horrors she witnessed and perpetrated, soured the perfect Turquoise Serpent she should have been.

I killed him because each time one of the squad dies, the good captain breaks a little more.

Akachi lost the thought.

Not Omphile. Not the assassin. Not once had Akachi seen even the hint of flaw or doubt.

The god-touched was untouched.

She never considered failure.

Probably never thought it was possible. Akachi took her in his arms and they cried together, defeated. He failed his god, failed his father. Again. For the last time. At least now, dead, there could be no more failure. It was over. He was released from the prison of expectations. Another dead and doomed soul.

Akachi craved oblivion.

Pulling away from Omphile, he fumbled at his pouch of narcotics. So many to choose from. Not jainkoei. He couldn't bear for his god to witness his failure. Narcotics to make him smarter or more aware. Narcotics for bravery or to open his third eye. Drugs for shape-shifting and dream-walking and to catch stained glimpses of the future. He'd already taken them all, and they were all useless.

Zoriontasuna. Escape into blissful euphoria. It was often used to achieve a balance with the other narcotics that might wind a nahualli too tight.

Akachi fished it from the pouch behind his belt and began stuffing it in the pipe.

Omphile watched, eyes hungry and desperate with need. "Will you share? Can we both escape?"

Akachi nodded, lifting the pipe.

Melokuhle slapped it from his hand, stomped it into the mud.

"No." Her eyes bled defeat, but there was more. Even beaten. Even broken. She would not surrender. "Death changes nothing."

"It changes everything," said Akachi.

"I trust Firash," Melokuhle said. "It doesn't matter that I don't understand. It doesn't matter that I don't like it, or that I hate you."

Akachi reeled in surprise. He'd had no idea. Her casually thrown condemnation stung.

How shallow was he that this disappointing woman's dislike left him on the edge of tears?

"You're a spoiled useless nahualli brat," continued Melokuhle. "Everything has been handed to you. You earn *nothing!*" She bared her teeth in a sneer of disgust. "I know who you are. I know who your father is." She poked him hard in the gut and he retreated before her wrath. "Firash told me I'd die seeing this through, and I have and I fucking will. I don't know what you're supposed to do, but you're going to fucking do it."

Akachi stared at the staff lying in the ash.

Cloud Serpent told me to kill the Queen's Heart.

Had he though?

His pipe lay in the ash beside the Staff of the Fifth Sun. It called to him.

Escape. Destroy yourself.

Amethyst.

Losing himself in the smoke wouldn't be enough. He had a dagger. He could take his own life. Here, in the underworld, would the obsidian claim his soul? Or would he die forever, never to be reborn. He prayed it was the latter.

The stone of self-destruction.

Forehead.

Heart.

Groin.

He felt the weight of the three stones. They crushed him, strangled thought with despair.

Amethyst.

That's what she put on my forehead.

He felt the lure of self-destruction, so familiar after his fight with that bright-eyed Loa assassin. So strangely compelling. Rather than putting something in him that wasn't there, it felt more like the stone opened his soul to its deepest desire.

He *wanted* to fail.

The stone did nothing more than allow him to be honest with himself.

There were two other stones. What were they?

Akachi struggled to remember.

Flint, over his heart.

The stone of conflict.

He'd read that it could be used to incite violence or, on a more personal level, to cause internal turmoil.

Melokuhle ranted on, raving at the burnt remains of trees, raging about how Serpents never broke, about how they were souls hewn from the very stone of Bastion. She believed none of it, he saw that in her eyes.

Omphile pressed herself to Akachi, moulding herself to him. A distraction. She licked his neck, nibbling and kissing. His focus splintered like cracks in jade.

I was…

What had he been thinking about?

Cracks.

The assassin took his ruined hand, slid it under her armoured vest. He held her breast with the stunted stubs of severed fingers. She leaned against him, moaned as he found a nipple.

"I said I was going to fuck you," she breathed into his ear. "And I'm going to. Dead. Doesn't matter."

Confusion and conflicting desire. He wanted her more than anything.

Yejide.

What would she think of him here, groping this Serpent in the underworld, cowering from his responsibilities?

Would she be disappointed?

She saw you as a stupid child, someone to pity.

Captain Melokuhle raged on, lashing out at dead trees, kicking up clouds of ash in her anger.

Omphile took Akachi's right hand, slid it awkwardly into her armoured skirt. His fingers found her wet and hot. She groaned in animal need, grinding against his palm until a finger entered her.

The other stone…

Hands fumbled at his robes. She gripped his cock and he grew hard. She stroked him as his fingers moved within her, as his ruined hand gripped her breast.

The other… stone…

Gods, he couldn't think!

The stone was pink! He remembered that. Pink stone placed on his groin. Where Omphile's hand was now. It felt so good. The soft fullness of her breast in one hand. Fingers of the other moving inside her, her groans growing in volume.

Where is her other hand?

She ran sharp fingernails up his spine, starting at the tail bone. Cold. Like stone.

Stone against his spine.

What was that third stone?

He couldn't focus!

He wanted her so bad, wanted to be inside her.

Kunzite! It was pink kunzite.

What the hell was kunzite?

Omphile's hot tongue, her grip on his cock, and the cold of her fingernails on his spine left little room for thought.

Cold like stone.

Distracting.

Kunzite was the stone of distraction.

On his groin. Where the assassin's hand was.

Fingernails dragged up his spine.

Cold, like stone.

Like obsidian.

She's going to kill me.

With the hand on her breast, Akachi shoved Omphile away, the fingers of his right hand slipping free. She staggered back but didn't fall. Grey eyes lit with mad glee, she stood over the staff. The assassin held his dagger in one hand.

"I was hoping it wouldn't be too easy," she said, spinning the knife in nimble fingers. "I was hoping you'd be worth killing." With her other hand she drew her sword.

"Captain," said Akachi, catching Melokuhle's attention. "Omphile killed Firash. She killed Lubanzi. She probably killed more."

Captain Melokuhle reached for her sword. Finding the scabbard empty, she frowned in confusion.

Omphile laughed with calm confidence. Armed with a sword and dagger, she was a Turquoise Serpent assassin facing two unarmed opponents. "Subira took your sword as you died. It would have made no difference, but she was never one to leave things to chance." She blinked as if startled by her own words. "Chance! Get it? She leaves nothing to chance and leaves everything to *chance*!" Seeing their confusion, she shrugged in annoyance.

Trying to piece together the disparate shards of thought Akachi said, "You're Loa."

"Gods you are thick," said Omphile. "Smoking Mirror touched me when I was six years old. I am his, strife, chaos and discord made flesh. He made me what I am. He made me the perfect assassin, a flawless murderer. He knew Southern Hummingbird, eternally predictable, would want me for his Turquoise Serpents."

Fists clenched, Melokuhle circled the assassin. "I'm going to break you in the old way. Every joint. Every bone."

Omphile snorted a mocking laugh but moved to keep both Akachi and Melokuhle in sight. "Smoking Mirror wanted me to make sure you got here, and I have done that. But..." She shook her head, lip curled in anger. "He chose a fucking Dirt as his Heart instead of me! Can you believe that? I'll show him. I'll kill you, and then do what he wanted you to do."

"You talk too much," said Melokuhle, dropping into a fighter's crouch. "Let's see if you're as good as you keep telling us."

NURU - NO MATTER THE COST

The nahual promise redemption and life after death. From the lowliest Grower to the highest priest, souls are purged and reborn based on how purely they lived their lives. Honour the gods, do your duty to Bastion, and live your next life closer to the gods.

But if the purged soul remembers nothing of its previous life, how would we ever catch them in the lie? How do we know we'll be reborn at all?

—The Loa Book of the Invisibles

Bomani led the way as if he knew exactly where they were going. Chisulo stayed at Nuru's side, close, but suddenly unwilling to touch her.

All my life I waited for him. I waited until it was too late, until he was dead.

Nuru took Chisulo's hand, startling him. "I'll never let go," she swore.

His lips smiled, but his eyes were all pain. "You're going to have to."

"I'll stay," she promised. "I'd rather be dead and with you."

Kofi's look of hurt discomfort cut her.

"I would never forgive myself," said Chisulo.

Nuru clung to his hand. "Somehow, I'll bring you all back with me. You'll live again."

Chisulo shook his head. "That's not your promise to make."

She couldn't accept that. Fuck the gods and their plans. *When do I get to be happy?*

Why should it fall to her to save the city? She was no one! Being Mother Death's Heart changed nothing. She knew no more sorcery than she had a week ago. The Queen was the real power. Nuru, on her own, was no match for a temple-trained nahualli.

Yet here she was, in the underworld.

Her boys had come to stand at her side, to fight for her cause, whatever it was. They hadn't asked. Whatever she fought for, they fought for too.

Chisulo, taking her silence as acceptance, gave her hand a reassuring squeeze. His strength gave her strength.

She saw the trap, understood her love for him was forever doomed. If she couldn't live up to his example—were she not willing to do the right thing, no matter the cost—how could he love her? To deserve his love, she would fight Bastion's war. She would fight for the Growers and the indentured and indebted and everyone the city had one way or another enslaved.

She couldn't give up because if she did, she'd lose him.

Knowing what she had to do didn't change how insane it was. Thinking she could kill the gods of Bastion, free humanity from their parasitic hunger, was madness.

He already died once, fighting for you.

Not this time. She had the god-killer. That baby she saw proved humanity didn't need the gods. She wasn't damning his soul. He'd be reborn!

She hoped.

"Bomani, you lumbering idiot," said Efra as they headed up another mud hill, "where are you leading us?"

Cresting the rise, he gestured down the slope. "I can always find a fight."

In the distance, dark shapes writhed through the night sky, occluding the ice spark of stars.

The muddy ground sloped down toward a torrential river of gore. In a world of night, devoid of all colour, the blood glowed a murky crimson, lit by the life force of those feeding it.

Armies gathered on each bank, facing their enemy. Hundreds of thousands of men and women, many wearing strange clothes and armour unlike anything Nuru had ever seen. From her vantage point, they looked like swarming ants, a seething crush of humanity.

Face Painted with Bells stood behind her army on one side of the river. Grown in size, she towered over the mortals. The ragged stump of her severed hand dripped smoking blood to the earth. About her waist she wore the Grandmother's skirt of dead snakes. They writhed in agonized unlife, their severed heads sewn crudely into place. Growers in filthy thobes fought side by side with Senators in silken robes. Nahual and Bankers marched together. All stood shoulder to shoulder in the mad press. Men and women. Countless thousands of children.

Across the river, Southern Hummingbird's army dwarfed that of the godling. For near one thousand generations of man, Father War had hoarded his souls. One thousand generations of fallen Hummingbird Guard stood alongside one thousand generations of Turquoise Serpents. Obsidian Swords. Flint daggers. Jade armour. They were an unstoppable force. In comparison, the godling's army looked pathetic, a filthy mob of diverse souls with nothing beyond death in common.

Where Face Painted with Bells' army comprised largely of people who'd never held a weapon, never been in a fight, every one of Father War's gathered souls was a warrior, trained in the arts of battle since birth.

They're dead. They're all dead.

The two armies blanketed the underworld from horizon to horizon. Nuru couldn't begin to comprehend the number of souls gathered for the slaughter. They should have been reborn, some of them many hundreds of times over. They should be populating Bastion, not gathered here to war for the gods.

Father Terror raised a great fire-spitting snake staff. Flames spewed into the sky, lighting the field of battle. With a roar, his army marched into the river of blood.

On the far bank, Face Painted with Bells screamed orders, and her own chaotic mob of dead charged into the river.

Great twisting serpents on gossamer wings of tattered souls fell from the night sky. Demons, familiars, lost spirits, fallen and forgotten gods summoned by ancient nahualli practising sorceries not seen in thousands of years. Tentacles reached from the mud, pulled screaming warriors from sight. The river of blood boiled as things, lurking beneath the surface, dragged souls under.

Smoking Mirror told her that those souls dying in the underworld were forever lost, never to be reborn. The horror of the tragedy she witnessed was too much. Each soul destroyed here was a soul that could never repopulate Bastion.

The two armies clashed in the frothing bloodwaters, crashing together like warring ant colonies. Sorcery rent the air, nahualli of every sect doing battle. Screams and cries of pain and rage and fear intermingled, a nightmare chorus of doomed souls.

Corpses floated away, spinning in the crimson current.

"There are more dead here than there are living souls in all Bastion," said Nuru, voice cracking.

Crushing doubt filled her. Her belief she could kill the gods and Bastion would survive was based on the fact she saw a baby! That was madness! It could have been born soulless, a monster like the stories from the Book.

"Efra," Nuru managed to force out. "Our plan." She cried from shame and horror at how close she'd come to destroying what she fought to save.

"What plan?" asked Kofi. He sounded small, lost.

Ignoring the Loa, Efra took Nuru by the shoulders. "The gods are flawed idiots. We only have their word that we need them."

"What if I'm wrong?" asked Nuru. "What if we need them?"

"You always want people to think they can't get by without you. It's a position of power. Just like you think you can't do this without me."

Nuru blinked at the scarred girl. "You're saying that's a lie?"

"Yes and no," answered Efra. "It's a lie you're telling yourself. I'm letting you believe it because it serves my purposes. The gods do the same thing."

Nuru considered her belief that she couldn't succeed without Efra's help. Had Efra somehow manipulated that?

Efra laughed, slapping Nuru's shoulder. "I get it now. You're always saying, 'I see you thinking about that.' Well, I see you thinking about that. You think you need me because I can and will do the things you think you can't. I need you because without you, I'm just a scarred little Dirt."

Just a scarred little Dirt? Even if she wasn't the Heart of Smoking Mirror, Efra could never be *just* anything.

"The things I *think* I can't do?" asked Nuru.

"You could do them," said Efra. "But if you did, you wouldn't be you. This way, you don't have to do them, and they still get done. You still get to be you."

"What the fuck is she on about?" asked Omari.

"I'd like to know that too," said Kofi, regaining some of his nahual superiority. "What plan? What haven't you told me?"

"You," Efra said to Kofi, "are going to have to make a choice, fat boy. I know you love her. Don't even pretend otherwise."

Chisulo bristled but said nothing.

"The question," continued Efra, "is what are you willing to sacrifice for her?"

Kofi looked from Nuru to Efra, carefully avoiding Chisulo's heavy gaze. "She is the Queen's Heart. I would sacrifice anything for her."

"No." Efra waved him to silence. "That's not Nuru you're sacrificing for, that's Mother Death. The question is, what would you sacrifice for Nuru?"

Kofi met Nuru's eyes and she saw fear and doubt there. More than anything, she saw love.

"I would sacrifice anything for you," Kofi told Nuru. "I would die for you."

"For her?" demanded Efra, "Or for what she is?"

"For *you*," Kofi said, not taking his attention from Nuru.

"You're lying," said Efra, sounding disappointed. "You priests care more about your gods than you do about people. You care more about your Loa agenda and taking Bastion from the nahual."

"I swear," Kofi promised Nuru, eyes locked on hers, "I would walk away from the Loa for you. You are everything."

Trapped by this declaration of love, of worship, Nuru couldn't speak. She was nothing, all flaws. A Dirt girl. She could never live up to what this young man thought she was.

"Would you abandon your god?" asked Efra.

Kofi twitched, darted the scarred Grower a confused look. "Why?"

The rest of the gang surrounded him, there to back Efra no matter what.

"That's not an answer," said Efra, relaxed and loose. "If you had to choose between Nuru and your god, who would you pick?"

She's going to kill him if he answers wrong.

Nuru wanted to warn Kofi, to say something—anything—to stop this.

She said nothing.

Kofi reached a hand toward Nuru, glanced at Chisulo, and dropped it. "I will follow you to the end. No matter what, no matter what you plan."

"We're going to kill the gods," said Efra.

The crash of battle and cries of the wounded and dying echoed up the hill.

"All of them," added Efra. "Mother Death as well."

"Long before there was a death god," recited Kofi, eyes closed, "people were born and lived and died. The gods inserted themselves in a pre-existing system that didn't need them." He opened his eyes. "That's from the *Book of the Invisibles*."

"See?" said Efra. "We don't need them. Listen to the fat nahual."

"It goes on to say," he added, "that the gods have been part of humanity's cycle of life and death for so long, that things have changed, that we now need them."

"The fat nahual is an idiot," said Efra. "Don't listen to him. Look, neither of you is seeing the obvious. Nuru killed Her Skirt is Stars, the god of childbirth."

"And yet children are born," said Nuru with dawning comprehension. "We don't need them!"

"What I wouldn't give to be squabbling over some shitty street with Fadil right now," said Omari, gazing down at the apocalyptic battle.

Everyone nodded.

"That really is a nice dress, Efra," said Bomani.

"You just like it because you can see my nipples." As always, she showed no hint of shyness, no embarrassment. She simply stated fact.

Bomani shrugged with a lazy grin. "If you'd have worn that back in the Wheat District, I'd never have got anything done."

"I don't remember you getting much done anyway," she answered.

Chisulo, attention locked on the battle in the river, said, "There is no defeating that force. Southern Hummingbird's army is better armed and armoured. Even their nahualli are trained in war."

Face Painted with Bells' army looked ragged and pathetic in comparison. Many were already fleeing the fight, a steady stream of deserters disappearing into the endless mud fields.

What can I do here?

The battle raged on, a crashing cacophony of destruction, agony, and death. Obsidian cleaving effortlessly through bone. Floating corpses formed islands in the river of blood.

They hunger for souls.

No wonder the god of the underworld always played an important role in the pantheon. Smoking Mirror would never willingly give that up. Did he think Nuru could win or change the course of battle, or had the god miscalculated? Had he not known about Southern Hummingbird's hoarded army?

"We can't win," said Nuru.

Efra watched the battle with narrowed eyes. "At every step, the gods and the nahual underestimate us. We've lived with the understanding that we are nothing for so long, we are failures before we begin."

"Are you saying we shouldn't try?" asked Omari.

"No," said Chisulo. "She's saying the way they see us will be their downfall."

"No, Omari was right," said Efra. "Yours sounds better though, so we'll go with that."

With nothing else to do, with no other ideas, Nuru drew the god-killer from her purse. Holding up the dagger, she said, "I need to get close enough to kill Southern Hummingbird."

No one asked how she would kill a god with a little knife.

"How do we get you that close?" asked Bomani, squinting at the landscape. "No forests. No cover. We can't sneak you over there."

"You need to call Mother Death," said Efra. "It's the only way."

Fear and hunger lit Nuru's gut. She was nothing, powerless in the face of the god. But that same god gave her power. She craved that strength.

"Once I call her," said Nuru, "I don't know if I can send her away."

Efra raised a scar-cut eyebrow in smug glee. "The gods can't war directly. She needs *you* to kill Southern Hummingbird."

All the narcotics Nuru took before Subira sent her soul to the underworld, awaited her will. The veil was everything and everywhere. Even here. Her allies in the smoke would come if she called. Her spirit animals stood ready.

They won't be enough.

Nuru drew the carving of Mother Death from her purse. Raising her hand, she displayed it on her palm.

"Mother Death will go to war. Stay here," she instructed her friends. "Stay safe."

"Your flanks are vulnerable," said Bomani. "I'll cover your right side."

"And I've got your left," said Chisulo.

"I'll guard your back," promised Omari.

Kofi dug an assortment of gems and stones from his pockets. "I'm ready. For once, maybe I can channel an emotion other than hate and rage."

"Shit," said Efra. "I was going to stay up here and watch."

AKACHI - A TERRIBLE PRICE

Growers, be sure you know the condition of your flocks, give careful attention to your herds; for the riches of harvest do not endure forever, and a crown is not secure for all generations.

When the hay is removed and new growth appears and the grass from the hills is gathered in, the lambs will provide Bastion with clothing, and the goats with the price of a field.

You will have plenty of goats' milk to feed your family.

—The Book of Bastion

The two Turquoise Serpents circled each other.

"Stay back," Melokuhle ordered Akachi, without taking her attention off Omphile.

The Captain, unarmed, feinted and ducked, looking for an opening to get her hands on the assassin.

Eyes hooded, a confident smile dancing perfect lips, Omphile moved with flawless grace. She ignored the feints, looked bored. "I'm waiting," she purred.

Melokuhle struck like a cat, a blur of motion too fast for Akachi to follow, and retreated, bleeding. She hissed in pain, blood pouring from a long cut in her forearm. For all the Captain's seemingly inhuman speed, Omphile was faster.

"I killed most of the squad," said the assassin. "It wasn't Loa assassins; it was *your* assassin. Every time someone disappeared while on guard, that was me. I killed Tukulu when the Loa ambushed us.

Remember how his blood splashed the back of your neck? I did it right behind you."

Melokuhle growled, flicked a clod of mud at Omphile's face with her toe, and followed it with a lightning-fast kick to the assassin's knee. She hit nothing, and again retreated, bleeding from a gash in her shoulder.

"I killed Firash," said Omphile, "while he was in the tezcat trance with pretty-boy."

Melokuhle attacked, feinting low with a kick, and throwing a spinning elbow strike.

The assassin swayed beyond reach and left a long red line on the Captain's other arm.

"I killed Lubanzi," Omphile said. "I led you to that church, knowing exactly what awaited us."

Again, Melokuhle attacked, lashing out with fast, sharp jabs. Her opponent bobbed and swayed around all of them, each time moving just enough she hit nothing. Flipping the dagger into the air, the assassin slapped Melokuhle across the face. The captain staggered back, eyes watering. Catching the knife, Omphile followed, stabbing and slashing, spinning graceful pirouettes, never where the captain thought, landing kicks to her ribs and gut.

The assassin drew sanguine art across Melokuhle's flesh with the dagger.

When she finally let up, Melokuhle stumbled from exhaustion, sucking raw and desperate breaths, bleeding from a score of shallow wounds.

"So?" asked Omphile. "Am I as good as I think?" Still relaxed, she looked far from winded.

Akachi hesitated, thoughts rushing. The captain was no match for the assassin. The fight would end the instant Omphile stopped toying with her opponent.

Should he join the struggle? Maybe with the two of them, they might overcome the assassin.

The veil stretched around him, his allies clawing at it, ready to come to his aid. He still carried his carvings. He could call them. He could become a savage puma, and ravage his enemy, feast on her flesh and blood! His mouth watered as he recalled the taste of the Loa assassin he devoured in the streets of the Wheat District.

No!

She'd touched him—just the briefest contact—with a stone of self-destruction. That had tainted his thoughts, driven him to terrible choices. And now, back in the land of the living, there was one resting between his eyes. He still felt its cold weight. Could he trust his decisions?

If I call my animal spirits, will I have the strength to banish them?

He knew the answer.

Fight or flee, his two choices. If he ran, he might escape the assassin.

And then what? Become a lost soul forever wandering the under-world?

Better than letting her gut me.

Omphile and Melokuhle clashed again, and the captain limped away, blood streaming from a long wound on the inside of her thigh. The assassin followed, hunger lighting her grey eyes. Every time Melokuhle got close, Omphile cut her.

The captain screamed in pain and rage, a long, loose flap of skin and severed muscle dangling from one arm.

Omphile is flaying her.

All this was a game to the assassin. The sword, still hanging forgotten in one hand, was insult to injury. She didn't need it.

Akachi focussed on the sacrificial dagger.

His sacrificial dagger.

The dagger that bore Captain Yejide's soul.

The dagger carrying Nafari's soul.

The Staff of the Fifth Sun, forgotten, lay in the ash. In pursuing Melokuhle, the assassin no longer stood over it.

Akachi bent to retrieve the staff.

The weight of ancient, calcified stone. Wood, older than worlds, carved to look like an eagle's talon, clutched the dull bloodstone.

The heart of a dead god.

Confidence filled Akachi's soul. Subira's petty stone sorcery was nothing before the power of the gods.

Doubt and fear fell away.

Meaning to crush her skull, Akachi attacked Omphile from behind. She must have sensed him or seen something in Melokuhle's eyes. With impossible speed, flawless animal grace, the assassin turned as he struck, ducking beneath the wild swing, and landing a savage kick to the inside of his right knee. The leg buckled, and he screamed in surprise and pain.

Kneeling, Akachi swung again. Completely missing the assassin, the staff struck her sword, shattering it.

Seeing her chance, Melokuhle threw herself on Omphile's back, wrapping her legs around her waist, and grabbing the wrist of the hand holding the dagger. Staggering, Omphile fought for control of the knife, driving vicious elbows into the Captain's exposed gut.

Climbing to his feet, Akachi limped after the two.

With her free hand, Omphile grabbed one of Melokuhle's wrists and twisted until the bone snapped. God-touched, she fought with inhuman strength, bending the forearm until splintered shards tore through flesh. Teeth bared, the Captain made no sound, smashing her forehead into the bridge of Omphile's nose. Reeling from the blow, blood gushing from her shattered nose, Omphile ripped her arm free of the captain's grip and drove the dagger into Melokuhle's belly, tearing it savagely sideways.

Akachi hit her from behind, swung the staff with all the muscle in his slim body. Calcified stone met bone and Omphile crumpled, landing on her back.

Raising the staff, Akachi brought it down, chopping like he bore a stone axe, into the side of her skull. She made no move to defend herself.

Akachi lifted the staff to strike again and hesitated. The assassin lay limp, blinking one eye. He'd crushed the occipital bone over the other and it sagged in gory ruin.

Omphile coughed a bloody laugh. "Lucky," she sputtered, red frothing her lips. "Broke my neck."

"Kill her," said Captain Melokuhle through gritted teeth. She knelt in the mud. One arm hung useless, a shredded wreckage. The other held in her guts. Or tried to. Slick loops of intestine slipped past her failing grip.

"You've still lost," said Omphile. "Firash told me you die."

Akachi lowered the staff, leaned against it like a crutch. "I've died twice already."

He stood in the underworld, the Staff of the Fifth Sun once again where it belonged, in his hand.

Nothing could stop him.

Omphile coughed more blood and spat. "Can you believe Smoking Mirror chose someone other than I as his Heart?"

For the first time Akachi thought he heard genuine emotion. "He chose Efra because he knew you would fail."

"Efra," said the assassin, grimacing. "What does she have that I don't?"

Omphile's question was a good one. What *did* Efra have that the assassin didn't?

Nuru. That's what Efra has.

Smoking Mirror's Heart stood side by side with Mother Death's Heart.

Father Discord. The Enemy of Both Sides. Of *course* he planned betrayal.

Have I been hunting the wrong Dirt this entire time?

He'd been so fixated on making sure the Queen didn't return to reclaim her realm, he'd all but ignored Efra, Smoking Mirror's Heart.

The Staff of the Fifth Sun took his worries, crushed them to nothing.

If Efra was with the street-sorcerer, he would kill them both, forever end their souls.

Captain Melokuhle, kneeling in the ash, guts sliding from the great rent in her belly, coughed blood. With a red grimace of pain, she crawled to sit at Omphile's side. The assassin rolled her eyes to watch the approach. For once, she said nothing.

Melokuhle is done.

The Turquoise Serpent would never again stand, or fight. Weakened by her efforts, her good arm fell to her side. Coils of intestine slipped free.

"Fuck," she muttered, staring.

The assassin said nothing.

Why is Omphile so quiet.

Her silence seemed wholly uncharacteristic.

"You go on," said the captain, voice a whisper. "I'll sit here. With my friend."

The assassin's eyes closed, her lips moving in what looked suspiciously like prayer.

Even beaten and broken, Akachi couldn't believe Omphile could resist gloating.

Unless…

"She's waiting for Subira to pull her soul back to the land of the living," said Akachi. "If Subira calls her back, she'll be fine."

Omphile's beautiful grey eyes flashed open in panic.

Melokuhle managed a wan grin before coughing more blood down the front of her shirt. "Oh, she's not going anywhere." She held Akachi's sacrificial dagger. "Unfortunately," the captain said to the assassin, "I don't have time to do this right."

"Captain," said Omphile. "If you spare me, I'll have Subira bring you back too. Neither of us need die. I swear it. I swear to all the gods, dead and alive."

"Even if I believed you," said Melokuhle, "even if there was some way I could absolutely know for sure you spoke truth…" Rage lit her eyes like fire and she showed bloody teeth.

Slowly, ever so gently, the captain slid the dagger into the helpless assassin's chest.

When Omphile lay dead, Melokuhle offered Akachi the knife. "Her soul is in here. I hate that she will be reborn, but maybe in the next life she will be less of an asshole." She shivered, spitting more blood. "Maybe she can redeem herself."

Akachi stared at the dagger. So many souls in there. Some good, some bad. Some outright evil. "I could kill you," he offered, wondering if he could. "You too can have another chance. Otherwise, you're gone. No rebirth."

"I'm done. No longer will I be a plaything for the gods."

She was weak. He could take the choice from her. A quick stab, and it would be over. Someday she'd be reborn, none the wiser.

"Bastion can spare no souls," he said.

"If you fucking try," said Captain Melokuhle, "I swear I will kill you."

Nodding, Akachi stepped away. "I'm sorry," he said.

"Fuck off." She slumped back, weakening. "What is that staff you cling to? Every time you start looking worried about something, your knuckles go white and you become a strutting cock." She grunted a pained laugh. "Like now."

Her words, which usually would have wounded, slid off him.

She was dying. Akachi saw no reason to lie. "It is the Staff of the Fifth Sun and bears the heart of a dead god."

Melokuhle seemed unimpressed. "In the stories, all the ancient arte-facts come with great powers and demand a terrible price."

He hadn't thought about it, but she was right.

"It doesn't matter," he said, feeling that heavy stone certainty fill him. "I am Cloud Serpent's Heart," he told her. She couldn't hurt him now. "I will pay the price, whatever it is."

Drooling blood, she said, "You change when you're holding it. You're more confident."

"Confidence is good."

"Doubt is good too," she said, closing her eyes.

NURU - VERMILION RAGE

There are ancient weapons, forbidden by the gods, hidden in the Priests' Ring. Some are simple, works of mechanical principals. Some are vile, bits of dead gods and fallen sorcerers. Some are holy artefacts, blessed by the First Nahual, the L'Wha.

—The Loa Book of the Invisibles

Nuru knelt in the mud, the sharp bones of buried dead stabbing her knees. Chisulo, Omari, and Bomani stood arrayed around her, watchful, protective.

Her boys.

Her family.

Her dead.

Only Happy was missing. She prayed his soul was somewhere safe, that someday he'd be reborn.

Kofi stood apart from the others and she couldn't begin to guess what went on in the young man's thoughts. The Loa nahualli turned his back on his god, the Loa, and everything they'd worked for. It was too much. Everyone he knew. All his friends. His mother. He walked away from his entire life for Nuru.

He barely knows me.

He hadn't seen her flaws. It was a weird tendency she'd noticed common to a lot of men. They saw what they wanted to see. They pretended their lives and relationships were what they wanted them to be, blinding themselves to the reality. Was it easier than trying to make changes?

What do I feel for him?

The priest was handsome enough, and he clearly worshipped her, though it felt unhealthy. She felt trapped by his unreasonable expectations. He cared. She had no doubt he'd sacrifice himself to save her. But he also used Growers like they were nothing. He had power and he was reckless.

Kofi and Chisulo were so different, it left her reeling.

Where Chisulo would always do the right thing, Kofi would commit terrible crimes if she asked. It was a kind of power she'd never before experienced. Like the way the Loa leapt to obey her commands. If she was honest, she liked it. All her life she'd been Nothing Nuru, Powerless Nuru. All her life she'd cowered from the nahual, hidden away who and what she was.

Where Kofi would help her no matter what she decided, Chisulo would be disappointed if she did anything less than fight to save Bastion.

You ran a damned street gang dealing erlaxatu to lazy Dirts, you sanctimonious hypocrite! she imagined yelling at Chisulo.

Even then, even as a nothing Dirt street thug, he'd always done the right thing, always been ready to help those in need.

Kofi loved her so much he would never give her up, never abandon her. He'd kill his own god for Nuru.

Chisulo loved her so much he would give her up if he thought that was what was best for her.

Why was it always about them?

My feelings should matter.

She didn't love Kofi. She loved what he offered.

Taking a deep breath, Nuru placed the carving of Mother Death on the ground before her. She concentrated on the figurine.

Here, in the underworld, her heart might not beat, her blood might not rush through her veins. But somewhere, in a reality increasingly less real than this hellish place, her body swam with narcotics.

The distant screams of war faded, became a background hum of agony.

The carving grew in detail, filled Nuru's mind, became her world. Glistening spider's legs, jagged and jointed, barbed with obsidian, knees jutting past a bulbous body. Sanity swallowing black, impossible night, a gaping wound in the fabric of existence. It danced, almost dainty, hardly touching the ground. Predator grace. Mesmerizing in its oil-slick rainbow beauty. Gut churning in its stuttering nightmare twitch. The torso, that of a young woman, curved up from the spider's body. Flawless beauty, impossible perfection. Nuru couldn't believe she'd carved anything so gorgeous. A goddess. Full breasts, round and firm. Long arms taught with muscle. Onyx flesh. Slim fingers tipped with obsidian claws.

The delicate artistry of the Queen's face broke Nuru's heart. Nothing could be so glorious, so worthy of worship. Full lips. Head held in a regal bearing. Hair like the night sky, a silken curtain of gossamer sable, hung long and straight, brushing the curve of her hips as she moved.

That face. That horribly beautiful face that Efra said was Nuru.

Untouched by life and all its pathetic worries.

The face of a god. The face of the Mother of the Universe.

Mother. The only word that meant anything.

But not all mothers cared for their young.

Like the river of blood, Mother Death's eyes retained their colour. Vermilion rage.

Ancient memories of a long-dead world seeped into Nuru as she lost herself to the god.

Father Discord assassinated She Who Shines Like Jade and the weather ran rampant and unchecked for a thousand years. Storms tore the world, drowning continents, laying waste to civilizations mightier than anything Nuru could imagine.

Mother Death's memories of rain reached back through time. She saw a sky black with thunderheads, a torrential downpour smashing the earth, drowning a world. She saw great bodies of water that went on forever, heavy with life. Waves crashed against a jagged shoreline, devouring rock in endless hunger. Great raging rivers pulled down mountains a thousand times more ancient than Bastion. Thick jungles, where it rained constantly, reached beyond the curve of the world. Towering trees brushed the sky with thick canopies raucous with birds.

Water was life.

For the first time glimpsing the true scale of the world, Nuru saw the truth: Bastion, the pinnacle of creation, the Last City of Man, the final refuge of life in this reality, was a pebble worn smooth by wind and sand. Every year she grew smaller, fell in on herself. From sand she came, and to sand she would return. Bastion wasn't some great achievement; she wasn't a gift from the gods. The Last City was a prison, a menagerie for humanity built upon the last source of water.

One after the other, over tens of thousands of years, Smoking Mirror killed every god with some link to weather. After each murder the Obsidian Lord gifted the Queen with something stolen from the dead god. After the death of the Lord of the Third Sun, she gained a minor hell populated by souls who had drown or died of a few specific diseases.

Amurru, the storm god. Khonvoum, the Setting Sun. Tarḫunz, Lord of the Vineyard. The rain god Tó Neinilii. Ukko, god of the harvest. On and on. Father Discord killed more weather deities than there were now gods in all Bastion's pantheon. Mother Death, the one god who might have stopped him, did nothing, her silence purchased with gifts of souls and blood and hells.

The Queen of Bastion played her part in killing the world.

Horror at the endless crimes of the gods grew in Nuru.

The gods deserved punishment.

She would be the blade of retribution.

Nuru's friends stared up at her in awe and horror, retreating before her terrible beauty. She towered over them. Eight legs twitching and dancing, a breeze of dead souls moved her hair, wafting like plant-life in long-dried oceans.

Mother Death studied the landscape.

Her servant, Face Painted with Bells, fought on the shores of the great river, Apanohuaya. The godling's forces, drawn from the myriad dead, crumbled before the larger, more skilled army arrayed against them.

There, on the far bank of the river, stood Southern Hummingbird.

Mother Death knew a rage born of millennia of starvation. Father War had played his part in banishing her. Glorious, ravenous hunger filled her. The fool god was here, manifest in her realm. She would slaughter his army, devour every one of his hoarded souls. She would end her errant child. The pact be damned. She created it and she would break it. Today began the last war of the gods. The Queen would feed on her children. She would claim their names and aspects. She would be all.

It was their own fault. There were no longer enough souls populating Bastion to support even the few remaining gods.

I will be a pantheon of one.

Nuru screamed in horror at the god's intentions.

She saw humanity as the gods saw them. Flashes of understanding, a bleed-though of perception, blood soaking through cotton.

We are insects, ants.

Nuru drowned in divinity. Even as she lost herself, she revelled in the power of this most ancient sentience.

Now that her husband, Father Death, was gone, the Queen truly was the last of the Rada Loa, the first gods of man. Primal, she was the fear in the darkest night. The obsession with fire, worship of warmth and pain, life and destruction. Dread of the deepest waters, where the unknown lurked. Ever mutable, she changed as humanity grew and evolved. She was never one god, but tens of thousands, wearing different names and guises through time. Squat stone pyramids, stained with blood, in lush jungles. Writhing, wriggling lives impaled on wooden spikes and raised to the skies in tortured offering. Great halls of stone, floor carved deep with runnels. Ten thousand men and women knelt, throats held willingly over the troughs, awaiting the blade. One man with eyes of stone passed from person to person, opening their throats. They bled, staying upright until weakness felled them.

They bled for her, and she dreamed in blood.

All this Nuru saw and more. For it is easy to underestimate the ant.

Fear me. For I am death, the destroyer of worlds.

After twenty-five thousand years of feeding off forgotten gods, demons, and the lost souls thrown from Bastion's Sand Wall, the Lady of the Dead had returned to claim her realm.

Small souls gathered around her, not worshippers, but not enemies. When she turned her attention on them, all but one fell shivering and sobbing to the ground. She recognized that one. Smaller than the others. A tight-pent bundle of rage and destruction and lust. Long ago, in a long dead civilization, there'd been a symbol of duality: a circle carved into dark and light. Good and evil. Law and chaos. Right and wrong. A scar carved this bright spark soul like that symbol.

"You walk on both sides," the Queen told Efra. "A choice unmade."

There was more, layers of past, a history written in pain and blood and longing and an inability to belong, but Mother Death didn't care to look deeper. For all she liked this little ember, it was nothing.

Scar curling her lip, Efra glared up at the god, unafraid.

For a moment, the Queen considered squashing her, more on principle than anything.

I need her, Nuru told the god.

Giving this nothing life to her Heart was an easy choice. More important enemies awaited her attention.

Down below, corpses of the dead choked the Apanohuaya river. Face Painted with Bells' army crumbled before the onslaught of Southern Hummingbird's superior force. The battle for the underworld would soon be lost.

Mother Death gloried in the moment. Her errant children were cowards, bereft of imagination. They knew the pacts, knew the appalling cost of breaking them, and shied from anything that might bring them close. Father War and the godling faced each other from across the river, but neither dared enter the fray. Manifested here, outside of the Gods' Ring, they were vulnerable.

Mother Death had no such qualms. Hers was a rage without bounds. It transcended reason, obliterated everything except the thought of vengeance. She would be victorious, she would reclaim her throne, and her city.

The Destroyer of Worlds went to war, and six small souls followed with her.

The Queen of Bastion descended to the river, wading into bloody waters. She cut straight through the centre of Southern Hummingbird's army, heading directly toward the god. Obsidian-barbed legs stabbed out at anything that got in her way. She flicked the impaled corpses free, sent bodies spinning to splash into red waters. Her ascended godling's army rallied behind their Queen, followed her into battle. Pumas and jaguars charged in from the shore, tearing their enemies apart, feeding on ravaged flesh.

A nahualli skyvyrm snaked through the night sky, long lines of ribs showing through tattered flesh. It spat fire and bone-melting bile on everything. Mother Death pounced like a hunting spider, snatched it out of the air. She tore it apart, littering those below with its innards. Landing amidst the enemy, stabbing and slashing, she sent bodies tumbling. The Queen wore blood like the slickest dress. Every soul snuffed was a soul devoured. No need for a sacrificial altar when they were this close.

The bright spark lives of her Heart's friends gathered around, reforming their honour guard. There were less than there had been, but that was nothing.

Trapped within the god, Nuru saw only that which Mother Death saw. She railed, helpless, as a massive puma crashed into Omari, and the Finger went down, disappearing beneath bloody waters. Chisulo and Bomani charged to his aid.

Mother Death moved on, leaving them behind.

Turn back!

Father War noted the Queen's advance. Cleaving a path through his army, her intent could not be more obvious. Southern Hummingbird grew in stature until he towered the height of one hundred men. He grinned madness. For too long he had been cooped up in the Gods' Ring. Finally, a worthy opponent!

He should be terrified.

Where Mother Death saw nothing but her enemy, Nuru saw a god who had come prepared.

This is her realm. He should flee.

Father War drew a sword the length of ten men. Even here in the underworld, reality writhed around that terrible blade. So crammed it was with millions of years of harvested souls, the black glass bled foul smoke. Entire worlds, realities, stripped clean of life. Gods and demons. Father War murdered them all to make his weapon.

Nuru saw the folly of her plans. Her god-killer dagger was nothing compared to this sword. Thinking she could kill Father War was purest folly.

Flee! she screamed at Mother Death.

The Queen ignored her.

A mighty sea dragon rose out of the bloody river in challenge, and Mother Death shredded it apart. Nuru caught flashes of the war behind her. Face Painted with Bells, beset by Turquoise Serpents, was retreating. Chisulo, Kofi, and little Efra fought back to back, surrounded by generations of long dead Hummingbird Guard. She saw nothing of Bomani or Omari.

Chisulo!

He would die again, never to be reborn. He would die for her.

No!

She couldn't allow it.

She wouldn't.

A long figure stood on a distant ridge of exposed rock, overlooking the battle. Stained robes of red, white, and black. She knew that shape, saw it in every nightmare.

It was the Cloud Serpent nahaulli she fought in the Wheat District. They'd left him mortally wounded and bleeding out in the street. Was he one of her dead come to haunt her, or had he somehow survived and followed her here, a faithful servant of The Lord of the Hunt?

His presence could be no coincidence.

This is a trap.

Nuru's first thought was Smoking Mirror, but his Heart was about to die, slaughtered by Southern Hummingbird's army.

Somehow, all this had been arranged.

Nuru understood the depths of her failure.

AKACHI - THE END OF THE FIFTH AGE

The coward questions. The coward flinches from his duty, hides behind reasons and excuses. The coward wants to know why. *The coward stalls and calls it deliberation.*

The brave man has faith, his belief armours him from doubt and failure. The brave man doesn't ask why because he knows. *The brave man acts.*

—The Book of Bastion

Staff of the Fifth Sun clutched in his right hand, Akachi watched the battle raging in the river below. The stump-fingers of his ruined hand twitched in helpless sympathy. Corpses choked the bloody waters, piled deep, became the islands upon which men and women fought to make more corpses. Mountains of dead.

The outcome was predictable, a forgone conclusion. Southern Hummingbird's forces would overwhelm the lesser army of Face Painted with Bells. Nothing in the godling's arsenal would change that. Her pathetic stone sorcerers were nothing in the face of temple-trained warrior-nahualli.

Strange stars wheeled overhead in patient grace, vicious knife wounds in the curtain of endless night. This was not Bastion's night sky. He saw not a single recognizable constellation and couldn't begin to imagine what that meant.

Akachi's right hand ached from holding the staff so tight. Loosening his grip, he let it lean against his chest. His skull ached around the missing eye, a bruised throb.

In his dream, Bishop Zalika told him that The Lord killed his brother, the god of the sun. Akachi found that same crime referenced in the copy of the *Book of Bastion* in her chambers, though it had been cut from later copies. The fall of the Fifth Sun heralded the end of an age, the death of the world.

She said he was tricked into killing his brother.

A strange dream sent him to the cathedral. Though she hadn't shared details, Zalika said she'd dreamed too. Unlike Akachi, she questioned the source of their dreams. She mocked him for his faith.

For all Akachi hated the Bishop, she wasn't a liar.

It felt different than when Cloud Serpent visited me on the altar.

Looking back, everything about the dream and what happened after felt wrong.

Zalika. Finding the book and the specific passages.

Subira and Omphile were servants of Smoking Mirror. They'd gone to great lengths to get him to the underworld.

Was the Obsidian Lord behind everything?

Imposible!

Doubt.

Fear.

His hand moved to grip the staff once again.

"The stones," he whispered.

He was still dead, still lying on a cot in Subira's church. The stone of self-destruction still lay between his eyes. And there was flint, the stone of conflict, over his heart!

That's why I doubt!

'Bring the staff to the place of eternal night,' Zalika said in his dream. The underworld.

He stared at the horizon. "I shall bring the sun to the underworld."

Akachi watched as a battalion of Turquoise Serpents in sorcerous jade armour cut their way toward Face Painted with Bells. The godling was gorgeous, eyes glowing like two candles in the endless night, polished stones sunk in flawless flesh. The hand Akachi bit off during their battle still showed chewed fragments of splintered bone. The Serpents overran her soldiers and hacked the godling apart with stone swords.

A strange sadness took him, and tears tumbled free; gods shouldn't die. She might be his enemy, but this felt like the death of a world. The pantheon was too small to begin with, and now, after the death of The Lord and Her Skirt is Stars, could ill-afford to lose more.

The veil tore with a scream, and the Queen of Bastion returned to the underworld.

Akachi stood rooted in awe and horror. Here, she was a thousand times more powerful than what he'd faced in the Wheat District. In the filthy streets of the Dirts, she'd been a terrifying monster, a demon. Manifest in the underworld, in *her* underworld, she was a god. She was *the* god. She was the first and the last. She birthed the universe, and it would be she who, in the end, destroyed it.

Mother Death carved a path through Southern Hummingbird's army, heading directly for the god. Death and misery followed in her wake, souls rent and devoured, fragments of bodies scattered.

Would she dare break the pact forbidding war between the gods?

His thoughts raced. If she did, the other gods would have no choice but to do the same, if just to protect themselves. The last war of the gods killed the world. If it happened again, Bastion would surely die.

I have to stop her.

This must be why Cloud Serpent wanted him here.

The Staff of the Fifth Sun felt cold and heavy in his fist, calcified wood, dead hundreds of thousands of years. Or longer.

Heat bled from him, his right hand numb and cold.

Crack the sky. Grinding glass in his skull. *Kill Mother Death.*

"Kill the Queen? She is the Mother of the Universe."

She is the Destroyer.

Akachi reeled in horror. The sight of Face Painted with Bells' death broke his heart.

Call the sun. Save humanity.

How could he contemplate such a crime?

Did you lose a hand and an eye to take the coward's route now?

"No!"

He risked everything for his god. He would hold to his faith.

Down below, Mother Death slaughtered thousands of Father War's troops. Thousands of souls who would never again be reborn.

Akachi clung to the staff, begging for the certainty he needed.

Call the Fifth Sun. Viciously sharp black stone scraped his thoughts. *Bring about the end of the fifth age.*

The Queen of Bastion drew inexorably closer to Southern Hummingbird, and the war god rose to face her, the glee of battle lighting him like a thousand suns.

The pact will be broken. The gods will war. Bastion will die. Only you can save her.

He had no choice. To preserve the pact that protected the Last City, he must stop Mother Death.

Akachi lifted the Staff of the Fifth Sun.

The heart of a dead god beat once, a great pulse of power smashing the nahual to his knees. Far above, the sheet of night tore.

NURU - DUST

Sometimes a religious text is just that. Sometimes it's a guide of sorts, an attempt at assisting a few hundred thousand souls to exist in an enclosed and slowly dying system. Sometimes it's circular, demanding faith and yet not having faith in those it demands faith from. Sometimes it's an attempt to awaken those souls to something beyond religion.

—The Loa Book of the Invisibles

The Queen of Bastion savaged flesh, shredded souls.

Devouring.

Ever devouring.

Blood sheened her naked torso, slick gore painting her curves, turning her raven waterfall of hair into a sanguine river.

Nebthet. Kālarātri. A thousand names reaching back through time.

The Lord was but a pretender to her throne. She was the one true god of death.

The Destroyer.

Nuru railed and screamed and begged Mother Death to turn from her enemy and was ignored. Surrounded by Birds, Chisulo, Efra, and Kofi fought back to back. Soon, they would be overrun and slain. Forever dead. Never to be reborn.

What threat could Nuru offer the Queen?

Desperate, Nuru realized she had one ploy to play: *Mother Death needs me.*

Bomani always used to say, 'Never bluff. Always carry out your threats.' If he said he would do a thing, that thing fucking well got done. Usually in the bloodiest and most violent way possible.

Nuru found cold calm.

Save Chisulo and the others, she told Mother Death, *or I will walk out to the Sand Wall and step off. I will banish you to the Bloody Desert.*

Two twitching bodies impaled on one obsidian leg, Mother Death stopped.

If they die, promised Nuru, *I die. You might be in control now, but once the narcotics wear off, nothing you can do will stop me.*

The god didn't move.

Test me, said Nuru. *Go on. Test me.*

Shaking her leg free of corpses, Mother Death turned and charged back toward Nuru's friends. An otochin blocked her path, a muscled monster with a long necklace of fetishes bolstering his strength and speed. A gore-splashed sword in hand, scores of bodies lay littered around him. The nahualli threw himself in her path, teeth bared in a snarl of bloodlust, stone blade raised high. The Queen punched a barbed leg through his skull shattering bone and brain and leaving ruin. She discarded the headless body and kept moving.

A twig in a torrential river, tossed by impossible currents, Nuru saw the world in mad swirling slashes of vision. The god killed without thought. Anything that got in her way died.

The Cloud Serpent nahualli stood on that distant hill. Hands raised, he held something over his head. Where Mother Death knew no fear, Nuru knew better than to underestimate the young man. Should she try and turn the god in his direction? Would killing the nahualli solve anything? If he followed her here, hunted her from the Growers' Ring to the underworld, nothing short of utter destruction would stop him.

As the Queen reached Nuru's friends, the sky broke, tore apart like someone shredding a thobe with sharpened flint.

Mother Death staggered and turned, finally seeing the young nahualli on the hill. Holding a long staff, he made a cutting motion with it, a wild swing. A gash tore reality, opened the blanket of night like a ragged wound. A stone, mounted at one end of the staff pulsed crimson, left slashes in Nuru's vision.

Those nearest the nahualli came apart, crumbling. A sudden roaring wind scattered their ashen remains.

Like a rock dropped in a puddle, a wave of destruction swept out from the nahualli. It left dust and ruin in its wake. Obsidian swords fell to black sand.

The wave swept toward them, inexorable. Unstoppable. Utter devastation.

Nuru stared in horror.

No.

All those souls, gone. Enough to repopulate Bastion several times over. All snuffed in an instant.

"Kofi!" screamed Efra. "Get us out of here! Now!"

Eyes locked on Nuru, Kofi raised a carnelian stone of the deepest red. Somehow, even though she stood as Mother Death, the Loa priest saw *her*, the woman within. Love and worship, and none of it was for his god. Right or wrong, he would do anything to save Nuru.

No matter the cost.

"I love you," he said. "I'm sorry."

She saw then what he and Efra planned.

"No!" screamed Nuru.

With no time for thought, she lunged toward Chisulo, trying to grab him so that whatever sorcery Kofi worked to save her, might save him too. Her fingers tangled in the grey of his thobe, stiff cotton, stained and filthy.

Their eyes met as the sky lit bright.

I have you!

Chisulo fell to dust.

AKACHI - EVISCERATED SKY

Whoever is not with us is against us, and whoever does not gather with us scatters. And so we tell you, any sin and blasphemy can be forgiven. But blasphemy against the Pantheon will not be forgiven. Anyone who speaks a word against the Nahual of Man will be forgiven, but anyone who speaks against the Gods of Bastion will not be forgiven, either in this age or in the Sixth Age to come.

—The Book of Bastion

The eternal night sky ripped and Akachi stood bathed in divine light.

A weight fell from him, a darkness he'd become inured to. Sick soul-staining rot faded to nothing. He felt light and free. Staff raised over his head, the sky above opening to the blaze of the Fifth Sun, he gloried in doing his god's work. Euphoria rushed through him, washing away the cobwebs that had clogged the corners of his mind for so long. For the first time since Zalika called him to her chambers and sent him out to the Wheat District, he felt clean. Unstained.

Black sand poured from his robes, piled at his feet.

Brow furrowed in confusion, he stared at the dwindling pile as the wind took it away.

Creeping understanding.

Numb horror.

The dagger.

He remembered the foul feel of the knife as Zalika handed it to him, heavy with souls. Somehow, he'd grown accustomed to it, barely felt its rot and decay.

Blind to its evil.

Deaf to the screaming souls it carried.

Ignorant of its stench.

A gust scattered what remained, a dark cloud spinning in the wind and diffusing to nothing in a heartbeat.

His sacrificial dagger.

Captain Yejide.

Nafari, his best friend.

All those souls.

Gone.

As the sky tore and the Fifth Sun dawned in the underworld, light swept across the landscape below. Every soul the light touched fell to crimson sand. Every shard of obsidian became black dust.

Hundreds gone in an instant.

Thousands.

More.

I killed them.

All those souls robbed of all chance at rebirth.

Yejide, his love, gone. Ash. He'd never bring her back, never see her again. He killed her more completely than Efra ever could have.

The light of the Fifth Sun swept across Southern Hummingbird's army, left bloody dust in its wake. It washed across Father War, and he too was dust.

I killed a god.

Deicide. The most terrible crime. The Book didn't even prescribe a punishment for it, it was so unimaginable. The great wound gutted the sky, eviscerated night.

Father War and his army a dissipating mist, the light devoured Mother Death's forces next, as it raced toward the oldest of the gods.

There was no stopping it.

Riven, the night shredded apart, the wound growing.

Understanding crushed Akachi to his knees.

When the damage above was complete and the sky bright with light, every soul in the underworld would be gone. Dust.

This was *his* doing.

This was *his* crime.

I did as I was told.

The plaintive cry of a child, helpless before the consequences of their actions.

Kneeling in the dust of Yejide, Akachi screamed at the eviscerated sky.

Great swirling clouds of sanguine ash and sand obscured his vision. More souls than all Bastion. And he murdered them all. Forever.

What was faith worth now?

When Akachi performed his first sacrifice, a Grower who stabbed one of his Hummingbird Guards, he'd wondered if sheer scale of atrocity might absolve him of sin. Such had been his horror at taking a single life. After, he puked, and fled to the numb safety of erlaxatu.

He knew the answer now.

Akachi laughed as the underworld came apart around him.

Where can I escape to this time?

There weren't enough narcotics in all Bastion to help him flee the responsibility.

Sobbing and laughing, crying, and begging for release, Akachi prayed that he, too, might dissolve to nothing.

"I did as I was told!" He shook a ruined fist at the raging sun tearing its way through night. "It's not my fault!"

NURU - VENGEANCE

There are truisms even the gods must accept. Existence is cyclical. Birth, death, rebirth. A beginning, an end, and a new beginning. The cycle is greater than all. Before each new beginning there must be an end, a moment of near perfect nothing. Yet even that nothing is flawed.

There is one god greater than all the pantheon, greater even than the Queen and her husband. In the end, the god of decay always wins. For it is his mercurial state which shall bring about the next rebirth. He is a liar and a trickster. He both loves and loathes. His power is the sleight of hand of the charlatan, and the unbridled destructive might of chaos.

Through him the Age of the Sixth Sun shall be born.

—The Loa Book of the Invisibles

Nuru returned to herself in stages.

For a long while she clung desperately to the nothing she always believed herself to be, a feather of thought fleeing reality on the winds of nightmare. The cold grit of stone on her back grew in her consciousness, became an anchor dragging her down into the horror of what awaited. Cold damp, the wet smell of mildew. In contrast, a flickering light, yellow and warm, teased her eyes. The scent of candles. Not filthy ox-fat like the illicit ones she traded for in the Wheat District, but clean and pure like the nahual used.

Dust, running through her fingers.

Chisulo.

Her boys were gone.

Losing them the first time broke her heart. In the days following, she'd been wrapped up in survival, embroiled in her insane plan to kill the gods and free Bastion. She'd shied from thinking about them, fled the pain.

Hating the gods, plotting their death, Nuru still took comfort in knowing her friends would be reborn. She might never see them again, but their souls would live on. Sometimes, she'd imagined Chisulo as a boy, remembering how he was back in the crèche. Always filthy. Usually in trouble. Always there to take care of his friends.

It was you, not me, who bound us together.

He'd been wrong about that. He made them better. He made them want to be better.

The whole reason she was here in the Senators' Ring was to make Chisulo proud, to do the right thing for all Bastion.

What did that matter now?

If he would never be reborn, what was the point in making sure there was a city worth being reborn into?

Her fist clenched, trying to hold on to Chisulo as he came apart, as he slid through her fingers.

Gone. Forever gone.

What was left? Was there anything to fight for, any reason to go on?

"I'm sorry," said Efra.

Grudgingly, Nuru opened her eyes. Efra stood over her. The scar carved her face in half, twisted her mouth.

"As soon as you started talking about going to the underworld," said Efra, "I knew we had to have our own way back. When Chisulo showed up, I knew you'd never willingly leave him."

Nuru stared at Efra in horror.

She did this. She planned it.

"It wouldn't have worked anyway," Efra said, rubbing at the scar. "He had no body to return to. Where would his soul have gone?"

Is she right?

"I see you thinking about that," said Efra. "You'll never know the answer. You can be angry with me, or you can forgive me, or you can thank me for saving your life." She tilted her head in consideration. "Or some mix of the three, I guess."

"There's nothing left," said Nuru. "He's gone. He died because of me."

"Not because." Efra scowled down at her. "He died *for* you. It was a choice, and one he made knowing full well what it would cost." Her voice rose in anger. "Don't you fucking *dare* rob him of that!" She grabbed Nuru, dragged her into a sitting position. "He sacrificed himself for you. Now what are you going to do to earn that?"

She was right, and Nuru hated her. Chisulo knew exactly what he was doing. She'd seen it in him from the moment she suggested she might save him. He knew dying there would be an end to his soul and hadn't hesitated because he knew she needed him.

Kofi still lay motionless on one of the altars, the slight rise and fall of his chest the only sign he wasn't dead.

"What's the point?" Nuru asked. "We can't win. You saw Southern Hummingbird's army. I never could have got close. We can't kill the gods."

"Is Father War dead?" Efra asked, knowing the answer. "Yes. Are we dead? No. So don't tell me we can't do this."

She said it like everything happened according to plan, like she and Nuru tricked everyone into being exactly where they were at exactly the right time.

She's crazy.

"Southern Hummingbird was the god of war," said Efra. "None of the other gods have armies."

She sounded too certain.

"How do you know?" Nuru asked.

"Did Her Skirt is Stars have an army?"

Thousands of children. Laughing. Playing. Running in fields of endless clover.

Dying.

Nuru shook her head.

"The others will be easy," said Efra.

Nuru pushed her away. "You're insane."

Efra shrugged, untouched by her words. "You need a reason to keep going? Fine. How many Grower children have been turned out of crèches? Who is going to make sure they grow up free? Chisulo died because he believed in you." She looked at the floor. "*I* believe in you. Please, don't let us down."

"You're saying what you think I need to hear," accused Nuru.

Efra barked a harsh laugh. "I couldn't decide if you'd go for that, or for the 'Do it for bloody vengeance' speech."

Vengeance.

Vengeance for all the centuries of abuse. Vengeance for the mothers robbed of the chance to know their children. Vengeance for the whippings. Vengeance for the sacrifices.

"Vengeance will do," said Nuru. "At least for now."

"That was my preference too," admitted Efra.

Kofi groaned, cracked an eye open. Seeing Nuru, he bared his teeth in a grimace of guilt and pain. "Sorry," he said. "I should have said something before."

"I told him not to," said Efra. "I told him if you knew, you'd resist. You'd die and it would be his fault."

"Could we have saved Chisulo?" Nuru asked. "Could we have saved his soul, brought him back with us?"

Kofi looked to Efra. "I don't think so."

It wasn't the answer she wanted, wasn't the answer she needed to move on. As with everything in life, it lacked finality, lacked closure.

"Subira knew we were coming," said Efra. "She led us straight down here, no hesitation, no questions. I can't believe I didn't see it." She held up the flint dagger. "You two wait here."

"Where are you going?" asked Nuru.

"You know where I'm going. And you know what I'm going to do."

Kofi stood on unsteady legs. "We should stick together."

"You'll just get in my way, fat boy. Stay and take care of her," she gestured at Nuru. "I'll be back. And if I'm not, get her out of here."

"And go where?" Nuru demanded.

With a laugh, Efra shrugged. "I'll be dead, so not my problem."

Back straight, no hint of doubt or hesitation, she strode from the room.

Seeing Efra's knife reminded Nuru of her own. Touching the purse, she found the god-killer still within. Kofi got them out before it was exposed to the light.

"How did you do it?" Nuru asked. "How did you bring us back?"

"Efra told me I had to prepare. She said I had to be able to bring you back from the dead. There was only one way to do that. Among other things, carnelian is the stone of doors."

"Couldn't you have used it to get us there?"

He shook his head. "I couldn't want you to die. Tecolotl sorcery is all emotion. You need reasons—desires—for whatever you're trying to achieve." He looked away. "You can't do anything your heart disagrees with."

She remembered the way he drove the Growers against the Turquoise Serpents, the way he called Dirts to their death.

You were fine with that. It didn't trouble your heart in the least.

He might love and worship her, but he was terribly dangerous.

"That was a trap," she said. "The Cloud Serpent nahualli was waiting for us."

"The turncoat," said Kofi with a rueful laugh. He sat up, rubbing at his temples and wincing. "Subira lied about being Loa. She must have contacted him once we were drugged. He could have gone to the underworld from wherever he is in Bastion." He rubbed his chin in thought. "They were trying to kill Mother Death."

"But they killed Southern Hummingbird instead."

Or maybe that was part of the plan.

I will be a pantheon of one. Mother Death's thought.

The Cloud Serpent nahualli had been there waiting. It was he who called the sun, he who killed Southern Hummingbird and destroyed all those souls.

He tried to kill Mother Death and Southern Hummingbird.

Cloud Serpent must have had the same thought as the Queen.

There weren't enough souls in Bastion to support the pantheon. It wouldn't be long before all the gods had the same idea. They would war until only one remained, presiding over the devastated ruins of Bastion.

Horror filled Nuru. Bastion wouldn't survive another war. Killing the gods wasn't enough; she had to do it quickly.

"You said the stones were conduits for emotion," said Nuru, desperate for distraction. "You have to attain a mental state to use them. What emotion opens doors?"

"There are two," answered Kofi, "fear and desire. You run toward something, or away from it."

"Which was it for you?"

He smiled without humour. "Bit of both."

Nuru understood running away all too well. She couldn't imagine having something to run toward, some hope for the future beyond another crust of hardbread. "What were you running toward?"

"You," said Kofi.

She couldn't think about that right now. She'd lost too much. His loyalty was already too much of a burden. If she used him, she would be responsible for any death and pain he caused. And she knew he wouldn't hesitate.

Fingers, passing through sand.

Efra returned, silk dress splashed with blood. She carried a staff with a bloodstone clutched in carved eagle talon. It stood a full head over her.

Sliding off the altar to stand on shaky legs, Nuru said, "You're Smoking Mirror's Heart."

It was the wrong thing to do. It was the dumbest possible choice.

It was the right thing to do.

Kofi's eyes widened in confusion.

"I am," agreed Efra, face blank.

"You know what it means."

"Yes."

"How long have you known?" Kofi demanded of Nuru.

She ignored him. "Because you were listening in the barley warehouse, pretending to be asleep."

Efra nodded.

"Why didn't you say anything?"

Brow crinkled, rubbing at where the scar crossed her lip, Efra said, "Why didn't you?"

"I was afraid. Were you afraid of how I'd react?"

If she says she was, I know she's lying.

"No." Efra frowned at the staff's bloodstone heart. "We aren't what the gods make us."

"What are we?" Nuru asked, confused.

"We're what we want to be. They have their plans, but in the end we're free to choose." She grinned hard. "Nothing has changed. We're going to kill them."

Relief flooded Nuru. Planning to kill an entire pantheon of gods was infinitely preferable to opposing Efra.

Kofi looked from Efra to Nuru. "Are you insane? She's Father Discord's Heart! She's the enemy!"

Nuru waved him to silence. "Only if we aren't planning to kill the gods. I saw that staff," she added. "The Cloud Serpent nahualli had it in the underworld. He used it to tear the sky."

"He was the Heart of Cloud Serpent," said Efra. "He used it to kill a god. I figure it's better in our hands."

"He's here? How did you get it?"

"I killed him," said Efra. "Subira too. But the nahual know we're here. We need to leave."

She was right. There was nothing here for them. But where to now? Farther into Bastion, all the way to the Priests' Ring?

Do I trust her?

No. That would be foolish. This was jagged dangerous little Efra.

Trusting her was like trusting a rabid puma.

But I can't do this alone.

Efra took Nuru's hand and led her from the church.

Bewildered, Kofi followed.

AKACHI - SCALE OF ATROCITY

There can be no apostacy.
The soul without faith, without belief, serves no purpose.
It questions yet offers no answers.
It feeds not the gods.
There is no more dangerous soul.

—The Book of Bastion

Murderer.

Such a pale word.

So pathetic. So unable to convey the depths of Akachi's crime.

Uncountable mortal souls reduced to ash and dust. Father War, one of the dwindling pantheon's most important gods, gone. The Hummingbird Guard, the city's keepers of the peace, were no longer priests. The only militarily trained men and women in the city, and they were without leadership. Without divine guidance, mortals were dangerous and unpredictable. Would they obey the nahual? Was there anything to stop them from staging a coup and claiming the city for themselves?

Who could stop them?

Akachi stared at his ruined hand. *The Growers.* An army of Dirts. He wanted to laugh, to cry. He wanted to claw his remaining eye from its socket and crush it, penance for his sins.

Mother Death, the Queen of Bastion. The oldest god, the last of the Rada Loa. She birthed realities and lived beyond their deaths. He'd watched the sun sweep across her army, turn everything to bloody sand.

Red, like the desert.

The was no punishment for such a crime.

Flay his flesh. Smash his bones as the Guard did to errant Dirts. Take his limbs. Bleed him on the altar. Open his chest and cut free his heart.

Throw him from the Sand Wall, banish his heinous soul from Bastion's light.

He deserved all of that and a thousand times more.

No torment could be enough.

Akachi opened his eye and found himself on a cot in Subira's church, the Staff of the Fifth Sun at his side. Omphile and Captain Melokuhle lay on their cots, motionless. Dead.

Blinking, he was unable to do anything more. The stones lay upon him. The amethyst resting between his eyes felt like it bore a hole through his skull, vomited self-destruction and loathing straight into his brain.

Failure. Failure. Failure.

His sacrificial dagger falling to black sand, pouring from his robes and piling at his feet only to be whipped away by the winds of the under-world. Yejide, gone forever. Nafari. That Grower Akachi sacrificed for striking Gyasi. All those awaiting rebirth and redemption. Every last soul in the underworld, red dust.

Many of the Hummingbird Guard had carried obsidian knives. The Turquoise Serpents possessed ancient swords so crammed with souls they smoked and cut through stone and bone with ease.

Akachi wanted to laugh but couldn't move. Scale of atrocity. Sacrificing that first Dirt had stained him. He'd been horrified by the blood, appalled by his actions.

It was a crime beneath notice.

How many did I kill today?

There hadn't been such death since the Last War.

"You're awake."

Subira stepped close to stand over Akachi, a sacrificial dagger in her hand. Head tilted to one side, she stared down at him. Sadness, or regret. He couldn't tell. Didn't care.

Kill me. End this.

It was an escape he didn't deserve.

"So easy," she said, placing a cool hand on Akachi's cheek as if offering comfort. "He said it would be."

A tear ran from his eye.

Do it. Please.

She raised the knife over his chest.

Would the dagger someday make the journey to the Gods' Ring? What would happen if it did? He'd sundered the sky, brought the Fifth Sun to the underworld. Its raging light destroyed souls. Would Bastion's dead still go there, only to be snuffed the instant they arrived? Had he doomed the city he loved?

"Not yet," said Efra, striding into the room, a flint dagger in one hand.

Startled, Subira turned, bringing her own knife up in defence.

Wearing the clinging silk dress of a Senator, Efra stood utterly unconscious of her appearance. Like the scar that should have defined her, the crimson dress was nothing. The Artist was right. She was beautiful. She *owned* that scar.

Efra made no threats, showed no hint of fear.

Too calm. Too in control.

He'd thought Omphile the perfect assassin, but Efra would kill her in a heartbeat.

She's katle.

Any show of humanity from Efra was just that, a show.

Akachi remembered the way Subira stumbled when he mentioned one of the girls was Smoking Mirror's Heart, the way she asked if he was sure. At the time he thought her startled and horrified by the revelation.

No. She was horrified because she realized she sent her god's Heart to the underworld.

"If he wants things to end a certain way," said Efra, "he should consider letting me know."

"He?" asked the tecuhtli.

"He may think we are his slaves," mused Efra, "but he is wrong."

We Are His Slaves, one of Smoking Mirror's older, less used names.

Subira hesitated. "Who are you?"

"I am his Heart."

The nahualli fell to her knees, prostrated herself before the Grower. "I didn't know! I never would have—I didn't know!"

Efra studied the kneeling woman with narrowed eyes. Her scarred lip curled in purest hate. "You almost killed me. You almost killed my friend."

"I'm sorry," the tecuhtli sobbed. "I didn't know! I was told—"

"Your god is as foolish as the idiots serving him."

Subira gasped in horror at the blasphemy.

"How did you get here?" demanded Efra. "How did a servant of Smoking Mirror end up in a church of Father Death pretending to be a Loa sympathizer?"

Subira sagged in relief. "Infiltrating the Loa was easy. Father Discord plays a long game, plans generations in advance."

Efra grunted derision but said nothing.

"Believing me to be a talented slave-sorcerer from the Bankers' Ring," the nahualli continued, "they welcomed me into the fold. Once I'd climbed the ranks, I volunteered to be installed in Father Death's priesthood as a spy. This achy old bag of bones isn't my true body," she complained. "Using kyanite, the Loa tore my soul free and forced it into the body of a nahualli they captured."

"They call you the turncoat," said Efra.

Subira nodded. "Only the highest ranked Loa know the truth." She dared a glance at Efra. "Or, they think they know the truth."

Expressionless, Efra showed no surprise, no hint she cared in the least for her god's long-running plans. "You can't kill him," she said, nodding at Akachi.

His heart cracked in despair. Life was a far worse torment than any torture she might inflict with sharpened stone.

"He knows too much," said Subira from the floor. "Smoking Mirror wants him dead."

"Smoking Mirror isn't here," said Efra. "I am."

"He's broken," pleaded the nahualli. "Useless. He'll kill himself the moment he's able."

"Broken is good," said Efra. "I like broken. It's unpredictable. You, on the other hand, are useless to me. Sit up. I don't like talking to the back of your head."

Subira pushed to her knees with a grunt of effort. "Did I not serve well?"

Efra's lips pursed in thought. Shrugging, she said, "I don't care."

She cut the nahualli's throat, a deep gouge emptying the woman in a dozen heartbeats.

Trapped in narcotic paralysis, Akachi listened to Subira's last bloody gasping breaths.

Stepping past the dying woman, Efra leaned over him. She stared into his eyes as if searching for something. "I see pain, I think. Misery." She flicked the stones off him, contemptuous. "You killed a god." Her eyes widened. "Ah. You thought you killed two. No. Mother Death lives." Gently, she brushed a length of hair from his face. "A thousand generations of man spent preparing for this moment, and things still didn't work out as Father Discord planned." She laughed. "You know what this means, right? The gods are fallible. They make mistakes. Makes you wonder what else they may have missed."

Father Discord planned all of this. Had the god sent that first dream, pushing Akachi to go to the Northern Cathedral and claim the staff?

Cloud Serpent never mentioned the staff. The Lord of the Hunt never said anything about going to the underworld to confront Mother Death's Heart. The god's instructions had been vague. Find *her*. Kill *her*.

With sudden clarity Akachi recalled his god's visit as he lay upon the sacrificial altar in the church in the Wheat District. Horror took him. How many times had he thought about that moment? Why hadn't he paid more attention?

'The gods war,' Cloud Serpent had said. 'We are riven by discord.'

Akachi had taken it literally, thought it meant there was disagreement and strife between the gods. What if the Lord of the Hunt meant they were riven by Discord, by Smoking Mirror?

'Smoking Mirror has chosen his Heart. She is chaos. She will bring about the fall of Bastion, utter ruin. Humanity will die.'

Oh gods. He was telling me who the real enemy was. He was telling me which Heart was the more dangerous.

'Hunt the scarred girl," Akachi's god commanded. 'Cut out her heart, bleed her on the altar.' And finally, at the end, almost like it had been an afterthought, 'Hunt the sorcerer who bears Mother Death. Throw her from the wall, once again banishing The Lady.'

Cloud Serpent's instructions to his Heart hadn't been vague at all. The dream had confused him, made Akachi believe things had changed. They hadn't. From the very beginning, Efra and Smoking Mirror had always been the true danger.

"Nuru often says, 'I can see you thinking about that,'" said Efra. "I realized she meant that my expressions were easy to read. Now, I only let her think I'm considering something if that's what I want her to think. I started looking for it in others. You're surprisingly easy to read." She squinted into Akachi's eye. "I see you thinking about that. I see you understanding. That's good and bad." She sighed, leaning against the altar like they shared casual conversation. "I could kill you now."

Please. Please. PLEASE!

"You want that. You'd welcome it." She hefted the bloody flint dagger. "Not obsidian. No chance of rebirth. Though that might be true of everyone now."

Akachi didn't care, didn't want to be reborn. Dissolution was better in every way. Escape to nothingness.

"Smoking Mirror wants you dead," she mused. "But it's just us here. You understand what *that* means, right? *I* decide."

He stared up at her, helpless. *Please.*

"It means we have power," she explained. "His plans didn't work out the way he wanted. All his plans, from this moment forward, assume the Heart of Cloud Serpent is dead." She nodded to herself, grunting in amusement. "For a god of discord and chaos, he has an awful lot of plans."

Efra plucked the staff from where it lay at Akachi's side. Turning it in her hands, studying it from all angles, she said, "Ugly. But you understand why I can't leave it with you." She examined the bloodstone. "I had a dream about this staff, you know?" She glanced at him, eyebrow hooked, scar twisting her lips in a curious smile. "Do you have dreams? Do you listen to them? Dangerous things, aren't they? Anyway. In my dream I smashed it."

Akachi managed a 'Nurg!"

"No?" she asked. "Why not?"

He couldn't explain, couldn't make his mouth work. Truth be told, he wasn't sure which terrified him more, the idea of destroying such an ancient and holy artefact or losing it to this Dirt.

I need it!

He was nothing without the staff.

"Nuhr," he managed.

"I don't think I'm going to break it," announced Efra. "You killed a god with this thing. What else can it do?" She picked at where the scar crossed her lips. "I think this should be in hands a little less dangerous than yours. Less dangerous than mine too. At least, until I need it. I know exactly who to give it to." About to turn, she hesitated. "What do you think this will do to his plans? Do you think he'll know it wasn't destroyed? I think it'll be interesting to find out."

Staff of the Fifth Sun in hand, Efra left Akachi lying upon a sacrificial altar.

More than all his many failures, the loss of the staff savaged Akachi. He felt like he'd been eviscerated, spilled onto the dirty stone floor. The lack left him gutted, robbed of confidence. Hollowed by doubt.

Failure heaped upon failure.

He'd been manipulated and used, his faith turned against him. His obedience, which should have been a strength, should have been applauded, left him vulnerable. All his life he'd been told to obey.

Obey the gods.

Obey the bishop.

Obey the ranking nahual.

Obey his teachers.

Obey his father.

How did Cloud Serpent not see this? Why wasn't Akachi warned? How could his god fail his Heart so terribly?

Akachi's faith withered and died.

One of the fingers of his right hand twitched, the empty numbness slowly falling away as feeling returned.

He lay still, staring at the stone ceiling, as the itching stab-pain crept up his limbs. Hour by hour he regained more of himself, until his body was once again his.

Somewhere in the church of Father Death there would be a sacrificial dagger. A sharp edge. Anything he could use to end his misery. Maybe even right there, on Subira's cold corpse.

He's broken. Useless. He'll kill himself the moment he's able.

"Cloud Serpent!" Akachi called, his voice echoing down empty halls. "Your Heart calls!"

No answer came.

He no longer had enough jainkoei in his blood to feel his god. Fumbling at his belt, he remembered he'd eaten the last of it.

Abandoned. Alone.

He'll kill himself the moment he's able.

Akachi rose from the cot. He searched Subira, finding her sacrificial dagger. Returning to the cot, he sat staring at it, feeling the cold weight of glass in his hand.

The staff was gone and with it, his certainty.

Robbed of confidence, he had nothing left.

Nothing.

"Faith with certainty isn't faith at all," Akachi said aloud. "True faith can only be found at the bottom, in the hollowed-out gutted depths of a ravaged soul. There are a thousand parables about faith, but do any sing the praises of the untested?"

He understood.

I have been tested.

His faith had been pushed to breaking and yet something remained, a spark of stubborn rage.

Akachi's lips peeled back in snarl.

Efra was supposed to kill me. Smoking Mirror thinks I'm dead.

This was a test.

All of it.

It had to be.

Why else was he still alive?

This was a test that would break anyone other than a true hero. This was the kind of test he'd read about so many times in the *Book of Bastion*. He remembered thinking about how, in the parables, the tested never broke, never bent. He remembered how insane that seemed, how, at some point, the cost *must* be too high.

Akachi studied the stump-fingers of his left hand with his remaining eye.

"True faith can only be found at the bottom," he repeated, "in the hollowed-out gutted depths of a ravaged soul."

How perfectly that described him, like it was written for Akachi alone.

Was the cost too high?

"No," said Akachi. "True faith is what remains when the gods have taken everything."

GLOSSARY - THE GODS OF BASTION

Cloud Serpent (Lord of the Hunt): God of the hunt. As no one leaves Bastion, all hunting happens within the city. The most common prey is escaped criminals or fleeing debtors. His priests wear robes with thick bands of red, white, and black.

Face Painted with Bells: Once a powerful Loa nahualli, skilled in crystal magic, she was slain by Akachi. Once in the underworld, she set a trap for Father Death, luring him into a false war. Slaying The Lord, she ascended, becoming the newest god in the pantheon. While not a true death god, and not nearly powerful enough to hold the position of ruler of the underworld, she resides there as Mother Death's representative. Though only a godling, she is the god of assassins.

Feathered Serpent (Father Wind, Lord of Storms, Bringer of Knowledge): God of wind and sandstorms. His priests wear masks that look like bone skulls eroded by sand and wind.

The Fifth Sun (The Movement, Naui Olin, He Who Goes Forth Shining, Father of the Day, Lord of Eagles, Flint Tongue): Long ago, back when the world was young and alive, The Lord had a brother, The Fifth Sun. The Fifth Sun was the god of the sun. Father Death killed his brother and took his heart to make a powerful artefact for his most loyal high priest.

The Third Sun (Father of the Long Cave Beneath the Earth, The Lord of the Third Sun): God of rain and those who drown and die of disease. Long ago slain by Mother Death so she could claim his realm (and dead) as her own.

Her Skirt is Stars (Mother Life, Goddess of the Stars, Skirt of Snakes, Grandmother): Gave birth to moon and stars. Goddess of childbirth and women who die during it. Her nahual run the crèches where Grower children are born and raised. They wear the spines of snakes woven into their hair and clothes. Their vestments vary in colour, but always match the colouring of some deadly viper, depending on their particular sect.

Lord of the Root (The Healer, Lord of Wine): God of doctors, medicine, narcotics, herbs and hallucinogenics.

Lord of the Vanguard: (Lord of the Nose, Nose Lord) God of merchants, commerce, and trade. Primarily worshipped in the Bankers' Ring.

Precious Feather: (The Maiden, Mother of Flowers) Goddess of pleasure, indulgence, sex, female sexual power, and protector of young mothers. Her priests are strictly female and wear robes cut to show off and accent their beauty.

Sin Eater: (Mother Sin, Mother Purity, She Who Devours the Filth, The Four Sisters, Goddess of Dirt) Goddess of filth, guilt, cleansing, sin, purification, steam baths, midwives, and adulterers. She takes confessions and purifies or punishes. Her priests are always immaculately clean. Never dirty or sweaty, they bathe many times a day. They wear robes of flawless white.

Smoking Mirror (Father Discord, The Obsidian Lord, God of storms, God of Strife, Lord of the Night Sky, Enemy of Both Sides, We Are His Slaves, He by Whom We Live, Lord of the Near and Far, Father of the Night Wind, Lord of the Tenth Day, The Flayed One, The Jaguar God): He is associated with a wide range of concepts, including the night sky, the night winds, the north, the earth, obsidian, discord, jaguars, and strife. His priests wear black.

Southern Hummingbird (Father War, The Left Hand, The Dart Hurler, Father Terror): God of war. His priests are the Hummingbird Guard.

Turquoise Fire (Father Flame, Lord of Time, The Heat in the Night, The Light in the Dark): One of the truly ancient gods, Father Flame has dwindled in the last millennia. Now, his nahual are never seen outside of the Priests' Ring, and even rarely seen there. His nahualli are by far the most powerful tezcat, capable of seeing detail beyond other Diviners. His sole remaining church, the Temple of Duality is in the Priests' Ring. His priests wear robes of red with polished stones of turquoise woven into the fabric and in their hair. The colour of the stone denotes their rank. A bright, clean stone with no other colours denotes an acolyte. A stone shot through with thick veins of other rock, one that is lumpen, misshapen, and ugly, denotes a high-ranked nahual. They are also all marred by fire, burned and scarred. All tezcat who dare the rivers of time have seen a day where Bastion is gone, lost beneath the bloody sands, and all the world is dead. Such visions leave most insane, and drive the rest to suicide. Turquoise Fire's nahual never talk about what they have seen, never discuss the death of the Last City.

The Lady: (Mother Death, Lady of the Dead, The Queen of Bastion, The Falcon, The Great Mother, Nephthys, Nebthet, Mother of the Universe, Kālarātri, The Black One, The Destroyer, The Lady of the House) Cast from the city after the creation of Bastion she has lived in the Bloody Desert for over twenty-five thousand years, devouring those souls thrown from the Sand Wall. She is the eldest of gods, betrayed by her husband, The Lord.

The Lord (Father Death, The Lord of the House): God of death. His priests wear long cloaks of owl feathers. Current ruler of the pantheon. The Lord was lured into a trap by the godling Face Painted with Bells (a powerful Loa sorcerer who ascended after The Lord's death) and slain.

The Provider: God of fertility and water and lightning.

GLOSSARY - NAHUALLI (SORCERERS)

Huateteo (Spirit Guides): Have the power to bring people together or tear them apart. Utilizing aspects of the pactonal art of dream-walking, they can move people's souls into one of the neighbouring realities. Different realities have different rules. Some are conducive to unity and time spent in such will bind a group into a tight knit unit. Some are darker and subtly weaken the bonds of society. A powerful huateteo can, given time and the right narcotics, alter people's personalities, plant goals and ideas.

Nagual (shape shifter): Has the power to transform either spiritually or physically into an animal form. Nagual can completely become the animal or take on aspects or characteristics of the animal.

Otochin (Fetish Magic): Fetish magic is the creation of charms and wards, which can offer protection, imbue characteristics (strength, charisma, quickness, etc.), or be used as curses.

Pactonal (dream-walking): Allows the practitioner to enter or control the dreams of others. This can be used to send messages, nightmares, or threats. A powerful nahualli can kill someone in their dreams and the victim's spirit will die, leaving the body a living shell. Since it is common knowledge that the gods speak through people's dreams, this is particularly powerful/dangerous.

Peyollotl (Totemic Magic): The sorcerer must hand carve totems of various creatures and study them while taking drugs. They imagine (and later hallucinate) the creature coming to life. The more powerful the sorcerer, the more they can control their hallucination. Truly powerful nahualli, like those in Bastion's earliest days, can cause their totems to grow to immense size and do all kinds of fantastic things, like breathe fire.

Tecuhtli (Death Magic): Practised only by worshippers of The Lord (Father Death) and The Lady (Mother Death). There is great power and energy in death. The dead are ritually burned at the local temple so that an evil street-sorcerer doesn't steal body parts for use in dark magic. Curses, poisons, summoning and binding evil spirits, raising and talking to the dead are all aspects of death magic. A powerful tecuhtli can summon spirits from the afterlife and bind them to corpses. With Face Painted with Bells, a godling in service of Mother Death, effectively over-seeing the underworld, only Mother Death's tecuhtli can now practice death magic. They also now have access to Father Death's Library of Souls.

Tezcat (Divination): By taking the right mix of drugs (and with the right training) it's possible to see flashes of the future, the past, or even elsewhere in the present. All tezcat who look beyond a certain point in the future go mad and commit suicide shortly after. Rumour is they see a truly dead world, the ruin of Bastion sinking beneath the red sands of the Bloody Desert. Attempts have been made to ascertain the exact day the city dies, but too many nahualli died in the process and the experiment was dropped. Matters were made worse by the fact it's impossible to control how far forward you see with any real accuracy. Most tezcat are incapable of seeing more than a day or two into the future and are, there-fore, safe. But rare and powerful diviners occasionally turn up dead by suicide after accidentally looking too far ahead. Rumours say the rate at which powerful texcat are killing themselves is increasing, suggesting that the day of Bastion's death looms closer. They also claim that's the reason there are now fewer powerful diviners than there used to be. No one knows for sure if it's in the near future, or thousands of years from now.

GLOSSARY - SORCEROUS NARCOTICS

Aldatu: A powerful hallucinogenic mostly commonly used by nagual as it aids in shape-shifting. Mushroom.

Ameslari: A strong hallucinogenic. A trained user can enter the dreams of another if that person is also asleep. The fungus is grown in dark basements and must be eaten.

Arrazoia: Improves logical thought

Ausardia: Increases confidence and bravery.

Bihurtu: Most commonly used by peyollotl (totemic magic). A poisonous residue scraped off the backs of a large, black frog. Bihurtu connects the sorcerer with the world of spirit animals, allowing the nahualli to channel aspects (strength, speed, armour, etc.) of various animals.

Bizitza Izoztuak: Leaves the user conscious and alert, but immobilized. Distilled from the venom of a deadly viper, it is used as a tool to aid in deep meditation.

Egia: Reduces inhibitions and makes it difficult to lie.

Epelak: Cured petals from the epelak flower are used to open the third eye, found in the centre of the palm of a sorcerer's right hand.

Erlaxatu: A relaxing euphoria that numbs the user to the hurts of the world and leaves a peaceful feeling. Smoked. Most commonly available narcotic in the Growers' Ring as it can be grown hidden in fields of corn and wheat.

Etorkizun: Milky sap from a tree. Mixed with your own blood, this is used by tezcat in divination magic.

Foku: Sharpens all senses. Edible seeds. Improves retention.

Gorgoratzen: Allows user to recall even 'forgotten' events in great detail. Any memories made while under its influence will be incredibly sharp.

Jainkoei: Opens the soul to the will of the gods.

Jakitun: Makes user physically aware of their surroundings. Increased physical aptitude, balance, proprioception.

Kognizioa: Makes the user smarter, better able to focus on problem solving.

Pizgarri: User feels sharp and alert, and *very* awake. Helps with concentration.

Zoriontasuna: A euphoric. Common street drug (4th ring), mostly used as an escape from reality. A trained user can cause those around him to feel some of his high. It calms crowds, makes people mellow and happy. A leafed plant that is smoked.

GLOSSARY - TECOLOTL - STONE SORCERY

Unlike nahualli and street-sorcerers, the Loa don't need narcotics to power their sorcery. The sorcery lies within the stones, and can be accessed by achieving the right mental state. Learning Loa sorcery is a matter of learning meditation and trances. Some are more difficult than others, and different stones require different mental states (often emotion-driven) to access.

Tecolotl don't specialize the way nahualli do. This is the sorcery of youth and emotion. Once they learn to tap their potential, and access the power trapped in the various stones, they can use any. The skill comes in the form of being able to call up the requisite emotion when it's needed, the purity/strength/ depth of the emotion being felt. There are very few old tecolotl. This is the sorcery of youth and rebellion.

Take a Loa sorcerer's stones away, and they are helpless.

Some stones can be used over and over and have been passed down for generations. Others, however, are a one-time use, after which they shatter or crack and become useless. Such stones are incredibly valuable. There are, hidden throughout Bastion, secret Loa mines where they dig for new stones.

After twenty-five thousand years, these mines, limited by the underlying stone of Bastion, are largely tapped out. They dare not attempt to penetrate the stone for fear of breaking the wards that keep the dead at bay. At this point they are scrounging for scraps. This is part of the reason for the desperate power-grab. Ranking priests among the Loa have foreseen a time when there are so few stones in circulation among their members that rebellion will be impossible.

The quality of the stones can have a great effect on its power. A large quality stone, prepared by a master craftsman, will be massively more powerful than a small chunk of rock. Raw, uncut stones, such as those handed out to street-level grunts are of low value/quality. The high-quality cut and polished stones are reserved for high-ranked nahual.

Agate: Curses and protections.

Alexandrite: Cause obsessions, make subject delusional.

Amethyst: The stone of self-destruction.

Angelite: Abort unborn children and kill the sick and elderly.

Astrophyllite: The stone of torment. Drive the subject insane with nightmares.

Black Onyx: Cause nightmares, mental torment, and ruin relationships.

Bloodstone: Blood red quartz. The stone of gates. Opens the veil so the wielder may step through, pass between realities. The stone of noble sacrifice.

Carnelian: Comes in colours ranging from grey to orange to blood-red. Each colour has its own properties. In its deepest red shades, the stone is a portal to death, a doorway from the underworld to the reality of the living. A skilled sorcerer can use it to summon souls to inhabit corpses. Combined with other stones (such as obsidian) it can create armies of the dead.

Diamond: Create blindness, physical or spiritual. Causes confusion and disorientation.

Emerald: Drive subject insane with greed and selfishness.

Flint: Stone of Conflict. In the hands of a skilled Loa nahualli, this simple and common stone can be used to incite violence. A powerful nahualli can drive even large crowds to rioting.

Fossilized Shark Teeth: The stone of curses

Garnet: Stores many forms of energy. It can store wounds the sorcerer suffers. Those wounds can later be given to a subject. It can also steal health or strength or intelligence from a helpless subject. The sorcerer can use what the stone steals, burning through the energy. The subject doesn't recover lost energy unless the sorcerer returns it to them.

Goshenite: Stone of Unmasking.

Hematite: Mother Death's stone. Like obsidian, it can store souls. Even when trapped beyond the Sand Wall, Mother Death could communicate with her priests through this rare stone, and feed them some small sliver of her power.

Hyraceum: Stone of Domination.

Kunzite: Stone of Distraction.

Kyanite: Knife of the Mind. In the hands of a skilled practitioner, this stone can forcefully rip thoughts, memories, even personality from someone. Everything they are can be torn away and stored in the stone. The sorcerer can later access the stored person, questioning them. Truly powerful nahualli can drive the personality into a new body. It will exist over top of the original personality, able to control the host body, slowly fading over time. This can be used to install spies into churches, business, and political structures. Some nahualli can even pull specific aspects of a person (skills, memories, etc.) from the stone and take it into themselves.

Skystone (Meteorites): Increase the intensity and effects of other stones

Obsidian: Obsidian is used by tecuhtli in their death magic. This is the one kind of crystal magic not forbidden to the nahualli, though they don't think of it as such. The soul of anyone killed by obsidian will be stored inside the stone. The more souls inside the stone the more powerful it becomes. If enough souls are stored in the stone it begins to stain local reality. The obsidian swords of the Turquoise Serpents, Southern Hummingbird's elite, carry thousands of souls and are unbreakable. These swords can cut through anything, even the eternal stone of Bastion herself. The sacrificial daggers used by the nahual are always obsidian. They are regularly returned to the Gods' Ring at the centre of Bastion to be drained of souls. Those souls are then cleansed and made ready to be reborn.

Opal: Container and radiator of negative energy.

Pyrope: Fire stone: Raw stones can be used to create a bright and blood-red light. Cut stones can be used to start fires and even unleash firestorms, depending on the craftmanship. A pyrope stone with many facets and polished to perfection is a truly dangerous weapon.

Ruby: Clarifier or purifier of intent.

Sphene: Stone of Depression.

Star Diopside: The stone of truth.

THE WALLS OF BASTION

The Sand Wall: Separates Bastion from the Bloody desert.

The Grey Wall: Separates the Growers from the Crafters.

The Wall of Lords: Separates the Crafters from the Senators.

The Wall of Commerce: Separates the Senators from the Bankers.

The Wall of Faith: Separates the Banks from the Priests.

The Wall of Gods: Separates the gods at Bastion's core from the Priests.

ACKNOWLEDGEMENTS

As I watch the world devolve into a shitshow of epic proportions it is the people on this list who give me hope, who make me think there might be something to this species worth fighting for.

Carrie Chi Lough read this thing ~~three~~ four times. Her feedback reshaped the ending into something with (hopefully) some impact. Petros Triantafyllou (booknest.eu) found some rather embarrassing plot-holes I'd totally missed. This is a better book for their efforts, and I am indebted to them both. Thank you!

When I decided to narrate the *Black Stone Heart* audiobook I did so with great trepidation. The absolutely amazing Julia Kitvaria Sarene agreed to beta-listen the book. Happily, she's agreed to do the same again, and I'm uploading chapters to her as I record the Ash and Bones audiobook. You rock!

There comes a point in each book—at least for me—when the shine wears off and I wonder why the fuck I thought this was a good idea. Sometimes I question why I'm writing at all. Having people in your life willing to poke a head in the virtual window and say, "Yo, you good?" is critically important. David Walters (fanfiaddict.com), Jeff Bryant, and Tom Clews are good friends even though I've never met them in person. And all three of them need to finish the book they're writing.

Jon Adams has one of my book covers as a tattoo and is an awesome dude. He does a final read of every book, catching the small detail stuff that often slips past me. I am grateful for his help and owe him several beers.

Despite rumours, there isn't a cabal. If there was, I'd owe each and every one of them a debt of gratitude for their unrelenting humour. I'd have to talk about how excellent they all are. I'd probably even have to make a long list of names and then I'd forget someone because I'm an idiot and feel like shit. Happily, there is #nocabal.

Thanks to Sarah Chorn for editing this book (and several of my other books). She is a pleasure to work, twisted in all the right ways, and her love and support for authors and the fantasy community is nothing shy of phenomenal.

Felix Ortiz did the cover art (he also did *Smoke and Stone*, and *Black Stone Heart*). He is a consummate professional and endlessly patient (and lawdy do I test that patience!). His work speaks for itself. Folks say "don't judge a book by its cover" but with Felix on the job I'm more worried about writing a book good enough to earn that cover.

Adrian Collins and the amazing team at **Grimdark Magazine** are tireless champions of fantasy, dark fantasy, and that ever nebulous grim-dark thing I apparently write. Someday I hope we can all sit down to skull a tinny or twelve. Cheers!

As always, I need to thank my friends and family for being awesome, for being supportive even when I turtle-up and withdraw for days, weeks, or even months at a time. I love you guys.

And finally, a hyuuuuge thanks to you, the reader. Without you, I'd just be some crazy dude screaming into the abyss. I mean, assuming you're actually real, that is. Maybe you aren't.

glances into the abyss

Hello?

Mike Fletcher (June 3rd, 2020)

Made in the USA
Las Vegas, NV
25 February 2021